OF MEN & OF ANGELS

OF MEN & OF ANGELS

BODIE & BROCK THOENE

THOMAS NELSON PUBLISHERS
Nashville

Published in association with the literary agency of Alive Communications, 1465 Kelly Johnson Blvd., Suite #320, Colorado Springs, CO 80920.

Published in Nashville, Tennessee, by Thomas Nelson, Inc.

Except for recognized historical figures and family members, all characters are fictional, and any resemblance to persons living or dead is strictly coincidental.

Library of Congress Cataloging-in-Publication Data

Thoene, Bodie, 1951–
    Of men and of angels : a novel / Bodie and Brock Thoene.
      p.   cm.
    Sequel to Only the river runs free.
    ISBN 0-7852-8068-5
    I. Thoene, Brock, 1952– . II. Title. III. Series: Thoene, Bodie, 1951– Galway chronicles.
PS3570.H46032 1998
813'.54—dc21   98–13533
                                                  CIP

Printed in the United States of America

1 2 3 4 5 6 BVG 03 02 01 00 99 98

*To the Petherbridge family,
with love—Edward, Emily,
Dora and Arthur.*

PROLOGUE

It was the old, old tale that had come down ripened and sweetened like your pipe, with the ages. . . . And men and women were like children listening for the thousandth time, to the same tale; and could go without food or drink for fondness of hearing you tell them.

—Seamus MacManus

☙ Prologue ❧

The sun rose in blood on the morning of Good Friday, April the twenty-third, in the year of our Lord, 1014. The left of the Irish line pointed a cautionary finger toward the hill of Clontarf and the Irish Sea beyond. A dark cloud, black and angular as a raven's wing, boiled upward from the ocean waves to hang overhead like a harbinger of doom.

But whose doom was prophesied? Brian Boru wondered as he paced within his campaign tent. High King of All Ireland for more than a decade, Brian Boru was tall and robust for all his white hair and seventy-odd years. His entire life had been played out against a backdrop of battles, campaigns, and wars. Now, though he would not admit it, he was tired of the continual strife. He prayed that this one battle would be decisive, that it would free Ireland from the threat of the Ostmen, the pagan Vikings.

King Brian had outfought and outmaneuvered the Danes until they were pressed back against Dublin on the coast. But like any wolf when cornered, they had become even more dangerous. Worse still, King Brian's lookouts had seen bonfires all along the sand dunes, guiding in the long ships carrying Viking reinforcements.

The deep voices of the Irish goatskin drums began their summons: to victory or death. The rumble of the bodhrans started off toward the left, pounded toward the center, passed King Brian, and swept onward to the west. Like a wave rolling onto the shore, the throbbing pulse petitioned the very hills to come down and fight.

Facing the assembled Irish was an army of Danes led by their king, Sitric of Dublin, aided by the turncoat Leinster chief, Malmorda, and Earl Sigurd of Orkney. These men had conspired to overthrow King Brian and establish Sigurd on the throne of Ireland, even as Sigurd's cousin Canute was seeking to rule England.

Sitric had also summoned a sorcerer named Brodar from the Isle of Man to bring ten dragon boats of his fiercest handpicked soldiers to the fray.

The horde of Vikings and their mercenaries from Flanders and the islands totaled twenty thousand men. King Brian lifted his chin, with its snow-colored beard, and turned to face the south. The war horns of the Vikings were clamoring, throwing back the challenge to the Irish drums. *Only one host will survive this day,* they boasted, *and we will be the ones left standing.*

The flaps of the tent parted, and the war council of Brian Boru assembled for the last time before battle. Brian's son, Murrow, and his grandson, Turlough, were first into the pavilion. These were followed by the Irish captains Malachi and O'Toole and the rest. Coming in last, in deference to the others, was the Norman knight Miles de Burgo.

"What say you all? How looks the day?" King Brian demanded bluntly.

"We are outnumbered by some four thousand," admitted Malachi. "My force has not yet come up; and Ostmen ships landed more men the whole night long."

"Our line is stretched thin," Murrow agreed. "To keep them from flanking us at Drumcondra, I have had to weaken our center."

"The raven banner is on the field," O'Toole said, "woven by a witch and carried by that cursed Brodar. It is said that their god, Wotan, rode into the camp of the Vikings last night. He promised them that if they brought on the battle today when Christians are weakest, then they would win."

King Brian looked troubled. "And are you saying we should delay this struggle?" he asked. "For you have all given me gloomy counsel. Is there not one of you who feels we can triumph?"

De Burgo cleared his throat and then waited for the High King to turn and face him. "Your pardon," he said, "but I take exception to what I hear. There is no day on the calendar when the power of Christ does not surpass that of the false gods of the Danes. And what is more, the position of our enemy is flawed. Their back is to the river Liffy and split by Tomar's Wood. We can crush them between the river and the sea."

There was angry murmuring at this. De Burgo was a foreigner, a mercenary. Being from Normandy, he had Viking blood in his own veins; it made him suspect and distrusted. A little knot of chieftains whispered in low tones, and then Brian's son, Murrow, stepped forward. "Your Highness," he said, "Turlough and I agree with de Burgo. The day can be won with the forces at hand."

That reassurance was all King Brian needed. His eyes again flashing with their accustomed fire, he ordered the captains to return to their companies. "De Burgo," he said, putting out his hand to stop the Norman from leaving, "one further word, if you please."

At the back of the pavilion was King Brian's chair of state. Covered with a finely worked cloth, the throne was green and embroidered with the figure of a wolfhound. The king whipped the fabric aside, revealing what was hidden between the curved bows of the carved wooden legs. It was a chest bearing the king's seal: a sword lying at angles with a cross. King Brian opened the box. It was filled to the rim with hammered gold: coins and necklaces, rings and armbands. "It is the tribute money," he said. "If we win, I will distribute it to the heroes of the day. But if we fail, or if I should fall, it must be guarded against the future of my son and grandson. I charge you to bear it away from the fight, because I trust you."

His right arm held stiffly across his chest, de Burgo bowed deeply.

"In my absence," King Brian continued, "you are to deliver it to whoever brings you this word: 'Neither a crown nor a collar.'"

De Burgo bowed again, and the two men left the tent. The sun's rays were beaming down through the dark cloud, piercing the raven's wings with shafts of gold. "They tell me I am too feeble to lead the van," he said to the Norman. "So I will remain here and pray. I want you to keep by the side of my son, unless the other event we spoke of becomes necessary."

The tempo of the drums increased, driving the pulse into de Burgo's ears and the flush of battle into his cheeks. King Brian paced to a promontory before his tent and there, in the sight of the host, he plunged the point of a golden-hilted sword into the ground on one hand and a golden crucifix on a long hazelwood staff into the turf on the other. Tossing down a small sack stuffed with fleece, his only concession to his advancing years, the High King of All Ireland knelt and received his book of the Psalms. Opening the volume, and casting his eye on a page at random, he read in clear, measured tones these words:

> *Praise be to the Lord my rock, who trains my hands for war, my fingers for battle. He is my loving God and my fortress, my stronghold and my deliverer, my shield in whom I take refuge, who subdues peoples under me.*

Then, turning a page of the manuscript illuminated with gold leaf and colors of dark green and bright yellow, he continued,

> *Deliver me from the hands of foreigners, whose mouths are full of lies. . . .*

As he spoke this phrase, his head dropped forward in token of prayer, and the heads of the entire host of Ireland did as well. Then when King Brian elevated his face again, sixteen thousand swords flashed in the morning glare and the battle was joined.

When the two forces were still twenty yards apart, the Danes unleashed a cloud of flying dragons, thin throwing spears with foot-long blades that tapered to needle points. Five hundred javelins were flung. Half that number rattled harmlessly off the bosses of shields or were deflected by the weapons of the Irish. But the other half struck home, piercing leather jerkins and the flesh beneath. The soldier sprinting beside de Burgo took a spear point in the throat and went down without a word.

On the other side of the Norman, King Brian's son, Murrow, waved his sword in circles over his head, exhorting the attacking ranks to close up. A spear flashed toward Murrow's chest. De Burgo lashed out with his own shield, diverting the passage of the lance only inches from Murrow's heart.

Then the lines crashed together with the impact of rams butting heads. Having flung their javelins, the Danes likewise charged forward, swinging short swords and hand axes. The conflict instantly became five thousand single combats.

De Burgo parried the descent of an ax with his sword, then slipped the point of his weapon under the Viking's guard and into his ribs. A pair of Danes thrust at him from opposite sides with stabbing lances. The Norman feinted toward one, making the man give back a step. Then as the other enemy tried to puncture him from behind, de Burgo whirled out of the way and the two Danes perforated each other.

Chopping earthward on the shaft of another pike and knocking the weapon from the Viking's hands, de Burgo cleared a space around him enough to draw a breath. The situation was not good. Murrow had concentrated his attack on the center of the Viking line. The ends of the pagan ranks were curling around, threatening to encircle the Irish.

"Now," he called urgently to Murrow. "Now for the signal!"

At a wave of Murrow's left hand, a drummer behind the fray began a rapid rattle on a bodhran that was caught up by others and passed up and down the battlefront. From the extreme right of the Irish line, Turlough, King Brian's grandson, emerged with a thousand men from the shelter of a grove of trees. Then it was the Danes who were taken from the rear. As Murrow and de Burgo pressed them hotly from the front, the Viking line wavered and ran, only to find their retreat cut off by the river Liffy.

At the bankside, de Burgo stood face-to-face with Earl Sigurd. The Norman's sword was notched and jagged from blocking a rain of ax blows, but still he cut and thrust against the would-be king of Ireland. Sigurd and de Burgo hacked at each other, neither giving ground, until a whole line of Danes were thrown bodily into the river by the press of the Irish attack. His eyes widening in fear, Sigurd flung his weapon at de Burgo's head, then plunged into the river to escape.

Panicked at the onslaught and the flight of their leader, the Vikings crowded down toward the sea, snarling the ranks of their comrades and trapping themselves in pockets too cramped to swing their axes. The Irishmen encircled them twenty at a time, thrusting into the clusters with spears.

A brawny, blond Dane burst from such a clump of men and attacked young Turlough with a war ax. Throwing up his shield, King Brian's grandson tried to fend off the blow, but the stroke shattered the leather and wooden circle. Leaping in front of his son, Murrow took the next blow of the ax on his own shoulder. He died with the point of his sword protruding through the body of the Viking.

With a howl of grief and rage, Turlough in turn led the press that backed the Vikings toward the sea. When Malachi's men, late arriving at the battle, joined in the attack, the Danes gave up and ran for their boats.

The slaughter on the sand was horrific. Having ridden the incoming sea onto the beach, the Vikings had disembarked in the confident expectation of an easy victory. Now, in the rout, they were appalled to find that the falling tide had swept their ships away. Knee deep in surf, their metal shields and heavy weapons dragging them down, the Vikings were massacred by the lightly armed Irish.

"Go to my grandfather," Turlough ordered de Burgo. "Tell him my father is dead, but the day is won." As he uttered those words, an ax came spinning through the air, killing him in that same instant.

It was a double load of evil tidings that the Norman carried back to the aged king. Despite the victory, both his son and grandson were slain. From a hundred yards away from the camp, de Burgo could see that King Brian still knelt in prayer. He also noted a group of black-clad figures circling behind the pavilion and coming at a run toward it. "Betrayal!" de Burgo shouted. "The enemy is behind you!"

How had the Vikings discovered a way through the Irish lines? Where was the gap by which these assassins menaced the king?

At the head of the attackers de Burgo found his answer: Captain O'Toole had turned on his comrades and opened the way for the sneak assault.

The raven banner floated in front of the dark-clad men. It was clutched in the fist of a six-and-a-half-foot-tall figure whose raven black hair and beard were worn down to his waist and tucked into his belt: Brodar, the sorcerer.

The black-visaged man was a giant. Once welcomed by King Brian as a brother, Brodar was a Christian apostate who had embraced the pagan ways of the Vikings to win their favor.

As Brodar's warriors engaged the bodyguard of the king, O'Toole slipped inside the royal tent.

Brodar thrust his evil flag into the soil so he could draw his weapon from his belt. Raising the two-handed ax he called *Skullbreaker,* he slashed it downward toward the king. But King Brian was no longer kneeling. With the vigor of a man forty years younger, he grasped the gold-hilted sword and skillfully parried Brodar's swing.

De Burgo, meanwhile, was engaged with two of Brodar's henchmen. Though he fought as shrewdly as before, his thrusts seemed to have no effect on the black-clad Vikings. It was as if they truly were protected by vile magic.

Then the point of his sword caught in a linked ring of metal, and de Burgo knew the secret: these specially trained warriors were wearing chain mail beneath their tunics and cloaks.

Now he knew both their strength and weakness. De Burgo rapidly circled, thrusting and moving, keeping the Vikings off balance, crossing them into each other. Their armor protected them, but the additional weight made them clumsy and slower footed.

After circling constantly to the left, de Burgo suddenly reversed direction. One of his opponents caught the change sooner than the other. In trying to shift direction, he collided with his comrade.

In a flash de Burgo was atop the stumbling man, slicing downward at the space between the helmet flaps and the collar of the chain mail. A second later the man was dead, and his companion was running away.

De Burgo turned to see O'Toole emerge from the tent, lugging the chest of treasure. The traitor, having led the enemy into the camp, was taking the tribute money as his payment. Tossing aside his sword, the Norman grasped the hand ax of the fallen Viking. As O'Toole rounded the corner of the tent, de Burgo unleashed a whirling, spinning throw that buried the ax head in O'Toole's back. The chest, breaking open, scattered its contents over the ground.

King Brian, worn down by the massive size and strength of his adversary, gave ground. A mammoth blow from Brodar's ax forced the king down on one knee. As de Burgo jumped to intervene, the sorcerer raised his weapon for another stroke. Thrusting upward, King Brian impaled his sword point in Brodar's chest. But it was too late to stop the descent of the ax, and the ten-pound blade hit the king between shoulder and neck.

Both men were dying, and they knew it. From three feet apart they regarded each other with dulling eyes. King Brian motioned with his eyes toward the raven flag and crucifix. The banner of evil had fallen facedown, while the cross remained firmly fixed in place. "Any fear I have felt is ending," King Brian gasped. "But your terror, Brodar, is only begun."

Without a word the sorcerer toppled forward on his face.

De Burgo caught the slumping king in his arms. "Lost or won?" King Brian asked simply.

De Burgo told the king the awful news. Victory had come to the Irish, but at the cost of all three generations of the line of Brian Boru.

"Then take the treasure and hide it," the king commanded in a hoarse whisper. "Guard it against the day of Ireland's great need. Remember . . . 'neither crown nor collar' . . . remember." Then he died.

PART I

The great Gaels of Ireland
Are the men that God made mad,
For all their wars are merry,
And all their songs are sad.

—G. K. Chesterton

1

Spring came again to Ballynockanor. This first day of March, 1843, was the last day young Kevin Donovan would spend in County Galway. For a lifetime his heart had believed that only the endless sea lay beyond the shores of western Ireland; there was no other world outside the land of his birth.

On this final hour of his last day, sunset arced like a shining knifeblade behind the swell of the Maumturk Mountains, cleaving east from west, home from banishment.

Lit from below, twilight clouds glowed pink and violet, forming a bright canopy floating above the valley.

En route to the sea, the water of the Cornamona River lapped the rocks where angels sat and, in some unknown tongue, talked softly of miracles long forgot and prophesied of great and terrible events soon to come. But no one living in the townlands heard their words. Thoughts of tomorrow's good-bye drowned all recollection of recent wonders in Ballynockanor. How many miracles could one village expect, after all?

The solitary bell of the tiny Church of St. John the Evangelist tolled slowly. Echoing across the bowl of the valley, it beckoned the villagers and many other folk to Kevin's farewell supper to be held at Burke Hall in the manor house of widower Joseph Connor Burke and his infant son, Little Tom.

Above and beneath, behind and before the resonant gong, angel voices softly sang a warning. But the song was nothing more than a single resounding note to those walking up the long slope with parting gifts for Kevin Donovan's American wake. Who could know that tonight marked the beginning of terrible troubles and mighty deeds for the people of Ballynockanor and all of Ireland?

In the gathering gloom of twilight the strident voices of evil men clashed like thunder against the warnings of angels and boomed from the clouds far above Connaught. Everyone in Ballynockanor who heard the rumble looked sharply to the west and knew a mighty storm would soon be upon them.

It was a mercy they did not foresee the force of the approaching wind or guess who among them, in the end, would be carried away by its fury. To know the future would have crushed the heart of every villager who came that evening to Kevin Donovan's farewell supper, for there was not one family among them all who would not suffer.

And so it was that evening on the banks of the river Cornamona, angels wept as the last sliver of daylight vanished.

> *Lord have mercy!*
> *Christ have mercy!*
> *Lord have mercy*
> *On the poor souls of Ballynockanor!*

There was only one among the souls of Ballynockanor who sometimes understood the music on the wind that blew from the Seven Bens. But Mad Molly Fahey was fey, and today the aged woman had difficulty sorting out the importance of heavenly messages from the fact that she had scorched the final batch of frogs for Kevin Donovan's frog bread.

"They're at it again! Singin', singin', singin' till a woman is near loony with it. . . . What is it? Ye hear that?" Mad Molly cried, raising her gnarled hands in agitation above the coals on the hearth of her daughter's cottage.

Twelve-year-old Martin Donovan winked at his seven-year-old sister, Mary Elizabeth. The two Donovan siblings heard nothing but the distant church bell. Molly was always hearing things no one else heard, so Martin said in a soothing tone, "It's just the bell."

Molly spat, "And the whole chorus of heavenly host as well! Callin' a million to the roads for Ireland, they are! A penny for each house. It'll come to no good lest we be strong! *Lord have mercy!*" Molly spun around and scowled into Martin's face.

Martin nodded. "Kevin's friends at the pub. No doubt they've had a drop too much to drink, Molly. Sure, and they're practicin' sad songs to sing tonight at Kevin's American wake."

"Now see what they've made me do! *Lord have mercy.* . . . They've burned our . . . our . . . frogs, Mary Elizabeth! There be no power to cure sickness at sea if the frogs in the frog bread be burned!"

Mary Elizabeth shook her black curls and with a stick poked at the charred frogs smoking on the grate. They crumbled and fell onto the coals. "Aye, Molly. Poor frogs. No use a'tall. They're ruined, sure. Might as well bake the rest of Kevin's frog bread with ashes and flour."

Martin screwed up his face in disgust at the process. A full dozen flat, hard loaves of frog bread were cooling on the sideboard. Made with ordinary flour and roasted garden frogs pulverized to powder, the bread was guaranteed to ward off the fevers of a long sea voyage to America. Martin and Mary Elizabeth had been sent out to capture a bucketful of the unfortunate creatures. Mad Molly performed the executions with the hard rap of a stone on knobby noggins in spite of the noisy protests and tears of Mary Elizabeth.

It occurred to Martin that he would rather be sick with seafever than eat the stuff. Ah well, the bucket was empty. This was the last of it, and Kevin's supper would begin in less than an hour. Martin and Mary Elizabeth would be expected home to wash up and change clothes. There was no time to bake more bread.

"Bring more frogs!" Mad Molly instructed.

Mary Elizabeth smoothed her skirts and replied cheerfully, "There's no more. Martin and myself, we caught them all and you roasted up the last, you see." The child did not let on that she had, in pity, stolen back half-a-bucketful and, wishing them long happy lives and many tadpoles, had tenderly released two dozen green prisoners beside the lily pond.

"No more!" the old woman cried incredulously. "The traitors. They've turned us back! *Christ have mercy!* Hunger and sorrow! Villages tossed! Everyone at sea! They've emptied all of Ireland. *Lord have mercy!* No one left to croak at night! Only the old ones, and no one left to bury them."

Martin sighed as he pictured a wave of terrified amphibians leaping from the shores into the sea to escape the fate of their brethren. Something like St. Patrick driving the snakes from Ireland. "Not all of Ireland. Only the garden. No more frogs in the garden, Molly."

"Loaves and fishes! What're we to do? Poor, poor Kevin!" She hunkered down beside the hearth and gazed somberly into the coals.

"Twelve loaves'll last Kevin from here to America." Martin put a comforting hand on her bony shoulder. "Aye. And Kevin'll be glad to have 'em too. It's a fine present for his American wake, and he'll thank you for it, Molly. You've done well. He'll eat eleven on the way over and save one for his journey back to Ireland."

Mad Molly covered her face with her hands and whispered, "Can't you hear them singin', Martin? We'll have to be strong, or Kevin'll have no home to come home to."

The American wake of Kevin Donovan was as solemn an occasion as any Irish funeral ever had been.

Burke Hall was ablaze with light. Clooney's flute and O'Rourke's fiddle played a sorrowful tune. Clutching the sackful of frog bread,

Molly Fahey waltzed through the crowd, asking, "Have the banns been read? Are they married then?"

Everyone knew the madwoman was inquiring after the young widow, Kate Donovan Garrity, and the widower, Joseph Connor Burke. Some announcement of marriage between the two had been speculated upon in the months since Joseph's return from Dublin with the coffin of Brigit, Kate's sister, and the newborn child, whom he claimed as his own. But Kate rarely spoke to Joseph except to greet him at church. It was observed that she never raised her eyes to look into Joseph's pleading face. He could grow old and gray in her presence, and she would never see it happen. Since Brigit's tragic death, Kate had kept to herself. The two sisters had parted forever with much unspoken and unforgiven. Joseph was surely a painful reminder of the breach. Now, with Kevin leaving in the morning and the Donovan family losing yet another member, sorrow hung over Kate like a cloud.

Martin whispered to Molly, "There's no weddin', Molly; 'tis farewell for Kevin. Remember? The bread?"

"Aye. A wake is it? Who's died? No, no! Don't tell me, Martin darlin'. It'll come to me mind presently," she crooned softly.

Guests began to sing "The Water Is Wide" with such feeling that it brought tears to the eyes of the half dozen battle-seasoned British soldiers waiting outside to escort Kevin to his ship.

Three hundred friends and neighbors were in attendance with more arriving by the minute. Seated at the head of the room to receive condolences were Kevin and his family: Da, Mary Elizabeth, Martin, and Kate with Brigit's babe in her arms.

The ballroom was hung in black crepe, befitting the mournful night. A long banqueting table was laid out with food and drink. Clay pipes and bowls of tobacco were provided according to the custom of smoking a pipe in remembrance of the dearly departed.

The object of mourning was, in this case, fully alive and well. But to the thinking of the folk of Ballynockanor, Kevin's forced emigration to America was almost as good as being dead.

Annie Rose Field, sister of Mad Molly Fahey, had been hired as chief keener for the event. Her wailing freed up the general public

to sing and smoke and chat without the bother of having to weep.
Annie Rose, the most accomplished keener in all of Galway, sank
sobbing to her knees before the living corpse of Kevin as he spoke
to Father O'Bannon about the perils of America.

"Ahhhhhh!" Annie Rose moaned. "Kevin Donovan is lost to us!
Ireland has lost her dearest and best son!"

Kevin was not the dearest nor the best, of course. Violent, bitter,
and hotheaded, he was hated by the English authorities and considered by the Irish Republicans to be a loose cannon on the ship
of state. But he was, with the common folk, among the best known
of Irish rebels. His duel, fought over the honor of his sister Brigit,
the killing of Viscount William Marlowe; and the subsequent fall of
the Marlowe dynasty and the restoration of Joseph Connor Burke
to his estates were already the subject of many tavern ballads.

Annie Rose, a younger, more tidy version of her wild-eyed, grizzled sister, trembled as though Kevin were laid out cold and dead
on the table where the food was heaped.

"Cruel day! Cruel day! The leaf has fallen before the summer's
end!"

Father O'Bannon, who was attempting to pass along wisdom to
Kevin, scowled irritably down at Annie Rose. "Sha, woman! I can't
hear meself think!"

At his rebuke Annie stopped short and sniffed indignantly. "Pardon,
Your Honor, but I've been paid good money by Tom Donovan to
keen for his boy. And keen I must for at least another three-quarters
of an hour."

Tom Donovan, standing next to Kevin, agreed, "'Tis true, Father
O'Bannon."

The priest frowned in reluctant compliance. "Aye then, Tom. But
can the woman not take the racket outside?"

Puffing his clay pipe, Tom Donovan noted, "Sure, and she's paid
to make the English squirm a bit, the scum. They're takin' down
the names of Kevin's friends to arrest as possible rebels. Annie's
keenin' is certain distraction."

The priest concurred. "That's well thought of."

Tom Donovan winked at Annie. "Go on then, woman. Keen at

the feet of the queen's soldiers! Swoon and froth at the mouth a bit, if you've a mind to. They're Queen Victoria's lads, one and all, and too ignorant of our ways to know your tears are made of shillings. Wail so as to trouble their dreams with guilt for years to come. You can do it!" He cheered her on.

Annie Rose was capable of performing on a level to make the skin of even the bravest British soldier crawl. She appreciated the challenge and so left the great house to stagger out and fall prostrate with grief before the troops. She shrieked in anguish that penetrated the panes of window glass and caused the visitors to smile with approval. Her grief could not have been any more convincing or disturbing if Kevin had been hanged—which he nearly had been.

It was agreed by all in attendance that the exile of the elder Donovan son was a cruel mercy. Kevin's heart was planted here among the hearts of kinsmen and neighbors. The world beyond was wrapped in the blue shadow of the unknown. By order of the magistrate, Kevin was going to America, and that was the end of it. The matter was as final and irrevocable as death itself.

Come morning he would kiss his father good-bye with the certainty they would never meet again on this earth. Sisters, brother, and perhaps even the wee nephew, Thomas Burke, might one day cross the sea to the States, but how many years would pass before then? And what of the girl Kevin loved? Poor Jane Stone. Her father, the former steward of the Marlowe lands, rotted away in prison for his crimes, but none held John Stone's offenses against Jane. A Protestant girl she was and spirited away to Dublin by her family in fear she might elope with a Catholic. Loving her was against the law and reason enough to get Kevin transported. What hope had he of ever seeing her again?

There was a disturbance near the entry of the Great Hall. Chris Barrett, backed by other stalwarts of the townlands, was engaged in a shoving match of some sort, and a harsh note was interjected into the crooning laments. It was a bit early, Joseph Burke thought, for the liquor to be riling old jealousies and new disputes. As the host of the evening, he felt it his duty to intervene.

Barrett was shaking his fist in a bearded stranger's face. While the younger man's visage was red and angry, the newcomer was remarkably impassive, his brawny arms folded across a massive chest. A shock of coal black hair merged with a full beard, and his bulk made Barrett and the others look like willows beside an oak.

"Get out, I say," Barrett demanded. "We don't want your kind here."

The stranger cocked his head to one side as if listening carefully but without concern to Barrett's diatribe. Barrett pushed still nearer until the two men were almost touching.

There was the slightest movement of the alien's right arm, a mere dropping of the limb toward his waist, and Chris Barrett was on his tiptoes, his cheeks blotched between anger and a sudden deathly pallor.

"What is the cause of this disorder?" Joseph inquired softly. "This is a wake, not a donnybrook."

Something flickered briefly in the light—steel, by its gleam—then disappeared beneath the broad plaid sash encircling the unknown man's waist.

Stepping back a pace and then another, Chris Barrett remarked, "This . . . this *Tinker* . . . came in and made free with the vittles and the punch. I told him we did not want his dirty, thievin' Tinker hands on the bread of honest folk, and he should take himself off at once!" The summary mingled indignation with outright disgust. The epithet *Tinker* was uttered with as much loathing as if the word were synonymous with dung.

The bearded giant spoke at last in a deep rumble. "Beg pardon, your worship. I was told in Clonbur that tonight's gatherin' was open to everyone in the townlands."

"To all belongin' to the townlands, aye!" Barrett retorted. "But not to a will-o'-the-wisp, horse-stealin', foul blot of a . . ."

"That will do, Barrett," Joseph instructed. "I'll handle this." To the traveler he said, "You heard rightly, but I do not know your name."

The Tinker bowed deeply. "Dermott O'Neill, your lordship, horse trader, at your service."

"Horse trader!" Barrett bristled.

"That will do," Joseph said curtly. "You are welcome, Mister O'Neill." Then as the Tinker bowed his way out of the group, Joseph added in a low voice to Barrett, "I'll have no brawlin' . . . but you may keep an eye on the silver for me."

Just as he dealt with one disruption, Joseph was alerted to another. The front door was flung wide and the arrival of a carriage announced. "Daniel O'Connell is here!" clamored the crowd. "The Great Liberator himself is come . . . clear from Dublin!"

With a swirl of his traveling cloak, Daniel O'Connell, called *the Emancipator* for his efforts to free Ireland from the yoke of anti-Catholic discrimination, swept into the hall. To the immense satisfaction of those present, the famous man embraced Joseph warmly. "God bless all here," he said in a booming voice.

"And did you come so far, Daniel, to see Kevin properly waked?" Joseph exclaimed. "How glad I am to have you."

"And how could I not add my blessin' to the departure of the young man whose neck I may modestly take some credit for preservin' unstretched? But here, where are my manners? Let me introduce you to my companions."

Following O'Connell were a pair of men. One, Osborne Davis by name, was a consumptive, hollow-cheeked thirty-year-old, with darting eyes that were the liveliest part of his countenance. "Cofounder and publisher of *The Nation*," O'Connell announced, referring to the leading newspaper that advocated repeal of the enforced union between Britain and Ireland. "A good man, for all that he is a Protestant. And here is his assistant, Garrison O'Toole."

"They are both welcome in my house," Joseph intoned, shaking hands with both the frail Davis and the storklike, mustached O'Toole.

Mad Molly capered by in time to hear the introductions. "Never trust an O'Toole," she loudly proclaimed. "'Twas the O'Toole betrayed King Brian in the time of the Danes. Traitors, every one."

O'Toole grinned thinly.

"Ah, pay her no mind," O'Connell said jovially. He bundled O'Toole, Davis, and Joseph up in the force of his personality and carried them across the room as if he were the host. The human waters parted before him and became a triumphal progress that ended at the punch bowl. To Joseph he muttered, "Sure, and it is not Kevin alone brings me to this wild corner of the world . . . but of that we'll speak privately later."

The singing and the smoking and the drinking and the talking and the advice-giving continued unabated for some time. Children were abruptly yanked upright and had their faces scrubbed before being dragged into the presence of the august Daniel. Knots of well-wishers formed around Kevin, cursing the English roundly but quietly, saving Father O'Bannon's attentive ears. No one wanted to do penance for too forcefully expressing common sentiment.

Only two groups within the crowd acted uninterested in mingling. Kate Donovan, after the briefest of greetings to Joseph, withdrew into her private thoughts. She saw to the needs of Brigit's baby as required, but otherwise took no part in the gathering. The other curious combination stood in the corner by the mantel. The Tinker, Dermott O'Neill, was engaged in surprisingly quiet but continuous conversation with Mad Molly Fahey. Perhaps the duo was not as unlikely as it first appeared. One was an outcast from society by reason of his gypsy ways and the disjointed prattle of the other was too wearing for long endurance.

With the baby sleeping on her shoulder, Kate observed Molly and the Tinker with a detached amusement. The old woman appeared quite coherent under the stern gaze of the newcomer, as though his rapt attention kept her mind from wandering too far from the subject at hand.

Kate was certain Joseph would regard the Tinker kindly if the fellow proved a calming influence on Molly Fahey. After all, Joseph was the only person in the county who treated Mad Molly as if she were in complete possession of her wits. Kate admired him for that, at least. He had never given up his memories of Molly as she had been before the sorrows had come upon his family.

Since his return from Dublin Joseph had taken Mad Molly into his care. In title, though not in reality, he had proclaimed Molly head housekeeper of the manor house, just as she had been in bygone days. At first her presence had a disconcerting effect on the other members of the housekeeping staff. But the fey woman did no harm, and the servants simply performed their duties over her and around her as though she were not there. Now here was this horse-trading O'Neill fellow talking to her as though they were fast friends.

Kate noticed Joseph in the center of O'Connell's political companions. With solemn looks he nodded at some comment, his eyes darted to Molly and the Tinker, then back again. He seemed pleased indeed.

Joseph was a kind man, Kate mused as she nuzzled the downy cheek of the baby. Why then did her heart still accuse him of complicity in the death of Brigit? How could she blame him ultimately for the duel that had cost William Marlowe's life and Kevin his homeland? Whatever part Joseph had in the dramatic turning of events in Ballynockanor, he had tried to set everything right. Why then could she not forgive him?

Perhaps it was because there was no calling back the tragedy. Kate had spoken to Father O'Bannon on the matter of her unforgiving spirit a dozen times. Although Kate's mind accepted that Joseph Connor Burke had done all he could for her dying sister, still, she could not let go of her own bitterness toward him. Brigit was dead. Kevin was banished. If Joseph had done the right thing from the start, none of it would have happened.

As if he felt her thoughts, Joseph raised his hopeful gaze to her. One hint of softness in her expression would have summoned him to her side. Instead, Kate looked away, lowered her head, kissed Little Tom, called "Tomeen" in the Irish, and turned her back.

She was grateful to hold the baby. While she rocked him, at least, his sweet innocence quieted her spirit and somehow shielded her against the darkness of the rest of the world. Was his life not worth everything? Everything!

It was rumored that if Joseph had not found poor Brigit the baby would surely have died as well. That was something in Joseph's favor, Kate told herself. But it was not enough somehow for her to let herself forgive and love the man again. She would never look at him without thinking of Brigit, gone forever without a good-bye; gone without a word of tenderness or forgiveness for Kate.

Kate breathed in the fragrance of Tomeen's skin and murmured, "Ah, Brigit . . . Brigit. He is so perfect. If only I had known. If only you were here, and I could beg your pardon and say I love you."

Impossible wish. Unanswerable prayer. What was done could not be changed, and Kate could never forgive Joseph Connor Burke for it.

Adam Kane entered the room, and the heads of the women turned in unison to watch him as he strolled toward Joseph and Daniel O'Connell to be warmly brought into the circle of political debate.

There was an air of confidence about the man, Kate thought, that drew attention to himself. Mrs. Clooney, Molly, Fern the house-maid, and Margaret the cook were impressed.

Kane had been hired by Joseph at the recommendation of Daniel O'Connell as the new steward of the Burke estates. A pow-erfully built Dubliner of about thirty-five, he stood ten inches more than five feet and was swarthy of complexion with dark-brown hair sprinkled with gray. His eyes were green, and his jaw square.

"A handsome man, that," admired Mrs. Clooney. "And my Aidan says he is an able fellow. A jewel, a gem of a man. He rode out two days ago and after lookin' the farm over he's lowered our rent three shillin's."

Fern, who was chucking Little Tom's chin, remarked, "The low-ered rent is due entirely to our own Squire Joseph, Missus Clooney. Isn't that so, Kate?"

"Such a decision would come from Squire Joseph," Margaret interjected. "But there's no denyin' the steward's handsome."

Kate said nothing. It was always wise in such company to listen rather than speak. Sad experience had taught her that any comment about a single man, whether pro or con, would be headlines for the gossips the morning after.

Molly eyed the man with an appraising squint. "But the name of the fellow! It's there in the name. Adam was the first man. Cain the second."

Mrs. Clooney pursed her lips in thought. "Sure, and he's K-A-N-E. It ain't spelled the same. Not a'tall."

Molly shrugged off the argument. "He's also a very able fellow, so ye say, Missus Clooney?"

Fern sighed in exasperation. "I never understand a word of what you're sayin'."

Molly proceeded nonetheless. "Well, which one is he, I'm askin'? Adam was a follower. Cain was a murderer. Abel was a fine fellow with a lot of blood to spill. So which is he?"

Mrs. Clooney summarized. "Adam. Cain. Abel. He's handsome as the devil! And were I young and single and didn't have twelve children . . ." At this she gave Fern an approving nod.

Fern giggled, then her eyes widened in horror. "Lord have mercy! He's comin' right to us."

And so he was. The able Adam Kane, handsome as the devil, was indeed passing through the crowd of tenants, shaking hands and gabbing but also casting sidelong glances toward the cluster of blushing females.

Kate did not blush but gave him a steady look of amusement as he greeted his admirers. Fern curtsied and could not bring herself to speak. Margaret offered him the hospitality of the manor kitchen at any hour. Mad Molly lifted her skirts a bit as though she were treading through a mud puddle and circled around him.

"Which one are you?" she queried.

"I am Adam Kane, late of Dublin, and I've met you three times, Molly Fahey," he replied, taking her bony fingers in his large, square hand.

He made as if to kiss her fingertips, but she shrieked and fled.

He remarked with a wink at Kate, "I often have that effect on women." He bowed slightly. "And you are Kate, the daughter of Tom Donovan and the aunt of the young squire Little Tom here."

"That I am," Kate replied cautiously. Adam Kane was far too adept at charming conversation and entirely too familiar with strangers for her to trust him completely. "And you are the new rent collector."

"Indeed. Chosen not for wit, but for a pleasant smile." Another sweeping bow to Fern, Margaret, and Mrs. Clooney. "And as this lovely Missus Clooney will tell you, it is hardly an odious task considering the fact that I am steward for a man like Squire Joseph Burke. And he has commanded that the rents in the townlands be lowered."

"'Tis true. Aye. 'Tis true." Mrs. Clooney twittered like a bird—a large accomplishment for one as large as herself.

"And when will you be comin' out to assess our lands?" Kate asked. She was plainly not impressed by the gallantry, although it was always a pleasure to see a fine-looking man with a sense of humor about himself.

"Considerin' the departure of your brother tomorrow, I thought I'd leave it to yourself. Squire Joseph says you're the one who manages the dairy and so will most likely be on the grounds."

"And so I am." Little Tom squirmed in her arms and squawked a protest. Kate replied curtly, "Come when you like. Just not tomorrow, sir. We'll none of us be up to it with my brother leavin'." At that she gave him a brief curtsy and walked off toward Kevin.

Behind she could hear the worried voice of the new steward. "I shouldn't have asked on such a night. There now, I've made my first enemy."

Kate congratulated herself. It was always wise to keep a man as handsome and cocky as the able Adam Kane off balance.

Patrick Boyle, a tenor of renown, had come all the way from Cong to share his blessed voice. He had already performed "Lough Erne's Lovely Shore" three times during the evening, but he obligingly agreed to render it once more. There was some clatter outside the manor house: more late arrivals from Castletown, no doubt. Boyle signaled the musicians and in a high, clear ringing tone sang,

When I was young and foolish,
My age bein' twenty-four,
I left Lough Erne's lovely banks
And to Boston I sailed o'er.
And there . . .

He got no further with the last rendition because of the clamor of shouts and angry curses that came from outside the hall to drown out the festivities within. A rifle discharged, and the explosion brought both music and conversation to a halt. At that instant armed men, their faces blackened with burnt cork, appeared in the entries and at the French doors leading onto the terrace. A full dozen pushed through the front hall, propelling the hapless and weaponless English soldiers before them like the tide in Galway Bay sweeps a clump of seaweed up the shingle.

"God bless all in this house, exceptin' these English spawn and the blood-suckin' landlord," cried their leader. He was cloaked from head to foot in black, but there was no mistaking the pistol with which he demanded attention. "We'll have a different tune, if you please," he exclaimed. "Sing for us, 'The Men of Ninety-Eight.'"

Boyle remained silent.

"Sure, and I know you know it well," the commander of the night riders suggested. "Here, I'll start you off:

Full forty years have passed and gone
Since Irish men they stood
On the green hillside of Erin
And for freedom shed their blood.

Tom Donovan stood and fiercely confronted the chief. "What is the meanin' of this? We are gathered to wake my son, not to incite rebellion."

"Sit down, man," commanded the leader of the Ribbonmen with a wave of his pistol. "Why is this sad occasion bein' held in the house of your oppressor?"

"And what foolishness is this?" Daniel O'Connell retorted. "Do you not know that the Burke is one of us and the rightful heir to the land hereabouts?"

"One of us?" the terrorist said with scorn. "There is no landlord livin' can be trusted, nor can any man who says one may be. Listen to me, you cowards. Why is this foul deed bein' permitted at all? Why do you not rise up in wrath instead of bein' meek lambs to the slaughter? Kevin Donovan, ride with us this night, and be free of English law and exile."

Kevin, his face twisted with hostility and hope, started forward. He was at once pounced on by Father O'Bannon on the one hand and Daniel O'Connell on the other. "It is not for lawlessness that you were spared the noose," O'Connell said loudly.

"Think, man," the good priest agreed. "Will you bring destruction on your kin and neighbors? Have no part with these rapparees, I beg you."

Kevin stood wavering between the desire to escape banishment and the very real threat to his family and friends. "I have given my word," he replied at last. "I do not wish to go, but I am bound."

"Bad cess to you then, I say," declared the Ribbonman with a curse. "And to all you spineless curs. You deserve to be tossed, and your homes burned to the ground. Hear me, especially you, O'Connell, with your fine words and your faith in English law: this country will run with blood before Ireland is free; don't think it won't. Tonight is just a warnin': trust no landlord nor any who say that peace with the English can be had without breakin' the chains of slavery. You are traitors, else, and will be treated as such."

The soldiers were forced to strip to their undergarments, and a great heap of uniforms was tossed on the fire within the stone hearth. Then, having taken the weapons and the horses from the British, the band of Ribbonmen disappeared into the night.

The English captain confronted Joseph Burke. "It is well that Kevin Donovan did not choose to escape," he growled, "or it would have been worse for you. Don't think I don't know how you set us up for this to happen . . . sending that wailing woman out to distract my men while we were surrounded and disarmed.

A full report of this outrage will be on its way to Dublin before morning."

It was, everyone said, the most memorable wake, American or otherwise, that had ever been held in Connaught. While the captain and one unfortunate soldier remained behind, wrapped in blankets, to shoot spiteful looks and seething glances at Kevin Donovan and Joseph Burke, the other four embarrassed guards quick-marched back to the Castletown barracks for replacement uniforms.

Great crack it was, to see the British shamefaced in their underdrawers. But for all the merriment and the poor jokes at the expense of the soldiers, there was an undercurrent of hostility and uncertainty. The challenges issued by the Ribbonman were repeated and retold and filed away for spreading at first light to the villages roundabout and beyond. One wag noted that given the speed of gossip, the report of the evening would undoubtedly be in the pubs of Dublin before official word reached the British authorities in Dublin Castle.

The upshot was that as many questioning looks lit on Joseph and Daniel O'Connell from the villagers as from the pair of English. It was with relief to Joseph that the wake finally ended in the wee hours of the morning with the departure of the Donovans and the reclad sentries. Baby Tomeen, perhaps the only guest totally oblivious to everything that had occurred, had long since been whisked off to bed by Miss Susan, the black nursemaid.

Joseph intended for the political discussion suggested by O'Connell to adjourn to the yellow withdrawing room, but when the crowd finally disappeared, he was too exhausted to move. Instead he, together with O'Connell, Davis, O'Toole, and Father O'Bannon, remained amid the debris of the wake. Crumbs, spills, overturned chairs, and a forgotten sack of frog bread littered the Great Hall. One sleeve of a soot-covered red uniform was outstretched across the hearth as if vainly trying to crawl from the flames. A trio of sergeant's chevrons on the fabric called to its former owner, but he would doubtless have no wish to reclaim it, Joseph thought.

O'Connell levered himself upright out of an armchair and surveyed the ruins. "Quite a party you throw, eh, Joseph," he said, grinning. "Shall we to business now?" The men drew up a small circle of chairs nearer the fire.

Joseph gave his assent, wondering if his wits were clear enough to joust with O'Connell. Joseph also brooded on the fact that he had spent an entire evening in Kate's presence and had not exchanged above three words with her. What if she shared the opinion of the Ribbonmen? Should Joseph have exerted more effort to help Kevin escape banishment? And he was partly to blame for Brigit's death. His lack of a timely warning about the lecherous Viscount Marlowe had contributed to Brigit's ruin and led thereby to the duel that was ending in Kevin's departure. He shook his head to escape these morose thoughts, only to find that O'Connell had addressed him. "I'm sorry, Daniel," he said. "What was that again?"

"I said," O'Connell repeated patiently, "that it appears you are in the thick of the Repeal fight whether you acknowledge it or not."

The other three men muttered their assent to this assertion. "The fact is," O'Connell continued, "to oppose the Ribbonmen without an alternate plan is to be seen as pro-English."

"How does that follow?" Joseph challenged. "I have revoked the most unjust of the rack rents and redressed other wrongs here in the county."

"Nevertheless, it remains that sentiment is runnin' high against all things that smack of English rule. To give that rapparee his due, blood will surely follow if a peaceful move to self-government cannot be found. You have, perhaps, read my Mansion House speech of February?" O'Connell spoke with as much modesty as the politician in him ever allowed. "Fiery and to the point," Garrison O'Toole noted. "Knocked the complacent on their ears."

Joseph waited, expecting and dreading what was coming.

"When the British forced the Act of Union on us in 1800, they took away not only our parliament and our right of home-rule; they took away our dignity. 'You are not fit to govern yourselves,' they said. And you have seen how they preach that doctrine in the

National Schools. We need to be shed of the Union. And now," O'Connell continued, "the tragedy of Brigit Donovan and its aftermath have set the stage for Repeal."

Joseph looked up sharply at that, thinking of Kate and not of Repeal at all.

Noting the response, O'Connell hastily added, "Not that any of us regard it as any less a tragedy, but it is still true: the actions of the Marlowes represent what is wrong with this country, with its foreign overlords and foreign government, and you, my young friend, are sung of in the same ballads."

"'Tis true, what Daniel says," Father O'Bannon agreed. "The whole nation thinks of Brigit's death as the story of all Ireland under the English, and that means you are involved, like it or not."

"And it will continue to be trumpeted," Osborne Davis asserted. "In every issue of *The Nation* and as many other broadsheets as we can load and fire. Our methods differ from those of the Ribbonmen, but not the desired outcome."

"What do you want from me?" Joseph asked wearily, looking around the hall as if seeing the impending loss of what he had so lately regained.

"Support Repeal here in Galway. Lend your voice to the rallies. Travel in support of the Repeal movement. Prove the Ribbonman wrong. Speak out boldly about the justice of the cause, and prove to other landlords that Repeal does not mean lawlessness or a loss of their rights. Show that you and other propertied men uphold our cause. In short, be my lieutenant in the lands west of the Shannon. You know your country's history well enough to know that the west has always been the strongest province at resistin' tyranny and the first to welcome the prospect of liberty to the shores of this island. The west has always contributed the hottest fuel to the fires of freedom. But," O'Connell continued, "the west wants rousin'. Someone who will hoist them up out of their indifference and into the full heartbeat of Repeal . . . and that leader, I'm thinkin', is you."

"But there is yet so much that requires my attention here." Joseph tried to imply that his first duty was to his child and to the people of the Burke lands, but he was really worrying, *How will I ever reach Kate if I go away from here?* "I will have to think on it."

"There is no time," Davis urged. "The rally schedule begins in earnest this month. The assembly of delegates for a Repeal assembly is already planned for next December."

"Not planned," O'Connell corrected with a broad wink. "It will be a *spontaneous* gathering. Anything else might be construed as seditious."

"Perhaps," O'Toole observed, "the young landlord, now that he has recovered his own, does not have the stomach for a fight. Perhaps the rapparee was right."

Joseph bristled at the implication, but Father O'Bannon spoke up on his behalf before he could respond. "Now then, none of that. We are all united here. Sure, and Joseph has been through much already. He must act carefully so as not to alienate the other landlords to whom he might show reason and justice."

The only thing Joseph could do was lamely repeat, "I'll think on it."

Davis and O'Toole were disposed to argue further, but O'Connell stood and offered conciliatory words. "That is all we ask now," he said. "And so, gentlemen, if we may impose on our host to show us the way, let's to bed."

"Good night," Father O'Bannon said to Joseph at the door. "Fret as little as may be. God will yet lead the way." He paused, then added significantly, "In every matter."

As Joseph put out the last of the lamps and ascended the stairs toward his bedchamber, he noticed for the first time that not all of the guests had departed. Rolled up in a thick cloak in the darkest corner of the Hall was the horse trader Dermott O'Neill.

If he is awake, he may have heard what passed here, Joseph mused. *Ah well, of what political persuasion is a Tinker anyway? He does not even have a village to which he owes allegiance, let alone a country.*

2

The morning of good-bye came too soon for Kate. She had not slept all night, but labored over Kevin's ironing and the darning of his socks while Kevin's pipe and conversation with Da at the hearth died away to silence and waiting. Like a man condemned to the gallows Kevin fought sleep throughout the night. To the rhythmic thump of the iron he dozed off, then jerked himself awake and dozed off again.

Kate watched him, remembering when they were children together. She carved the vision of these last hours into her memory. Why had she never stopped to notice the curl of his brown hair across his forehead, or the detail of his broad, calloused hands? It was far too late to capture the wasted moments.

The light slid over the hills from the east. Kate could not hold it back nor keep it from carrying Kevin far away to the west. With the sun came the certainty that some good-byes are forever.

Martin and Mary Elizabeth, still dressed in their duds from the

American wake, slept on the hearth rug at Kevin's feet. The soldiers, accepting the hospitality of the Donovan barn, were up. The jingle of bits and spurs announced the end of the wait.

The ordinary juxtaposed with the unbelievable. Kate spoke calmly. "Would you like a cuppa tay then, Kev?" But her mind cried in torment, *The last cup he will taste by the hearth of home! Can it be that I will never see him again?*

In a hoarse voice Kevin replied, "Aye. Thank you, sister Kate." He did not dare say what he was thinking lest they both break and fall to pieces.

"I've finished the mendin' and the darnin'. Clooney says it'll be cold on the sea, and you must keep your feet dry. Remember my words now."

"I'll remember." His gaze was fixed on Mary Elizabeth. Was he wondering how old she would be before he ever laid eyes on her again? If ever he did.

Da stirred and jolted awake. His glazed eyes stared at the window. "So it's come, has it?" he muttered, pulling himself upright. "Sorry, Kev. I dozed a bit." At the sound of horses' hooves on the yard Da's face betrayed a fragment of horror, as though he had seen death through the glass and not just daylight.

"I didn't mind you sleepin' . . ." There was more Kevin wanted to say, but he dared not. Kate read his thoughts. *I didn't mind you sleepin' while I watched. I'll remember you peaceful, dreamin' here around me when I am far away and there is no other comfort to my soul except the memory of you here at the fireside.*

Kate caught his eyes, and with a look she forbade him saying aloud what they all knew.

Shoving a cup of steaming tea into Kevin's hand, Kate forced herself to do the commonplace things, the necessary things. He ducked his head and stared into it, then gulped it down so he could pretend the brimming of his eyes was because he had burned his mouth.

"I'll have a cup if you please, Daughter," Da asked in a voice too cheerful.

Martin awoke. Pulling himself upright and hugging his knees, he stared gloomily at the coals but said nothing.

Then Mary Elizabeth stretched. "It's mornin'." She sat up and touched Kevin's knee. "I'm glad you haven't left yet, Kev. I've got a present for you."

Now here was some relief, thought Kate. Mary Elizabeth, who did not understand what Kevin's banishment meant, scampered off to the bedchamber and emerged holding a small oilskin-wrapped packet. "You must not forget my caul." She placed the gift reverently into Kevin's hands. "You will not drown if you have this with you."

"Aye." Kevin acknowledged soberly in recognition of the belief that a baby delivered with the birth caul over its head would never drown. The caul itself, saved and passed along to anyone traveling on the sea, would also protect the traveler. "A fine honor. I'll send it back to you soon as I reach New York."

"Be sure you do, Kevin Donovan. I'll need it when I come to America."

Mary Elizabeth's certainty made Kevin smile. He put his hand on her forehead and said openly, honestly, "Come soon, Mary Elizabeth. Before you grow up and become too full of sense. For I'll miss your fine way of makin' everythin' seem logical even when it isn't a'tall."

Mary Elizabeth did not understand the compliment, but she thanked him all the same, throwing her arms around his neck and kissing him loudly on the cheek.

"And I'll miss havin' the handsomest brother in Ballynockanor! Will you find gold in America and send it home to us? Molly says for you the streets in America will be paved in gold."

Kevin exhaled. "If Mad Molly says it's so, then who am I to doubt it?"

As though conjured up at the mention of her name, Mad Molly's shrill voice sounded in the yard. "Vermin!" she shouted at the soldiers. "What have ye Sassenachs done with Kevin! Where have ye stowed him!"

"Speak of the devil," Da remarked wryly and lit his pipe.

Martin and Kate went to the window. Mad Molly was throwing handfuls of dust at a trooper who cowered behind the barn door.

"What Daniel O'Connell could do to the English with one thousand Mollys," Martin suggested.

"And what's she doin' out persecutin' the queen's poor soldiers this early in the mornin'?" Da joined them to watch the scene.

Martin sniffed and grinned at the sight of a lumpy canvas sack bound with twine. "She's come all the way from Castletown with Kevin's farewell gift."

Kevin looked pained. "She made me swear by Mary I'd eat it. I forgot to bring it home. . . ."

There was no escape.

"Frog bread," Martin and Mary Elizabeth said in unison.

From high above the village of Ballynockanor, beside the weathered stone cross of St. Brigit, Joseph watched Kevin Donovan take leave of his family, his village, and the land of his birth.

His chin high and proud, Kevin stared straight ahead as he sat atop his horse. He would not look to the right or the left lest the image of faces well loved, and now forever lost, make him splinter. The people of his life lined the narrow, rutted lane and raised their caps in hurrah as the queen's soldiers bore him away from home.

Kate hung back by Father O'Bannon at the front of the cottage. Martin and Mary Elizabeth, shouting farewells, trotted alongside the procession. Tom Donovan, his thin frame straight as a shovel handle, stretched his hand in blessing toward his son.

This was the way of it in an Ireland held captive by England, Joseph thought. A man like Kevin, defending his own sister against wrong, was banished forever from his homeland. For the sake of honor Kevin had lost everything and everyone he loved.

"God go with you, Kevin Donovan." Joseph made the sign of the cross. "You are a better man than any of us who stay behind in Galway. Aye, Kev, brother. You're better than myself. For now that my heart has found home again can I risk losin' it for a cause? Even for the cause of freedom?"

The cheers of the farmers and their families were carried up to the ancient cross on the wind. The voices and the vision were engraved forever into this granite sentinel. One day the stones of Ireland would cry out what they had witnessed, and God would judge each case in righteousness. Until then, Joseph knew only that his heart hungered for its own patch of earth; this place called *Connaught* . . . his home.

The dreams of his father now belonged to Joseph. What more could a man want than to raise his son in Galway, the land of wild beauty? Joseph turned his gaze on Kate as she entered the little whitewashed cottage. Perhaps one day she would love him again, and they would marry. Then perhaps there would be other children to love: his own flesh and blood running down the hills of Connaught, fishing in the river Cornamona, growing up and one day giving him grandchildren. . . .

Because of his own longing Joseph knew the heart of every tenant farmer in the townland that day: each held a vision of modest abundance, fields well tended, a pantry filled with enough to feed the family in the lean months.

Was O'Connell's calling for Repeal and the cause of an Ireland free from English rule bigger than all these other dreams weighed together?

Joseph could not answer the question. The deep desires of his own soul told him nothing was worth losing this place and this time and those he had come to love.

Joseph practiced the words he would speak to Daniel O'Connell, "I can't help you with Repeal. Irish union with England can be tolerated in Connaught since I am squire. It'll not harm my tenants. I can't risk everythin'. There are folk who need me here, fields to tend. I have a son to raise. I am content with the smallness of my life."

Even as he recited the sentiment he thought of Kevin. For the sake of honor, everything familiar was lost. Was it worth it?

Below Joseph's vantage point, Kevin and the soldiers topped a rise and then vanished from the view of Ballynockanor. The farewell ended. There were crops and livestock to tend.

The line of villagers along the road broke and scattered toward their own lives.

Tom Donovan, his hands upon the shoulders of Martin and Mary Elizabeth, walked back the way he had come. Father O'Bannon, looking older than usual, limped toward the Church of St. John the Evangelist.

Wrapping his cloak around his shoulders, Joseph strode down the slope toward the stone chapel. He would tell Father O'Bannon his decision.

Father O'Bannon was unusually glum as Joseph entered the vicarage.

"Sit down, sit down!" he invited with a flick of his fingertips.

Joseph pulled a stool close to the fire and extended his hands. "'Tis a cold mornin'."

"Aye. And a sad day as well for those who had to see their dear brother depart forever. Lord have mercy. 'Tis a kindness that God does not let us see our future. I baptized that boy, confirmed him, and gave him his first communion. Who could have known what would come of him? And who can know now what the future holds?" Father O'Bannon prepared tea. "And where was yourself this mornin'?"

"I watched from the cross of St. Brigit."

"I had a feelin' you were observin'. And when will you take to the road for Repeal and O'Connell?"

Joseph tucked his chin, embarrassed by the bluntness of the question. It left him no room for excuse. "I've decided my place is here."

O'Bannon sloshed the hot brew on his hand. "Stay here, lad? What're you sayin'? There's history to be made for Ireland and her people. Will you miss it?"

"I've been given a second chance at my life. A home, a true family. The things I imagined were lost to me forever, Father. It's a dream for me to be here. Can I risk the loss of the dream now?"

The priest sighed heavily and sank into his chair as if Joseph had laid a heavy burden upon him. "Aye, a dream. We of the west stay here asleep while the Irish nation beyond our own tiny border suffers."

Closing his eyes he lifted his face toward the dusty rafters and slowly recited,

And if, when all a vigil keep
The West's asleep, the West's asleep—
Sing oh! Poor Erin well may weep;
That men so sprung are still asleep.

A heavy silence followed. Joseph turned his eyes to gaze out the window to where sunlight played on new grass.

"I want my life, Father. And a life for my son. Here in Galway."

"A life for your son, is it? A life under continued English tyranny and arrogance? The tyranny that banishes his uncle? The arrogance that defiled his mother?"

"If I stay out of it we'll have peace here in the Burke lands. Security."

"History past tells a different tale, Joseph."

"They can write Irish history well enough without me. I am a simple man. I want nothin' more than what I've been given."

"They'll take even that away sooner or later if you don't march now with O'Connell. The time is right."

"It'll happen in Dublin. Not in Ballynockanor."

Father O'Bannon rocked and considered his words for a long moment. "History only seems to take place in capitals and marbled halls. That's because the winners write it. The winners are often guilty, and so they bear witness to nothin'. The truth dies with the men who loved it. The lies sit upon dusty shelves in crumblin' books and are taken for fact by those who come after."

"That may be so, Father. But I can't change it."

"Ah, but that's where you're wrong. For God commands that true history is to be written on the hearts of men. Christ taught us to pray, 'Thy kingdom come, thy will be done on earth as it is in heaven.'" The old man held his finger up like a candle. "Think of it, Joseph. From the time of St. Patrick, we Irish were the ambassadors of Christ on earth. It was Irish monks who built monasteries to preserve the literature of the ages. Our missionaries ventured into pagan England to convert their kings and then to all of Europe to carry the Word of God to the nations. That is our history."

"Aye. It's true. Every word of it."

"Sure it is. Then came the English to repay us. A long story it is, beginnin' way before that vile king, the eighth Henry of cursed memory, who broke with the church so he could divorce, marry six times, steal the lands of the church, and have the wealth of the monasteries in his own pocket. Or shall we speak of the Puritan tyrant Cromwell? Our land attacked, churches destroyed. Our people persecuted with a savageness surpassing that of the first-century pagan emperors. England was victorious and so wrote her own version of our history. Aye, Joseph. I've seen the reports. After murderin' Irish Catholics, Cromwell's soldiers wrote home that strippin' our bodies they found tails six inches long. It was received as fact because it eased the consciences of murderers to think we were not human. The Irish, you see—scholars, missionaries, those who preserved the church through the darkness of the ages—were written about as if we were only half men. Do you not see it, lad? They degrade our heritage yet today. Lazy drunkards they call us! If we let the English masters write Christian and Irish history, then the truth of who we are will be lost."

"Isn't it enough I've started an Irish school for the children of Ballynockanor and Castletown? And this in defiance of English law?"

"No. It is not enough. For as long as English statutes rule in Ireland they can close your school by force if they've a mind to do it. Queen Victoria is, by law, the head of the Church of England and of Ireland. We Catholics have no right to educate our children as we see fit."

"They're more likely to leave us in peace if I *don't* stand up."

"Peace? What would Christ have you do when your nation bows its neck to suffer at the hands of wickedness?"

Joseph argued, "He said, 'My kingdom is not of this world.'"

Father O'Bannon countered fiercely, "Without apology He rebuked evil men and drove the moneychangers from the temple. He taught us to pray for God's will to be done on earth as it is in heaven. Can we pray and not strive to correct injustice? Can we ask for God's will to be done and not work for a nation where God's compassion and His righteousness are held sacred above all else?"

Joseph clasped his hands in agony as Father O'Bannon's words uprooted his apathy. "I long for safety."

"There is no safety for Ireland without justice. There is no human dignity for the Irish without freedom! Our conquerors believe we are ignorant fools descended from apes. They strive to keep us poor and uneducated, weak and terrified. We, who are created in the image of God, who preserved the Holy Word, and cherished learnin' through the Dark Ages, have been slandered to the world by the very English nation our Irish church fathers converted to Christ!"

"What can I do, Father?" Joseph asked quietly. "I am only one man."

"Important movements are born of one good man joinin' another and another until there are a million gathered upon the road for the sake of righteousness! You are the son of your father. Ireland needs your voice," corrected the priest, and then he recited the second verse of the poem,

> *But—Hark! Some voice like thunder spake:*
> *"The West's awake! The West's awake"*
> *Sing oh! hurra; let England quake*
> *We'll watch till death for Erin's sake!*

A daily average of eighty children from Castletown and Ballynockanor attended classes on the Burke estate. Although any school in Ireland except the official English National School was against the law, Joseph Connor Burke ignored the edict just as he had done in the early days when he was schoolmaster of the parish hedge school in Ballynockanor.

The refinement of educational lawbreaking had come a long way from the one-room school with the sod floor and the smoking turf fire. Classes were now held in the west wing of the Jacobean manor house. Martin's class was in the walnut-paneled library with high, plastered ceilings and more books on the bookshelves than he had ever dreamed of reading. Unlike the National School in Castletown, every child was freely given a pair of shoes and proper clothing to wear. A hot meal of stew and bread was served at midday. Even the poorest children in the parish held their heads up with pride when they entered the great house. No longer could harsh English masters demand the recitation of the poem, "Children of the dust must not be proud. . . ." No more were the children constrained to repeat, "I am a happy English child. . . ."

Joseph had spoken openly about the matter after he reclaimed the estate. He called the new institution *St. Brigit's School.* The name was discussed by the gossips in the market square, and it was decided that this was as much for his wife's memory as for the Irish saint. Even though Joseph Connor Burke was born to the title of *Squire and Landlord,* the farmers and their wives could plainly see that the fellow must have truly loved poor Brigit Donovan. Although they tipped their hats, curtsied to him, and called him "sir" and "Your Honor," that did not mean Joseph Connor Burke was not a bereaved husband with feelings just like any other widowed man. And was the wee babe not half Donovan? One of their own kind? *Himself has a heart, landlord though he may be.*

As for Joseph's policy on the school, it was much applauded by everyone but the authorities.

He had read his statement from the pulpit as Father O'Bannon nodded sagely.

"Catholic or Protestant, the children of Galway are Irish. Though the classes will be taught in the English tongue, there will be no punishment for speakin' the Gaelic."

There had followed much cheering and Mad Molly shouting, "Glory be!"

Joseph had continued, "The school and its benefits are my gift to the tenants of the Burke lands. Education is the only way to combat misery and poverty." There were more cheers and the universal thought that he might also have added the words: *and to combat the English!* "By the time wee Tom is grown, it is my wish that every man, woman, and child in the townlands will speak, read, and write as well as the scoundrels who sit in parliament in London. *Nay, better!*"

This sentiment nearly blew off the new slate roof from the Church of St. John the Evangelist. Joseph Connor Burke was proving himself to be cut from the same cloth as his dear murdered father had been, *God rest his soul, and isn't it a pity the good always die young. . . .*

To achieve his goal Joseph hired four teachers from Dublin and a schoolmaster named Daly. It was accepted that the children came for the food and clothing first and education second. No matter. Even clods with the tiniest intellects were learning a bit of Latin and how to read, write, and cypher. A few months after Joseph Connor Burke's bold enterprise had begun, the new school was packed with Protestant children as well as Catholic children.

To the dismay of Miss Rush, the National School headmistress, the brooding brick edifice of the government school was empty of all but the children of government officials, Church of Ireland clergy, and soldiers. Wretched woman that she was, Miss Rush condemned St. Brigit's School and wrote petitions of protest to the proper authorities at Dublin Castle. She had heard that the children were allowed to ask questions in class and that laughter was permitted. The shame of it! And was not the squire, Joseph Burke, encouraging laziness by providing food and clothes to the little Irish beasts? She warned Dublin that no good could come of this—none. The end would be open revolt against the proper authorities!

Martin secretly hoped Ribbonmen would burn her school to the ground. "Aye!" Martin exclaimed when he heard the content of her letter. "Let the revolt begin with us wee Irish beasts addin' a bit of hot tar to the ruffled feathers of Miss Rush!"

Mary Elizabeth, ever the gentle lamb, followed the example of Daniel O'Connell's movement and rejected violence. Instead she turned to prayer to deal with the wicked. Invoking the Almighty, she requested that the ugly inside of Miss Rush would become evident on the outside. It was interesting to Martin that within the month the schoolmistress became as fat as Clooney's sow and unusually hairy after that. The mustache on her upper lip thickened so it might have been the envy of any soldier in Galway except that she took to shaving surreptitiously.

With the exception of that one curiosity nothing came of Miss Rush's complaint. Dublin Castle remained silent, and St. Brigit's School flourished.

3

Kate did not hear his footstep nor the approach of his horse, but when she turned from hanging out the washing, there was Adam Kane studying her from the corner of the house.

His presence startled her. She gasped and put a hand to her cheek. He laughed with true enjoyment as though he intended to surprise her.

"It's you, is it?" This time there was no pretense to the edge in her voice.

He doffed his top hat and bowed. "Aye, Madame. The . . . what was it you called me? Tax collector?"

"Rent."

"That's true. Indeed I am. And a more pleasant or happy batch of tenants a steward has never seen than you in Ballynockanor."

She caught her breath. "You've got the sneaky tread of a collector of rents, Mister Kane."

"I'll take that as a compliment."

"I didn't mean it as such."

"One day you might change your mind about me. I'll hold a positive thought in that regard."

"You may hold whatever thought you like."

His smile broadened. "When it comes to yourself I will hold many thoughts, Miss Donovan."

He was flirting with her openly. His forwardness made her self-conscious. She tucked her scarred hand beneath her shawl. "Not Miss Donovan. Didn't they tell you I'm a widow? My husband's name was Garrity."

"Widow Garrity." He tested the title and frowned. "May I not call you Kate like everyone else in the townlands?"

"Sir, there's no one in the townlands who hasn't known me from childhood."

"And some of us wish we had."

"You're a bold one."

He shrugged. "It comes with the position." He paused a moment and added, "Squire Joseph said you were beautiful. Fern told me about the fire that took your husband and mother and injured yourself."

"Indeed you are steppin' over the line of propriety."

He disagreed. "I'm an honest man is all. I want the air clear between me and yourself when I see you."

"Why should that matter?"

"Gossip is that the squire had an eye for you. That once you looked kindly toward him. And that now you hate him dearly."

"Gossip!" she retorted. "Bein' sucked into the bog of talk so soon are you, Mister Kane?"

He waved her protest away. "I'm thirty-five years old and a single man. That's old enough to sort out what is fact. Fact is, you are a fine-lookin' woman, Kate. I thought so the first time I laid sight of you. The fire did not diminish the obvious. Fact is, the squire has no claims upon your heart. Fact is, I may well wish to court you."

She swallowed hard. An honest man. A blunt man. Or was he something else?

"You may wish whatever you like," Kate replied. "Fact is, I may well join a nunnery and be done with the likes of you."

He laughed. "That would not keep you from thinkin' of me."
He looked around at the house and the barns and the sheep pens.
"In the meantime, Squire Joseph, whose heart you've broken in
two, says there'll be no rent on Donovan land."

She interrupted angrily, "He says that, does he?"

"Indeed. His in-laws shall pay no rent."

"Yes, we shall. Else who in the townlands will pay our share? I'm
no fool. Squire Joseph Burke must collect rents from his tenants to
pay his own rent to the Crown. The Donovans will not be the only
ones in the townlands not meetin' their obligations. Tell that to the
squire."

"Shall I tell him anythin' else?"

"Such as?"

"That when I mentioned his name you blushed?"

"It's indignation about such foolishness that brought the color
to my cheeks."

He gave her a knowing look. "I think you yet have the squire in
your heart."

That pronouncement did indeed cause her to flush. "You're too
bold, Adam Kane. Tell him no such thing. Joseph Connor Burke,
nor any man, has a place in my affections. Nor shall have."

Closing one eye he held up his hands and pretended to look at
her through a spyglass. "Thar she blows!" he exclaimed. Then with
a wink he bowed again, proclaimed three shillings off the Donovan
rent, and took his leave.

It was too late at night when Joseph arrived in Waterville, County
Kerry, to ride the last ten miles to Daniel O'Connell's country house
at Derrynane. Instead he took a room at an inn on the edge of
Ballinskelligs Bay.

The next morning, well before light, he was off again, riding the
black hunter over Coomakista Pass. On his right hand the sand-
bordered inlet opened onto the deeper blue of ocean. As the road
climbed the heights, Joseph got occasional glimpses of the Skelligs,

islets floating on the swell like green and white speckled ducks paddling toward the shore.

Though arriving at Daniel's home just at the breakfast hour, Joseph was informed by the white-haired steward that O'Connell was already out in the uplands of his property, preparing for a hunt.

"Already?" Joseph questioned, not certain if he had heard correctly.

"To be sure," the servant replied. "The master is often out before daybreak," and he proceeded to give Joseph directions to O'Connell's most likely "roost," as he put it. The instructions included turning left at the clump of willows and then bearing "a wee bit north till you reach the stone fort, but if you come to the lightnin' blasted oak, you've gone too far."

The climb up the hillside was steep, and Joseph stopped to catch his breath. A gray mist hung across the vale like a slanting curtain, pulled back to reveal half of the peaks over the way and mysteriously concealing the rest.

A quarter mile beyond the slumbering heap of boulders that marked the remains of a Bronze Age stronghold, Joseph located Daniel O'Connell. The Liberator was seated on a rock slab shaped like a table, the five-ton lid of an ancient chieftain's burial place.

"Ho, Daniel," Joseph called.

"Saw you comin', Joseph," O'Connell returned. "I'm just finishin' up. Be right with you."

Spread out across the top of the tomb were a half dozen newspapers, a heap of correspondence, and a notebook. O'Connell opened *The London Times* to the editorial page, read furiously, scribbled a few notes on his pad, then threw the paper aside. Two more papers, *The Nation* and *The Illustrated News*, were treated in similar fashion, as were a fistful of letters.

"And is this your office, then?" Joseph asked when the flurry of activity had subsided.

"Can you think of any better?" O'Connell replied, sweeping his hand around the valley and the craggy peaks. "It is never the same twice," he observed, pointing out how the interplay of light and shadow on stony heights and rocky clefts, on stream courses and tree copses was ever changing, vibrant with life. "Sometimes I don't know how I ever leave here," he concluded. "But then you said much the same about your estate, and yet here you are. Will you join me for breakfast?"

Beside the massive boulder was a basket. When opened it produced oat bread, butter, cheese, boiled eggs, fried bacon, and a flask of still-steaming tea. Daniel O'Connell swept his paperwork into the emptied wicker hamper and proceeded to eat with as much gusto as he conducted his correspondence. Joseph joined him.

"As glad as I am of your company," O'Connell said around a mouthful of bread and cheese, "you have not come all this way for purely social reasons. Tell me your mind."

Joseph recounted his recent discussion with Father O'Bannon and the struggles between his desire to live quietly and the prodding of his conscience. "After all was said, it was plain as day," he summarized, "that I could not rest easy while others were puttin' everything they possessed, even their lives, on the line."

"And . . . ?" O'Connell prompted when Joseph's words slowed.

"And bein' a Burke, recognizin' myself as bloodless and indifferent did not set well with me," Joseph stated grimly.

"No more than it would have with your father," O'Connell murmured.

"Mark me, Daniel," Joseph said, "my first duty is still to my son and next to the people who look to me, and that means I may not be traipsin' about the whole length of the country . . . but if I can be of value by actin' as your lieutenant in Connaught, then I'm your man."

"Well done!" O'Connell said, applauding him. "Stout lad. I had no doubt you would come along. Who'd want to miss out on the admirable adventure, eh? Now here's what I want: make a schedule that will take you around the whole country west of the Shannon. Speak to the wardens and the collectors of the Repeal rent to encourage them. Oversee the transport of the money from the province to Archbishop MacHale in Tuam; he'll forward it from there. Above all else, be ready to speak of Brigit."

Joseph agreed, though he thought the last request would clearly be the most painful. To shake off the disturbing images that flooded his mind he changed the subject. "I heard your steward say that you were up here huntin'," he remarked. "But clearly one of us was mistaken: no horses and no hounds."

"Ah," Daniel said with a laugh. "Don't let little details like that be botherin' you. *Ridin'* to the hounds is for the patrician houses like yours. As for the hounds themselves . . ." He gestured off down the slope toward a stand of oaks. A huntsman in green was struggling upward with a pack of russet-and-white beagles. "I am too sly a fox to approve of catchin' my own kind. But you are in time for my kind of hunt," he offered. "Around here we follow on foot . . . after the hares."

The area south of Trinity College, Dublin, along Harcourt, Nassau, and Dawson Streets, was home to booksellers, printers, binders, and newspaper offices. The printshop that produced *The Nation*, the paper of the Repeal movement, was located in that same vicinity. If the Georgian building on Baggott Street in which it was housed was shabby and unprepossessing, it had the advantages of cheap rent and a close proximity to the park of St. Stephen's Green.

Osborne Davis, editorial writer and one of the founders of the paper, came into the printer's with a sheaf of papers in hand. "O'Toole," he said to his assistant, "our next issue will mark the five-month anniversary of the paper. Since our critics said that we would not last sixty days, I want to gloat a little. Let's run again the poem from the first issue."

Davis, a Protestant from Cork, was keenly aware that for the Repeal movement to succeed, a sense of being Irish had to bind together those of differing religious backgrounds. To achieve this end he wrote and encouraged others to write poetry about the heroic deeds of Irish folk heroes.

O'Toole gravely accepted the sheet of foolscap Davis was waving, which read,

We want no swords, no savage swords
Our fetters vile to shatter
Let all who hear repeat the shout
That freedom is the matter.

"This is very good," O'Toole said deferentially, well aware that the doggerel was Davis's own composition. "But can we not sound a little more strident, a little more forceful?"

O'Toole's sister, Beth Anne, emerged from the composing room, a slide of lead type in her ink-stained fist, in time to overhear the discussion. "Poet's Corner is already set for the next issue," she complained. "Listen:

As lightning begets thunder
Blood will have blood and swords hew asunder
Hereditary bondsman, this is your lot:
Who would be free, himself must cleave the knot!

"In honor of the Galway City Repeal Rally," she insisted.

"May I remind you both that our offerings must stress the peaceful nature of the movement?" Davis replied. "It serves no purpose if we are closed down for being too militant. Nor will talk of blood and battles win the complacent tradesmen over to the cause."

Garrison O'Toole shrank from debating with his chief, but not his spinster sister. "But this is not a call to arms now," she protested. "It's adapted from a Daniel O'Connell speech back in '38. Almost his very own words."

"That may be so," Davis remarked with a pained look, "but on the eve of the meetin' when the authorities are payin' close attention, it is absolutely essential we not sound overtly belligerent. Let us consider that the end of the discussion. Garrison, I want you to go to Ulster for me tomorrow. There are some important papers that Duffy needs to see at once."

Garrison O'Toole looked troubled. "I'm sorry, Osborne," he said. "But I thought you knew. Family matters take me away from Dublin tomorrow. I'll only be gone four days at most. Can the papers wait till my return?"

"If necessary," Davis replied. "There is no one else I care to trust but you. Make the journey as soon as you return. Now I'm off to see O'Connell."

"I will," O'Toole promised, ushering Davis to the door of the printshop. "I'll see to it personally." After walking the editorial chief halfway down the block toward Merrion Square, he returned to his sister. "Now what are we to do?" he worried aloud.

"Is there any question?" Beth Anne said with assurance. "Mister Davis has his head in the clouds, conferrin' with the Great Liberator. We'll run 'The Hereditary Bondsmen' poem as planned. If he complains, we'll say it was an unfortunate oversight, or that his instructions were never clear. We will see to it that this paper has the writin' it truly needs, in spite of what the editor thinks."

Five miles from the heart of London, past the Vale of Health, and beyond the top of Hampstead Heath with its commanding view of the city spread out below, was a public house known as "The Spaniards." Its precise age unknown, The Spaniards had been home to at least two centuries of intrigue. In its time it had harbored outlaws, Jacobins, those on the run from the parliamentary army and those who supported it. In 1780 the tavern had furnished the rendezvous for the Gordon rioters in their quest to tear down the nobility, beginning with Earl Mansfield's nearby home, Kenwood House.

On that occasion the cavalry arrived in time for the elegant country estate to be spared, and the terrorists dispersed. But the plotting and scheming that took place in The Spaniards continued almost without interruption—just changes of cast.

It was an unusual group that gathered in the oak-paneled back room of the pub. Burtenshaw Suggins, assistant to the Lord Chancellor of Ireland, found it convenient for his purpose, since he and Secretary Edward Lucas were staying at Kenwood. The third official, Charles

Trevelyan, assistant secretary of the Treasury in Prime Minister Peel's cabinet, had ridden up from his home in Eton Square.

The reason for the clandestine appointment had more to do with the fourth member of the gathering than the three British administrators. There were plenty of government offices and conference rooms in Whitehall that would have served, but the nameless last element of the quartet was a British spy operating in Ireland who did not want to be seen going into an official building.

Indeed, he had slipped into The Spaniards by the door leading to the stable ten minutes after the arrival of Suggins, Lucas, and Trevelyan.

"Well?" Suggins demanded. "Is it a tempest in a teapot as we thought?"

The operative, his cloak pulled high up around his neck and his hat pulled low across his forehead, spoke in muffled tones through the scarf that covered his face. He was taking no risk that even a chance encounter might cause him to be later recognized. He answered with the certainty of one who traveled freely in the inner circle of the Irish movement to repeal political union with England.

"The situation is dangerous indeed. The planned assembly of Irish tenants will take place next week in Galway City, my lord. Daniel O'Connell's advance men are throughout the whole nation south of Sligo. He has wardens in every parish, sometimes three or four. Protestant and Catholic poor alike hold but one opinion. There is not a tenant family in southern Ireland who does not support breakin' off with England and reestablishin' an Irish parliament in Dublin."

"Just arrest O'Connell and have done, I say," Suggins sputtered. "The man is a seditious rebel and ought to be hanged."

"The man," Trevelyan corrected dryly, "is the past Lord Mayor of Dublin and a current duly elected Irish member of our parliament here in London."

"The Irish representatives to our English parliament are an ineffective minority and subject to ridicule," Suggins said.

"English opinion is not the issue here. O'Connell is the most popular man in Ireland," the agent added. "It would be a disaster to move against him openly, at least for now."

"I agree," Lucas concurred. "O'Connell is a canny politician. His speeches, though fiery, contain nothing that would hold up in court. No, we must wait till he makes a misstep."

"Or cause one?" Suggins added pointedly. "How long do we dare let this movement grow?"

"Is O'Connell susceptible to bribery: money or titles?" Trevelyan inquired. "If we lop off the head, the body will surely die. What do you say, Mister O'Toole?"

"No names, my lord," the operative, Garrison O'Toole, cautioned, anxiously twisting a silver ring inscribed with a Celtic cross. "Even here O'Connell has friends."

"Very well then," Trevelyan noted. "Can O'Connell be bought off?"

"Indeed not, my lord. It was tried two months ago. He gave up the mayoralty because he could no longer afford the trappin's, yet crowns and guineas would not move him. As for titles? The sweaty Dublin mob would have made him mayor for life, but he means to dedicate himself to repeal Irish union with England. Of course my sister . . . my associate . . . and I will do what we can to push O'Connell's movement into something treasonable, but so far they are bein' very discreet."

There was a brooding silence in the room. Trevelyan stared up at the fleur-de-lis of the pressed tin ceiling. Then he asked, "Of course the cause is popular among the Irish tenants. What about the Irish-born gentry? Is there any menace there?"

"There is one who will bear watchin'," O'Toole said. "Joseph Connor, Lord Burke of Connaught. He is the widower of the girl ruined by Viscount Marlowe."

"That one?" Trevelyan snorted. "Burke, eh? Well, Burke's a fool! Marry a whore and then claim the child as his own? If he's a sample of the wise leadership of the Irish separatist movement, then we have nothing to fear."

There was a chorus of chuckles around the room, in which all except the spy shared. "Do not underestimate the power of sentiment," O'Toole observed. "Brigit Donovan alive was a whore—of no consequence. Bridgit Donovan dead is a martyr—a cause célèbre.

Her husband and the baby are the livin' reminders of an English landlord's insult and high-handedness. And Burke has agreed to act as O'Connell's deputy in the west."

Trevelyan held up his hand in submission. "The point is, can we deal with this fool, this Joseph Connor Burke? May he not yield to flattery or cash? Can we not discredit him among the Irish peasants he supports?"

There was an echo of agreement in the room.

Suggins said, "If we can get him to denounce O'Connell's movement as ill-timed or poorly considered, too rash you see, that will put an end to the halo over him and this martyr Brigit."

The three government officials looked at O'Toole. Understanding their intent he said, "We have an agent in the area. We can try many avenues, my lords, but what if Burke is not open to either bribery or persuasion?"

Lucas and Suggins, who would be leaving for their return to Ireland in the morning, turned to face Trevelyan. Everyone knew he spoke for Prime Minister Peel. "England lost the American colonies in similar circumstances. The Americans resented our parliament having control over their laws and lands. History must not repeat itself in Ireland. We cannot have titled landowners openly supporting the notion of rebellion among the Irish tenant farmers," he said. "The government will approve *any* steps necessary to silence Joseph Connor Burke. Drive a wedge in O'Connell's movement, and we defeat O'Connell."

4

Martin found his attention wandering out the window to the fountain across the Burke driveway. He and the other boys of his age-group, Alan O'Rourke, David Clooney, and seven more, were gathered around Schoolmaster Daly at the rear of the library. Within the west wing of the manor different ages were reading, studying lists of spelling words, or doing cyphers on slates.

For Martin's group, it was history. Martin was certain Mr. Daly was a good teacher. In fact, when it came to reading stories aloud, or poetry, the Dubliner was even enjoyable. But history was boring at the best of times, nor did Daly have the knack of enlivening it.

At the moment, the instructor was reviewing the penal laws that suppressed the Catholic religion prior to the Act of Emancipation. "The Irish Catholic," Daly intoned, "could not own a horse of value greater than five pounds. He could not vote. He could not buy land, inherit land, or be gifted with land by a Protestant."

Martin yawned, ducking his head quickly to hide his face. Mister Daly was not as mean as Mrs. Rush at the hated National School in Castletown, but he still swung a willow branch when he thought it helpful, and willow branches still stung, regardless of who did the swinging.

"These laws . . . ," Mr. Daly continued, then stopped abruptly. As Martin watched, the instructor's eyes bulged and a huge sigh escaped the man as if he confronted an overwhelming task.

Even before darting a glance over his shoulder, Martin suspected the cause: around the doorframe of the passage into the hall poked a wiry mass of tangled hair. Following this tangled profusion was a wizened face and then eagerly darting blue eyes.

The rest of Mad Molly rounded the corner and entered the schoolroom. She seated herself at the rear of the group, bobbing her head pleasantly and saying nothing. Molly made the teachers nervous, and she in turn appeared to dislike them, but she harbored a special resentment toward Daly for an undiscovered reason.

Instructor Daly, Martin saw, was not convinced that this quiet arrival was anything other than the calm before the storm. The teacher leaned over to David Clooney and whispered, loud enough for Martin to hear, "Go get the squire."

David's exit took him past Mad Molly's seat. As he passed she stretched out one arm to bar his movement. Then stroking his hair with her other hand she murmured, "Poor, dear boy. Poor, poor lad," and then she let him proceed.

"As I was sayin'," Daly resumed, "these laws were themselves revoked by later laws."

"Mighty fine boots," Molly muttered, leaning sideways out of her chair and fixing her eyes on Daly's footwear.

"Because Catholics were not permitted an education, this very school would have been . . ."

"I've often wondered who masters the schoolmaster," Molly pondered aloud. "Ye cannot serve two masters." Her body still extending parallel to the floor, she widened one eye to its fullest, roundest orb while squeezing the other so tightly shut as to almost fold her face in half.

To Martin it seemed that she was aiming an imaginary cannon at Schoolmaster Daly.

"These laws were changed by an act of parliament," Daly continued tenaciously, resolutely staring over Molly's wrinkled presence at a map of Ireland hanging on the back wall. "In other words, unjust laws were repealed. Just as my good friend, Daniel O'Connell, insists for the present movement, these changes took place without bloodshed."

Molly bolted upright and waved her hand. Though she was not part of the class, it was impossible to ignore her. "What is it, Molly?" Daly inquired with another long, drawn-out breath.

"Without bloodshed, did y'say? What about the men of '98? What about the poor boys of the United Irishmen?"

"Armed rebellion always leads to more repression," Daly said firmly, trying to turn this interruption to his advantage and keep control of the class. "Bloodshed . . ."

"Bloodshed, indeed!" Molly exploded. "What about when they took Father John Murphy, him who had tried and tried to keep the peace? I'll give you bloodshed! They hanged him, and then they burned his body in a tar barrel and cut off his head and spiked it on a pole. And then they . . ."

Finally it was Mad Molly herself who was interrupted, much to the disappointment of Martin and his friends. This was the liveliest history class they had ever had.

Joseph Burke laid his hand on the woman's shoulder, and she subsided. "Come with me, Molly," he said gently. "Don't you know you're needed in the kitchen?"

"Potatoes," she said almost automatically. Then glaring with some of her former fire, she looked at Daly and said, "Mighty small potatoes, if you ask me. Who masters the schoolmaster? Oh! Tool of the devil, he is, that he is."

Molly allowed herself to be led from the classroom.

Mr. Daly, face flushed and composure destroyed, said, "It has grown quite warm in here, I think. We will take a ten-minute recess for some fresh air."

It had been a long, hard day for Kate. The market square of Castletown was crowded with farmers and their wives, and the gossip of the day concerned Brigit. Would the village not let her rest in peace?

Kate had heard the speculation, of course, that Joseph Connor Burke was the true father of Brigit's child. She had not believed it at first. But now wee Tomeen seemed to resemble Joseph more each day. The cleft in Little Tom's chin, the curve of the cheek, and the expression in his eyes all had the look of Joseph.

Mrs. Clooney's observations had a ring of truth in them. Kate found herself thinking through the possibilities of when Joseph might have rendezvoused with Brigit. He'd had ample opportunity.

The very thought of such a thing angered her more than ever. The idea that a man like Joseph had once thought himself fit for the priesthood! Had he not made overtures to Kate? Then why not Brigit? There was only one consolation: he had done the right thing and accepted paternity of the baby.

She felt nothing but loathing for Joseph as she turned onto the Burke estate to deliver cream and butter and pick up Mary Elizabeth and Martin after school.

To her right the stables loomed. Darkly handsome, the steward, Adam Kane, stepped from the barn to watch her passing. Kate kept her eyes fixed sternly to the gravel path. Why let the fellow know his look made her uneasy?

School was not yet out. Margaret called to her from the kitchen as she took the butter and cream from the cart.

"You've time for a cuppa, Kate. Come in, girl. Your wee nephew's here by the fire. Come in! We're all here."

The kitchen was indeed filled with familiar faces. Mad Molly, unusually quiet this afternoon, sat watching by the hearth as Miss Susan nursed Little Tom. Fern, the housemaid, chopped onions for

Margaret, who had served as cook since the old days. Darby, the ancient manservant, polished the silver.

"God bless all here." Kate carried the dairy goods directly down the narrow steps to the cooler. A cup of steaming tea was waiting for her when she returned. Fern made a place for her at the servants' table, and Miss Susan passed Tom to her for the burping.

Kate kissed the soft head, feeling comforted by the child. "It's like seein' young Brigit when I hold him," she said aloud, then immediately regretted her words.

Margaret gave her the smile of one who knew more than she could say. Kate had been seeing such smiles from the gossips in Castletown. She ignored it.

Fern, without much wit beneath her curly brown hair and maid's cap, said what Margaret had not. "I think he looks more like Squire Joseph every day. Bless me, I do!"

Kate kissed the baby again and pretended not to hear.

Darby tilted his bald head in agreement. "Of course he looks like the squire. I saw the squire at this same age. Of course we called him Connor then, but never mind that. This child, but for the red curls, is the very image . . ."

Molly began to rock. "That he is! That he is! Little angel. Never mind the trouble, or how he came to us. The very image of wee Connor Burke."

Miss Susan, her warm, chocolate-colored eyes full of pity for Kate, said nothing about the baby's looks. "Never seen a better baby," she commented. "Lord knows it don't matter who he look like. Got his daddy's quiet soul, I think."

Inherent in this discussion was the unspoken speculation abut the circumstance of Little Tom's conception. Had the Squire taken Brigit before William Marlowe seduced her? Was this what made him give up his calling to the priesthood? He certainly had everyone in the townlands fooled!

Kate felt sick and unhappy by the time she ordered Mary Elizabeth and Martin onto the cart for the ride home. Kate had longed to take the baby from Joseph and raise him in the Donovan cottage as Brigit would have wished. The evidence of Joseph's paternity certainly changed everything. It explained Joseph's actions in Dublin. So he was not a saint. He was not as selfless as everyone had believed. Never mind. Joseph had every right and obligation to raise Tom as he saw fit.

The small study was at the end of the corridor on the second floor above the ground at Burke Hall. It was not paneled and spacious like the library now in use by the school, but it was a comfortable place to work and full of good memories.

Stretching, Joseph rubbed his eyes as he leaned back in the chair. A glance at the wall clock showed he had reason to be tired; it was after midnight. There was never enough time to get everything done in the daylight hours and still keep up with letter-writing and reading. Under a six-inch-high carved replica of the stone cross of St. Brigit that stood on a hill above Ballynockanor was a stack of a half dozen completed replies. Held in place by a red leather-bound volume entitled *Scientific Methods of Modern Farming* by Thomas Jefferson were a dozen more letters awaiting his responses.

The pressure on Joseph's time had increased as soon as he admitted he was going to Galway City for the Repeal rally, and not just because he was to be away. Daniel O'Connell sent him tons of correspondence: newspaper accounts of speeches, plans for organizing Connaught into efficient cells of active Repealers, and suggested names of other landlords whom O'Connell wanted Joseph to contact. Nor was information only arriving for review. Joseph's opinion about proper locations for future west country rally sites was also solicited, as were the identities of solid citizens among the middle and upper classes who could be counted on to support Repeal.

Daniel O'Connell always made his associates feel they had joined a holy crusade, a righteous quest for justice. No matter how many times Joseph protested his lack of expertise and knowledge, O'Connell insisted he was the Galway Repeal machinery's most important cog. This persuasion prodded Joseph to read one more memorandum, write one more reply.

As he lit a candle before extinguishing the lamp in the study he picked up a clay pipe that had belonged to his father. Joseph had found the pipe dumped into a box of his father's personal things. Part of the stem was broken off short, but the aroma of his father's tobacco still lingered in the bowl, and the scent always carried Joseph back to childhood. Many times as a boy Joseph had awakened to the smell of tobacco smoke drifting up to his bedroom. If he got out of bed and padded into the small study he was sure to find his father working late, huddled over account books and pondering another plan to aid the struggling farmers of Burke lands. How Joseph wished he had his father around to consult still. He laid the pipe down and headed for his rest.

The tall bed with the four dark wood, spiral-carved posts was not without memories either. It was here that Joseph's father had died, poisoned by his brother-in-law. Fifteen years after the tragedy, Joseph had crept secretly into that very room at night to pin a warning to the headboard above his sleeping uncle. Tonight was not the time for any such reflections; there were too many immediate, practical concerns. Joseph drifted off to sleep considering the advantages of Clifden over Kinvarra for the location of a future Repeal rally and whether he should investigate growing flint corn as animal feed.

As if to redirect his waking reflections, his dreams were full of Kate. Images of the manor house filled with children who were not village offspring, but his own and Kate's, swirled in Joseph's sleep. He heard the patter of their feet on the stairs and awoke, smiling at the thought.

A floorboard creaked in the silence. It was probably Miss Susan up feeding Tomeen. Joseph continued to smile, thinking of the infant with the curly red hair. Then the wooden joint groaned again.

His eyes snapping open, Joseph listened carefully to the darkness. The tread was too heavy to be the nurse and seemed to come from the opposite end of the house from the nursery. The quarters for the servants were quite distant, above the kitchen.

Some unknown was in the house, someone with a reason to be stealthy about his movements.

Swinging out of bed, Joseph picked up the candle but did not light it at once, then reached for the sturdy hazelwood walking stick that leaned in the corner. Dressed in his nightshirt he headed quickly to check first on the child.

At the door of the baby's bedroom he knocked, and Miss Susan opened the door. "Have you been awake with Little Tom?" he asked in a hushed voice.

Miss Susan matched her reply to the tone of the question. "This baby so well fed he ain't gonna wake up b'fore mornin'," she whispered. "Is there trouble?"

"Intruder," Joseph said tersely. "Lock the door, and don't open it unless you know it's me."

By the time the bolt clicked in the lock, Joseph was halfway along the hallway. At the head of the stairs he listened again, but heard nothing.

Then there came the faintest rustling of papers, like a mouse rattling in a sack of grain. It was coming from the direction of the small study.

Creeping forward slowly, Joseph passed the slight bend in the corridor where a later masonry addition had been joined onto the original ancient house. Once around the corner he made out a faint glow coming from under the door to the study.

Two paces forward and a beam complained of the weight under Joseph's own feet. Instantly the light ahead was extinguished. The door of the study crashed open, and there was an explosion of footsteps.

The need for quiet abandoned, Joseph rushed toward the office. Racing steps echoed Joseph's own. He ran with the walking stick extended in front of him like a spear.

The flight of the trespasser reached the servants' passage, and a door banged open. Then the noises plunged headlong down the steep flight of stairs toward the ground floor.

How many were there? Were they armed? Joseph remembered the ominous warning issued by the Ribbonman captain but dashed forward anyway, heedless of danger to himself. On the third tread from the bottom of the stairs, Joseph's foot slipped. The stick flew from his hand, clattering downward, crashing into the panel that concealed the maids' access to the Great Hall.

Shouldering through the entry, Joseph instinctively ducked, wary of a blow from behind the carved portal. He ran into a table, groped for an iron from the fireplace, and spun around, seeking the prowler.

The clatter of footsteps on flagstones drew his attention toward the terrace. A French door was ajar. In the blackness of the night, no one could be seen outside, though the noise of retreating feet still rattled over gravel and the cracking of brush.

In the open doorway, Joseph paused. There was no way to follow farther without stopping for a lantern, and no good sense in doing so either. He carefully locked the entry, then took down the fowling piece that hung above the fireplace. Lighting a lamp, Joseph checked to see that the weapon was loaded, then made a circuit of the doors and windows. All were secure.

After rousing the sleeping servants, Joseph ordered a careful search of the rest of the house. No other intruders were found, and nothing was seen to be stolen.

Joseph went back to the small study. His desk had been ransacked, and the papers were gone. His letters and the correspondence from Daniel O'Connell had been removed.

On the floor, crunched into fragments by some heavy boot, were the remains of his father's pipe.

As Joseph cleaned up the mess in his office he was intensely aware that his fear had not been for himself but for Little Tom. Perhaps it was his own sense of longing for his father or perhaps anxiety for the safety of the baby that made Joseph lift the infant from the crib and carry him off to his bedchamber.

No matter the reason, Joseph was comforted by the warmth of the tiny bundle that lay fast asleep in the great bed beside him.

Joseph left the candle burning on the night table, partly as a warning in the event the intruder would consider returning, but mostly so he could stay awake and gaze at Little Tom.

Bright red locks peeped out from beneath the yellow knitted cap. Joseph touched a curl with his forefinger and whispered, "Sure, and you're the very image of herself, Tomeen." The child bore the features of his mother: fair complexion with rosy cheeks and red curls, the small perfect mouth and blue eyes.

Joseph was grateful that the child looked so much like Brigit, a mercy from God. That fact allowed the townsfolk to look at Little Tom and think of his mother. The older ones had known Brigit from infancy. Everyone had admired her beauty. The child had inherited well from the Donovan line. The true identity of the baby's father did not matter to Joseph. The question of William Marlowe's paternity or the possibility of countless other men who purchased Brigit's body for their pleasure was of little consequence compared to the life of Little Tom.

Joseph's ambitious dreams and former plans weighed nothing in the balance of this one soul. Love for the baby had supplanted everything Joseph once considered important. His thoughts of entering the priesthood? Tomeen had become Joseph's congregation of one. Inheritance? The wealth of Ireland and the world could not purchase one tiny finger of sweet Tomeen.

It was remarked upon in the market square of Castletown that Joseph Connor Burke was a doting father, indeed. His affection raised the question that perhaps he had known Brigit too well before she ran off to Dublin with Viscount William Marlowe.

Mrs. Clooney was heard to say that perhaps Joseph had been better acquainted with Brigit than anyone thought. "Have you ever seen a man so smitten by a child? It's his own flesh and blood, I tell you. And could that not be the reason he went searchin' for the girl and set it right by marryin' her?"

Joseph was actually pleased by the rumors that portrayed him as the true father of Little Tom. Though Father O'Bannon knew the truth of it, he did not put a stop to the talk. The priest was the only other living soul who knew the facts, and Joseph encouraged him, for the sake of Tomeen, not to answer the speculation.

There was, of course, the matter of what Kate believed about Joseph. Did she look at him and imagine he had seduced Brigit and fathered her child? Did she hate him for that imaginary crime as well as everything else?

Joseph stroked the cheek of his son and whispered, "And what if she does? What does it matter, Tomeen? You're heart of my heart, though your face is the mirror of your mother. You're worth a city and worth all of Ireland to me, boy. Worth Kate's disdain and my reputation if it comes to that. My penance, you are truly my own, firstborn of my heart. I promise I'll protect you even if I must live without Kate's love."

Joseph found Father O'Bannon tending the rosebushes in the churchyard of St. John the Evangelist. The short, balding priest turned at the squeal of the iron cemetery gate, squinted into the morning sun, then waved broadly as he identified his visitor.

"A fine mornin', to you, Joseph," he said, tossing aside the turf spade with which he was shoveling manure. He dusted his hands on the flour-sack apron tied over his cassock.

"I'm sorry to interrupt your gardenin', Father, but I'm in sore need of advice and don't know where else to turn." Because they were such close friends, Joseph launched into the tale of the previous night's intruder. When he had recounted what was taken he concluded, "My first thought was to call for the new constable, but then . . ."

Joseph's voice trailed off into the shake of Father O'Bannon's head. "It is best to reason this out first," O'Bannon warned. "The new policeman is not Constable Carroll, God be praised, but he was appointed by the magistrate over in Clonbur, and that judge is no friend of Repeal."

"Meanin'?"

"Meanin' that if what was taken pertained to your work for Daniel O'Connell, there's many in the pay of the English would not shirk from thievin' to read it."

"But it was of no consequence."

"Ah, but how would they know that unless they read it first? Anyway, have you considered that it could be one of the servants in your own household?"

Picking idly at the lichen growing on a carved stone bearing the name *Boyse,* Joseph replied, "No, they appeared genuinely asleep until wakened by me. Besides, there was scarcely time for one to circle the house, reenter at the servants' wing, and get into bed." This conclusion was offered firmly, but it still lacked conviction, even to Joseph. "I was rememberin' the threat posed by the Ribbonmen at Kevin's wake," he said. "If they invaded my house once, they could surely do so again."

"That gang of thugs?" O'Bannon snorted, frowning down at his boots. He picked up the turf spade to tap the mud from the soles. "Aye, it's possible. If they think you're in league with the English, then they might mean to prove it by readin' your mail. Still, I don't think it likely. Their kind like to put on paint and travel in mobs."

"But if someone should boast of it in the parish," Joseph persisted, "no doubt you would come to know it."

O'Bannon shrugged. "I'll keep my ears open and will inform you, exceptin' of course it comes by way of the confessional. But I tell you, Joseph, this is not the doin' of any man from this parish. It smacks of political deeds beyond poor wee Ballynockanor."

"Not from this parish," Joseph mused. "What about that hairy, hulkin' Tinker? He was lurkin' about after the wake the other night. Might he be the one?"

O'Bannon dismissed this suggestion. "And would he still be camped over by the brook? I saw his wagon there meself this mornin'. Sure, and he would be miles from here already. The last thing any Tinker folk want is trouble with the authorities. But heed me now," O'Bannon said seriously, laying his thick hand on Joseph's arm and gazing earnestly into Joseph's face. "You know I stand shoulder-to-shoulder with you always. But watch your back. You are no longer Joseph Connor, destitute student of divinity, but the Burke of Connaught, and a friend to the Liberator. Watch your back, I say. Ye have enemies y'have never met."

5

Castletown, the market community at the heart of the Burke lands, was divided by the river Cornamona. A stone span called Charity Bridge connected the two banks. Across the river to the west the coach road rose as it wound through the blanket bogs toward the peaks of Connemara. Away east it dipped and hugged the shore of Lough Corrib until it reached Cong on the border of County Mayo.

As Joseph trudged toward Castletown along the highway from the Burke estate west of the river, he reflected on how far from this tiny corner of the world he had been and returned. After young boyhood on the estate, he had been sent away to boarding school and then had attended seminary in Dublin during the period of his uncle's usurpation when Joseph was thought to be dead. He had traveled abroad in France and elsewhere, and now he was back. In all that time, how many of the villagers had been farther from home than the horse fair in Tuam, scarce twoscore miles away? For that matter, how many generations of Ballynockanorians had ever seen Galway City, and it lying an easy day's sail down the length of Lough Corrib?

Though he had fine black hunters to ride and carriages for his use as the hereditary lord, the Burke of Connaught, Joseph preferred to walk. He enjoyed seeing the lands and the fields and the hills from ground level and at a slower pace. The plainer truth was, he already felt sadly separated from the people he had called friends, and he did not wish to exaggerate the division. Except for the school he was sponsoring, too many people treated him with too much deference.

Unfortunately, even walking was not a cure-all for the divorce caused by rank.

"Good day, your lordship," beamed Lem O'Shaughnessy from the doorway of his linen shop. "I've just received a shipment of the finest damask from Ulster if you'd care to step in."

"Not today, Mister O'Shaughnessy, thank you."

Feeney, the proprietor of men's clothing was even more direct, coming out of his business with a hat in one hand and a jacket in the other. "Best new tweed . . . London fashions . . . I just happen to have your lordship's very sizes here about me." He popped the hat on Joseph's head and would have thrust the coat on him as well if Joseph had not hastily pled a prior engagement and, returning the hat, crossed to the other side of the street.

There was no respite even from those who did not have goods to sell. Michael Erne, examining an ox beside the town fountain, plucked at Joseph's elbow. "What d'ya think, your lordship?" he inquired. "Red Will Kiley wants me to buy this ox off him. Is the beast sound, d'ya think?"

"I have no special gift for judgin' oxen, Mister Erne," Joseph responded.

"Ah, but your lordship is a scholar and a well-traveled gentleman," Erne insisted. "What would such an animal be worth in Dublin?"

"I'm sure I don't know," Joseph said, excusing himself yet again.

Then there were the others: the ones who had no wish to curry favor with the landlord; the ones like Barry Fitzpatrick, who lounged in the alley beside Watty's Tavern and spat noisily as Joseph passed. Fitzpatrick muttered something to his mates, and they laughed over their pints of stout. There were those to whom the Ribbonman's injunction against landlords was already second nature.

The Green Bough Coaching Inn was Joseph's destination. It was not a pub to which the common folk of Castletown resorted, being an establishment that catered to those who had money enough to travel. Its only local clients were the gentry who deliberately wanted to separate themselves from the tillers of the soil.

Joseph's attendance at the Green Bough was not by his choice. He had been summoned to a meeting there proposed by two of his fellow landlords: Squireen O'Shea and Colonel Mahon.

Little Squire O'Shea was a Catholic, of sorts, who owned some land that adjoined Joseph's to the north. He was a slightly built man, dark where Joseph was fair, with fists scarcely big enough to raise the tankard he was clutching when Joseph entered. "Welcome, your lordship," he exclaimed, rising from the table where he and Mahon were sitting. O'Shea's respectful tone resulted from the fact that he had sublet grazing land from Joseph's uncle, and he wanted Joseph to renew the lease. O'Shea was a notorious fence-sitter, anxiously watching out for his own advantage and seldom committing to anything on principle. He was sweating, probably because he also leased land from the other occupant of the table.

Mahon, who remained seated, was a retiree from the British army who had seen service in the Napoleonic wars. He had been rewarded by the Crown with lands to the east of Burke property, on the far side of Ben Levy. Whiplike and sneering, he was fiercely anti-Irish, anti-Catholic, and anti-Repeal.

"I imagine you know why I desired this meeting?" Mahon asked, smoothing an imperceptible wrinkle in his silk cravat. A crystal tumbler of whiskey was beside his elbow.

"No," Joseph said, sitting down. He chose to ignore the fact that Mahon neither stood nor invited Joseph to sit.

"It's this blasted Repeal nonsense," Mahon said, snorting. "It's bad enough that such lawless and treasonous sentiment is allowed free expression, but now these proposed rallies! I mean, excuses to leave off work and take a holiday, what? Curse that O'Connell and his rhetoric, telling my people that they can run their own affairs. Not that I am referring to present company, of course. I mean the uneducated peasants, a superstitious lot, prone to lying and drinking."

"How sadly true that is," O'Shea concurred. "So easily misled and confused by fancy words."

These were the other landlords whom O'Connell hoped Joseph could persuade to favor Repeal. "At present the people of Ireland are ill cared for by the Westminster government," Joseph said cautiously, trying to ignore the caustic remarks and talk common sense. "To be fairly apportioned, Ireland should have 30 percent of the House of Commons seats. Since England is not disposed to increase the number of our representatives, it is logical to have an Irish parliament directing Irish affairs."

"Give our land to the pope, you mean," Mahon said scornfully.

"There is no change in land ownership contemplated in any proposal I have seen," Joseph remarked.

"You have seen?" Mahon said with disdain. "And when the pigs are in the parlor, who will tell them to keep out of the pantry? Need to put a stop to it, I say. Besides, there are those who will make it worth your while, eh?"

O'Shea bobbed his head in agreement until he saw the way Joseph's face darkened, then he abruptly bowed his chin into his ale as if to lap from the mug.

"Colonel Mahon," Joseph said. "I have no reason to wish us to be enemies, but my position on Repeal is very clear. I think that the greatest good for the people of Ireland—*all* her people—will come from self-government. Anything that makes the English parliament recognize that truth I will support. If the rallies have that effect, then I support them as well. And no bribe," Joseph leaned hard on the word, "will change my mind."

O'Shea slurped noisily and said nothing.

"Bah!" Mahon puffed. "You are a traitor to your country and to your class. You and that school. Rest assured, Dublin Castle does not take kindly to giving bog-trotters notions above their place. Good day to you. Are you coming, O'Shea?"

Joseph sat in silent thought for some time before he realized that he had been left with the tab for the drinks. As he exited the coaching inn he passed Barry Fitzpatrick, who was still entertaining his friends. "I say it again," Fitzpatrick loudly proclaimed, "you can't trust any landlord . . . not one. They look to their own and have no regard for anything but money."

Joseph genuinely liked Adam Kane. The man was knowledgeable about farming in the rocky soil of the west. Most important, he got on well with tenant farmers who had been raised for generations to hate the agents of the landlords.

An affable fellow whose father had been a compatriot with O'Connell, Adam Kane fit in well among the people of Ballynockanor and the Burke lands.

This morning Joseph walked with the steward in a field that had been used for grazing for generations.

"It's fertile, sure, though it looks as rocky as the rest." Joseph stooped and scooped up a handful of soil.

"Years of manure," Adam said, pointing at Joseph's hand. "That's what'll do it."

Joseph threw the dirt down and laughed. "I could grow wheat on my palm with such soil."

"That you could, Squire. But what do you have in mind?"

"I plan on dividin' this forty acres into eight sections for testin' eight different strains of wheat."

"Man cannot live on potatoes alone. Is that it, Squire?"

"A loaf of bread is a luxury among the farmers in Galway. Irish grain is shipped to England where it feeds English cattle. I'd like to change that."

"A noble goal."

"As for the potatoes, next autumn we'll bring in a new strain. Twice the spuds per acre."

"I'm for it. The way your tenants are obeyin' the Lord's command to be fruitful and multiply I'd say we'll need the crop to keep up."

"This field . . . meanin' the wheat experiment . . . I'd like to put you in charge of it. I need a man I can trust while I'm away. Are you able?"

The two men walked a few more paces before Adam replied, "That I am. But I need to tell you somethin', Squire. Speakin' of trust . . ."

"Be open."

"Talk is . . . and I know talk is talk, and it may be nothin' a'tall . . . but all the same, talk is that you've had an eye for Kate Donovan."

"I'm fond of her."

"Fond enough to marry."

"If she would have me. But she . . ."

"Talk is she hates you, Squire. I'm sorry, but there's the truth of it."

Joseph clasped his hands behind his back and fixed his eyes on the far horizon. "So that's the talk, is it?"

"That it is. And so, Squire, that bein' the case . . . and you plannin' on bein' away . . . honesty compels me, one man to another, you see. Squire, I'd like to court the woman, and I'm certain she's interested in it as well."

Silence. The thought of Kate with Adam Kane settled in on Joseph like a weight. "I have no claim on her."

Adam clapped him on the back and sighed with relief. "I'm glad to hear it, Squire. I couldn't see you ridin' for the cause of Repeal with Kate Donovan in the back of your mind and then comin' home to find she's in love with myself."

"In love with you?"

"That's right. It wouldn't be right. If you trust me with the wheat field here, Squire, then it's only right you know I have plans for Kate Donovan. I'm thirty-five years old, and it's time I marry. She's a handsome woman but for the fire. Her hand doesn't put me off. She's got fine breasts, a trim waist even without corsets, curvaceous hips, and a lovely face. She's been married before and so knows what to expect in a man's appetites. I've asked hereabouts, and Aidan Clooney says her husband was a well-contented man. You know what that means. So I'll have no doubts on what she's capable of on that score. Children. Children. No doubt she'd be grateful to have a man like myself for a husband. That's my plan anyway, and I thank you for givin' it your blessin'.'"

"You'll not have my blessin', Steward," Joseph shot back. Adam had talked about Kate as if he were describing a prize heifer in heat.

"But Squire, you said . . ."

"If she'll have you . . . if she loves you, then I have nothin' to say. That's what I said."

Kevin had often ridiculed Kate for tending the graves of ancient Donovans. But this was, for her, a ritual of spring. Each year, spade and rake over her shoulder, Kate returned to the churchyard to tidy the row of graves in the Donovan plot.

Entire lifetimes of work and worry and memory lay buried under a thick carpet of leaves. Generations of Donovan songs and fireside stories lay dormant beneath the accumulation of winter debris. It was Kate's task to scrape away the layer and expose the ground to sunlight and to life.

New grass, periwinkles, and primroses would grow from the dust of those who once sang and prayed and suffered here. The winds of summer would come and gently strum each blade of grass and leaf and blossom. Bleached bones and stilled voices would once again be translated into the hum of angel music. A choir of verdant greens, one hundred shades of red, blue, and violet would shout of glory to God from the churchyard! The living parishioners who passed by on their way to pray would see colors more vivid than the gray of leaning headstones. They would smile in the direction of a grave and remark on the primrose blooming where tears once fell. This was certain proof that grief grew pale beside the colors of life and finally faded away entirely. Names and dates eroded on the headstones evoked no sorrow from the memory of the living.

Kate knew this because she had grieved for those she had lost, and the ache had diminished over time. But it was still too soon for her to feel peace as she passed Brigit's tomb. There were too many reminders, too many regrets, too much left forever unresolved and unforgiven.

She had not begun her task when Father O'Bannon bustled around the corner of the church. "Good mornin', Kate!" he called. "Is it spring, then? I'm never certain until I find you here."

She attempted a smile, but her gaze flitted to the stone crypt of the Burke family. The priest caught the moment of unconcealed aching on her face.

"Brigit helped me last year," Kate remarked.

"Aye. That she did." Father O'Bannon's tone softened. "And this year she's in a place where there's no winter."

"Will there be no end to good-byes?" Kate said, revealing the darkness of her mood.

Father O'Bannon grimaced at the comment. He sank down on the stone bench beside her and put a hand to his back in complaint. "No," he answered in a matter-of-fact tone. "Me sainted mother used to say that we didn't come into this world at the same time, and we'll not be leavin' at the same time either." He nodded once. "A fact of life."

"I envy Brigit."

"Envy!" He rebuked her self-pity. "Envy that poor benighted child who made every wrong choice in her short life and died before she lived?"

"I don't envy her life," Kate snapped. "I envy her peace."

"It was a hard-won peace." Father O'Bannon's patience ran short as often happened when his lumbago bothered him. "Now she's dead. And some other woman will be raisin' her child. Envy! Kate! You've been breathin' too much turf smoke, girl. Where's what little wit God gave you?"

His rebuke stung her. "Won't you let me grieve a bit, Father?"

"Grief is one thing. Daft talk is another. Speak sense, girl. 'Tisn't the peace of the dead you envy. 'Tis somethin' else eatin' at you, I'll be bound! Or I've not been your confessor these many years."

"All right then!" Tears brimmed in her eyes. "It's himself, her husband I'm angry with!"

"Joseph."

"Aye. That's his name. At least part of it. He never was honest with me. And life would have been much better if he'd never come to Ballynockanor."

Father O'Bannon ran his tongue over his four teeth and squinted in disdain at her words. "Better, you say?" he cried sarcastically. "Sure, and if he hadn't come home, who'd be lord in the manor now? Marlowe. And what would have come of your poor foolish sister and the wee babe? This holy chapel! Wouldn't it be tossed and all of the village scattered to the four winds? 'Tisn't Joseph Connor Burke you're hatin', Kate. 'Tis yourself you've made into your heart's enemy. Aye. You've not forgiven yourself, and so you cannot forgive your neighbor. Even though your neighbor never harmed you."

"He harmed my family."

At this the priest reddened. His eyes grew wide, and he sputtered, "Your family, is it? The fightin', brawlin', proud-as-the-devil Donovan family are we speakin' of? Squire Joseph harmed your family? How? Over the years you've done that well enough without Joseph." He did not let her reply. "Harmed you, is it? By wipin' out Brigit's disgrace at the cost of his vocation and the appearance of his own honor and . . . the cost of losin' your love? Nonsense!"

"He can't lose what I never gave him."

The old man shook his head as though he could not believe what she was saying. "This is myself you're speakin' to. You deny you were fond?"

"A bit."

"You deny you loved him?"

"I didn't know him."

"You still don't know him, or you wouldn't let your heart commit false witness against him."

"I? False witness!"

"Aye. The very word. Thou shalt not bear false witness. Smash, bang! Kate Donovan, you've slaughtered the eighth commandment!"

"I'm not confessin' to any such thing!"

"Then you've a blot upon your soul, and you'll not be comin' forward for the Holy Eucharist to make mock of the blood of Christ until you're put right."

Kate glared at him in fury. "If I had any sense a'tall I'd be a . . . Protestant!"

He crossed himself in horror at the thought. "As if they'd have you. Sha, woman! You're headstrong enough. Aye. Rebel! That you are! Tom Donovan's daughter! Kevin Donovan's sister, and may God help America when your rebel brother reaches her shores! But I've said what I meant, and I meant what I said. Don't bother playin' the wronged damsel, for I'm not buyin' that spavined horse. Kevin did what he did and is banished to America. Brigit did what she did, and she's gone. Joseph did what he could to save your brother and your sister, and how have you thanked him? With your hatred. False witness indeed. You've nearly killed the poor boy with your cold fury." He stood up suddenly, wincing at the pain in his back. "Let me know when you want to make confession. Otherwise I'm firm in my resolve. Now get on with you. Clean your old graves and dig one for your heart, for you're all talk and self-pity and no love a'tall. Tinklin' brass! A clangin' . . . bell . . ."

With that pronouncement he waved his hand irritably at the bell tower as though he were brushing away a fly, then limped away toward his cottage.

Kate scowled after him. "Sure, and his lumbago has shut the door of the church on my face!" She leapt to her feet and grabbed up the spade, swinging it like a club. "And here's for you, Joseph Connor Burke. Now you've made my priest cross with me too!"

6

A chill wind was howling down out of the west, giving Joseph plenty of reason to think that his reception at the Donovan cottage might not be the warmest either.

Despite the numbing effect of the gale and the threat to his earlobes, he went literally hat-in-hand to the Donovan barn. His father-in-law, Tom, was aware of his impending visit and had gracefully gathered Martin and Mary Elizabeth and taken them on an unexpected and wholly unnecessary trip into Castletown.

The time of day being what it was, Joseph expected to find Kate about the milking. Sheltered in the lee of the whitewashed barn, Joseph heard the tinging sounds of milk hitting the pail, confirming his expectations.

Joseph lingered outside before entering the low portal. He recalled the time he and Kate had together managed the difficult delivery of a bull calf in that very spot, a bull calf happily gamboling in one of the Donovan's leased fields. Leased from him, he pondered. He was now the Donovan family's landlord.

On that occasion he had seen the damage done to Kate's arm by a long-ago dreadful fire; he had seen it, and yet the glimpse of her injury was far from the strongest memory of that day. Instead, Joseph recalled that episode a year earlier as the time he knew for certain he was falling in love with Kate. Knew it and feared it; he had believed himself destined for the priesthood. But God had prepared other plans. *God grant,* he thought prayerfully, *and Father O'Bannon be right, that there is yet a path forward from where we are now.*

Whether he had inadvertently spoken aloud or whether perhaps Kate had been alerted by the chattering of his teeth, the ringing of the milk bucket stopped, and Kate called out, "Is someone there?"

"Aye, Kate," he responded with a hearty cry and a quick rap on the doorpost, as if he had but that moment arrived. "It's Joseph. May I come in?"

She assented with a reply that was to Joseph's thinking even colder than the weather. "Of course," she said briefly. "It's a fierce day outdoors for any livin' thing."

"I see you're milkin'," Joseph began awkwardly.

She did not even deign to reply to such a transparent observation.

"Well, then," he said, stumbling for words. "That is, I've come . . ."

"I can see that," she acknowledged. "But what for? And where's your hat and scarf and heavy coat? If you take the chill you'll not be holdin' Little Tom, mind."

"Oh, nay, never," he agreed vaguely, wondering how he could overcome so much hostility. "The baby is well enough," he offered, seizing on that subject as a favorable one.

"And did you come all the way here to be tellin' me that? Sure, and I saw him for myself yestere'en."

With that last hopeful avenue forestalled, Joseph saw no other course than to plunge right in. "Kate," he said, "Daniel O'Connell has me goin' about the west country, speakin' for Repeal. I will be away from here some times . . . perhaps even travelin' to Dublin."

"Oh," she said without apparent interest or concern, "you'll not be takin' the baby in this weather, I vow. Even a man must have some sense where wee ones are concerned. And did you come then to ask for my help with the child? You know you have that even without the askin'."

"I know, and I thank you for it," Joseph mumbled, "but that is still not the reason I called."

Kate stood up from the milking stool, placed a hand to the small of her back to ease the ache, and patted the rust-colored moilie. "If this is to be a long visit we'll move in by the fire," she said. Her tone strongly suggested that it was an unwelcome interruption to her work.

"No need," Joseph replied. "It's but a brief question. You already know that a great Repeal rally is to be held in Galway. Now widower I may be . . ."

Kate's spine stiffened so abruptly that Joseph stopped in alarm, then hurried on. He felt himself buffeted more by the force of her gaze than by the intensity of the storm outside. "But you, Kate . . . Brigit was your sister. And Da and Martin and Mary Elizabeth . . . you should be there. You are better to represent your Brigit than I could ever be."

"Parade my sister's shame and tragedy around in public like some tavern song?"

"Not a'tall. Brigit's memory is cherished by the whole nation. She will be honored, this I can promise."

There was no change to the broomstick rigidity of Kate's backbone. "And who do you think will do the milkin' and the dairyin' if we all go gallivantin' 'round the countryside? There's rents to be paid, you know."

Cringing again, Joseph almost ducked back outside, and he shuffled his feet like a bumbling youth. "That's your decision, is it?"

"It is," Kate pledged forcefully. Then she added, "But I know menfolk must be about politics, and I expect Da will want to go. My offer to help with Tomeen is still good."

Joseph brightened. "And will you stay to the manor? You would be most welcome. Miss Susan will be glad of your . . ."

"Indeed I will not!" Kate retorted. "The wet nurse and the child may stay here at the cottage with me."

"Yes . . . I . . . of course. Good day to you then."

Joseph forgot the low height of the door and bumped his head on the beam as he departed.

No matter what Joseph said to himself about Kate in broad daylight, at night he dreamed of her. He dreamed of himself with her. It was always the same.

They walked together along the banks of the Cornamona. Night birds called from clefts in the rocks.

He smelled the fragrance of her skin. Desire flowed through him like the rush of the river's current. There was no light but Kate. Her skin glowed like a lantern through her thin, white cotton shift. He followed her to a place beneath the willows where the grass was warm and soft. She stood behind him, her breath stroking his back, arms wrapped around his middle. As they sank down together, she pressed against him. He turned to touch her, aching to fill her, only to find she was gone. And the light vanished with her.

When daylight came Joseph could not see Kate in the flesh without remembering the dream. Knowing she hated him, he remained smiling and calm around her on the outside. But in reality he was dreaming, wide awake, and aching on the inside.

Then there were times Kate held the baby in the crook of her arm and bent to whisper in Little Tom's ear. Joseph watched intently, and pretended to enjoy the domestic scent. Truth was, Joseph was wishing for Kate's soft mouth to move against his skin; he was hungry for her lips to brush his forehead. The thought made him dizzy. He would have gladly traded places with Tomeen.

At confession Joseph told Father O'Bannon the truth; he was tortured by her nearness and by her absence. In spite of the pain of it, wanting Kate's love and desiring Kate's passion was a sweet agony he would not relinquish. Nor could he give up hope that his longing might one day be satisfied. He was holding tightly to his sin.

Father O'Bannon remained unimpressed by Joseph's transgression. He explained that God often began His plan for holy matrimony and procreation through dreams and imagination. If anyone looked at the absolute facts of wedded bliss there would be no short-age of priests and nuns, he added. True love, said Father O'Bannon, was nine parts vision and one part reality. There was no other way it could function. He cited 1 Corinthians 13:4–7.

"Dream on, Joseph, if the pain makes you happy," Father O'Bannon said. "Love is its own penance."

In addition, Father O'Bannon promised he would pray that Kate would have a dream or two of her own about Joseph; and that she would also suffer.

After all, God was still in the business of miracles.

The household was sleeping when Joseph entered the foyer of the Great Hall. Candles burned low in the dining room. The long table was set for one with wine, cold meats, and cheeses on a plat-ter. He was more tired than hungry, but his stomach growled loud enough to remind him that a man could not live on melancholy alone. Scooping a handful of food onto the plate, he shoved the wine bottle into the pocket of his jacket, took up a candle, and made his way toward bed.

The ache of weariness and loneliness filled Joseph as he climbed the broad, winding staircase toward the bedchamber. Light from the candle illuminated the stern faces of family portraits on the walls of the corridor. He stood on the landing to study his father's image. Joseph had found the painting in a dusty corner of a storage room and had restored it to its rightful place beside a picture of Joseph's mother. Of the two, Joseph saw more of himself in the clear blue of her eyes, fair hair, and complexion. And though his mother had died before his father, Joseph found it easier to recall details about her. Even in the last days of her illness she had made him believe she would be with him forever, love him always.

Joseph had not realized how deep his loss had been until he moved back into this wide, empty house that her living presence had filled and overflowed in his boyhood. Memories long suppressed became as sharp as morning sunlight in this place.

Joseph wondered how different life might have been if she had not died so very young. This thought brought him full circle back to Brigit. To the baby. What would Little Tom's life be like, growing up alone without a mother or brothers and sisters in the old house?

"Lonely." Joseph uttered the word that, more than any other, defined his own life. Better the tiny cottage of the Donovan's, full of warmth and caring.

A baby's cry emanated from the near end of the corridor. So Little Tom was awake. Joseph nodded slightly to the portrait and made his way toward the nursery.

Through the door he heard the soft, crooning voice of Miss Susan singing about a mockingbird. Joseph knocked hesitantly.

"Who's that?" called Miss Susan.

"Joseph. Is Tomeen unwell?"

The door was flung open. The infant on her shoulder, Miss Susan smiled and stepped aside. "It's your daddy, honey. He came to say good night."

Miss Susan had no last name. She was nearly six feet tall and quite lean from two years of nursing babies that were not her own. Her dark skin had a sheen like polished wood. Joseph knew she had escaped slavery in America and had come to Ireland as wet nurse to the child of a Quaker family. She mentioned once that she was comforted by the infants she nursed but had never spoken about what had happened to her own.

At Joseph's hesitation the woman glared at him. "Well, come ahead on. You lettin' the night air in. Close the door behind you."

Meekly he entered the room, the domain of this strong-willed black woman who handled Little Tom with the confidence of someone who knew about babies.

"Am I keepin' you up?"

Miss Susan cocked an eyebrow at the plate of cold cuts and the neck of the wine bottle. "Your baby boy like to eat late just like his daddy. He just been fed 'fore you come." She placed the child on the changing table and went to work. Little Tom renewed his frustrated wail. "Hold your horses, honey. Miss Susan workin' fast as she can." Over her shoulder she said to Joseph, "Good strong baby. Eat real good. Growin' real well."

Joseph always felt intimidated by the way she slung the child easily from one hand to the other. "He looks like his mother."

Miss Susan sensed her employer's trepidation and so spoke to him as though he were a child himself to be ordered around. "Everybody sayin' he look more like you every day."

The comment pleased Joseph. Though it could not be, he would promote the talk of it. "Aye? My chin, perhaps."

"His eyes," Susan said flatly. "Look at the way this baby boy look at you. He's yours all right. Anybody can see it in his eyes." Snapping her long fingers she pointed to the rocking chair by the fire. "Sit," she commanded.

Joseph obeyed. Miss Susan placed Little Tom over his shoulder. "He's grown just since this mornin'."

"Pat him easy like. Little Tom like to drain me dry. He got another burp in there." The child obliged with an enormous belch.

Joseph looked pleased. "Sounds like he's been down at Watty's Tavern."

"Oh, he's a good'n, Mistuh Joseph. You gots you a good boy. He be wantin' a mama, though." Miss Susan beamed. "All this chile need is milk an' honey. I gives him milk. He needs a mama to give him honey lovin'. I love on him, but it ain't the same. Naw, it ain't the same."

Her admonition shamed him. "I . . . I . . . ," he stammered, brushing his fingers over the soft red curls. Then he said quietly, "I'll be gone a while, Miss Susan."

Her face fell. "Well, well. Jus' when I thought we was gettin' somewhere."

He continued. "I must. Duty . . ." Closing his eyes he drank in the scent of Little Tom's skin. What would life be if he could raise his son in peace and freedom? "That is . . . I spoke with Kate Donovan today. . . ."

"Uh-huh. That be good news," Miss Susan said approvingly.

"I feel it's best if you and Little Tom stay at the Donovan cottage while I'm away."

"With his aunties and uncle and granddaddy. Them Donovans sure do love this chile. Now that be real good, Mistuh Joseph. Better'n this big, empty barn. But I tell you what Little Tom need. He need himself a mama. Now Miss Kate . . ."

He interrupted more sharply than he meant to. "Kate Donovan would not be agreeable to that notion, I'm thinkin'. And I'll thank you not to mention it while you're there. She'll be mindin' the dairy shorthanded. Your help will be appreciated."

"Yessir. I notice she don't take kindly to you. Margaret in the kitchen say since you this baby's true daddy Miss Kate hate you more'n ever on account of this baby's mama bein' her sister. Well, other fishes in the sea. Forget her. Find yourself a good woman an' marry an' give this child what he need."

With the sounds of singing and recitation echoing from the west wing of the manor, Joseph smiled as he stepped out the rear and headed toward the stables. Tomorrow was the day of leaving for Galway City and the Repeal rally, and he intended to supply horses for himself, Tom Donovan, and Father O'Bannon for the journey.

Though possessed of several fine carriages and a two-wheeled phaeton with a top that folded down, none of these were to be used. After the abrupt departure of Joseph's uncle to the lunatic asylum, the coachman and footmen, Dubliners all, had taken their leave and returned to the capital. That was fine with Joseph, who disliked putting on airs, but it made carriage travel awkward. He could have driven the team himself, but knew his passengers for the Repeal assembly would never allow it—no more than he would suggest that either his priest or his father-in-law act as his chauffeur.

Halfway to the stableyard he heard the noisy squawking of Old Flynn, the ancient master of horses for the estate. Flynn seemed to be angrily denouncing someone. This was a puzzle because with the departure of Kevin Donovan, there were no other yard hands about. Moreover, the dispute was so one-sided, Flynn's strident tones alone being heard, that Joseph wondered if having Mad Molly around the home was infecting others.

Entering the passage into the two-story barn, just beside the canvas-shrouded fire pump wagon, Joseph stopped midstride in astonishment. The barn, till yesterday sadly in need of cleaning and mucking out, was shining and orderly, even swept. But this unexpected tidiness was only the beginning of wonders. Old Flynn, blackthorn stick waving like a one-bladed windmill, was shouting at the burly, black-bearded form of the Tinker. Even more amazing was the Tinker's complete lack of response. He was dandling the hind leg of one of the brood mares across his knee as if rocking an infant. And to set the cap on the marvels, the horse, normally a skittish, high-strung beast who would not have tolerated Flynn's screeching without much hopping and plunging, was holding perfectly still.

"Flynn!" Joseph barked sharply. "Flynn! What is this?"

The aged man was deaf, or partly so, and it was not until Joseph moved into his line of vision that the torrent of words and the whirl of the shillelagh stopped.

Flynn began at once to answer Joseph's inquiry, even though he had not heard it expressed. "I caught yon blackguard muckin' about with the horses, your lordship," he charged. He shook his stick at the Tinker, though O'Neill was only six feet away. "And he won't leave off, neither. I come in here an hour since, and he was sweepin' and totin' like there was no tomorrah. When I asked him what he was about, he would not answer me, except to grunt and go on wheelin' the barrah. Then, he spotted Glenys there, favorin' her leg like, an' he nips into the stall without so much as by-yer-leave, and now he's messin' with her. And he won't stop!"

"All right, Mister Flynn," Joseph said soothingly. "Calm down. No harm's been done. I'll handle this. Mister O'Neill, what are you up to?"

The Tinker slowly lowered the leg of the horse, patted her flank, and then turned. "Your mare has a bowed tendon," he said. "She won't be sound less she gets off hard surface and onto good turf."

"It's not a bowed tendon," Flynn exploded. "No such thing. She's got a bit of a stone bruise, that's what!"

"Mister Flynn," Joseph said, "I think it would be best if you go on about your other duties for a time. I'll call when I want you again."

Flynn left, but not without much hostile muttering and many black looks over his shoulder.

"Show me," Joseph demanded.

O'Neill first slid his hand up the length of the horse's backbone, then whispered in her ear. Before the Tinker had even bent beside the injured leg, the mare had already raised it from the ground, as if in obedience to a spoken suggestion.

"Your lordship will notice the slight swellin' here," O'Neill pointed out. "And watch this." He tapped the frog of the hoof's sole with the bone handle of a knife that appeared from nowhere. "You see," he said as the horse stood unflinchingly still. "No bruise. But now this." The Tinker gently squeezed the leg, and the animal shuddered but otherwise stayed quiet.

"Very impressive," Joseph commented as O'Neill straightened up. "But what about the cleanin'?"

The Tinker shrugged. "I'm a horse trader without any horses to trade. You're a horse breeder without a stablehand. Perhaps we can help each other out a bit."

"You mean you'd stay to muck out stalls and ride exercise and work for Flynn? I warn you, there's room and board, but the pay is meager, and the abuse may be great."

Both men grinned into each other's amused eyes.

From the far end of the passage a squeaking voice sang, "Dermott O'Neill knows the beasts . . . great and small, he knows them all."

Mad Molly, of course, Joseph thought. *How does she come and go so quietly for being so noisy wherever she arrives?*

"Dermott O'Neill," she continued, "speaks with angels. Dermott the Ruthful, he is called. Think to shame him, they do, for sparin' the man of God. But God promises him the kingship. Aye, so He does."

Molly had a way of referring to long-ago events in the present tense. Just then, Joseph knew, she was connecting the Tinker with an Irish king of the same name who had been dead for twelve centuries.

O'Neill spoke softly to Molly, and the old woman grew silent. Joseph could not hear the words, but they sounded like a mixture of English and Irish, but with something else added in, musical and unknown. Joseph knew that Tinkers had their own language, but he had no idea Molly Fahey would recognize it.

"And now, your lordship, you'll be wantin' me to drive your carriage to Galway City tomorrow," O'Neill said.

"No," Joseph corrected. "I am minded to go by horseback. But I will want you to take the carriage out tomorrow. After lessons, you take Molly here, the nurse, Miss Susan, Tomeen, and the two Donovan children over to the Donovan cottage. I think you should stay about the Donovan place and help out with the feedin' and milkin', though you will have to sleep in the dairy shed."

"Sure, and it's all one to me," O'Neill acknowledged. "Now, that bein' the way of it, you'll be wantin' the black for your own self, the stout broad-backed bay for Mister Donovan, and I think, the gentle mare for the priest. Is it so?"

Joseph contented himself with a nod. It was not clear which was a greater wonder: that O'Neill could unerringly assign horses and riders without having seen any of them ride, or that he already knew who was accompanying Joseph away for the weekend.

Mad Molly capered ahead of Joseph back toward the house. On the way she was singing, "Dermott O'Neill speaks with the angels, knows all the beasts, friend to them all, kind to the least."

7

The morning was contrary. The sky could not decide whether to rain or shine. Clouds made sly passes between the sun and the earth, causing light and shadow to shift across fields and fences in confusion. On their way to school on the Burke estate Martin and Mary Elizabeth, in an effort to warm away the chill, played tag with the sunlight as it broke through in patches on the road. Kate watched them hopping away and felt their absence as they disappeared over the knoll. Da, like every other man in the countryside, was gone with Joseph to the gathering in Galway City.

Like the day, Kate was restless as she led Daisy, the little milk cow, to the stanchion and balanced herself on the stool. Tugging away at the teats, Kate's mood must have passed through hide and udder and affected Daisy, who mooed incessantly and stamped her hind leg through the milking.

"And what have you got to complain about?" Kate asked the cow. In truth Kate knew she was speaking to herself. She recounted the hopes that had been followed by losses. True love and marriage to Sean and then the fire that had taken his life and scarred her forever. Mother and infant brother taken on the same night.

"And did I not learn to live with that? Without hope of children of my own? Without the love of a man?" she said aloud.

Then Joseph had come. He had reawakened the possibility of love in her. She had dreamed of him, longed to be held again. In this very barn the day the calf had been born he had touched her accidentally, and the flood of warmth had coursed through her in a way she had never dreamed of feeling again.

Then there was Brigit. Joseph had wed her in Dublin, and Kate had put him forever from her heart.

"And did I not learn to live without the dream?" she asked. Daisy bellowed a mournful response. "It was only a dream, you see. An unsubstantial thing it was, and I can do without wantin' somethin' I can never have."

She told herself this even as the light broke through again and shone through gaps in the thatch to pierce the gloom of the barn and stick in the earth like spears all around her. And with the shafts of light came a spark of realization. How lonely her life was.

Da off to the meeting. Mary Elizabeth and Martin at school. These brief partings she could manage because they would be back soon enough. There was washing to do. Cooking and cleaning and loving them by keeping them clean and fed and making sure they were in church on time. But one day they would leave her and not come home. Martin would marry and have someone else to care for him. Mary Elizabeth would marry and go off to care for some man. And Da? One day he would die in his bed or be kicked by a cow or fall off the road and . . .

Kate breathed out sorrow and leaned her face against the warmth of the moilie. There was comfort in the touch of a living creature. "Like Sean. Like Mother. Like the baby and Brigit. Aye. And like Kevin too. Gone." There was a hole in Kate's life where love trickled out and flowed away.

What use was anything when no one stayed near enough for a woman to love in the cooking and the washing and the ordering of their daily lives? *Though I speak with the tongues of men and of angels yet have not love. . . .* A grand concept love was. A fine sentiment. But love at a distance, love for those who had died or gone far away was not the same as darning socks or keeping the fire burning on the hearth. *Love is patient. Love is kind. Love puts up with many abuses. . . .* One day those whom she cared for would not need that kind of loving, and then Kate would be altogether alone. Aunt Kate. What would it matter if she was patient or kind or put up with anything?

The return of that realization frightened her. Before Joseph had reawakened hope in her she had been content with the thought of living her days alone.

A smoldering resentment filled her. What right did he have to awaken hope in her? Her fear of loneliness, her reconciliation to a life without close-up loving, had been manageable before he intruded!

"It's the fault of himself I'm in such a state today," she said, yanking too hard on the teats. Daisy stamped in unhappy response. "Well then. I'll master this like I have mastered other things. Aye. You'll see. I'll never give in to lovin' a man again."

At Burke Hall, the corridors were more quiet than was usually the case. Today one half of the students were absent. Martin knew this was because of Mr. O'Connell's meeting. A number of the children had remained on the farms to tend to chores in the absence of fathers and older brothers. In other cases, entire families from the parish had gone to the gathering. Those students who remained behind were somber and subdued. For the first time since its inception, Martin made a mental note to ask Kate if he could stay home rather than sit through lessons in the vast echoing library of the house.

After school, on the gravel path leading to the stable, Mary Elizabeth was unusually quiet. Her lower lip was out. Blue eyes brooded.

"And what's the trouble?" Martin asked.

"Didn't you notice, then? Sure, and 'tis no wonder he has the school in his house. It must be a terrible gloomy place when we all go home. It's too big."

"Aye. That it is."

She made a face. "An awful waste of space. I don't like it so empty. Lonely, it is."

"Aye." Martin contemplated what it must be like to get out of bed in the middle of the night and walk all the way to the kitchen for a glass of milk. A man would be thirsty again before he got back to bed. But then there were servants to bring milk up from the kitchen. Somehow Martin could not imagine their Joseph calling for a servant to fetch him anything, however. To Martin's way of thinking there was only one useful servant in the household. That was Miss Susan, who nursed Little Tom so well that the baby was round and plump like a tub of butter.

Mary Elizabeth continued, "I wouldn't like it one bit if I were himself."

"Like what?"

"He'd best marry again and fill the rooms with children. And then I will come and take care of them."

Martin snorted with surprise. "Wherever did you hear such a thing?"

"Missus Clooney."

"Missus Clooney has so many children she doesn't know where to put them. If she was a sow and her babies were piglets then Mister Clooney would be a rich man. She grinds out babies like little sausages."

"Aye. Well, she'd misplace them altogether if she lived here. As for me, I like a wee cottage with lots of people in it. The Clooney house is not a lonely place. Anyway, Missus Clooney says Kate's a fool for not seein' Joseph loves her. Missus Clooney says there's plenty of women on the lookout for such as himself, and they're willin' and able to console him. She says he's a fine catch, and she'd wed him herself if she did not have Mister Clooney and twelve children."

"Then Missus Clooney'll have to marry with him. Kate never will," Martin concluded.

"Aye. Kate liked Joseph better when he was a poor man, I'm thinkin'."

"She never liked him. Not a'tall," Martin argued. "Kate never liked any man but Sean."

"Da. Kevin. You. Father O'Bannon." Mary Elizabeth tallied them on her fingers. She stopped midtick as a resolution came to her. "I'm not comin' to school tomorrow."

Irritated, Martin tried to resume the former discussion. "Kevin! Da! Myself! Father O'Bannon! She's not likely to like Father O'Bannon enough to wed him!"

"I'm not comin' to school, and you can't make me. Miss Susan and the baby will be at our cottage, and I want to be home when home is not so empty as it has seemed lately. I like it when we're all cozy, and there's a bit of chat goin' on in the kitchen. And I can hold wee Tom."

Martin shook his head in resignation. It was no use debating with Mary Elizabeth. Her brain had made an about-face and was marching off in another direction. He tried to follow. "You've been lonely, have you?"

"Aye," the child confessed. "The cottage is too quiet without Kev and Brigit, Martin. Did you notice Tomeen's got red hair too?"

"Like Brigit, is it?"

"Aye. Curls too. Sure, Martin, and it's the very same."

It was late afternoon. Certain of spring, wild geese flew north, high above the field where Kate drove the cows toward home. A biting wind stung her cheeks as she turned her face up to watch the straight arrow of the flock across the gray sky. How did they know, with the winds still blowing cold, that it was time to come home again to Lough Corrib?

It was faith that held them on course; the timeless certainty that summer waited for their return. If only her own faith could be so pure and her journey so clear, she thought.

It was nearly dusk when the milk cows plodded through the barn doors, each turning into her own stall. Above their mellow mooing Kate heard a snatch of singing from the road.

"That'll be Miss Susan and the children, then." She patted Daisy on the rump and set the milk bucket aside. She was grateful for the arrival. Martin could help finish the evening milking.

Stepping out into the twilight as the closed carriage pulled up in the yard her smile of greeting turned to a frown. Perched upon the driver's seat sat the huge bulk of the Tinker. His dark, brooding eyes regarded her angry expression without concern. He did not so much as tip his hat to her as he set the brake, leaped to the ground, and moved to stroke the nose of each horse and speak to them soothingly in the secret language of the Tinker race.

Mary Elizabeth called from within the carriage, "Kate, it's Little Tom here on my lap. I held him the whole long way!"

Kate did not reply to the child but demanded the attention of Dermott O'Neill. "I'll thank you to speak either the English or the Gaelic in my presence."

The corner of the Tinker's mouth turned up slightly. "I was not speakin' to yourself. And the horses would not understand."

Kate was seething. What was such a man doing driving such precious cargo from Burke Hall?

Everyone respectable knew the truth about Tinkers. They were drifters, liars, and thieves—not to be trusted!

"And what are you doin' with Squire Burke's horses and carriage?"

"I've delivered your brother and sister. Your wee nephew and the wet nurse."

"By whose authority?"

"And Squire Burke has told me I'm to stay here and help out with your herd."

"Squire Joseph Burke does not speak for me, and I need no help." She might have added that she wanted no help from the likes of the Tinker.

The Tinker did not reply, although he understood clearly that he was not welcome. As Miss Susan emerged from the carriage he unloaded a carpetbag and a bundle of bedding, which he set inside the door of the cottage.

Martin eyed the man suspiciously and said in a low voice as the

Tinker climbed back to his perch again, "Joseph's hired him on for the stable."

Kate regarded her brother with disbelief. Had Joseph Burke lost his mind? To bring such a one as this into his household? And this when every able-bodied man was gone to Galway City?

The Tinker took the reins up and stared straight ahead as though he could understand neither English nor Gaelic. He would not reply to questions but simply waited for Mary Elizabeth and Little Tom to be lifted from the vehicle. Far above, wild geese honked as they flew in formation toward the Lough. The Tinker raised his eyes and hand in salute, one traveler to another.

Kate asked Miss Susan, "Is it true?"

Miss Susan nodded once, and with a glance of disapproval at the bearded giant she took Little Tom from Mary Elizabeth and hurried into the warmth of the cottage.

Mary Elizabeth piped as she jumped down, "Joseph hired Mister O'Neill to take Kev's place in the stable."

Kate stepped back and put her hands protectively on Mary Elizabeth's shoulders as the Tinker glanced down to make certain everyone was clear. With a word in an unknown tongue, he urged the horses into movement, backing and turning the carriage in the compact yard with the slightest motion of his hands on the reins.

Martin commented with respect, "Tinker he may be, but he knows a bit about horses."

"It's a dark wisdom his kind possess. I'll have a word with Squire Joseph Connor Burke on this matter," Kate said through gritted teeth as she watched the carriage go.

Another woman in the Donovan house. It had been so long, almost a year since Brigit had run away. Kate was glad of the company of Miss Susan, though the tall, efficient nurse spoke little in the first day of her arrival.

Kate milked the cows morning and night.

Miss Susan separated the cream and churned the butter.

Kate drove the moilies to the far pasture.

Miss Susan had the meal ready and the children washed when she returned.

Kate mucked the stalls.

Miss Susan swept the floor, boiled the laundry, and ironed the shirts.

Kate had difficulty understanding the American dialect. Miss Susan grew weary trying to explain each word more than once. Therefore the two women passed the time with a minimum of conversation. Yet Kate welcomed this quiet companionship. It crossed her mind that they were so competent with the organizing of children and work that it would not matter much if the men of Ballynockanor stayed away forever. But that was not to be. The men would come rumbling home, triumphant in their politics and outrage. Blustering and cursing and making vows, they would bring it to the supper table with them, and peace would be gone.

The men's return the two women sat beside the fire. Martin and Mary Elizabeth were in bed. Little Tom nursed contentedly at Miss Susan's breast. His red curls and rosy complexion contrasted with the rich, dark cast of her skin. He reminded Kate of a perfect peach on a shining, mahogany tabletop.

The word *beautiful* escaped unbidden from Kate's lips.

Miss Susan smiled. "Yes'm, he is a perty baby."

"It was yourself I was meanin'. Your skin."

"You mean you never seen a colored woman 'fore me?"

"Never."

"Well, glory be. Folks back home'd never believe it. In Georgia there are more colored folks than white, I reckon. White folks free. Colored's always slaves."

"If there are more of your people, sure and why are they still slaves?"

Miss Susan raised her chin, laughed, and gave Kate a knowing look. "Down South us folks is like Irish folks and English, I reckon. 'Cept they buy us an' sell us. Break our families lest we be strong. Keep us ignorant lest we be smart like they is. I got away, though. Miss my man and my chilluns somethin' fierce." At that she gazed down sadly at Little Tom, stroked his cheek, and rocked a little more vigorously as she recalled her own.

The revelation that Susan had children still in slavery shocked Kate. A thousand questions filled her, but she did not dare ask. Susan shook her head from side to side as though trying to clear her mind of memory. Then she began to talk in a low, singsong voice.

"First they sell my man and our oldest boy off down the river," the words came slowly. Kate struggled to understand the meaning. "I grieved for them so, I wasn't no use to nobody. They sell me away from my other two younguns. All the while I'm carryin' another chile inside. Lawd Jesus guide me. I get away up north to Boston. Freedom. Has my baby too soon . . . po' little thing. She didn't have strength to face this mean ol' world. Jesus take her home. My milk come in so strong my breasts is like to break like melons. Missus Beecher knows the Sheffields, English Quaker folk, in America. . . . Missus Sheffield got no milk for her baby boy. Lawd knows I need that baby boy, an' he need me. He was like to die. Good folks, the Sheffields. They take me in. I nurse baby Will these two years past. Then Little Tom here comes, and his mama dies . . . Lawd knows why I'm here. That night your sister pass on, I hear Little Tom a'cryin', and my milk drop strong as ever. Now the Lawd bring me to this town . . . I cain't even say the name of it. Don't matter. Don't matter. Lawd knows this baby need me, and that's all any woman wants . . . to be needed and to love, ain't it, Miss Kate? Not even so important to be loved by somebody else. But just to love somebody. Ain't that what the Lawd put into us gals? And what is we to do when there's nobody in need of us no more?"

Somehow shamed by Miss Susan's searching eyes, Kate nodded once and rose to tend the fire, her crippled hand plainly visible in the light. Susan let her gaze linger in unconcealed curiosity on the scars. She had told her story. Would Kate reciprocate? For a moment Kate's own loss hung on her lips. But she could not bring herself to share aloud the grief and the fear they both knew too well.

Miss Susan broke the long stillness. "I cain't be this baby's mama. He need a mama. I done told Mistuh Joseph he best be findin' him a good woman to marry." She let the words linger in the room.

"You plum scared to love, ain't you, Miss Kate? Scared you might lose somebody again, ain't you?"

Tears brimmed in Kate's eyes. She resented the truth. Miss Susan's heart had found the crack in her soul where joy drained away. "Sure, Miss Susan, and there's only so much a person can hear. Say no more to me, I beg you. . . ."

Miss Susan reached out and took Kate's ruined hand in her own. "I got to say it, honey. . . . A woman's love is like a deep well, ain't it? We didn't dig it. Didn't make the water flow. Jesus done that. And always there's more inside than we can drink alone. So many thirsty people out there waitin' for a cup. Miss Kate, I been watchin' you every day. Gal, you gonna drown your own soul if you don't find a bucket and give some of this away." With that, she guided Kate's fingers to Little Tom's soft curls and pressed them there.

8

The origins of Galway City, located between the salmon-spawning flow of the river Corrib and the dark sweep of the Atlantic Ocean, were lost in the mists of time. There had always been a settlement at the ford of the stream, but it was the de Burgo clan, Norman knights, adventurers, and progenitors of the family Burke, that raised the village to the level of an important seaport and trade center in the early 1100s.

Within a century, two things happened to the city: it had prospered enough to attract hordes of pretentious English and Welsh and Norman settlers while the Burkes had become as Irish as any O'Flaherty or McMurrough. As such, the Burkes were no longer welcome inside the walls of the town they had promoted, so they thumbed their noses at the fourteen clans of newcomers and joined the Gaelic-speaking suburb named the *Claddagh* across the river.

It was within the Claddagh, at the home of its mayor, or king as he referred to himself, that a meeting on the eve of the Repeal rally took place. Gathered in the two-story stone house were Daniel O'Connell, Osborne Davis and Garrison O'Toole, Tom Donovan and Father O'Bannon, and Joseph.

"Thank you for joinin' us, Mister Donovan," said O'Connell in welcome. "We are resolved to take the first steps to see that what happened to poor Brigit will never be repeated."

Twisting his round wool cap in his calloused hands, Da asked, "And how many people will come to the meetin', do you think?" Upon being told that the lowest estimate was sixty thousand he inquired anxiously, "Will you be needin' me to speak to the crowd, then?"

"It would be an honor to yield you the podium," O'Connell said with obvious pleasure.

"Oh, nay!" Da objected swiftly. "That's all right."

"Very well," O'Connell agreed. "But you will sit on the platform with me and be introduced. As will you, Joseph. Now, what remains? The wardens are all selected and are even now receivin' their instructions from Mister Daunt."

"And the soldiers?" Davis asked. "Has there been any official response? Have they brought in more troops?"

O'Connell shook his mane of dark hair. "Relations with General Braddock are most cordial. He understands that we want nothin' more than to assert the privilege of every British subject to petition for the redress of grievances. We are well within our rights to ask parliament to repeal a statute that we find repugnant and unworkable."

"And it won't hurt to show them how large an army we could raise if we wanted," Garrison O'Toole added, rubbing a finger over his thin mustache. "Why, the entire muster of queen's troops in Galway cannot be half of what we will turn out in tomorrow's meetin' alone."

Sternly, O'Connell said, "We will not even hint at such a thing! We have gone out of our way to stress our peaceful intent. The broadsheets tacked to every tree and fencepost for thirty miles around emphasize that fact."

"Nor would I have permitted my pulpit to be used to advocate attendance at this rally if any suggestion of force had been made," added Father O'Bannon.

"I still say that the threat of violence is not the same as the action," O'Toole argued. "If the British tremble a little, so much the better. Besides, force is something the most uneducated farmer can understand, it having been used against them often enough." Turning to Joseph he insisted, "Doesn't the story of your wife's tragedy cry out for justice?"

The room was hushed, waiting for Joseph's reply. "Brigit's memory is not honored if we plunge this country into civil war. We need influential people to adopt our cause. That will never happen if we cease to be a peaceful assembly and become a ravenin' mob."

"Yes, but . . ."

"That will do," Osborne Davis said to his colleague. "To quote Daniel's Dublin speech, 'Not for all the universe contains would I, in my country's cause, consent to the effusion of a single drop of human blood.'"

"Except my own," O'Connell added. "Except my own. Such is exactly the tone we must and will maintain."

The sound of breath whistling between the teeth of Mary Elizabeth attested to the fact she was asleep. So were Miss Susan and Tomeen. Martin was dreaming in the men's end of the cottage. The Donovan home was still indeed, the turf burning low, with scarcely a crackle or spark.

Kate, who was sitting alone by the fire, had allowed her tea to grow cold. She raised a poker from the embers and plunged it, sizzling, into her cup, then returned the iron to the coals. Kate realized it was time for her to be asleep also, but it had so far eluded her. She was replaying what Miss Susan had said. Kate argued with the recollection in words that she had not even spoken aloud to the nurse.

Daisy lowed out in the barn, and Kate, still reflecting on the need to give love, on wells without buckets, wandered teacup in hand toward the window.

She drew back in alarm. A half dozen or more men with torches and painted features glided toward the cottage like sinister wraiths.

There was a sharp rap at the door.

Through the barred entry, Kate called out, "What is it, then?"

"Message for the Donovans," was the reply. The words were pitched low and hoarse, as if the speaker were trying to disguise his voice.

"Who are you, and who is the message from?"

The speaker outside the door became impatient. "Open this door, unless you want us to break it down. Hurry up, then. It'll be the worse for you if we have to use force."

Roused by the noise, Miss Susan came into the room with Tomeen pressed against her. Kate hissed for her to get back in the corner by the fireplace.

Trembling, Kate retrieved the fire poker. Holding the orange-glowing spike in front of her, she stood guard in front of Miss Susan and the child.

At a shouted order, a score of heavy blows hammered against the panel. The latch burst, and the door flew open.

Into the room came a soot-blackened man. Two more stood guard outside with blazing brands. They wore long, shapeless cloaks and slouch hats pulled down around their ears. The leader carried a club.

"We've come," he said, "for the child of Brigit Donovan."

"Never," Kate swore, waving the poker so that it hissed in the air. "You cannot have him."

"Why should the child of the martyred Brigit be raised by the tainted hands of a landlord?" the captain said. "Why do you defend the traitor, Joseph Burke? Your own sister dead, your brother banished . . . give us the child to raise, and he will grow up to strike for the vengeance he deserves."

"Get away from here!" demanded Martin's shrill voice. He charged out of his room, swinging a slat from his bed. The thin lathe connected with the Ribbonman's arm, and he howled and whirled around. Lashing out with a booted foot, he connected with Martin's face, knocking the boy backward into the wall. The intruder lifted the cudgel he carried to deliver another blow.

"Stop it!" Kate shrilled, lunging forward to hold the glowing poker under the eye of the attacker. "Stop it, or you will lose your sight! I swear it."

Slowly the Ribbonman lowered the club and dropped it, then raised his hands, palms outward. "We mean no harm to any of you, unless you interfere," he declared. "But it is wrong for this child to grow up under the thumb of an English-lovin' spawn."

"You are wrong," Martin asserted from where he sat on the floor, his hands pressed to his cheek. "Joseph is with O'Connell."

"O'Connell," the outlaw sneered. "Parcel of wind and compromise. He'll sell us out, first chance. No, boy, your brother had the right notion . . . kill the English; kill the landlords."

"Well you ain't takin' this child," Miss Susan vowed. "'Sides, you cain't feed him less'n you got me, an' how you gonna travel with a black woman, huh? You got a disguise gonna keep folks from knowin' me?"

This argument disconcerted the bandit chief. He backed up toward the door to confer with his comrades, only to find that they were no longer in place. He turned to see where they had gone, only to return a moment later, propelled by the point of the Tinker's finger.

"You will leave now," the great, bearded form announced. "You will go from here and not bother these people again. Do you understand?"

The arrival of those who were coming to Galway City for the rally began before daylight. Though the speeches were not scheduled to begin until noon, by six in the morning the roads into the town were clogged with people on foot and arriving by donkey cart. Three-quarters of the crowd were men, but the quarter that remained of mothers with babes in arms and grandmothers carried pickaback by their sons soon reached a significant number. Long before twelve o'clock was rung in the bell tower of the collegiate church of St. Nicholas, well over one hundred thousand souls swelled Eyre Square to overflowing and lined the streets of William and Mary that led to the site.

"Fine thing," Da observed, pointing at a police constable on a street corner and the sign over the officer's head. "A fine thing to have to march down an avenue named for William of Orange, and he one of the cruelest Protestants after Cromwell." Tom Donovan was referring to the Dutchman, who in 1690, after succeeding to the English throne, dashed the last Irish hope of a Catholic monarchy by defeating King James the Second at the Battle of the Boyne.

It was Father O'Bannon who corrected Da. "Nay, Tom," he said. "Think not on that. We are neither Catholic nor Protestant here today, but Irishmen. What we do here and what follows will have King Billy spinnin' in his grave if we get it right."

This may have been true in the minds of O'Bannon and the other leaders of the Repeal movement, but there were still those businesses on Shop Street and High Street and Quayside whose shutters were closed and barred. Some belonged to people attending the rally, but others were surely disgruntled loyalists opposed to Repeal. A few stores were even so bold as to have orange banners fluttering outside accompanied by signs stating "No Repeal."

Joseph was pleased to notice that no vandalism was offered to any of these contrary opinions. The throng moved at an orderly, if slow, pace. Men wearing armbands that said "Repeal Warden" were posted at every intersection to give directions, assistance, and make sure no disruptions occurred. Though the local constabulary was out in force, there was nothing for them to do, and no redcoated soldiers appeared.

As they reached Eyre Square, Father O'Bannon took his leave. "At every corner of the square there is an altar set up," he said. "My colleagues will be holdin' mass every hour till noon to pray for peace and freedom, and I must join them."

Daniel O'Connell, with exquisite timing, postponed his own arrival until the other dignitaries were assembled on the platform and the first stroke of twelve began to roll over the hushed crowd. O'Connell emerged from a nearby inn where he had been waiting and mounted a carriage. With Repeal wardens parting the mass of bodies, O'Connell was drawn around the square, tipping his hat and waving as one hundred thousand voices called out, "Long live the Liberator! God bless O'Connell, and God bless Ireland!"

Mounting the stage at the east end of the park, O'Connell cordially introduced the honored guests one by one, explaining why each was present. Archbishop MacHale, Osborne Davis, Garrison O'Toole, and the rest were each acknowledged by polite applause. He had Tom Donovan and Joseph stand together, but he got no farther than their names when a roar went up from the crowd. "God bless the father and the widower," the people cried, "of the sainted Brigit!"

It took ten minutes for the tumult to subside, and when it did, Da made the mistake of waving his cap and bowing to the crowd, which set off another ten minutes of demonstration. Da at last sat down, but Joseph, disliking the scrutiny of thousands, descended from the stage and stood at the bottom of the steps at the side.

O'Connell spent no additional time warming up the crowd. He outlined the goals of Repeal: a government for Ireland made up of Irishmen, but a nation that would still be part of the British empire. "God save the queen!" he cried. The wardens responded lustily, as instructed. The reaction from the rest of the multitude, if not as prolonged and boisterous as before, was still warm and approving.

All around the square enterprising merchants operated carts and stalls selling drinks and food. Less than half a block from the stage was a booth offering hot gingerbread. Joseph, who had not eaten that morning, felt his stomach rumble as the aroma of the spice cake drifted past.

O'Connell elaborated on how Repeal would be achieved: there would be at least forty meetings throughout the length and breadth of the country in 1843, after which a formal petition would be signed for presentation in the House of Commons.

As Joseph's attention was drawn to the gingerbread vendor, he noticed some sort of disturbance there. There were too many people in between for him to make out its nature clearly.

"And what must you do?" O'Connell asked rhetorically. "You must organize your street, your village, your parish. We want, nay, we *will have* three million Repealers by August. Think of it, my friends. In just four months from now one out of every three Irish men, women, and children will be marchin' in step with us toward Repeal. So I am here to recruit. But instead of your takin' the queen's shillin' as a soldier, I want you to *give* your shillin' for Repeal. We impose no hardship, but every household that is able should set aside one penny each month for the Repeal rent. A single pence, friends. Is that too dear a price for freedom?"

The shouts of "NO! NO! Pennies for Repeal!" ringing throughout the crowd seemed loud enough to carry clear to London.

"Stop, thief," Joseph distantly heard the gingerbread vendor cry. "Stop him! He stole my moneybag!"

Toward the closest alley leading away from the square dashed a lean, straggle-haired man of perhaps twenty years of age. To all but those nearby, the baker's shouts were lost in the roar of the crowd, and no one moved to intercept the cutpurse. Clearly in another twenty yards he would round the corner into the narrow byway and escape. Instinctively, Joseph broke from his place and ran headlong toward the thief.

A blue-coated, gray-haired constable, stationed across the street, also heard the outcry and moved to intercept the robber. The escaping man barreled into three unsuspecting women who were listening to O'Connell's speech, knocking them to the ground. But his flight was impeded enough for Joseph and the policeman to converge on the brigand. The thief began yelling, "Help me! They're tryin' to arrest me for yellin' 'Down with the English.' Help!"

The constable flung himself on the young robber and wrapped both arms around the felon's knees, bringing him crashing down on the cobbles. The cutpurse slipped a finger-length, fang-bladed knife out of his sleeve and slashed at the officer, who knocked the weapon aside with his forearm.

Joseph grabbed the wrist of the knifehand and struggled to keep himself and the patrolman from being stabbed. He was relieved when three male bystanders joined the fray. The new arrivals seized all three struggling figures.

Then, to Joseph's shock, they turned the thief loose, and he scampered away into the crowd. "For shame," one of the newcomers said, shaking the constable. "Why are you chasin' down a slip of a lad for shootin' off his mouth?" There was a hostile murmur of agreement from the others.

"No," Joseph protested. "You don't understand. He stole money."

An additional three burly forms joined the altercation. Instead of seizing on either thief or policeman, they made directly for Joseph. One of them wrenched Joseph's coat up over his head, so that his identity could not be determined by other onlookers.

A boot crashed into Joseph's ribs, and another stomped him between the shoulder blades. His cry to them to stop, that they were making a mistake, was driven out of him by the blows. He could scarcely croak. Then he was dropped in the gutter while the other attackers continued to maul the constable. "Shall we teach this English lackey some manners?" Joseph heard one of them ask. "Flog him or hang him?"

"No!" Joseph shouted, overcoming the crushed feel in his middle. "He could have been killed tryin' to stop the thief."

"And shall we teach you a further lesson too?" another of the antagonistic crew suggested. The speaker was missing his two front teeth and had his nose pushed sideways like a boxer's.

It might have turned out even worse if the gingerbread seller had not arrived at that moment, accompanied by Garrison O'Toole. "You great clots!" the baker shrieked. "You've let the thief escape. Turn loose of this man and the officer before I meself charge you with aidin' and abettin' a criminal!"

As if by magic, the six who had interfered melted away into the thousands. The baker assisted the constable while O'Toole brushed off Joseph's coat. "I saw what happened," he said. "You've a heroic bent, Joseph Burke, and you make fine copy. But you'd best give up takin' the part of constables, or people will be thinkin' you must be either a traitor or a spy."

PART II

No more I'll hear your sweet song, in the
*   dewy milking bawn,*
With the kine all lowing around you, in the
*   pale, red light of dawn;*
Some other maid will sing those songs, while
*   you are in the clay—*
Oh! Blessed God! my heart will break for
*   Mary of Loch Rea.*

—Michael Hogan, The Bard of Thomond

9

News of the nighttime visit to the Donovan farm dimmed the enthusiasm of the men who returned from Galway City. This was more than a threat to Joseph Burke and Little Tom, the tiny heir of his estate. It was meant to be a threat against O'Connell and the Repeal movement itself. What use was a gathering of peaceful Irishmen if rapparees rode from the wildlands to threaten women and children while their sons and husbands were away? There were many bitter rovers living in the hills among the Ribbonmen. They would gladly see O'Connell dead, hope of peace destroyed, and war declared against the British.

No matter how important the cause, what man would risk the safety of his family for it? This was discussed at length in O'Flaherty's Pub in Ballynockanor as well as Watty's Tavern in Castletown on market day.

Clooney sipped his pint of bitter. "And who's to say, Tom Donovan, what they might have done to Kate if the Tinker had not come upon them?"

"The Tinker!" declared O'Rourke. "I say he's one of them. Sure, or why would they turn back?"

At this comment a hum of understanding swept through the crowded tavern. Tom Donovan nodded grimly. "He put a stop to it, that's certain. Though I can't say why or how he done it, lads."

The side door opened, and Martin Donovan entered. "Da!" the boy called. "Tobin is in the square askin' after the bull calf."

"Here I am." Tom waved over the heads of the crowd. "And Tobin should know where he'd be findin' me."

The crowd parted, rough hands reaching out to pat Martin as he passed through. The black bruise on his face made him a bit of a hero. Stout lad to defend the women against armed men.

"I told him you were at a political meetin'," Martin breathlessly explained. "Tobin says he'll have none of it. Ribbonmen burned the farmhouse of three Repealers over in Mayo who marched with O'Connell. Tobin says he intends to keep his mind on cattle."

From the back of the smoke-filled room another shouted, "And cattle we will be if we give in to the English or to a band of violent outlaws."

Someone else cried out, "They're our own kind, fightin' the way they think best."

"Fightin' us? Fightin' O'Connell? Threatenin' to steal wee Tomeen?" objected Tom Donovan. "No thank you, sir! They're not my kind!"

A cheer rose in favor of this sentiment.

"Perhaps O'Connell's way is the way of cowards," came the retort. "Why will the man not gather an army to fight?"

A low, dangerous rumble was the response from the majority. This was a familiar sound to any who had been present just before a riot. Feelings were running high in favor of O'Connell and against the tactics of the night riders. There were too many O'Connell supporters for the dissenter to argue with. The door opened and shut as he slipped out.

To other topics. "Tobin has never been a man for politics," Da explained in a patronizing voice. "His grandfather sat it out during the '98 and was well rewarded for it. When his neighbors were transported for rebellion, the old man inherited their leases. O'Connell's way is the best, that's sure. No blood. No violence. We have a stir-rin' time at the meetin' and keep our farms."

Clooney reached out and lifted Martin's bruised face to the lamplight. "What did they do to you, lad?"

"Kicked me. I ran to stop him and . . ."

"Was there anything you recognized about the villain, Martin? Could he be one of us?" Watty leaned over the bar and peered down at him.

Martin put his fingers to the mark, and his forehead creased in thought. "The one who kicked me? Not from Ballynockanor. Not from Castletown either. Not a poor man either. He was wearin' boots, you see. Fine boots. With a silver cap on the tip of the sole."

The information caused an uproar in the assembly. What outlaw in all the world could afford boots? Ribbonmen, like the poor farmers of Ballynockanor, wore leather shoes called *pampooties* in the winter months and went barefoot during warm weather. Expensive boots were for English soldiers, constables, and landlords.

"Perhaps he stole them," O'Rourke concluded.

Martin thought about the scene a moment longer, then said, "Aye. Likely, I suppose, but they were all wearin' boots, sir. Just at my eye level they were. Fine black leather. Polished too."

When Joseph went in search of the Tinker, he could not locate the man anywhere. The barn, the tack rooms, the loft, the paddocks; Dermott O'Neill had disappeared. His suspicions mounting, Joseph tapped on the door of Old Flynn's cottage and asked if the Tinker had been seen.

Flynn grumbled and griped again at having to work with a vagabond, thieving, up-to-no-good traveler. When pressed for a straight answer, he grumpily acknowledged that O'Neill had asked leave to return to his caravan, which was parked at the bottom of the west pasture. The stablemaster admitted that O'Neill had done the required chores, including two that came to Flynn's mind as afterthoughts, before taking leave of the stables.

The walk across the sloping grassland gave Joseph more time to think about what he was going to say, but settled nothing about what he *would* say. He was grateful for the Tinker's timely intervention at the Donovan cottage, but wary of how O'Neill had come to be there and why the Ribbonmen had so readily obeyed.

When the rounded top of the Tinker's wagon came into view, Joseph stopped once more. A whirring, rasping noise reached his ears, and when he walked forward another ten paces he saw its cause. O'Neill was seated at a grinding wheel, the foot treadle spinning the stone. His back was to Joseph, and he was bent over his work, sharpening a knife. Beside him on the ground, carefully aligned on a scrap of leather, were a dozen more knives. The least was palm sized, while the largest had blade and hilt enough to be called a modest sword.

Even though the wheel had not faltered and Joseph had advanced no farther, the giant man spoke. "Good evenin', your lordship. Is there somethin' amiss with the horses?"

"No," Joseph acknowledged, clearing his throat with a guilty cough as if he had been caught spying on the man. "No, Flynn tells me everything is fine with your work. How did you know it was me?"

Rising from being hunched over the stone, the Tinker said, "Comes of livin' outdoors most of my life. Senses like hearin' and smell get keener." Then dismissing the subject as if his nonexplanation was all he would offer, he asked, "Was there somethin' you wanted then?" O'Neill thumbed the edge of the six-inch-long blade he was grinding and pursed his lips thoughtfully.

"Aye," Joseph said, "I wanted to thank you for protectin' my son and the womenfolk t'other night."

"Ah, that." The Tinker received this praise with a flick of his hair, like a horse tossing its mane. "It was nothin' really."

"So you say," Joseph persisted, "but still, I'm grateful. How did you come to be there, so many miles from here? Did you hear a warnin'? Did some lad's tongue slip in a pub?"

O'Neill held the knife so that the gleaming blade reflected the orange rays of the setting sun into Joseph's eyes. "No," the Tinker said at last. "It just came to me on the wind. It comes of . . ."

"Livin' out-of-doors," Joseph finished. "Yes, I see." Then he forced himself to ask the rest. "And if you don't mind me askin', why did those rapparees obey you so readily? Big as y'are, they still outnumbered you six to one. Yet Martin says all but the leader fled as soon as you arrived, and their captain soon after. Martin says the bandit chief looked terrified of you."

Grinning, the Tinker said, "Have y'not noticed then? I have a way with dumb brutes. I guess I just spoke their language."

There was no way to probe without voicing his suspicions, and that step Joseph was unwilling to take. "I'll say thank you again, then. If you should hear any threats to any of my kin or friends, I'd appreciate you tellin' me about it."

"Indeed I will, your lordship." O'Neill had already turned back to the wheel and was burnishing the other edge of the blade.

"Why do you have so many knives?" Joseph asked in parting.

"It's a hobby of mine," the Tinker replied. "I make them. Besides, a man cannot tell when a blade might be useful." Like the Tinker's other replies, this was really no explanation, but it was all he seemed prepared to provide.

The whisper for Repeal had become a bold cry in every tavern, inn, and crossroads of the Province of Connaught. The west was indeed awake.

The fact that freedom from England might come without her direct assistance irritated Mad Molly. She informed Joseph of the inequity of it as she cleaned the ashes from the kitchen hearth.

"And myself, Molly Fahey . . . who am chief and foremost house-keeper, cook, valet, coach driver, harvester, seamstress, and gardener in the House of Burke . . . have not been asked to lift one finger to help the greatest cause since the rebellion of '98!" At this declaration she jabbed at the air with her ash-covered index finger, then paused, looked at the digit as though it were not her own, wiggled it, and put it in the water kettle to wash. "Now, now . . . Where was I? What? What? What?"

Molly was being unusually lucid, Joseph thought. Sipping his tea at the thick, scarred kitchen table, he assisted. "You were sayin', Molly, that nothin' ever gets done around here without you."

This pleased the old woman. She smiled toothlessly, her lips puckering as though she would kiss him. "Sure, and that's me very point! Repeal! A penny tax a household to be collected for the cause. But what you have to make them give is an extra poor box in the back of Father O'Bannon's chapel. Have we not been brought up to pay our poor taxes to someone who comes to the door of a cottage and says, 'Pay up or die, if you please!'"

"Aye, Molly. But this is a different sort of collection, woman."

"Not a'tall! Ask Dermott O'Neill! Sure, and he heard them singin'!" she declared, holding up the ash bucket as though this were the very receptacle to receive Repeal pennies. "They say we poor folk must pay our pennies to support O'Connell and Repeal of the union with England or we die, sir! A million strong for Ireland on the roads! And strong we must be! There's nothin' else for it! Or the Irish will die hungry." She lowered her voice to a whisper. "They told me clearly, Joseph Connor Burke. Clearly, clearly, clearly, they said! What's wrong with Joseph, they asked? Is he afraid?" Her head wagged in negative reply. "I defended ye, Joseph. . . ." She brightened. "But ye need me, Joseph, for none can hear the angels but the Tinker and myself."

"I do not doubt you, Molly."

"Then I am the official Repeal Tax Collector in the townlands?" She leaned in close. "They'll not refuse when I ask them to give. They think I'm mad, you see, and so they fear to disappoint me since I've been charmed by the fairies."

Joseph knew there was no talking her out of it. "It isn't a tax."

"Whatever it is, I'll get it. I've got a plan! A vision as to how to make them give up their hard-won pennies. Trust me, Joseph Connor!"

"Then I create the post of Ballynockanor Officer of Repeal Rent just for you. You may go about takin' donations. What will you need, Molly?"

She bobbed up and down and clapped her hands happily. "I thank ye for the honor! I told them you would, for you're a kind man and a gentle man and a man of reason!" She lost her place in the excitement and knocked on her head to jar the thought loose again. "What do I need? Nothin' a'tall that any official wouldn't have. A carriage and the Tinker to drive me, if you please. A new, blue serge frock and a green silk sash with REPEAL written upon it."

"Shoes?" Joseph grinned down at her bare toes.

"Shoes? What? Would you have them thinkin' I'm English? No shoes. But one more item. Aye! Two worthy assistants. Martin and Mary Elizabeth Donovan will do!"

"It's done, Madame Repeal Rent Collector."

She clung to his arm and squinted up at him in adoration and gratitude. "You'll never regret it. I'll make the farmers pay like that vile steward John Stone used to do . . . may he rot in prison! If they do not support Repeal, I'll threaten them with a madwoman's curse and throw dust into the air! Oooooh. That puts them a'twitter every time. The dust is a likely touch. Fear. It's always best to make the people pay their taxes in the way they're accustomed to."

The wind that swept across St. Stephen's Green in Dublin was damp and chilly. Nevertheless, Osborne Davis had insisted that his meeting with Garrison and Beth Anne O'Toole take place out-of-doors, so that the other employees in the printshop could not overhear his criticism.

"I won't have it, do you understand?" Davis said forcefully to O'Toole and his sister. "We cannot publish a headline that reads 'Galway thousands vow: Repeal or Death!' It never happened, and it gives Dublin Castle entirely the wrong notion of the tone of the meetin'."

"But did Daniel O'Connell not make them repeat an oath to pledge their lives for Repeal?" Garrison O'Toole asked. "I was there; I heard it."

"It's not the same thing at all, and you know it," Davis fumed. "Now it is bad enough that you ran that blasted poem over my disapproval. This banner is even worse. There are Repeal meetin's already scheduled for Sligo, Mullingar, and Cork. Do you want the Chancellor and Lord Lieutenant Grey to proscribe them? To kill the movement before it's fairly begun and arrest us?"

"But O'Connell himself speaks of sheddin' blood for freedom," Beth Anne observed. "Are the common people to be denied hearin' that sentiment expressed?"

"O'Connell said he would not spare his own blood, but refused to consider spillin' the blood of anyone else. He pointedly disavowed any show of force, any threat."

"But what is an assembly of one hundred thousand men clamorin' for breakin' away from England if it is not a show of force?" Beth Anne challenged. "How can *The Nation* be the voice of Repeal if we are always shilly-shallyin' around?"

The color rose in Davis's pale cheeks, and an explosion seemed imminent. Visibly he forced himself to take a deep breath before replying. "We all want Repeal to come soon," he said. "We all feel the yoke of British servitude. But this movement is as much an appeal to the British common man as to our own. Convince the English clerk, crofter, and physician that we are peace-lovin' but determined to control our own destiny, and they will be sympathetic. If they perceive Repeal as an act of rebellion, some kind of popish plot, then they will cheer as the cavalry rides us down with sabers; they will applaud as the cannons are unleashed on our gatherin's. That is exactly what our enemies want." He pondered, sighing heavily. "Mark me, now, I do not say you are altogether wrong or alone in your thinkin'. Many in the movement want us to be more bold. Daniel himself has trouble holdin' back at times, the fire-eater. We must be cautious and circumspect."

O'Toole's head bobbed in token of submission, but a defiant spark remained in Beth Anne's eye. Osborne Davis did not see the nudge Garrison received in the ribs from his sister's elbow.

"By the by," O'Toole said with a start, "I understand that Burtenshaw Suggins and Edward Lucas are the chief government operatives watchin' Repeal."

"Oh?" Davis said with interest. "Do we know what their plans are now? Is the iron fist about to be revealed anyway?"

"My sources say they are keepin' a close eye on the rallies, but will take no action yet. I have heard they will make a swing through the west country, to see for themselves what the mood of the people is."

"Have they published an itinerary?"

"It is not supposed to be an official trip," Beth Anne corrected. "The reason they give out is that they are accompanyin' Lady Fiona Shaw, that's Edward's cousin, to her estate in Limerick. Oh, but one specific stop has been mentioned."

"And what is that?" Davis inquired, turning up his coat collar.

"You must not say anything to O'Connell about this," O'Toole urged. "It would only cast doubts on someone he loves very much, and I'm certain there is nothin' disreputable goin' on."

"Who are you speakin' of?" Davis demanded.

"Why Joseph Connor Burke, of course," O'Toole announced. "Lucas let it be known particularly that they were callin' on the Burke of Connaught. But it must certainly be a harmless visit."

"Yes," Beth Anne added. "And that vicious rumor, linkin' the young squire with the Lady Shaw. I'm sure there's nothin' to it. Imagine, the man heralded by O'Connell as the spirit of Ireland, consortin' with the relation of a British official."

M ad Molly looked grand indeed in her new Repeal Rent Collector's dress. She was especially proud of the bright green silk sash with the bold print letters spelling out REPEAL on the front and back. Joseph had a lady's black silk top hat brought for her from Galway City. A green scarf, perfectly matching the sash, was tied around the band.

With her hair pinned up beneath the hat, Martin thought Mad Molly Fahey looked almost as sane as anyone could expect a madwoman to be.

He told her so. "Molly, you've never looked so grand since you first were daft."

"And same to you, Martin," she returned proudly.

Martin and Mary Elizabeth, though dressed in their ordinary clothes, were also awarded green sashes to designate their exalted positions as assistants.

Dermott O'Neill, the Tinker, would have nothing to do with elaborate displays. "I'm no more than a stablehand. What do I know of such things?" He wore his tattered coat and trousers. A shapeless, brown hat drooped over his brooding brow and made his dark visage even more menacing.

The official carriage of Mad Molly and her assistants was an antique pony cart trimmed in banners proclaiming the cause. On one side was the admonition, "MARCH FOR IRELAND! FOLLOW O'CONNELL!" On the opposite side was the declaration, "PENNIES FOR FREEDOM! A COIN FOR REPEAL!"

Molly had argued for a message more stirring and motivating. "And why can it not say 'PAY OR DIE'? Or at least, 'YOUR PENNY OR A CURSE'?"

Joseph vetoed her request.

This morning the Tinker hitched Gideon, the diminutive gray pony, to the cart. Mad Molly, her naked toes covered with dust, strode around the vehicle with her hands clasped behind her back in a Napoleonic posture. "Aye! The very thing!" she cried with delight after the inspection. "A beauty! A beauty! Ain't she, Mary Elizabeth? If Queen Victoria herself is sellin' oats in the market square today, why she'll see this coach and bow her wee small head and pay a penny for Repeal!"

"That she will, Molly," Mary Elizabeth crooned as she stroked Gideon's nose.

Martin was certain the English queen would not be in the Castletown Market Square selling oats. It was, however a grand sentiment. He was still not clear on what they would be doing in Castletown. It was market day, and the square would be packed with farmers from the surrounding townlands. Mad Molly stated that she could round up as much as two pounds from such a mob, but the exact strategy for the collections of Repeal donations had not been spelled out.

"And what will you have us be doin'?" Martin queried.

"Look handsome, me boy-o!" was her reply. With a stern, demanding squint at the Tinker she declared, "I'll drive the cart, if you please."

The Tinker shrugged acquiescently and helped the woman to the driver's seat. Climbing wordlessly in behind her with Mary Elizabeth and Martin, the Tinker pulled his hat brim over his eyes and leaned back in the corner as if he were asleep.

Molly sat high and stiff like a state coachman. "The glory of the Lord and of Gideon!" she cried. Snatching up the whip she tapped the pony on the rump, and the cart jolted off down the lane. She kept her faded blue eyes fixed on his ears and did not let him have his own way. The animal plodded toward the main road. Martin was about to state that he could walk faster than the pony when Mad Molly cracked the whip above the pony's skull and gave a war whoop!

The ride into Castletown was wild and jolting. Mary Elizabeth, her face alight in the delicious experience of being so near to the possibility of being killed, pointed at Martin and laughed. "You're white as a sheet! Martin's white as a sheet, Molly!"

"I told him he needs more sun." Then she shouted, "Ye need more sun, Martin!"

He smiled uneasily and saluted. The Tinker, lolling about with the motion of the cart, appeared still to be sleeping. Or had he died? Martin was about to tap Dermott O'Neill on his broad shoulder when the Tinker raised his chin slightly, black eyes fixing on Martin from beneath the hat brim.

With a gasp Martin drew back.

Molly called to him again, "Are ye havin' fun, then, Martin?"

Through clenched teeth Martin grinned and nodded.

The madwoman, too distant to touch him, stretched out the whip and tapped him gently on his head. "You're a fine lad. That ye are. They all say so."

The swirl of dust that followed the single pony cart into Castletown could have been that of a host of Bible-age chariots. Before the trap even crossed Charity Bridge, the people in the market square were pointing toward the spiral of pink haze that swept upward over the sun.

Nor did Molly let the headlong rush of the beast falter at the first cluster of tables and benches that marked the outer ranks of the trading day. Whooping and clattering, the pony cart burst on the Castletown scene, with Molly and Mary Elizabeth doing the whooping, while the Tinker leaned carelessly back against the bullhide frame and Martin hung on for dear life.

Scattering fishmongers and oat merchants, shoemakers and dealers in pottery, the arrival of the Queen of the Repeal Rent Collectors set Castletown on its ear. One moment it was an ordinary market day, and the next business was suspended as a crowd gathered around the cart.

While the poor pony shuddered and trembled, Molly swung the whip around her head with the noise of a thousand agitated hornets. "Pennies for Repeal!" she demanded as the whirring finally died. "This is the day the Repeal rent is due. Bring your pennies for Ireland and for freedom."

Someone at the rear of the crowd tossed a penny toward the cart. It rattled on the floorboards, and Mary Elizabeth picked it up. Molly stretched out her hand for the payment. "Whose picture is on it?" she inquired.

"It's the queen," Mary Elizabeth said, turning the copper over in her palm.

"Render unto Caesar the things that are Caesar's and unto Repeal the pennies that are for Ireland," Molly cried.

"Truly eloquent," announced the Tinker as he stood up, took off his hat, and held it out like a basket. "Now is the time to bring out the pennies you were meanin' to give, but kept forgettin' to carry to the church."

"Clooney!" Molly announced, singling out the musician with a stab of her whip. "Play us 'The Men of Ninety-Eight,' while my associates pass amongst you to receive the payment." Clooney looked as if he would rather go back inside Watty's Tavern, but once caught in Molly's glare he was skewered. The sound of Clooney's flute was soon marching over the market square.

"Heaven be our shield," burst out Father O'Bannon, tucking up the hem of his cassock with one hand and forcing his way through the crowd. "What's the meanin' of this? Molly, have y'lost what little sense y'had left?"

Dermott O'Neill went to the priest's side. "Do but have patience, Father," he counseled. "Only listen to her speak a moment before you judge."

"Do not say you mean to give tomorrow," Molly warned, looking Dan Tobin right in the face. "Do not say y'have no penny to spare when there is a stockin' under your mattress with twelve shillin's in it." This was addressed to Barry Fitzpatrick, who shuffled his feet and looked away. "Do y'not remember what came upon Ananias and Sapphira when they lied to the Lord?"

"Y'see, Father," observed the Tinker, "she preaches well. She's but doin' part of your work this day, and with the squire's blessin' at that."

So Father O'Bannon stepped aside as Martin, Mary Elizabeth, and Dermott O'Neill passed among the crowd collecting the Repeal rent. Molly continued to harangue the assembly from the cart. Though they would not admit it, many quaked a bit with the dread of Mad Molly's dire predictions and were moved to donate thereby.

And those who were not, Martin noted, were certainly inspired to contribute by the forceful light in the Tinker's dark eyes.

∽ 10 ∼

M artin Donovan loved May Day. By Irish tradition, it was the hinge of the year—the first day of summer, and best of all, a holiday from work and any thought of school.

For the first time since the preceding autumn, the hearth fire in the Donovan cottage was allowed to go out. Rising early in the morning, Kate had removed the ashes and swept the hearth. In place of the glowing turf she stoked the stone ring with flowers: early roses and late daffodils, pink cranesbill, and the soft blue of spring gentian that blossomed in the cracks of the rocks near St. Brigit's cross.

Martin saw it from his bedroll beside his sleeping da and knew it would be a gloriously perfect day.

May Day was also Gale Day, the twice-yearly occasion when rents were due to the landlord. For the only time in Martin's memory, his father actually spoke well of the approach of Gale Day. He did not begrudge paying Joseph Connor Burke for the lease of the pastures. "Sure, and fourteen shillin's an acre is a fair price," he declared.

"And himself bein' such a fine man, I would pay without grousin' should it be twice as much!" Then he added with a wink at Martin, "Well, maybe only a wee bit of grousin'!"

This year the Gale Day payments were to be made in a pavilion set up in the yard of the Burke estate. This was itself a noteworthy change: the Marlowes had required everyone to assemble in the main square in Castletown, where the sour-faced steward, John Stone, collected the rack rent under the shadow of the gibbet hanging outside the courthouse.

So it was that Martin, Kate, Da, and Mary Elizabeth trooped happily to Burke Hall, and the sounds of laughter and music reached them when they were still a half mile away. There was dancing going on and much merriment, and as far as Martin could tell, everyone was having a grand bit of crack, with the possible exception of the landlord himself.

Squire Joseph, formally dressed and wearing a silver stickpin carved in the likeness of the Burke arms, was seated at a high table inside the tent. Adam Kane stood at his side. As each tenant advanced and, doffing his cap, presented the rent payment, Joseph stood in acknowledgment and bowed deeply, looking stiff and uncomfortable.

Annie Rose Field, Mad Molly's younger sister, returned to visit Ballynockanor for the May Day celebration. She was well remembered from the American wake of Kevin Donovan as the woman whose keening scared the breeches off the British soldiers.

When Tom Donovan saw her coming he remarked to Aidan Clooney, "Think of it, Aidan! A woman of such passion might have done well enough performing to suit the likes of himself, old Bill Shakespeare. Team her up with Molly, and there would have been no need for *three* witches in *MacBeth*."

Clooney said he had not yet heard the ballad of the witches of *MacBeth*, but if Tom would hum a bar he could certainly play it on his flute.

"And here they come, speak of the devil!" Clooney jabbed his flute in the air toward the approaching sisters.

Mad Molly, arm in arm with Annie Rose, marched through the

crowded square to where O'Rourke, Clooney, and O'Brien, the blind piper, had assembled their small band to play.

Annie Rose, who was a rational woman except when she was paid to keen, locked eyes with Clooney and proclaimed, "Ye didn't know me sister and meself can sing a duet fit to bring tears from the eyes of a stone saint. But here we be, the two of us. A pair we are . . ."

Molly nodded happily. "A pair. A pair. Two shoes make a pair. Pare the apples, said he . . ."

"Shut your gob, Molly," Annie Rose instructed kindly. "We're goin' to sing for the kind people, for I know they never knew ye had the voice of an angel!"

Molly extended her bony finger upward, raised her eyebrows, and said quietly, "Aye. But I can't sing. I'll not tell them of the tribute, sister. Little wee Connor will need it by and by. Aye, they've all come, bringin' the boru, the tribute. But Clontarf pays for all, sister. Clontarf pays for all."

Martin heard this banter. Though it was the ravings of a mad-woman, he recognized Molly had managed to compound ancient tales with modern circumstances. Boru was the Gaelic for *tribute,* and paying rent was like bringing tribute to the High King. Even the reference to Clontarf made a twisted kind of sense: the High King of All Ireland, Brian Boru, Brian of the Tribute, had met his death defeating an army of Vikings at the Battle of Clontarf.

Annie Rose nudged her sister hard in the ribs and said to Clooney, "She loves to sing. She's not always been daft. There are shreds of her mind left, and music is the key . . ."

"No key. It's a wall and no lock a'tall." Molly rapped her knuckles hard against her sister's skull. "You can tell it's hollow by the sound. I've known it all along."

Annie, who responded to the rap by soundly batting Molly in return, smiled sweetly at Clooney. "There now. She's off again. Play the May song quickly, or there'll be no calmin' herself, and she may do battle with the maypole or with yourself."

The threat of Molly unleashed caused Clooney to quickly put his flute to his lips and begin the "Sweet May" song.

O'Rourke joined him on the fiddle with a rousing introduction.

Molly's faded eyes brightened at the melody. Annie Rose winked as the two began to croak in a most imperfect harmony:

May, Sweet May, again is come,
May that frees the land from gloom.
Every branch and every tree
Ring with her sweet melody;
Hill and dale are May's own tributes.

At this phrase Molly smacked herself hard on the cheek and cried, "Shut me mouth! May's tributes! There! I've said the word, and there are thieves and villains who would have it all! May's tributes! Hush, Molly Fahey. They'll kill for it!"

Molly would not be hushed, not even by herself. She continued to tell herself to hush, and yet she would not.

The song was ruined. Though Clooney continued to play and O'Rourke to fiddle, the vocal experiment came to an end. Molly danced away, calling for Mary Elizabeth and Martin, who scurried off to hide.

Annie Rose was left scowling. She sniffed and wiped her nose on her sleeve. "Well then, gentlemen, upon me word, it was her favorite song as a child. I was hopin' to bring me sister's mind back from the chicken coop, but she's gone. Aye. Gone. Gone. Gone. Her eggs are scrambled, and there's an end to it."

With a sigh Annie Rose wandered after her.

Clooney, wide-eyed, lowered the instrument from his mouth and said, "With a voice like that, why should the woman be paid for keenin'? Such screechin' is enough to *raise* the dead and bring tears to the eyes of the livin'!"

Martin, safely hidden under the layer of green boughs and rushes that decorated the musicians' stage, readily agreed.

Some weeks after Gale Day, Joseph was seated in the yellow withdrawing room. The door was shut, not because the noise of the children in the other wing of the mansion irritated him, but because he needed to think. On his desk was a personal letter from Dublin that had arrived in the morning post. It was from Edward Lucas, secretary to Burtenshaw Suggins. He and a traveling companion would be journeying through the county and would enjoy the pleasure of stopping over at Burke Hall. It did not specify a date.

Lucas, once a close friend of Daniel O'Connell, was clearly on the opposite side of the playing field when it came to the issue of Repeal. Joseph suspected the visit would be more than social, and he resented it.

To the experience of being almost beaten or lynched at the hands of overzealous Repealers had been added Garrison O'Toole's warning that Joseph was appearing dangerously pro-English. The additional burden of this latest unwanted intrusion in his life by those who undoubtedly thought he was anti-British was almost more than he could bear.

There was a diffident tap at the door. "Pardon, your lordship," said Fern timidly, well aware Joseph had given strict instruction he was not to be disturbed. "Pardon for intrudin', but there's two gentlemen and a young lady say you're expectin' them."

"A lady? Two gentlemen, Fern?" he repeated as a question. It was unlikely either Colonel Mahon or Squireen O'Shea would be calling. Who could it be? "And did they give their names?"

"Oh, aye," agreed Fern. "And a terrible great heap of titles an' names they have too. More'n I can remember, I'm sure."

Titled lords, here at the jumping-off point into the wilds of Connaught? It could only be Lucas arriving early. "Well, show them in, girl," Joseph said, hastily restoring some order to his cravat and straightening his waistcoat.

The two men and the woman that the stuttering Fern ushered upstairs were instantly recognized by Joseph. One was Edward Lucas. The other was the assistant chancellor himself, Burtenshaw Suggins. Between them was Lady Fiona Lucas-Shaw, first cousin to Edward. Graceful, fair of hair and complexion, Fiona was in her own way a force to be reckoned with among the mighty in Ireland. For a time,

like every other young man in Dublin society, Joseph had imagined
he was in love with her. At the age of seventeen he had danced
with her at a ball. She was four years older than Joseph and a heart-
stopping beauty. The poet Maurice Jepson wrote of her,

> *Like a merchant who has ventured*
> *All his fortune on the sea,*
> *So in thee my hopes were centered,*
> *Destined soon a wreck to be.*

For weeks after the one dance, Joseph had considered convert-
ing to the Church of Ireland so he could court the older woman.
Then the poet Jepson killed himself in despair over her rejection.
Good Daniel talked sense to Joseph. Such a woman was not interested in romance or poetry or conversion for love.

Ah, but for money Fiona had converted to Catholicism and married well, an elderly, wealthy man. Soon after, she was happily widowed. In the meantime Joseph's calling to the priesthood had driven
infatuation from his thoughts. Now here was the woman who drove
poets to suicide and young men to Protestantism! She curtsied before
him. He was amused as he took her hand, kissed it, and greeted her.
Somehow the image of himself at seventeen stumbled gawking and
gasping into his mind. He almost laughed. If anything, she was, at
twenty-nine, more beautiful than she had ever been. But Joseph was
past poetry and infatuation.

Lucas and Suggins, both lofty officials of the British government
of Ireland, were guttering candles in her presence.

"My lords," Joseph said, bowing them into the room. "I had no
idea you were coming so soon. I beg your pardon for not being
ready to receive you."

"No matter," Suggins replied with a dismissive wave of his hand.
"We are en route to Limerick and Lady Shaw's estates. We decided
to drop by and offer our congratulations on the recovery of your
patrimony. You remember Lady Shaw, of course."

Joseph's eyebrows elevated slightly, but he raised no further query.
Castletown was scarcely on any direct route to Limerick. What was

the real reason these two high-ranking officeholders would come out of their way to see him?

He shook off the doubts by remembering his manners. "Lady Shaw. Could anyone forget? Eight years it has been. What was it the poet wrote? '*I fondly dreamt that heart mine own.*'"

At his recitation she blushed and averted her bright blue eyes from his amused gaze. "Please, sir. I was very young."

There was a tinge of sadness in her voice that made him regret quoting the verse.

"You'll surely be stayin' the night at Burke Hall?"

The trio assented, and Joseph ordered the rooms be made ready and the cook notified that there would be three guests for dinner.

After tea had been ordered and delivered and some pleasantries about the weather and the lamb crop had been bantered about, Fiona asked if she might be shown to her room. The trip had been long and she was weary, she said. Joseph rang for Fern, who led the elegant guest to her quarters. The scent of her perfume lingered in the room.

Suggins nodded toward Secretary Lucas and the genuine cause of the interview was revealed.

"We understand," Lucas offered lightly, as if the topic were of only passing interest, "that you attended the O'Connell assembly in Galway City."

No mention of the word *Repeal*. Perhaps the very expression was anathema.

"I did indeed. It was peaceful and orderly and quite well attended. Perhaps one hundred twenty thousand in total."

Suggins sniffed. "Dear me," he said. "How that number does grow and grow! I think the original estimate was somewhat nearer twenty thousand. But there is an excusable tendency to exaggerate these popular movements, eh?"

Joseph admitted he had no way of knowing the actual number.

"Just so," Lucas continued. "A passing fancy that will occupy people only until the demands of farming require them to do less gallivanting about."

"I doubt it very much. The call for home-rule is extremely well received across the country and will continue to grow even more powerful."

Lucas looked at Suggins, and a distinct expression of distaste passed over both countenances. "And you yourself will continue your involvement?" Lucas asked haughtily. "We were certain that a promising young man with the heritage of the Burke of Connaught on his shoulders would not do anything to jeopardize his position."

That was as thinly veiled a threat as ever Joseph had heard. Jeopardize his estate? How? Joseph felt compelled to speak up on behalf of his foster father, Daniel, and the cause of Repeal. "People who can scarcely afford shoes are makin' do with even less and givin' up their pennies for Repeal," he said. "The British government must not underestimate the desire of the people for self-rule."

Leaning forward, Lucas inquired, "So this parish collects the O'Connell tribute?"

This scathing remark was apparently a reference to the Repeal rent. "Certainly," Joseph agreed. "A penny per household every month."

"A pity," Lucas said, shrugging. "To see the poor farmers so taken in as to part with their hard-earned coppers. Don't you think a word from you would put a stop to it?"

Joseph was getting angry. "It's not for me to say how my tenants direct their pennies," he said firmly. "Besides, why would I oppose the worthy cause? I am myself a subscriber as well as the senior collector for the west."

"Dear me." Suggins sniffed again. "How unfortunate. You will certainly wish to rethink the wisdom of such a course; it sets such a poor example, don't you think?"

"My lords," said Joseph, standing up, "I think you should know that just because I have succeeded to a title confirmed by Her Majesty's government does not mean that I am any the less Irish. It was my father's title before it was mine. I know from experience the effects of misrule."

Lucas rose also and assisted Suggins in levering his bulk out of the armchair. He then opened the door just as a group of schoolchildren were singing in the Gaelic,

How sweet is our green land, how useful the sod, here
beside the rivers and the mountains made by God.

"That racket," Lucas commented. "Is that the alleged school we
have heard you are operating in opposition to the National School
in Castletown?"

"It is the school for the children of my tenants, yes," Joseph
allowed.

"My, my, and in the tongue of ignorance and superstition," Suggins
commented. "We must look into it further. And now, if you will
excuse us. It has been a long journey."

The retreat of the two government officials to their rooms was
every bit as abrupt as their arrival. Joseph returned to the yellow
withdrawing room to ponder some more.

Mahon had openly proffered a bribe. Now Suggins had given him
an explicit warning. He had been admonished to avoid supporting
Repeal, or the ruling party could make things difficult indeed.

But why should they care so about him? Joseph wondered. Out
of those who favored Repeal and many who were much more active
in its pursuit, why select Joseph Burke in poor and faraway Galway
to caution so firmly? Was it because they also regarded the west
country as crucial to the rebirth of Irish liberty?

The notion made Joseph recommit himself to the struggle, to wonder what more could be done. And as he admitted to himself, it made
him wonder from which direction the next assault would come.

When he studied his fields, the needs of tilling and planting, lambs
in want of care, he saw everything clearly. Farming was unmistakable. Even the right of children to be educated and to be instilled
with pride in their heritage was obvious.

Why was it that everything beyond his fields was dimly understood and confused? It was so difficult to be a rational man in a
world that embraced lunacy. And worse than how it tumbled his
thoughts was how it oppressed his spirit.

Joseph was still sitting and reflecting long after Fern tiptoed into
the room to light the lamps and warn him that the evening meal
would be served in an hour in the dining room.

Lady Fiona, navigating the corridors by instinct and sound, had located Little Tom and Miss Susan in the nursery. There she had spent the afternoon with the child in her arms.

Joseph found them together as he dropped in on his way to change for dinner. Fiona, bright and smiling, cooing baby talk to Tomeen, looked up in happy surprise at Joseph's entrance.

"He's a grand boy, Joseph!" she exclaimed, turning the baby around and propping him on her lap where he reached for his toes.

"You're here, are you?" Joseph could think of nothing else to say.

"This is the most entertainment I've had since leaving Dublin. Poor Edward and Sir Stuffy have discussed politics all the way from east to west."

"Aye," Joseph answered cautiously. "Nor have they left off the talk of it here."

She absently kissed the top of Little Tom's head and prattled on in a way surprisingly Irish to Joseph. "Tomeen has been regaling me with stories of America that Miss Susan has taught him."

"Has he now?" Joseph took the baby from her arms. Without the child a self-conscious formality crept back into her manner. Suddenly she did not know what to do with her empty hands.

"That he has," Fiona replied, looking away. Did she feel foolish, or did she blush because of Joseph's frankly approving gaze?

"And what have you been tellin' Lady Fiona about America?" Joseph asked Little Tom.

Miss Susan replied, "He been flirtin' with the Lady. He told her Georgia ladies would like to die to have such complexion as she got. She a regular Georgia blossom." Miss Susan winked and laughed. "Sun so hot there in the summertime ladies always got to have some-body fannin' to keep the heat away. Suppertime two boys stands either end of the table with big feather fans an' shoo the flies away. Oh my. Everybody all eatin' at the same big table. Rich folk treat younguns like the poor folk does here. Chilluns all 'round, crowdin' in at the table. Mama at one end an' Daddy at t'other. Ain't like here where folks in the big house keep their younguns hid away most times."

Fiona arched her eyebrow and cocked her head in an expression of amusement at the image. "I'll remember the American fashion in dining if I ever have children of my own. Seems deadly dull for the children though, doesn't it?"

"Children at the table is first an Irish custom," Joseph corrected. "The children are everything to us Irish. They are the only true wealth of a man."

"Even better. I *am* Irish, after all."

This was a defiant remark. However true it was, Joseph had always considered Fiona Lucas an English transplant. Her family had, after all, sided with the power of the British Crown since the days of the Ulster Plantation. "Have you ever taken a meal in a cottage with your tenants, Lady Fiona?" He regretted the sharpness of the comment the instant he said it.

"Sure, and did you not know, Squire Burke? My mother was . . . a tenant." She cut him off. With a glint in her eye she rose, touched Little Tom's cheek, and whispered, "Stay sweet, little one." Implied in the advice was that Joseph had not stayed sweet. "And will you be bringing your wealth to the dinner table, Squire Burke?" She smiled and, knowing she had won the contest, swept from the room.

They heard him coming when he was still more than a quarter mile from Ballynockanor.

It was Adam Kane. Yelling and waving an envelope over his head as he rode at a full gallop toward the house, he drew Kate and Da, Martin and Mary Elizabeth from the four corners of the room.

"It's the steward," remarked Martin without enthusiasm. Martin did not approve of the man's intentions toward Kate.

"A handsome fellow," observed Mary Elizabeth. "But still not as fine as Joseph." The child cast a purposeful look at Kate.

"He'll do," Kate agreed, understanding the motives of her siblings. "But it's Fern who's in love with him."

Da, wiping his hands from the cheesemaking, exclaimed, "Fern, is it? The little housemaid with the wee brain of a chicken?"

"That's the one," Martin confirmed. "Sure, and she follows himself around the gardens and brought him tea when he was surveyin' Joseph's special wheat field and supervisin' Mister Clooney at the plowin'."

"Fern is welcome to him," Kate pronounced, winking at Mary Elizabeth.

"Babies don't just come. Not like baby Jesus and the Virgin Mary!" Mary Elizabeth protested. "Alice Clooney told me. So if you don't like Adam Kane and you won't have Joseph, how are we supposed to have any more children to play with around the place?"

Da cuffed her gently. "None of that, girl! You'll have to make do with Little Tom and Martin and visitin' the Clooney's. Now leave Kate in peace."

Mary Elizabeth's reply was lost as Adam Kane cantered up to the front of the cottage, brought the horse up short, and stepped onto the ground before the mare was fully stopped. He was performing as surely as a little boy walking a fence displays his prowess for a girlfriend.

Adam was panting as if he had personally been running as strenuously as the horse. Da took note of this, patted the lathered mare, and raised his chin slightly in disapproval.

"I've brought you news." Adam bowed to Kate.

"Sure, and has O'Connell declared war on England?" Da asked. "Or has the queen proclaimed the liberty of Ireland?"

"It's not that dramatic. The Galway mailcoach brought it as far as the manor." Adam extended the letter. The family gathered around and gaped down at it in wonder as if it were a message from heaven.

"Kevin's handwritin' it is." Kate gingerly took the rumpled envelope by one corner as Mary Elizabeth clapped her hands and hopped from one foot to another.

"Kevin's alive, Kate," cried the child. "He didn't drown in the great, wide sea!"

Da, his voice choked with emotion, said, "Praise be to God Almighty! Sure, and it's come a long way."

"Take it in beside the hearth!" Martin directed. "We'll read it where we last were a family together."

Kate led the way, followed by Mary Elizabeth, Martin, Da, and Adam Kane, who tied his horse to the hitching rail.

The precious correspondence was placed on the mantel while Kate made tea. It was, thought Martin, something like looking at an uncut cake and savoring the thought of the taste before taking a bite.

Adam seemed as eager as the family. He perched on a stool, his large hands on his knees and his face alight with anticipation. By virtue of the fact that he had delivered the document, the Donovans included him in the proceedings as though he were one of them and knew Kevin like a brother.

Steaming cups of tea poured, silence fell as Da broke the seal and extracted a thick sheaf of papers covered front and back, margin to margin, with Kevin's scrawling handwriting.

Da examined the first page with a frown. Everyone held their breath. Was Kevin well? Had things gone badly?

"What is it, Da?" Kate asked with trepidation.

Tom Donovan's brow furrowed. "It's me eyes. I can't read a word of it."

A collective sigh of relief rose up as Kate took the thing from Da's hand and began to read aloud the account of the long sea voyage and arrival in New York.

> *By the time we staggered from the stinking hold of our ship we were all brothers and have sworn that if success comes to one of us then we will bring the others along. I have stayed with friend Henshaw who is from County Tyrone and a Protestant, tossed for his part in United Ireland.*
>
> *Just off the boat I spied a gold sovereign lying on the ground. As I stooped to pick it up, Henshaw exclaimed, "Friend Donovan, what are you botherin'*

with a solitary coin for? Let's be movin' on to where the whole pile is waitin' for us."

A wee bit of humor, that. We who have newly arrived and are everywhere called "fresh fish" and sneered at, soon learn that things are not easy even here in America.

In point of fact the poverty was extreme for the Irish in New York. Kevin went on for four pages about the crowding and the shortage of housing. The Donovans applauded when at last Henshaw and Kevin found lodgings.

We occupy a bit of a room with six other lads of various counties at the rear of a shabby building. Our stories are much the same. We have a fine view of the back of a large rooming house. The folks over the way give us all the chance in the world, for they don't close their shutters. Directly opposite our window is the room of Mrs. Abbott who is a widow and has visitors at all hours of the day and night to console her. The room beneath contains a new-married couple, I think. The next has a room where two old maids are having a consultation. The devil put it in our heads to disturb their peace of mind. We have a long tube with which we can propel a putty ball a long distance, as true as a gun. The first shot struck the window—slap!—which caused them to draw back and probably utter a shriek. We had our blinds closed so they could not see us. One got up, put on her spectacles, and looked out. While she was looking we slapped the window again. She drew back and folded her hands in despair. The two worthies are now sitting in their old places looking at the stains of putty on their glass and vowing vengeance no doubt.

The passage was read to applause and laughter, Adam Kane guffawing with such gusto that he held his belly and moaned for the pain it caused him. Wiping tears of amusement from her eyes, Kate poured another round of tea and went on with Kevin's tales of finding work as a hod carrier for a bricklayer and stories of the local Irish tenant committees that gave as much grief to the American landlords as they had the English squires back home.

He finished his report cheerfully,

> *Tell Mary Elizabeth that her caul saw me over the sea. I'll not return it yet. We hear of great gatherings of the people of Ireland. Talk is that O'Connell is near to bringing Repeal to victory and shattering the Union with England. When it happens I'll come home again, and I'll need the caul once more for the long voyage back to Ireland. All of us who are exiled pray for that hour to come!*

And so the welcome communication ended on that note. Even in America the stories of O'Connell and the Repeal movement were news!

Da stood slowly and stretched himself in contentment. "America! Hooligans! A grand adventure for my boy. But you see how much he still longs for home."

This was directed at Adam who studied the pattern on his teacup. "Don't set your heart on it. This I know. If Repeal fails there'll be many more of us leavin' for America."

"Yourself?" Da asked.

"It's in my mind. There's land there to be had for the takin'." He fixed his gaze on Kate. "A man could get rich and live a happy life in America if he had the right woman at his side."

There could be no doubt whom Adam Kane had chosen to emigrate with when the time came. Kate did not like the inference, but she could not stop the talk of Adam's intentions toward her.

Kevin's letter was read in its entirety at O'Flaherty's Pub and Watty's Tavern and at St. John's after mass on Sunday. It fired the sense of excitement in many a young man in the village. It also increased tenfold the zeal in support of O'Connell and the coming Repeal meeting at Mallow. The cry rose up, "Repeal the Union! Bring our banished boys home again to Ireland!"

Little Tom remained in his nursery at the dinner hour, much to Fiona's amusement. She waved her hand at the large, silver candelabra, fine china, and crystal goblets and remarked wryly that just as Joseph said, the wealth of every true Irishman was visible at his table.

Darby, who had served at the house for thirty years, brought up bottles of wine dated 1820, which had been stored away in the cellar since the days when Joseph's father was squire. Margaret, the cook, shuttled Mad Molly quickly off to her daughter's cottage and spent the day preparing roasted lamb with mint, pheasant stuffed with mushrooms, and fresh salmon trout from Lough Corrib.

There was enough on the table to feed ten households among the tenant farmers. Fiona made that exact comment with a look that assured Joseph she did not mean it as a compliment. Neither of her traveling companions noticed her gibe or Joseph's blush.

"I suppose such dainties as these would make the tenant farmer sick," she added, carving the pheasant into tiny pieces.

"Lord, yes!" agreed her cousin Edward. "They live entirely on a diet of potatoes, my dear. They would not know how to digest such rich food."

Silence. The clink of silverware against the china. Joseph, chagrined by the knowledge that the houseservants would repeat each detail of the menu and the conversation, felt ashamed.

At length Fiona spoke again. "I hear there is an outbreak of some dreadful disease of the potato on the Isle of Wight. Did you have any details of it, Edward?"

"Turned the entire potato crop into a mass of rot. They'll be hungry there next winter, I can tell you, begging at the door of the queen's summer palace, eh?"

Sir Suggins drained his glass and with a jerk of his head summoned Darby to pour more wine as Margaret brought a second course to the table. "If the blight comes here, the whole country would starve, I expect. And that would put an end to Mister O'Connell and the

Repeal movement! How's that sit with you, Squire Burke? The politics of Ireland hang upon the potato crop, eh? Isn't that so, Edward?"

"These peasants have nothing else to eat. I hear American slaves have a better diet than Irish farmers. Ask the Negress, Burke. She'll verify, I'm sure. But there's little chance of the blight reaching these shores . . . unless some landlord decides to bring it to Ireland himself. Plant a few diseased potatoes here and there. An interesting way to thin out the unproductive tenants, don't you agree, Burke?"

Joseph did not reply. A sidelong look between Darby and Margaret caught his eye. It was plain to Joseph that the conversation was carefully staged to alienate him from those who worked in the house and farmed Burke lands. Tomorrow every word of this discussion would be in full sail on the winds of Connemara. He finally responded, "In these parts, there's enough food for all. And so there will always be while I stand in my father's boots, sir."

Suggins waved away the somber reply irritably. "Aye. You've proved that well enough with the little beggars in your school, haven't you?" Suggins gulped the lamb. "You feed them as well as all this? Lamb. Trout. Pheasant. Splendid. Splendid, I say."

Fiona was suddenly repentant of the ridicule she had introduced. "It is fine," she said quietly. "And I must apologize, Joseph. The jest has turned ugly."

Suggins and Lucas stared at her in disdain and disbelief.

"What's a few potatoes more or less?" Lucas offered brightly.

Fiona rounded on her cousin. "Everything, it seems. And it *is* noble of Joseph to feed the children of his tenants."

Suggins coughed into his fist. "Quite enough, then. No harm intended. Irish potatoes are quite safe from the blight, Fiona. Edward meant no harm, nor did I."

As if to dispute him, a flash of lightning lit the night outside the window. Thunder cracked close by. Fiona gave a little cry.

"There's someone out there," she cried, blanching. "A horrible face!"

She pointed out the window as the lightning flared again. In the glare Joseph glimpsed the grim visage of the Tinker glaring in through the window.

"There it is!" Suggins gasped.

Joseph excused himself and, taking Darby into the hallway, said, "Go see what the devil he's doin' out there spyin', will you, Darby? Tell him Squire Joseph wants him back at the barn where he belongs. At the instant, if you please!"

Rain began to bucket down, pounding on the glass panes and running rivers from the gables. Joseph waited in the corridor until Darby returned, drenched and muddy.

"Tinker said he was out for a smoke. He's gone back, sir. Tinker'll not be lightin' his pipe outdoors in this weather."

Joseph was inexplicably troubled, first by the conversation but more so by the dark look of the Tinker. "No, that he will not. Thank you, Darby. We'll take brandy in the music room."

"Aye." The aged servant nodded, then added, "You know they'll not be travelin' to Limerick tomorrow with the rain comin' down in sheets. Should I tell Margaret and the others they'll be stayin' over till the weather clears, sir?"

"Aye. Another day. But pray for sunshine, Darby."

It was suppertime at the Donovan cottage. How empty the table felt now, without Kevin and Brigit. The four remaining Donovans had difficulty filling the empty spaces left in ordinary conversation. Brigit had always known everything about everyone and told all she knew whether it was true or not. Kevin had always enjoyed a spirited argument over politics and landlords. What could liven up the evening meals without the controversy Kevin and Brigit used to bring so easily to the family gathering? Dinner had become deadly dull of late.

Mary Elizabeth determined to wake her family up again. "There is a Lady stayin' at Joseph's house," she piped as she spooned a potato cake onto her plate.

"A new maid, do you mean?" Da asked, taking the bowl from her.

"No," the child insisted. "Not a *woman*, Da! But a real Lady!"

Martin noticed Kate sit up a little straighter at the supper table. Her expression betrayed curiosity mixed with troubled thoughts. Martin nudged Mary Elizabeth in the ribs, urging her to silence, but the signal only pushed the information out of her mouth in a rush.

"Two gentlemen and a lady. All the way from Dublin, they are. Come to see Joseph now that he's important. That's what Fern the housemaid said to Margaret in the kitchen. Then she told Molly, and Molly said . . ."

Kate pretended the gossip was entertaining but of no consequence. "Sure, and I suppose Joseph will have many sorts of gents and ladies come to call now that he's one of them."

Mary Elizabeth frowned. "He's not one of them a'tall! Silks and satins and top hats on the gents. Not a'tall like Joseph!"

"Aye," Da spoke around his mouthful. "He's our own kind, Kate. You should have seen him dealin' with the rabble who mistook his intention, sure. But he handled it well. He's one with the plain folk and no mistake. He'll take no note of the sympathizers of the Crown nor their overripe, prune-faced ladies. Sows dressed in silk. That's what they are."

Martin swallowed hard at his memory of the slim, beautiful lady dressed in a pale-green satin cape sweeping up the stone steps of the manor house. There was nothing remotely reminiscent of a sow about her.

A sideways glance informed Kate that Da's assessment was incorrect. "Well then, Martin," she chided. "What have you got to say about the lady?"

"Tell them, Martin!" Mary Elizabeth demanded. "They won't believe me."

"Believe what?" Da asked.

Kate leaned forward slightly. "What is it, then?"

Martin waved his hand in front of his face as if he were brushing away a fly. "The Lady from Dublin is . . . very . . ."

Da banged his knife on the table. "Aye, lad? Out with it!"

"I've never seen the like of her," Martin blurted.

Mary Elizabeth gloated. "He's not tellin' because all the boys are smitten. They gawked at her. She's . . . golden! Aye! That's what she is, golden!"

"English, is she?" Da continued to eat. Kate was quiet after that, distracted by the information.

This was a query Martin could handle. "She's Irish, all right. A Dubliner accent. I heard her speak when they walked around the grounds together."

"They who?" Da encouraged.

"Who do you think?" Kate snapped.

Mary Elizabeth took up Martin's halting recitation. "Recess it was. We were outside. And there was herself hangin' on to Joseph's arm like she was afraid to walk on her own two dainty feet without fallin' down. And the path without so much as a pebble to trip her up!"

Da shrugged. "Well he's a man, ain't he? Put a pretty woman on my arm, and I'll walk." Tom Donovan winked at his son. "Golden is the word, is it, Martin?"

Martin could not disagree. "Aye, sir. That she is."

"I don't like her there with our Little Tom," Mary Elizabeth pronounced.

"Little Tom?" Kate sparked.

"Aye," Mary Elizabeth continued. "There they strolled as plain as the nose on your face. Joseph and herself with Miss Susan and Little Tom trailin' along after. Then the two gentlemen as well. And what do you know? Beside the yew trees the Lady calls to Miss Susan and takes Little Tom out of Miss Susan's arms. Then the lady carries our baby the rest of the way!"

Martin said optimistically, "Sure, and at least she wasn't clingin' to Joseph anymore."

"I don't want her touchin' our baby," Mary Elizabeth argued. "Little Tom is ours, and Joseph is ours too. She's givin' him the look."

"The look?" Kate inquired.

"Aye." Mary Elizabeth nodded and turned her head coyly and smiled sweetly in imitation. "Like Brigit used to do when Tim Mulrooney came into church."

No more needed to be said. After that Martin noticed that Kate looked pale and sad as she cleared away the dishes. Martin was certain Kate never liked Joseph at all. But Little Tom in the arms of another woman who was not a woman but a Lady? The thought of this, it was clear, made poor Kate very unhappy indeed.

Kate was still angry when she went to bed. This was a mercy. Anger was a tangible relief against the loneliness she had felt for months.

She turned her face toward Brigit's empty bed where the moonlight pooled on the smooth coverlet. She let her mind drift back to the times when Brigit had not come home until long after curfew. Her thick red hair had been loose and wild around her face.

Kate had known Brigit had been with a man. But had it been Joseph? While Kate had been dreaming of him, wanting him, loving him, had Brigit been lying in a tangle with him in the straw? Was wee Tomeen truly Joseph's own baby?

The question made her feel somehow betrayed. Turning her head toward the wall she traced the patterns of the limestone wash with her finger. Years before, when she had fallen in love with Scan, she had on this very bed scratched his initials and a heart onto it with a penknife. In daylight she hid the carving with a pillow and uncovered it each night to trace it again and again and wonder what it would be like when he made love to her. Only a faint line of the heart remained beneath new layers of whitewash. But the longing to be loved returned to her stronger than ever.

She sighed. How could she love a man who was so without honor? If the talk was true, then he was as bad as William Marlowe, and Kevin should have shot him dead as well.

And if the talk was false? Kate still had reason to hate him. Why then did she close her eyes and imagine him just above her? Why did she reach into the air as if to pull him down to her? How could she envy poor Brigit for having been loved by him? And despise him for loving Brigit, as he must have done since they were wed?

It was a jumble of confusion. She would not allow herself to think of his mouth on her mouth or his hands exploring the lonely places of her body.

"Blessed Jesus!" she prayed softly. "Have mercy. Deliver me. For the more I want not to think about him the more I think about him."

Mary Elizabeth rose up in a stupor. "What you sayin', Kate?"

"Nothin'. You're dreamin', Mary Elizabeth. Go back to sleep."

Mary Elizabeth obeyed at once, falling on her pillow and snorting once before her breathing fell into a regular rhythm again.

Kate tossed restlessly as the moonlight slipped across the room. Hours passed, but her longing for Joseph did not diminish. Her disobedient thoughts explored possibilities for a hundred nights with him and then began again.

She could not say what hour of the morning it was when she finally slept in sheer exhaustion from her imaginary escapades. When the rooster crowed just before dawn she groped her way from bed, washed, dressed for morning mass, and left the chores to Da and Martin.

For having had no pleasure in the night, she certainly had a wagonload of sins to confess!

Father O'Bannon seemed pleased to see her. It crossed Kate's mind that he almost took pleasure in her haggard expression.

"Back to church already, Kate daughter?"

"To make confession."

"Not sleepin' well?"

"Not a'tall. Not a wink!" She lowered her voice. "It's himself I couldn't stop thinkin' of. Squire Joseph. Terrible wicked dreams, and I wasn't even sleepin'!"

The cleric studied the desperate agony in her eyes. "Lust is it, Kate?" The way he said the word shamed her to her toes. He clucked his tongue. "Make no mistake. Lust in an unmarried woman is a shortcut to the devil's own house."

"Lord have mercy," she said, crossing herself. "Can we not go . . . inside? I'll tell you in private."

"Sure, sure, sure." He led the way to the confessional, drew the curtain, and listened for half an hour.

He prayed with her. Was pleased to welcome her back in the fold of the church. Gave her a long list of charitable deeds to accomplish. Good works would wear her out and get her mind off her sin, he said.

"And Kate, daughter, there's no help for it. The Scripture says it plainly. If you burn with lust, the only thing to do is marry and make some poor man rejoice that a sinner is restored."

This last brought Kate up short. She studied the flagstone of the church floor. "There's talk about . . . who's Tomeen's father."

"Only God gives life, Kate. As for our Joseph, like Saint Joseph in the Nativity, he came along after the fact. Be merciful."

11

The morning after Joseph suffered through the trial of having dinner sauced with Lucas's sarcasm, Suggins's heavy-handed humor, and Fiona's changeable moods, he felt in need of relaxation. Breakfast having been previously announced for nine o'clock, there was no reason Joseph should have to endure their company a second sooner than necessary.

Leaving his study and avoiding his guests by descending the back stairs, Joseph made his way out the rear of the house before the mantel clock chimed eight. Between the manor and the stables, a low stone wall enclosed an area of recently tilled soil. In some map of his uncle Marlowe's, the tract was shown as being intended to become a formal garden in the English mode. Joseph had other plans for it.

With a volume of Jefferson's writings in hand, Joseph paced off the length of an imaginary furrow. Stopping at the far end, he observed how the cypress trees stretched long, shadowy fingers toward the opposite side of the enclosure. According to Jefferson, sunlight was of prime importance to what he had in mind. With a tape measure Joseph studied the length of the shade, frowned up at the sky, and scribbled a few notes in the margin of the book.

From across the wall Lady Fiona commented in a musical, teasing tone, "They say Queen Victoria's grandfather was called *Farmer George* for his great interest in things agricultural. Are you attempting to revive the custom among the gentry?"

This was uttered so pleasantly that Joseph chose to take it as light banter. "No," he corrected. "It is not a fashion with me; I *am* a farmer."

Fiona picked her way delicately over the stile, watching carefully where she placed her elegant, high-heeled shoes. At first involuntarily, and then deliberately, Joseph used her moments of distraction to study her. Fiona's straw-colored hair glistened in the morning light, accentuated by the paler yellow of the high-waisted dress she wore. Nor was her hair the only thing accentuated by her costume; its cut also showed off her figure to full advantage.

She glanced up in time to catch Joseph staring. Flustered, he looked away in embarrassment and dropped the tome of Jefferson.

"And is this your 'prattie patch'?" she taunted. "All good Irish farming families have them, do they not?"

Clearing his throat to hide his chagrin, Joseph chose to regard her question as serious. "No," he said, "just the opposite, in fact. I intend to make this an experimental garden."

"That sounds clever," Fiona commented with a smirk. "What does it mean? Or is it a quotation from the radical American Jefferson?" She gestured toward the book Joseph had awkwardly retrieved.

Because Jefferson's ideas about freedom and equality had been widely quoted during the course of the French Revolution, he was not well thought of by the Anglo-Irish aristocracy. "It is one of Mister Jefferson's ideas, yes," Joseph agreed. "Many of the remarks passin' as dinner conversation last night were idle chatter, but there was one glarin' truth: Ireland is overdependent on the potato. Oh, it serves us well, but we need to learn to grow other crops. That's what I intend tryin' here. This patch of ground will be for testin' different grains to see what the yields will be. In a few years, when I've reached some conclusions, I can help the folk of the townland better their lot."

Brushing a rock off the wall with a gloved hand, Fiona sat down before speaking again. She regarded Joseph with suspicion. "Are you serious about aiding your tenants? This is not a pose for Sir Stuffy to take back to Dublin Castle, is it?"

"Indeed not," Joseph said firmly. "My father and I had long talks when I was a wee lad about makin' Connaught bloom like a rose. I intend to carry on with his dream."

Her look of skepticism changing to one of genuine admiration, Lady Fiona Shaw added, "Then you'll be in need of a wife. Someone to share your dream with you, for you to talk over your plans with and console you when your experiments fail."

"Yes," Joseph replied awkwardly, "I suppose I will at that."

"You are an interesting man, Joseph Connor Burke. Too bad the roads are passable already. You have made an intriguing figure, one not to be fully known in a two-day renewal of acquaintance."

Completely uncertain how to reply to this, Joseph contented himself with a bow and a murmured acknowledgment. "But it is nearly time for breakfast," he observed. "Let me escort you back inside."

Without argument, Fiona allowed Joseph to take her arm and lead her back toward the wooden steps that climbed the rock fence. Joseph preceded her over the stile and then turned on the other side to help her across. Since he was holding both her hands and carefully assisting her down the last three steps, it was surprising that her heel caught on a plank. With a low exclamation, she swiveled in his grasp and fell, tangling her legs in the ten-inch fall.

"Lady Fiona," Joseph said with concern, "allow me to help you up. I can't fathom how that happened. I'm so sorry."

He raised her to her feet again, but when she put her weight on the right she winced in pain. "I'm afraid you'll have to help me into the house," she said. "I think I've twisted my ankle."

And there she was, Martin's "golden Lady" leaning heavily on the arm of Squire Joseph.

From the milk cart Kate observed the two as they slowly made their way up the broad steps of the manor. The Lady was limping—the perfect picture of feminine helplessness.

"Sure, and have you ever seen anythin' more disgustin'?" Kate asked the pony. "If Squire Burke is such a fool to be taken in by such a woman, then she's welcome to him." She snapped the reins down on the rump of the pony, who jogged briskly toward the manor house. This was the day Kate always brought cheese to Burke Hall and gave Martin and Mary Elizabeth a ride home. The pony knew his way to the watering trough outside the kitchen door.

A committee of servants were peering out the window as she arrived: Margaret, Darby, Fern, Molly, the Tinker, and Miss Susan with Little Tom.

"You saw her, did y'not?" Margaret inquired. "Herself, I'm meanin'. Oozin' like butter on a hot day. And for all her fancy words, talkin' down to the rest of us like we was birds in a cage."

"Aye," Darby said glumly. "Golden and honeyed she may be, but there'll be no good come to us from this visit."

Kate snorted. "And why does himself not send her packin'? Is he so thick between the ears that he cannot see what she is about?"

"He a man," Miss Susan said meaningfully, to which Margaret and Fern nodded their assent. The Tinker smiled through his beard, and Mad Molly played with the green Repeal sash and crooned softly.

"Then let her have him, I say," Kate declared. "They deserve each other."

"Sha!" Margaret and Mad Molly said in unison. Molly returned to admiring her image in the curved sheen of a copper pot.

"You doesn't mean that, girl," Miss Susan said, passing the infant to Kate to hold.

The Tinker offered, "There is a far more deadly game goin' on here than the sportin' of male and female. Those who caused that woman to come are the same who would turn us out upon the road for spillin' gravy on their trousers."

Fern blushed and studied a tiny scuff mark on the tile floor.

"But what's to be done?" Kate asked. "Can any of you go to the man and say, 'For your own good, Squire, y'need to send this serpent away'? As for me, I have enough to deal with: poxy cows and their milk dryin' up."

"Cowpox," Mad Molly said. "Molly Fahey had it when she was a lass, didn't she?" she asked her reflection.

"Ain't there somethin' to be done to save the squire from the clutches of this Jezebel?" Miss Susan wondered refocusing the conversation.

Darby, Margaret, and Fern looked at each other in uncertainty.

Finally the Tinker broke the silence. "What say you, Molly Fahey? About this highborn wolf in sheep's clothin'?"

Grinning toothlessly, Molly plucked at her ribbon, arched her eyebrows, and cackled.

On the first day of Fiona Shaw's extended visit to the Burke estates, Joseph was pleased to have her company, if a little embarrassed at being seen with her. She was interested in *everything*. She wanted to see the stables, the brood mares, the hunters. Though the Tinker ignored her and would not remain in her company, she made Old Flynn stutter and puff out his chest at her compliments.

She asked Darby for a tour of the wine cellar. Margaret was cajoled into parting with the recipe for the stuffing with which the cook prepared the pheasant.

Joseph was interrupted at his letter writing by her questions regarding Repeal. What would be the nature of a new Irish parliament? How would the members be chosen? Would the Repealers be satisfied with controlling only their domestic affairs, or did O'Connell envision sending emissaries abroad as if Ireland were a sovereign nation?

In short, the entire household was in an uproar, and Joseph was getting no work done, whether for farming or Repeal. He began to suspect that her attendance was part of a plot hatched by Lucas and Suggins to either spy on him, catch him speaking something indiscreet, or merely to destroy his productivity.

Besides all that, her physical proximity was distracting.

By the third day of her stay, he was distressed by her continued presence. There was no graceful way to ask an injured houseguest to depart before they pronounced themselves fit, so he had to think of a means to make her want to leave.

As a way of getting free, Joseph suggested that he could not neglect his duties to the Repeal movement and would have to be absent from the manor, touring the province. Fiona replied that she was prepared to accompany him on his rounds. She was eager, she said, to view the tenants as political activists. It was an entirely new thought.

As a chess match, it was a draw.

It was on the return from their visit of Allintober, on the sixth day of Fiona's visit, that Joseph concluded something would have to be done soon. The speed of gossip in the townlands being what it was, everyone in Allintober had heard that Lady Fiona Shaw would accompany Joseph to their village. They knew who she was, who she was related to, and the politics of her near connections. Joseph was on the verge of losing his influence for Repeal because of Fiona. At Allintober all sixteen families registered their disapproval by staying home; no one came out to hear Joseph's appeal for the penny-a-month Repeal rent.

Driving the pony cart back from the village, the course took them along a sunken road where the banks on either side loomed up over the height of the trap. The route was extremely rutted and uneven, and Joseph slowed the pony to a walk so as not to jounce Fiona unnecessarily. Once he thought he caught glimpses of something flashing blue and green through the willows that lined the earthen banks, but when he turned his head to look directly, whatever it was had vanished.

At the top of a ridge, where the sunken road turned sharply west before plunging downward again, the unmistakable wail of a banshee burst out of the shrubbery. The pony reared, shied, backed, fought the reins, and finally came to a standstill, lathered and puffing.

"What was that?" Fiona cried, almost as wide-eyed as the pony. "It had an unearthly sound."

The answer appeared: a blue-serge-clad form wearing a green sash inscribed "REPEAL." Mad Molly leaped from the top of the dirt embankment to land three feet from Fiona's side of the cart, her bony index finger extended toward Lady Shaw's trembling face.

"*She* has not paid the rent!" Molly proclaimed. "She has not paid. When will she pay the penny? Render unto Caesar that which is Caesar's, and render it now!" Molly bounded forward, her outstretched palm coming to rest under Fiona's chin. "Pay up!" she demanded.

Fiona shrunk away from the wild-haired apparition. "But I don't have my purse with me," she pleaded in terror.

"She doesn't have the rent," Mad Molly crooned, low in her throat. "She does not have it. She spent it on perfume and frippery. Well, then."

Molly bent low toward the ground, all but the curve of her spine disappearing from sight.

Fiona made the mistake of leaning forward to see what the crazy woman was up to. "What are you doing down there?" she inquired, just as Molly rose up with a handful of the red dust of the roadway.

"There!" she exulted, flinging the dirt forcefully into Fiona's face and curls. "A blessin' for ye: may each speck o'dust become for ye a penny so ye will have the rent when next ye are asked."

Alternately stammering and shrieking, Fiona wiped her eyes and spat dust from her mouth as Joseph handed her his handkerchief and tried not to laugh. In the confusion, Mad Molly melted back into the brush.

"What . . . what was that?" Fiona sputtered in a trembling voice.

"That," Joseph explained calmly and seriously, "was the esteemed Madame Commissioner of the Repeal Rent. She's really effective at collecting donations, and while her Repeal duties have kept her away for some time . . . she's my housekeeper."

"Joseph," Fiona said when she could speak intelligibly again, "my ankle is feeling much better. I believe I will be ready to take the Limerick coach tomorrow."

The clink of silverware against china and the watchful presence of the servants in the room made the evening meal awkward. Joseph was certain Molly's appearance on the road had been planned in the kitchen. Did Fiona suspect she had been a deliberate target?

Her manner was cold and distant, and yet Joseph was certain there was something she wanted to say to him. Between the partridge and the lamb she said lightly, "It's a pity, Joseph. It really is."

"Aye." He pretended to understand her meaning. "I'm glad you're well enough to travel, but it's sorry we are you're goin' tomorrow."

She glanced at Margaret. "Is that so? Well, that's not what I was speaking of, but rather the fact that there seems to be, among the people here, a resentment of their betters."

"There's none better than themselves, Lady Fiona." Joseph raised his glass with a wink.

"Those who run this country would disagree."

"They don't live here, now do they?"

"Not anymore. But it's known that things might change."

"Say what you've come here to say, woman. It's taken far too long. Just speak your mind . . . or the mind of whoever put you up to this."

She sat ramrod straight, pale in her resentment of the brusque, condescending tone in his voice. "As you wish. You're bound to lose everything if you persist on your course with O'Connell for Repeal."

"Everythin', is it?"

"Your family holds its lands as a lease from the Crown of England, does it not?"

"That is so."

"Then you are as much a tenant as these simpletons who rent their little plots of land from you."

"Aye. We are equal."

"What happens to them if you lose your lease?"

"The Burke lease is good for another one hundred and twenty years. I'm not likely to lose it."

"There are ways, Joseph. They have ways to do whatever is required."

"And that, Fiona, is the reason I work with O'Connell for Repeal. The law in Ireland should not be based on the whims of an English parliament, or its overseers, in England. My lease of lands, which have been Burke lands for centuries, should not depend on my opinions. That is what freedom is about."

"I am the gentle voice of warning, Joseph."

"You are the whisper of temptation."

"Then yield and be saved. Yield and you will keep what you have. Everything you hold dear will still be yours."

"How can you know what I hold dear?" He held up a spoon that glinted in the light of the gleaming candelabra. "Silver? Riches? The trappin's of a country squire? Before I became myself again I ate with a wooden spoon upon a pewter plate and was content."

"The lands. This house."

"What profit is it for a man if he gains the world but loses his own soul? Weigh what I have in the balance with what I believe, and possessions are nothin'. My soul is what I value most. It is the one thing you and your kind can never take from me. Or from the people of Ireland. My soul belongs to Christ. The soul of Ireland has belonged to Christ from the day our fathers heard the holy word of God preached yonder on St. Patrick's mountain. For hundreds of years you've been tryin' to destroy that soul, but you'll not win."

"You're a fool, Burke."

"That may be, but I am Christ's fool, not England's."

"You'll lose all you possess."

"I'll give all my possessions if I am asked to do so. But I will still have what I most dearly love."

"I forgot you had once intended to be a priest, to take the vow of poverty." Lady Fiona stood abruptly. "I have done what I could to warn you." She turned to go, but stopped a moment. "I am sorry for you, Burke. Things could have been easy for you."

"If you believe that, Lady Fiona, then you don't know how hard life is when a man sells his soul for the sake of comfort."

Located between Dublin Castle and the Ha'Penny Bridge over the river Liffy was the Stag's Head Tavern on Dame Court, just off Dame Lane. The pub was built in the 1770s—long enough for the nicotine of the pipe smoke to turn the white-painted ceiling dingy amber where it was not outright blackened.

Though members of the government frequently had recourse to the comforts offered at the Stag's Head, on that particular evening the two men who slipped into a second-floor room did so by the back stairs. Sir Burtenshaw Suggins and Charles Trevelyan were late arriving at the conference with Garrison O'Toole.

O'Toole was seated midway between the room's two doors, ready to bolt if anyone unexpected should enter by either portal. "It is past time for you to be here," he complained as soon as Suggins and Trevelyan were in and the door shut and locked. "Were you followed?"

Suggins laughed. "My dear fellow, have you not noticed the water dripping from my coat? It is pouring rain outside. No one is abroad on a night like this, but we came through the alleyway just as you requested. And now, to business."

He and Trevelyan drew chairs alongside O'Toole's, beneath the fixed stare of the stag's head over the mantel.

"What about the campaign to push O'Connell into being rash in his speeches or in print?" Trevelyan asked, crossing his slender legs at the ankle and steepling his fingers.

"It is goin' nowhere," O'Toole said. "O'Connell is always on the verge of sayin' somethin' for which he could be charged, but he has an uncanny knack for drawin' back right at the brink. As for the paper, Osborne Davis has been watchin' us like a hawk. No edition gets released without his, Duffy's, and Dillon's say-so. That's why I must be so careful, my lords. They are already suspicious of me."

Trevelyan ignored O'Toole's pathetic plea. It was apparent from his sneer that he believed spies and traitors were useful but disreputable tools, much like chamber pots. "Well, keep trying," he ordered. "If we cannot trip O'Connell up, we will have to bring him down in some other way."

"These cursed meetings are getting bigger all the time," Suggins complained. "Two hundred thousand, three hundred thousand. Just because they are quiet and orderly now does not mean they could not become a ravening mob. What will happen if the whole country believes we are too cowed to do anything? Then it will be too late, I tell you." The official stared at O'Toole, and when the turncoat dropped his gaze, Suggins gave the stuffed deer a look full of enough animosity to almost make it avert its glass eyes.

"If only there were some way to make these provincials stay home and tend to their farming," Trevelyan remarked with a long-suffering sigh. "If they would just keep to their place, all would be well."

"Aye," Suggins agreed. "It's too bad there is no flood or famine or plague. Anything like that outside their doors would cause them to forget politics in a hurry. . . . Plague," Suggins repeated thoughtfully. "Like the outbreak of smallpox at Kilmainham Gaol?"

"That would do the trick," O'Toole said. "I hear they are droppin' like flies in there. Oh, I'm sure your lordships have been vaccinated; so have I and all educated city-folk. But out in the country, why, it'd be another story altogether."

"Can you imagine how perfect Ireland would be without the Irish?" Suggins observed, raising his eyebrows in appreciation of his own wit. "Not you, O'Toole, or your admirable sister. No, the bogside paddys, I mean. No more fifteen children packed into one-room shacks scratching out potatoes from five acres of dirt. Why, in a generation the land would recover enough to raise every manner of crops, and the well-to-do squires that remained would be relieved of their responsibility for collecting pennies for rent. Just think of it."

From the studious frown on O'Toole's sharp features, he was plainly thinking furiously. "You know," he said slowly, "smallpox is transmitted by touch. I have read that the Americans gave infected blankets to some inconvenient Red Indians. . . ." He concluded suddenly, favoring Trevelyan with a meaningful glance.

"O'Toole," Trevelyan said sternly, "you must increase the pressure on O'Connell, or we will be *forced* to take additional measures. See to it at once."

∼ 12 ∼

Every male above a certain age from Castletown and Ballynockanor was going to the Mallow rally. Even though Mallow was farther away than Galway City, there was an increasing sense of being part of something significant, something historic. Boys too young to comprehend Repeal or self-rule or freedom were told to pay attention anyway; they would understand someday. They would not want to tell their grandchildren that they had failed to be a part of the most significant popular movement in the annals of Ireland.

What with the summer well begun, the potatoes growing but still too early to harvest, it was a perfect time for that most unusual of Irish experiences: a holiday.

Mallow, on the river Blackwater, was famed for its fishing and its horse racing. But on that June day, it had no trouble believing that all its future notoriety would come from the fact that its population of a few thousand souls was swelling to more than a quarter of a million.

"Sure, and it's a glorious day," Father O'Bannon commented to Joseph. "What's a little rain on such an occasion?"

"Aye," Tom Donovan agreed, untangling Martin, three young McMurrough lads, and five Clooney boys from Joseph's carriage. Father O'Bannon had insisted that the lads of Ballynockanor go to the meeting. According to him, if they were old enough to fill an adult place in a church pew and were past their first communion, they were old enough to count as adults at Repeal rallies.

One of the ways in which Joseph decided he could be of use to the Repeal movement was through helping arrange transportation for those who otherwise would have had to walk. For the people of the Burke townlands, it was a grand adventure. "And useful," Joseph remarked to Garrison O'Toole. "Nothin' will make us grow faster as a country than a sense of how grand this whole realm is. My grandfather's tenants grew up thinkin' their allegiance was to Ballynockanor. My father's thought they belonged to Connaught. But Martin will know he has a whole nation to be proud of."

"Aye, a nation," O'Toole grumped. "But will they think much of their leaders? How long will O'Connell draw back from pointin' out to this army that they *are* an army? Already some among the more radical, not me, you understand, but Dillon and Duffy, are talkin' of breakin' away from Daniel. And it's easy to see why they feel that way. Since Prime Minister Peel discharged all the Repeal-minded judges last week, what have we done to retaliate? Nothin', that's what. I've told Daniel my thoughts on it too."

"What would you have?" Joseph inquired. "Daniel arrested or an outbreak of civil war? One might lead to the other, you know, since who besides Daniel can control these thousands? Besides, the firin' of the magistrates may turn out to be a good thing. A whole slate of justices who had not yet declared for Repeal have resigned in protest."

Despite the rain, the platform was full of guests eager to be seen next to the Great Liberator. The hillside of the meeting was solid with people, with more crowding in, packing in, pressing. "Look," said David Clooney, pointing at a nearby wagon. "They're handin' out blankets yonder, free for the askin'."

"It's not cold," Martin objected. "What would you be wantin' a blanket for?"

"Because," David explained, "I can use it to keep the rain off me head . . . but also so's I can take somethin' home to remember this by. Here, can I have one, mister?"

"Where you from, me boy?" asked the heavyset, gap-toothed character handing out the bedding.

"David Clooney of Ballynockanor," the boy announced proudly.

"Well, then, Master Clooney all the way from Ballynockanor," responded the man, retrieving a folded coverlet from under the toe of his boot and thrusting it into David's hands, "here's one special for you."

The weather may have been gray, but Daniel O'Connell's speech was anything but dull. As if replying to O'Toole's concerns in the text of his oration, O'Connell soared into the grip of fiery emotion, and the thousands of onlookers went with him. "We wish no civil war. We shall keep to the ground of the constitution. But where is the coward who would not die for such a land as Ireland? Let our enemies attack us if they dare; they shall never trample me underfoot!"

"Saints preserve us," Father O'Bannon whispered to Joseph. "He is perishin' near the edge now."

"'Oh where's the slave so lowly,'" O'Connell quoted from a poem, "'condemned to chains unholy, who could he burst his bonds accurst, would pine beneath them slowly?'" There was a meaningful pause while O'Connell milked the drama of the moment. Then in a voice that could have reduced the walls of Jericho he declared, "I am not a slave!"

A thunderous roar of approval burst from the crowd. It rolled backward and forward like waves crashing on the seacoast, deafening those farther back in the throng. Then as his words were repeated from front to back a new outbreak of cheering swamped the gathering. And another. And another. And so it went, until the combined voices of a quarter million were howling.

It took twenty minutes for the multitude to settle down enough for O'Connell to continue. Joseph held his breath, hoping that in the interval O'Connell would come to his senses and soften the tone of his rhetoric. He looked at Father O'Bannon with raised eyebrows and got a concerned nod in return.

"They may trample on me," O'Connell continued in a honeyed voice. "But it will be the dead body of me they trample on, and not the living man!"

A full half hour of chanting ensued. "Repeal, Repeal, Repeal," was followed by "O'Connell, O'Connell," and "I am not that slave!"

Waving over the heads of many in the crowd were pitchforks, turf spades, axes, and blackthorn sticks. "It would only take one more word from him," Joseph said urgently to O'Bannon, "and the whole country would go up in flames."

Perhaps it was a good thing that the rain was falling heavier than ever as O'Connell concluded his speech at Mallow. There was no explosion, but every scrap of bunting, every blade of grass, was claimed by some eager spectator wanting a souvenir of the great "Mallow Defiance."

"See?" David Clooney said boastfully to Martin. "Glad I am I got this old, holey blanket. I'll leave it to my grandchildren with the story of this day!"

Daniel O'Connell's drawing room in the Merrion Square house, Dublin, was full of Repeal Association leaders. Osborne Davis was there, as was Garrison O'Toole. Even though the rallies were grow-ing in both frequency and size, with the next one in Athlone less than a week away, the topic on everyone's lips was *The London Times.* "Do you see what they say about you, Daniel?" Davis asked. "They say you are linin' your pockets with pennies stolen from poor farmers."

"That's not news." O'Connell shrugged. "I've been accused of worse. Besides, no one in Ireland believes it."

"Many of the Tory party consider everything this rag prints to be gospel," Garrison O'Toole offered, stroking the side of his stringy neck.

"And I remind you, Daniel," Davis insisted, "it is not just the effect on the Irish that concerns us. The movement is bein' ridiculed in front of the English common folk. Just look at this cartoon copied from *Punch*."

The caricature presented for inspection showed a well-dressed Daniel forcing a shabby figure to drop a penny in a box marked *RINT*. While O'Connell's left hand gestured toward the collection receptacle, his right hand reached inside to await the dropping penny.

"And do you see how ragged this fellow is?" O'Toole complained. "Why his breeches are out at the knees and the seat both."

"Never mind," Daniel argued. "We cannot stop them from sayin' or printin' whatever they like. More important matters draw our attention, like do we have enough wardens ready for Cork? We are goin' to have five hundred thousand this time; I feel it."

"There is one thing even *The Times* got right," Davis allowed. "They put the average size of the rallies at three hundred thousand. They call them 'monster meetin's.'"

"Monster meetin', eh?" O'Connell mused. "I like that, 'deed I do. They may hope to use the phrase to scare women and children, but I like it. Let's use it ourselves and see if we can't push the 'monster meetin's' up to a half a million souls."

Beth Anne O'Toole entered the room, plumping her ample form down on the sofa vacated by her brother and primping her dirty blond hair. She apologized for being late to the gathering. "I had somethin' took a speck of clearin' up."

"And you workin' so hard settin' type for papers and broadsheets," O'Connell said sympathetically. "Did you get your problem resolved?"

"That I did," she said. "Just a bit of bother with the Crown Rents office. Seems that there was some back tax owed on the printshop buildin' and some confusion about who owed it. Sure, and it was deliberate harassment. I had to straighten them out."

Everyone moaned in agreement. The British rent collectors were notoriously hard to deal with. When not being outright crooked, they were stunningly obtuse and incomprehensible.

Still, in their private thoughts, those in the room were certain that if anyone could straighten out the British bureaucrats, it would no doubt be Beth Anne O'Toole.

Kate was driving the milk cows down the road to the barn when she spotted Adam riding toward her. Even at a distance she could tell he was happy to see her. He raised his hat and spurred the big sorrel mare into a gentle lope to meet her.

"Ho, Kate!" he called.

She waved and stepped in front of her little herd of bovines as he neared.

She was genuinely glad to see him. "And what are you doin' so far from the precious wheat field?" she asked.

"Sure, and I was comin' to say good-bye," he replied.

Her expression must have displayed some disappointment. "You're leavin', are you?"

Her question pleased him. "So you do care."

"Not a'tall," she replied, patting the nose of the mare.

"Ah, well," he said, sighing. "I'll be thirty-six in three months, and I promised my mother on her deathbed I'd be wed before my thirty-fifth year was over. I was hopin' you'd help me honor the departed."

"Never make promises you can't keep, Adam."

"Give me some glimmer of hope, won't you, Kate?"

"You're leavin', you said."

"Galway City. Squire Joseph wants me to pick up a load of seed potatoes for the fall plantin'."

"Then you'll be back."

"That I will. And I'd like to have more to come back to than a lonely room and no prospect of love."

"Seed potatoes is it?" she said, changing the topic.

Adam scowled. "You're a hard woman, Kate."

She replied honestly, "That I am not, Adam Kane. But I've seen the heartache when a woman is too easily won."

He leaned forward in the saddle. The light joking manner disappeared. "Listen," he said seriously. "Hard times are comin' for the west."

"How do you know such a thing?"

"Ask Molly how she knows," he replied. Then, "I've got a bit of cash comin' my way. An inheritance, see? I won't be the steward of a rich man forever. It's America I'm thinkin' about. Marry me, and I'll take you there. Where Kevin is."

She slung an arm around Daisy's neck. "And who would tend my cows?"

"Blast the cows!" he exploded, sitting back again. "I'm tryin' to be serious with you. Can you not talk with me a bit without makin' crack about everythin'?"

"Look, Adam," she began to apologize, "it's a handsome offer . . ."

"That it is. And you'll have no better. I've got a promisin' future. I'm askin' . . . Never mind. You are indeed a hard woman." He looked away, whipped the reins around, and spurred the horse into a gallop up the lane toward Galway City.

Kate stood for a long time in the middle of the road and watched him go. She did not love him as she had loved Sean or Joseph. But could she not learn to love him? A new life in America. A land where there was no oppression. The thought was tempting. She carried the question home with her.

Sir Burtenshaw Suggins, seated in his plush office in Dublin Castle, looked down at his interlaced fingers resting comfortably on his paunch and announced his satisfaction with the way the campaign against Repeal was progressing. "A little more provocation by our agents, and O'Connell and his close associates can be arrested for treason," he said smugly.

Charles Trevelyan wagged a cautionary finger. "O'Connell himself is still too discreet and far, far too popular for us to risk moving against. Better we keep to the program of undermining his lieutenants."

Lucas concurred. "Take Burke, for example," he suggested. "We have arranged for him to be fined and brought up on charges for operating an illegal school."

"Quite right too," Suggins sputtered. "Breeding grounds of sedition and insurrection. It's too bad we can't do something even more definite about the young hellions; drown the cubs, and you need not worry about the lions, I say."

Trevelyan said carefully, "There may be something afoot right now in that regard . . . if it works. Mister O'Toole has put in motion a modest scheme."

Beneath his heavy eyelids, Suggins regarded Trevelyan with interest but said nothing.

"There is something else aimed at Lord Burke," Lucas said, not fully understanding the exchange between the two senior conspirators. "Suppose the Burke owed a massive amount of back rent on his property and could not pay it? I doubt he would continue to care about politics if the ground under his feet turned to quicksand."

"What a pleasant thought," Suggins bubbled, splashing brandy on his waistcoat in his excitement. "If only it were so."

"But . . . ," Lucas continued, "it seems that there was a terrible record-keeping error in the payment of Crown rents. He is five years behind on his lease."

"Five years!" Suggins exulted. "How very droll. Was this your idea, Lucas?"

"No, sir," Secretary Lucas modestly replied. "It seems Beth Anne O'Toole came up with that thought."

Both Suggins and Trevelyan applauded. "Deucedly clever, that woman," Suggins added. "Much brighter than her brother, useful as he is."

"Now," said Trevelyan, smiling, "have you seen the latest copy of *The London Times*? Listen to this poem about O'Connell:

> *Scum condensed of Irish bog*
> *Ruffian, coward, demagogue,*
> *Boundless liar, base detractor*
> *Nurse of murders, treason's factor.*

All three men laughed with delight.

13

It was nearly two weeks since the monster meeting at Mallow.

David Clooney, eldest among the Clooney brothers, was the first of the Ballynockanor children to become ill.

It was Thursday morning in geography class when he stood beside his chair to recite European capitals. Martin could plainly see David was sweating—wiping his brow with the back of his hand after Paris, painfully grimacing and rolling bloodshot eyes toward the ceiling before Vienna. Martin had often felt the same way himself when answering questions in class.

The surprise came when David Clooney put his hand to his stomach, groaned loudly, and fell forward in a faint. Alan O'Rourke commented that this was one way to get out of remembering the capitals. Schoolmaster Daly did not laugh. Rushing forward, the intense little man took David Clooney's wrist, felt his forehead, and gasped.

"The lad's on fire! Here! What's this?" Rolling up David's sleeve he examined a rash that extended up the inside of the boy's arm.

"Lord have mercy," he mumbled in a stunned voice. "Martin! Run fetch the squire! The rest of you outside! NOW!"

Will, Samuel, and Michael Clooney, stairstep brothers of David, refused to leave. The trio hovered over him in concern.

As Martin left the room he heard Master Daly ask in a solemn tone, "It's just as well you boys stay here away from the others. Have any of you Clooney children been vaccinated for the smallpox?"

Smallpox." Joseph repeated the verdict of Schoolmaster Daly. "Can you be sure of it, Daly?"

"I've seen it before. And there was an outbreak of it in Killmainham Gaol near Dublin just a month ago."

"But this is Galway. Could it travel so far? So fast?"

Daly looked at the Clooney brothers, the youngest of whom was softly crying. "Has David been outside the townlands, boys?"

Will replied, "Aye, Mister Daly. Sure, and you know we were all present at O'Connell's Repeal meetin' two weeks ago."

Daly nodded and turned to Joseph. "There's the answer to where it came from. It takes two weeks for the first signs. Sure, and it's smallpox. Scourge of the world, it is. I've been inoculated."

Joseph picked up David's limp body from the floor. "Myself as well."

"As has anyone from Dublin with any wit and education. But your people here in the townlands, sir . . . Ballynockanor's the backwater of the whole world. The question is not if they have been vaccinated, but if they even knew such a miracle has existed in the world for forty years."

Will reached out to take David's hand.

"Don't touch him, boy!" Daly cried, pushing the child away. "It's passed by touch!"

Samuel lowered his eyes. "We all share the same bed with David, sir."

The Tinker, drawn from his work by the voices of children banished to the garden, strode into the sickroom, took one look at Joseph and the schoolmaster, and disappeared again.

Moments later he reappeared with mattresses, pillows, and blankets heaped on his back. More were carried down to the library, and the room was converted into a hospital ward for the boys who, one after another, toppled to the disease.

David Clooney was put to bed in the same room where he had fallen. His brothers, overcome with chills and fever within two hours of David, were likewise placed on mattresses beside him beneath the towering bookshelves of the library. A half dozen others, including Alan O'Rourke, were seized with fever and nausea before noon.

The seemingly healthy boys in the class, Martin among them, were quarantined in another room while a decision was made about what course to take.

"You say none of the girls were at the meetin' at Mallow?" the Tinker questioned Joseph.

"Only the boys from the parish were allowed to accompany their fathers, and there was a huge outcry from the females at that."

"They'll thank God they stayed home by the time this is finished, Squire." The Tinker rubbed a hand over his forehead.

"You know this disease too well," Joseph remarked.

"That I do, sir. I've seen its work on a transport ship bound for New South Wales. Off the Canaries it hit. I'll not give the details, but only four out of every ten survived."

"How is it you were not stricken?"

At this, the Tinker gave a wry smile and pulled his shirttail up to show his back. It was deeply scarred with pock marks. "A man can't die twice from it."

"What should be done?" Joseph searched the faces of both men.

The schoolmaster rubbed his balding pate and shrugged. The question seemed to hang in the air: What could be done in such a tragic circumstance?

The Tinker knelt to touch David's fevered head. "Pardon, sir, but first we'll have to separate the sheep from the goats as it were, Squire.

If any have been inoculated they must go home. As for the rest? Quarantine and inoculation are the only hope, sir. If Mallow is indeed the place the boys picked up the pox, then we'll be seein' their fathers in here as well. The incubation period is twelve to fourteen days. We should board the girls someplace away from the lads. If we notice the slightest sign of a fever . . . That's how it begins. Chills. Fever. Sickness. And then the sores."

"The stable. We can set up a girls' dormitory there," Joseph said, nodding.

The Tinker stood and scratched his beard. "Aye. The weather is warm enough for it."

"We'll need help."

Daly gave an unhopeful glance toward the row of invalids. "We'll need a priest. And a gravedigger."

Tinker replied, "None should come to help if they are not protected from catchin' it. Not mother nor father must come near the pestilence. 'Tis worse with older ones."

"Would you ride for the doctor, Dermott O'Neill?"

"All the way to Galway City. Lord have mercy. We'll lose half of them by the time I fetch a surgeon back. You need what I know here, Squire."

Daly raised a timid hand. "I'll ride, sir." He cocked an eye at the Tinker. "Pick an easy mount for me if you will."

The Tinker clapped the instructor on the back. "Good man, Daly. Since you're safe from the pestilence you'll not be carryin' it with you to the poor of Galway City."

With the promise to meet Dermott O'Neill at the stable, Daly scurried off to his quarters to change.

"And what of Tomeen, my son?" Joseph asked the Tinker. "He can't stay here."

"I can't be sayin' if a single place in the west country is safe except the Donovans' dairy."

"Martin and his father were at Mallow. They're marked for death as any."

"There's no safer place in a smallpox epidemic than a dairy, beggin' your pardon. You know it's rare for a dairy family to get smallpox."

"So it is. I'd forgotten."

"I'll be takin' Miss Susan and the wee lad to the Donovans straight away. There'll be things we need from there, and I'll fetch them and hurry back. Whatever man of Ballynockanor or Castletown was there at Mallow, call them in, so they'll not infect their wives and daughters in their homes."

"What about . . . ," Joseph began a query.

But the big man turned on his heel and shouted back an order. "Fetch Miss Susan and Tomeen to the carriage for me." He paused a moment and held aloft a thick finger. "Bring Molly Fahey down to help tend the sick lads here. Sure, and the pestilence'll not touch her. There are others in the village who've had it once. They're safe. I'll bring 'em back to nurse the sick ones."

Kate and Da were in the barn tending to Daisy's infected udder when the clatter of horses and the crunch of carriage wheels sounded on the cobbles outside.

"Miss Kate!" It was the worried call of Miss Susan. "Miss Kate! Where is you, gal? Somethin' terrible took hold of the younguns at the school!"

Sprinting for the barn door, Kate and Da bumped headlong into the Tinker who pushed past them and made for the stalls.

Miss Susan, Little Tom in arms, remained beside the carriage. She shuddered and kissed the baby. Her expression spoke of death and terror. At the sight of Kate she began to weep softly.

"What is it, Miss Susan?" Kate inquired.

Da took Tomeen as Kate enfolded the woman into her arms. "Speak!" he demanded harshly. "Is it Martin? Mary Elizabeth?" He had lost so many children that he had come to recognize the smell of grim news before it was spoken.

"It's them Clooney boys. Down with the smallpox! Squire Joseph sent me and Little Tom out to y'all for safekeepin'."

"Where's Mary Elizabeth? Martin?" Kate urged.

"Squire Joseph and the Tinker say nobody else goin' home for a while. Mister Donovan, you 'sposed to get on back to the school to help with the chilluns. Miss Kate, Squire Joseph says you stay here with me and the baby. Let nobody in, he say. The judgment of God done come upon us."

The Tinker offered a sharp reply to her quaking words. "Mind your tongue, woman!" he commanded. "Do not ascribe evil to Him who can do no evil! Where sickness is, the Lord has also provided remedy."

Kate, who had forgotten Dermott O'Neill was present, whirled around. "What can you know about this?"

The Tinker glared past her, fixing his eyes on Da. "Tom Donovan. How long have these milk cows been infected?"

"Some days. Teats and udders."

The Tinker's stern features relaxed at the news. "Sure, and it's an answer heaven-sent. We'll have enough for every soul in the town-lands then."

"Enough what?" Kate demanded.

The Tinker continued as if he had not heard her objections. "Fetch me a dull knife and a bowl, Tom. There is no time to lose."

Da obeyed immediately and entered the house.

"And by what authority do you order everyone around at such a time?" Kate scolded.

The Tinker responded, "Give the child to Miss Susan, Kate, and come along to the barn with me. I'll be needin' your help."

Against her will she did as he commanded. Still resenting him, she nevertheless followed him to Daisy's stall.

"We'll lose her milk with this." Kate sighed.

The Tinker pulled up the milking stool to the cow's flank. "Fetch the lantern, woman." Kate did so. "Now hold it so I can see what damage there is." The light revealed teats and udder painfully swollen and covered with fresh scabs.

"Sure, and she'll go dry."

"There's salvation here for your village and Castletown as well."

At that instant Da returned with the bowl and knife. "And what do you intend to do?" the old man asked.

The Tinker carefully began to scrape the scabs from the swollen udder, putting the gore into the bowl.

Daisy protested, kicking out at the Tinker.

"She is your cow, Kate. Talk to her then!" Dermott commanded. "Tell her she is touched by the finger of God."

Kate refused to repeat such nonsense. She stroked the nose of the unhappy cow and crooned softly to her. Daisy rolled her brown eyes in terror at each stroke of the knife.

Minutes passed with the only sound being that like a man shaving with a straight razor. Finally the Tinker spoke. "Kate, have you had the cowpox?"

"Aye."

"Good. And you, Tom? I'm assumin' you've had it in sixty years among the milk cows."

"That I have," Tom said, as though the question were a silly one.

The Tinker continued, "And Martin?"

Kate frowned. "What has this . . ."

The Tinker insisted, "Martin! Tell me, has he had the cowpox?"

Kate nodded. "Could anyone tryin' to milk around such a mess as that not catch it?"

"Answer me straight, woman. Is the boy safe?"

"Safe?"

"Aye." Dermott straightened and stared up at her. "Have you never known why it is a dairyin' family does not catch the smallpox and perish like everyone else? It's this." He held up the scab-filled bowl. "You catch what Daisy has, and the lesser illness prevents the greater. You're forever safe from death by that pestilence."

Kate blanched. She had not known the reason behind the lore. "Well, then. You want it straight. We've all had it except Mary Elizabeth."

"As I feared." Dermott stood abruptly and marched past her and Da and into the house. Without explanation he picked up Little Tom and laid the child on the table. Then, as Susan swooned and Kate cried out a protest, the Tinker scratched the baby's arm with the tip of his own bone-handled knife and rubbed a bit of scab from the cow into the wound as the infant shrieked hysterically. Dermott O'Neill tore off a bit of blanket and used it to bind the tiny injury.

"You're as mad as Molly is!" Kate pushed the Tinker away, and Miss Susan rushed in to snatch away the wailing child.

Kate held her fists up to strike. Da stepped between Kate and the Tinker and tried to calm her. "Kate!" Da shouted. "Did you not hear the man, Daughter? If Little Tom catches the cowpox, then he'll not die of the smallpox plague."

Kate, still raging, stepped back. Her fists were clenched and her jaw set. "It's a dark knowledge you have, Tinker."

"Not a'tall." Dermott gave a short laugh, then turned to Susan, who cowered terrified beside the hearth and comforted Little Tom. "Miss Susan, girl." Suddenly his tone was gentle. "Do you want to live?"

"You knows I do."

"Then you'll have to let me prick your skin and touch the wound with this weaker sickness."

"You want to put that filth on me?"

"Aye. In all the world Satan has brought no greater scourge to mankind than the smallpox. It is the angel of death. This is the remedy of the Almighty." He held up the bowl. "That it is. Sure, and you know that those who look for wisdom find it in everything livin', all things growin'. Each plant and tree and creature contains some heavenly antidote against some evil. God has not left man without the answers. As strange as it seems, this scum scraped from the poxy teats of a milk cow will save your life, Susan."

As though in a trance, Susan smiled slightly, passed Little Tom to Kate, and rolled her sleeve up. She presented her bare arm to the Tinker, and he repeated the procedure.

There were three others in the townlands protected from small-pox. These accompanied Dermott O'Neill back to the manor house. Father O'Bannon, who had been vaccinated years earlier, the blind widow, MacDonagh, who had lost her sight to the disease as a young woman, and Kate Donovan.

Seated in the wagon, Widow MacDonagh raised her nose to the

wind as they approached the Burke manor house. "It's smoke I'm smellin'."

The Tinker replied, "Squire Joseph is burnin' anythin' the children have touched."

Father O'Bannon, who had not left off saying his prayers for the entire journey, lifted his head at last and made the sign of the cross. "May God have mercy on us."

At the turning onto the estate property a large crowd of parents waited outside the locked gates. The entrance was guarded by Old Flynn, who peeped around a granite pillar at the shouting mob of fifty people. Flynn timidly showed the barrel of a flintlock rifle. "'Tis for your own good. Squire says it's for your own good! I'll have to shoot ye if ye try to pass!"

The people clung to the iron bars of the gates, blocking the entrance to the property.

"Let us fetch our little ones out of there, Flynn!"

"You can't keep our children locked away!"

"Let them out!"

"Their blood upon your head and the head of Squire Joseph!"

The Tinker drove straight on, guiding the horse through the group as though they were not there. They broke and scattered. To each side curses were shouted.

Kate kept her eyes riveted on the thick plume of gray smoke that rose above the trees in the direction of the great house.

Familiar voices called to her. "Kate, girl! Will you send Alan out? Tell him his da is here," cried O'Rourke the fiddler.

Kate responded, "My own Mary Elizabeth as well as Martin are within! They've got to stay here for a while."

The Tinker confided to Kate in a low voice. "Tell them to wait here outside the gates. Tell them they'll need the touch of cowpox to save them and that Squire Joseph will be here at the gates to see to it within the hour. Tell them the well children of Castletown and Ballynockanor will be made safe from harm and the sick children will be made well as much as God wills and we are able."

Kate looked at him sharply, afraid to speak such positive words in the face of such awful reality.

"How can I say such a thing?"

"Tell them," commanded Father O'Bannon. "Do as he says, Kate, lest they riot and break through the barrier."

Kate reluctantly stood up and repeated the Tinker's words as Flynn unlocked the gate and swung it back only wide enough for the passage of the wagon.

Father O'Bannon stood beside her. "Fear not the pestilence that walks at noonday!" he cried. "Only turn your hearts to prayer! Now let us pass. Your children are in need of their priest!"

At this message the crowd fell silent and stepped back. Flynn clanged the gate closed behind the wagon and locked it tight again.

With a backward glance Kate saw their worried faces pressed against the bars. The smoke billowed ahead of them. It was Mad Molly tending the blazing bonfire of clothes, shoes, books from the library shelves, and benches from the school.

"The lads are billeted in separate quarters indoors," explained the Tinker. "Quarantined, they are. It started with the Clooney boys, then came upon young Alan O'Rourke who stayed at the Clooney cottage a time. We've separated the sick lads from the well. We're keepin' those who went to Mallow away from the girls. It had to be carried home from Mallow, you see."

The female schoolchildren, wrapped in the brocade fabric of draperies scavenged from the house, stood outside in a semicircle around the fire, watching their belongings turn to ashes.

Kate searched their solemn faces. Missing among them were the Clooney sisters and Mary Elizabeth.

Kate frowned. "The Clooneys, you say?"

"Aye. It started with the eldest, and the others dropped like flies one after the other."

"Christ have mercy! Mary Elizabeth's been sleepin' over with Alice Clooney the whole long week."

One look at Molly Fahey's troubled face told Kate everything. She did not need to ask about Mary Elizabeth. The truth was evident.

The Tinker strode ahead, entering the portal of the west wing. The old woman pitched a heap of skirts and underclothes onto the flaming books and wooden benches.

Mad Molly cried, "Ah, Kate! Kate Donovan! Where's your father? She's been cryin' for her father, ye see?"

Father O'Bannon put a steadying hand on Kate's shoulder. "Easy, girl," he whispered.

"Where is she?" Kate directed the question to Molly, who did not appear to hear it.

There were tears in Molly's eyes. "These tears, 'Tisn't the smoke, and don't you be thinkin' it. Sure, and wee Mary Elizabeth's me own little darlin' girl as much as if she were me grandchild."

From the ring of girls Darlene O'Rourke piped, "Me granddad went blind from the smallpox. Just like you, Widow MacDonagh. Now Mary Elizabeth's inside the library with the other sick ones. With my brother Alan and the Clooneys. There ain't one of them who ain't got it."

The priest comforted Darlene as Kate made her way to the door. "God bless you, child. Your da is out at the gate. He says to tell you all will be well."

"When can we go home?" asked another girl.

The question was left unanswered as the Tinker pushed past Kate with strips of toweling, a sharp knife, and the bowl of cowpox scabs.

"Father O'Bannon," O'Neill instructed, "I'll be needin' your steady hand and firm control with this inoculation."

"Sure, they'll not argue with their priest," Father O'Bannon agreed. "But are they . . . the sick ones . . . do they not have need of me?"

"Not yet. Now, healthy girl children first, then the strong, well lads inside, and then we'll see to their parents at the gates and those beyond."

Kate turned on the step and locked eyes with Dermott O'Neill. "Have you seen her?"

He lowered his voice. "Aye. And the Clooney children. The O'Rourke boy and your Mary Elizabeth. They have one thing in common. They've been sleepin' in the same room. There's hope for every other family in the townlands in that fact. Your wee sister's no worse off than the rest. It's a long, hard road from this terrible beginnin' to the end. Whatever the end may be for her, heaven now or long life on earth, she'll need your comfort."

Kate hurried to find Mary Elizabeth. The sickroom was so terribly still, thought Kate as she entered. The library classroom had been stripped of books and benches. Tall bookshelves were empty. High, narrow windows that looked out across the manor gardens to the fountain were closed. The air smelled of whiskey used for sterilization and of vomit.

Laid out on the floor at one end were the four Clooney brothers and Alan O'Rourke, their heads along the baseboard. The Clooney sisters and Mary Elizabeth rested on mattresses at the opposite end of the room.

Joseph's questioning had established that Margaret and Fern were safe from the disease. Fern mopped the floor with alcohol. Margaret sponged the girl patients with cool water.

Joseph, who barely glanced up as Kate entered the room, knelt beside Alan O'Rourke to strip the boy's clothes and place them in a basket with the other items to be burned. Joseph's eyes were bloodshot, his expression betraying grief. Kate acknowledged him with a wordless inclination of her head, then moved quickly to Mary Elizabeth's side.

The child was sleeping. She lay on her back, mouth open, eyes only half-closed. Dark curls were damp with perspiration; her breathing was shallow and ragged.

Kate longed to take her into her arms, but Margaret put a finger to her lips and warned in a whisper, "She's only just drifted off."

Sitting back on her heels Kate caressed Mary Elizabeth with her eyes. The delicate hands, normally so active, lay upon the coverlet with fingers spread like the broken bloom of a rose. The faint discoloration of the dreaded rash could be seen along her hairline.

Kate swallowed hard as reality slammed against her consciousness.

Ah, Lord. Don't take her. Not Mary Elizabeth, she prayed silently. *Christ have mercy! Spare us this one. Da could not bear it. And I . . . could I say good-bye once again? Spare the only Donovan whose life is untainted by sorrow.*

The firm grip of Joseph's hand on Kate's shoulder interrupted her. He motioned for her to come with him into the corridor. Her legs felt weak as she followed him out. He closed the door behind them, and without a word, he pulled her against him in a gentle embrace. She did not resist, but rested her cheek against his chest and listened to the steady drumming of his heart.

The two stood silently locked together. The resentment she had held for him for so long suddenly seemed without significance or reason.

At last he spoke. "It's been a long, hard day. Glad I am you've come, Kate."

She nodded, but her voice was choked by emotion.

He stroked her hair, needing nothing more from her but her nearness. "Mary Elizabeth's strong. Aye. There's great hope for the young ones. Only sixteen days, the Tinker says, before the illness runs its course in those who are infected. Twenty-one days before we'll know if we've kept it from spreading throughout the townlands."

Kate answered hopefully, "He and Father O'Bannon are seein' to the youngsters first, and then they'll be workin' at the gates and beyond."

Joseph whispered, "There'll not be one in Castletown or Ballynockanor without the mark of this terrible day upon his arm. Though we are many, we're branded with one wound. Can we not be one heart, then?"

She knew what he was asking, but she could not answer. Not yet. "I'm here, Joseph. We'll fight this together."

"It's a beginnin', Kate." He kissed the top of her head and released her. But he held her still with his eyes.

"I've been too harsh, I'm thinkin'."

"And I too. . . ." His tender reply was interrupted by the crash of the exterior door and Molly's howl in the hallway.

"Oh! Tool of the devil! That's what it is!" She rushed toward Joseph and Kate, her eyes wild. "He's not comin' back! He'll never be back I say! He sent it upon us to kill us, every one!"

Joseph grasped the woman's arms and gave her a shake. "Quiet now, old girl! The wee ones are sleepin' at last."

She lowered her voice to a broken croaking. Tears streamed from her eyes and ran down the gullies of her cheeks. "A long, cold sleep he's brought upon them! Tool of the devil is that one! Master of the schoolmaster! And then there's the potatoes. He'll kill them as well! A million on the roads with O'Connell! They want them hungry, don't you see! Hungry men can't march."

Joseph tried to comfort her. "Is it Schoolmaster Daly you're anxious about, Molly? He's gone to Galway City to fetch us back a doctor."

"Nay! Daly's gone to Galway City to speak with the spawn of Satan! And he'll never come back here again! Sweetly he speaks like an angel, but there's evil in that black heart. I heard the warnin'! Plain as the pox on his face it is! Don't you see? They've just begun to destroy, Joseph Connor Burke. Our wee children first. Now they'll close the roads to Ballynockanor. We're prisoners. So much for the west and O'Connell, Joseph. Pox today! Potatoes tomorrow. Keep us home, they will. Bury us in our own sweet earth! That's what they want! Ireland without the Irish. Dermott O'Neill knows what I say is true. Who will live and who will die. Poor wee Mary Elizabeth! No one ever listens to me."

At that she sank to her knees and would say no more.

14

Schoolmaster Daly arrived in Galway City flushed and out of breath. He had covered the thirty-five miles from Burke Hall in a constant state of apprehension and panic. Both man and beast were lathered by the time Galway Bay came into view.

The horrible discovery of the smallpox outbreak among the schoolchildren was communicated to the chief doctor at the clinic on Upper Abbeygate Street, but the result was not promising. "What d'ye expect me to do about it?" the physician replied. "The disease will just run its course. God willin' only half those folks'll die—more likely the entire village. I'll let the authorities know so that the town can be quarantined; there is naught else to be done."

In a daze, Daly stumbled away from the hospital, leading the horse he was now too shattered to remount. He came at last to Eyre Street to a bookseller's above which there was a one-room apartment.

Tethering the horse in front, Daly ascended the outside stairs. He pounded on the oak door, then rushed in without waiting for his knock to be answered. "Something terrible has happened," he gasped to the lone occupant of the chamber. "No one will have to worry about rebellion in Ballynockanor. They've the smallpox there!"

Garrison O'Toole rose from his writing desk, sweeping fragments of crackers off onto the floor. "Daly," he said, brushing crumbs from his mustache. "I wasn't expectin' you before next week."

"Smallpox!!" Daly gasped again urgently.

"Yes," O'Toole agreed, "so it worked. My own idea, that. Squire Joseph Burke will have his hands full for some time now, I expect. Of course this was just a minor attempt, but if it succeeds it might be worth repeatin'."

Daly's eyes bulged as if someone had grasped him around the throat. "You mean that you . . . this was deliberate? But the children . . . you never said anythin' . . ."

"Come, come, Daly," O'Toole said sternly. "When you signed the agreement to act as an agent of the government, you never quibbled at takin' the pay that was offered, did you?"

"I'll tell . . ."

"Oh, I don't think so," was the calm reply. "Do you think anyone would believe you knew nothin' about this? Or believe you at all, for that matter? There is that dreadful matter of you and that underage girl at your previous employment."

"It's a lie!" Daly shrieked.

"Written records are so much more impressive than idle gossip, wouldn't you say?"

Daly staggered out of the room and wandered off, neither seeing nor caring where he was heading. He was miles away, across the river Corrib on Gaol Road, before he even realized he had left the horse behind.

They must be made to come back to the manor," Dermott O'Neill said to Joseph. He studied Joseph's face for a long moment. "And you know what must be done? It gets in the thatch, you see. There must be no drawin' back."

"I know," Joseph said curtly, the bowl of gore and scrapings carefully balanced on his lap. "It will be done."

The Clooney cottage was located on the hillside to the east and above Ballynockanor proper. It was long and low, having on its front three exterior doorways facing south and no windows at all. The walls, built of rough, fist-sized, unmortared stones, were innocent of any whitewash, although the roof was bright with new straw.

The Tinker called out for Aidan Clooney before he had whipped the horses up the last incline in the grass track that led to the home. Ducking under the low doorway, Clooney emerged into the daylight as the wagon pulled up.

"What's amiss then?" he asked. His speech was rough, and he winced as he spoke. His reddened eyes and cheeks told the rest of the story: Aidan Clooney was already in the grip of the smallpox. "Is summat wrong with the children? My throat has been so sore I have not been able to play the flute these two days past."

"Yes," Joseph acknowledged. "Your children are ill, Aidan. We're takin' care of them at the school."

"God bless you, sir," Clooney said. "What is it that's afflicted us?"

Not wanting to answer that question yet, Joseph posed one of his own. "What about your youngest, and the missus? Have they gotten ill?"

"No, saints be praised," Clooney said. "I feel mighty rough, meself. God in heaven," he said with disgust when he looked down at the bowl Joseph handed to the Tinker, "what is this?"

"It is heaven-sent," O'Neill responded, "and may keep the rest of your family from takin' the disease."

Mrs. Clooney appeared at the doorway. Her broad face was clouded, and she had a child on each ample hip. "I heard," she said. "Come in and do what is needful for these wee ones and the one in the cradle."

Joseph drew Aidan Clooney aside as the Tinker entered the home to prepare the inoculations. "You will have to come back to the manor," he said. "Quarantine, you see. We've brought clothes for you to change into since all your other things must be burned. It's the only way to stop the spread."

An outraged cry of pain burst from the cottage. "Hold the child still, woman," Joseph heard the Tinker scold.

"It's bad, then? Very bad?" Clooney questioned.

"It's the smallpox, Aidan. But that serum from a pox-ridden cow gives protection."

"But wait," Clooney protested. "Protection, you say? But not to those who already have it. Mary and Joseph, what about the others?" The man was shaking and visibly pale through several days' growth of whiskers.

"We're doin' what we can for them," Joseph said. "Now take these clothes and go back of the house and change. Don't go inside again once you've changed."

"But I'll need to gather some things we will . . ." Clooney stopped as Joseph's earlier words sunk in at last. "All our things," he repeated, his voice trailing away.

"Everythin'," Joseph ordered brusquely, aware the man was near to shock and scarcely able to think clearly. "Don't fret about it now. Change clothes, and go stand by the wagon bed."

Joseph hoisted a bucket from the wagon and entered the cottage to a chorus of wailing children. Two were sitting on the floor by the hearth while the third, the littlest one, whimpered and snuffled in its mother's arms.

"Now, you," O'Neill said to Mrs. Clooney. "This won't hurt much."

The woman rolled up a sleeve to expose a beefy arm. "Do y'think after bearin' twelve children I'm feared of a wee scratch? But will it do any good?"

The Tinker answered the honest, calmly spoken question with a straightforward reply. "God has so arranged things that it takes a fortnight to take the smallpox but only ten days for the cowpox to catch hold. It is a slim margin, but it's still a divine reprieve."

"And otherwise?"

"Every day we live is in God's hands," the Tinker said. Left unspoken was the fact that from even mild smallpox, three out of ten people died. The more virulent strains carried off seven or eight out of ten.

Mrs. Clooney nodded, looking down at the tin pail in Joseph's hands. "Coal oil, is it? I thought as much."

"Take the children and dress them and yourself in the new things, then wait by the wagon," Joseph instructed.

When the woman had slung the infant in a shawl tied crosswise over her bosom and hoisted the other two again, she looked once only around the room and left.

"Do you want my help with this part of it, Squire?" Dermott O'Neill asked.

"No," Joseph said, shrugging. "See to them. This won't take long."

There was a pine chest across one end of the narrow space. A bit of looking glass perched on the mantel. Three heaps of feather bedding and a threadbare gray blanket occupied the wings of the cottage; there were no bedsteads.

On the shelves across the other end of the cabin were the Clooneys' precious things: a stack of wooden trenchers, Clooney's pair of wooden flutes, three unchipped mugs and five more that were missing their handles, and a prayer book.

Not able to look any further, Joseph started at one end of the cottage, sprinkling coal oil liberally on the meager furnishings and the low ceiling where the thatch hung down to shoulder height.

At the doorway he paused, extracted a match from his waistcoat pocket, and scraped it across the sole of his hobnailed boot. Its flame gleamed cheerfully in the shadow. Joseph dropped it into a pool of coal oil near the door.

The blaze was already licking the thatch and a plume of black smoke was billowing upward by the time Dermott O'Neill clucked to the team and the horses pulled away. Mrs. Clooney and the three children were nestled in the back of the wagon, covered in a blanket brought from the manor house.

Aidan Clooney stared at the pyre without speaking. From the spring seat he reached out for his youngest child. The Tinker, kindly but firmly, forbade the touch. "We must give them every chance," he said.

Only then did Clooney sob.

Within one day of the smallpox outbreak a troop of British soldiers arrived from Galway City to set up outposts along the boundaries of the Burke estate. The road from Castletown to Tuam was sealed with a barricade of an overturned cart surrounded by brush. The track that led from Ballynockanor up over the mountains was blockaded by stones scavenged from a fence. Armed pickets patrolled the perimeter of the townlands. Heaps of rocks were set to mark the line no one from inside could cross. The loaded rifles of the soldiers contained the certain penalty for any man, woman, or child attempting to leave the area. Already there had been a shooting: Joe Watty's dog had wandered too near the Castletown side of the barrier. As a warning, two sheep were likewise slaughtered up on the hillside above St. Brigit's cross. Though the meat from the animals might have fed a half dozen families, no one in Ballynockanor was allowed to fetch them back. Their rotting carcasses remained where they fell as an additional reminder that to come closer would result in death.

Neither the doctor nor Schoolmaster Daly returned from Galway City to the manor house, but the arrival of the soldiers convinced Joseph that Daly had reached the city.

Two days after the lines were set, the Galway mailcoach pulled up to the soldiers at the Castletown barricade with a sack of mail. The pouch was conveyed by a foot soldier some fifty yards into the interior. Joe Watty, cursing the sergeant who had killed his dog, was ordered forward to retrieve the bloated, stinking animal as well as the mail pouch.

Inside was a letter of explanation to the squire from the schoolmaster.

Joseph stood among the groaning children in the ward and read the message.

Squire Burke,
I shall not be coming back to your employ. I regret the
tragedy that has been perpetrated upon the boys who

were in my charge. Some evil comes upon mankind through natural, unavoidable consequence. Other comes through the devices of evil men. Understand my meaning. Their purpose, sir, is to end your hope of Repeal with despair. By now your people and lands are cut off. The west is awake and will be punished for it. Be warned. Division and suspicion seemed to be a noble tool to use against your cause. Fear is one thing; planned murder is another magnitude of strategy altogether. I swear I knew nothing of it. What I did was done for the nation. I am now quitting Ireland for a place where the murder of children is not allowed for political purposes.

Your servant,
A. M. Daly

Joseph felt the blood drain from his face. He crumpled the paper and shoved it into his pocket. He recalled Molly Fahey's shrill warnings. The madwoman had never trusted Daly. But why? Understanding flooded him. Schoolmaster Daly had been an informer. The stolen papers, the break-ins—all became clear. What else had Molly witnessed that she could not fully articulate? Fear and division were indeed a well-used tactic in the political game. The threat of the Ribbonmen against Little Tom at the Donovan cottage must have been staged by Daly. But a deadly contagion of smallpox deliberately passed to a child of Ballynockanor? The dark evil of such a strategy was almost incomprehensible.

Who had done this? Who had bribed Daly to inform and then bragged to him about paralyzing the west with smallpox?

The terrible thought followed that Daly had been recommended for the teaching post by Daniel O'Connell himself. O'Connell would have to be informed that someone he had trusted had proved a traitor. Perhaps there would be some way to apprehend Daly before he escaped Ireland. O'Connell would know how to get the truth out of the teacher, Joseph thought.

Dermott O'Neill rose from Alan O'Rourke's bedside. With a

shake of his head he indicated to Joseph that things were not going well for the boy. In an anteroom Aidan Clooney was also near death.

Joseph beckoned the Tinker to his side.

"Squire, you look like you've seen a ghost."

"A demon," Joseph returned. "Daly will not be comin' back."

The Tinker furrowed his brow. "I'm not surprised by the news, Squire."

"You never did tell me how you happened to be near the Donovan cottage the night the Ribbonmen came to take Tomeen."

The corner of the Tinker's mouth turned up. "Is it my suspicion of Daly you're askin' about, Squire?"

"If suspicion is what took you out that night."

"A peculiar fellow, Daly. You'll recall he asked me for a gentle horse to ride to Galway City?"

"That I do."

"The request was for your ears. The man borrowed your young bay the night of the raid on the Donovan farm."

"The high-strung colt."

"Aye, to be sure. Daly told me he had a family matter to tend to, and he took the bay. Managed the creature like he was born to its back. Schoolmaster Daly isn't what he seems, Squire."

"I'm sure of that now."

"That very night he told me he would ride to Tuam and that he needed a mount with some fire in his belly. Aye. But he didn't ride toward Tuam. I followed him."

"Why did you not tell me this?"

"I lost him in the hills above Ballynockanor. Then I saw the torches in the Donovan yard. You know the rest. I didn't see the bay among their mounts. I wasn't certain if Daly was with them."

The thought passed through Joseph's mind that the Tinker was not at all what he appeared to be either. But who was he? And why had he come to Connaught?

The messages that came by way of the Galway mailcoach in a leather pouch tossed into the no-man's-land of the quarantine barricade looked innocuous enough. There was a buff-colored envelope with no return address and a pale blue envelope sealed with the imprint of Her Majesty's Ministry of Quit Rents, Dublin. Margaret carried them both into the study on a silver tray, as if they were greeting cards.

Joseph, midway through a volume of medical studies, glanced idly at the correspondence, then read another page from Edward Jenner's treatise on vaccination for smallpox. Everything the Tinker had suggested was born out by scientific study: infection with cowpox provided immunity against smallpox.

Joseph had no big concern about the communication from the tax collector. The next payment due the Crown did not have to be made until the following Gale Day, the first of November. If the dread disease was indeed checked in a month, the Burke townlands had plenty of time to recover for the farms to prosper and the taxes to be paid.

He was still thinking about Jenner's conclusions and what the Tinker had said about God providing antidotes for every disease if humans just knew where to look as he reached into his desk. Joseph removed an ivory-handled letter opener engraved with a whaling scene.

Slitting open the buff-colored envelope, Joseph noted that it was from the board of trustees of the National School.

Sir, he read. *It has been brought to our notice that you are illegally operating an illegal school.* Joseph wondered if there was a legal way to operate an illegal school. *You are hereby ordered to cease-and-desist forthwith. There is already the matter of a fine of five hundred pounds for this offense, but ignoring this order will make you subject to additional fines of one hundred pounds per day for every day of noncompliance. To fully resolve this matter, you are hereby ordered to attend a meeting of this board to be held at Dublin Castle . . .* The letter went on to name a date only five days hence.

There was nothing to be done about it at the moment. Though himself vaccinated, Joseph, like the others in the Burke townlands, was a prisoner of the quarantine. He would write to the board and ask for a postponement of the hearing, and then he would appeal the penalty. As for the school, he was now in compliance with the order, whether he wanted to be or not. For the duration of the disease, there *was* no school.

It seemed that the hateful Mrs. Rush of Castletown's National School and the angry landlord Colonel Mahon had done their spiteful best.

Joseph replaced the school letter on the tray and opened the blue envelope. He scanned the first two lines twice before the content registered with him.

> *Lord Burke,*
> *It has come to the attention of Her Majesty's Commissioners of the Rent that payment of the Crown lease on the lands held by you is in arrears. The sum is now due and payable.*

Joseph was brought up short. His title and the transfer of his father's lands had been examined and confirmed by the Dublin courts. What was this about?

Farther on, the letter explained:

> *Your uncle, the honorable Lord Marlowe, owed back rents on the property as cited below. Due to an unfortunate oversight, this shortfall was not recognized until very recently. Inasmuch as you are the present holder of the Crown lease, it falls upon you to satisfy this account. You are hereby notified that you have until 1 October of this year to satisfy the arrears.*

Joseph was perplexed but still not unduly alarmed. His uncle had possessed the Burke lands for fifteen years. The rent collectors of the Crown might be lax, but for how long could overdue lease payments be left unaccounted?

The second page of the letter contained the answer.

Rents have been uncollected for some time, the message announced. *As of 1 March 1843, no payment has been made for a period of five years.*

The time span was astonishing. Five years of unpaid rents, all due within less than four months? The sum was incredible. It was *four thousand, five hundred pounds*, said the letter flatly, in black ink. Not including penalty and interest due of *six hundred pounds*.

There was little left in the Burke estate as far as cash was concerned. Lord Marlowe and his profligate son William had spent a great deal. What little remained after Joseph took possession had been invested in improvements to Burke holdings and for supplies and salaries for the school. There were no other savings. Joseph had been counting on a good oat crop on his own farm. The same for his tenants would enable them to make their rent payments to him of fourteen shillings per acre. Of course, those plans had been laid before the smallpox epidemic.

If the crop was satisfactory and everyone in Ballynockanor and the townlands roundabout recovered from the devastating illness sufficiently to pay what was owed, Joseph could look forward to an income of fifteen hundred pounds sterling—less than one third of the arrears.

His eye fell on the sallow page from the school board. When added to the rest, the five-hundred-pound fine seemed crushing. But even worse was the timing: Joseph could not believe that both poisonous communications would arrive in the midst of the pestilence strictly by coincidence. The forces arrayed against the west country were not content with causing disruption and turmoil; they were bent on nothing less than total destruction.

Joseph found Father O'Bannon tending the sick. The priest was spending time praying with as well as spooning warm broth and encouragement into each victim. Lifting their spirits, he always said, was his contribution to their healing. Illness could be faced; overcoming anxiety and despair was the real challenge.

The squire sincerely hoped Father O'Bannon could do as much for him.

"Father," he said softly, "would you be steppin' into my office with me?"

O'Bannon obliged at once. Aware Joseph could just as easily have spoken to him in the library or the hallway, the priest recognized the signs of distress and an urgent concern.

"It's this way, Father," Joseph began, lifting buff and blue envelopes from his desk. "The school has been proclaimed . . . forbidden . . . and I'm to answer charges for it." He shrugged. "That's as may be, since we have no school now in any case. But it came the same day as this." Joseph unfolded the letter about the Crown rents and extended it.

Striding to the window where the light shone brightly on the gloomy words, O'Bannon adjusted his spectacles down on his nose and read in silence. When he had finished he turned the missive over in his hands and whistled tunelessly through his few remaining teeth. "A bad business, this," he observed. "Came the same day as the other?"

Joseph acknowledged the accuracy of the statement.

"And just after the plague descended on us, lockin' us away from any chance to fight back?"

Again Joseph allowed that the priest's thoughts followed the same path as his own. "It can be nothin' but a conspiracy," he said. "Foul and blackhearted and, worst of all, inescapable. I have struggled with it for a night and a day, and I see no way out. I cannot raise the rents with people sick and dyin'. Even the untouched families will struggle with their payments while the quarantine disrupts commerce. Whoever has done this has us in a fiendishly clever box and hammered home the lid. And they have won; it is the end of the Repeal fight for me."

"Oh?" O'Bannon commented with a note of reservation in his voice. "Fiendish is the right of it. The devil himself is behind such deeds as these. But knowin' your enemy is knowin' how to fight him."

"Fight how?" Joseph said, slumping in his desk chair and toying idly with the letter opener. "We're finished before we've begun. There's no money to even fight with, let alone pay the back rent. It's hopeless."

"I see," remarked O'Bannon, staring at Joseph. His reading glasses made his eyes look owl-like and piercing. "So to give up is your plan then, is it? Joseph, lad, I will not preach to you any sterner than I would another, but sweet heavens! Humans have such short memories! When God has shown you the way out of one wilderness you thank Him, and then when you come to the next bit of dark forest you say, 'Where is He? He has abandoned me.'"

"Yes, but . . ."

"Hush till I'm finished. I do not permit catechumens to interrupt their lessons, and you are in need of renewed instruction." Joseph sat back in mute surprise at the vehemence in the priest's words. "Now then, where was I? Ah, here it is: circumstances are never as dauntin' or as damagin' to us as how we take on about them. There is always somethin' to be done. And the fact that the fiend has trotted out this weapon to use on you means two things: first, the fight you are in . . . Repeal, I mean . . . must be very important, and so you must go on with it in any way you can. Second, you can take comfort that despair is the worst thing he can spring on you. Things can appear to grow worse, but if you conquer despair, no deeper pit remains to trap you."

Joseph was afraid to speak even when the flow of O'Bannon's words ceased, for fear of another reprimand. When it became obvious that the priest was waiting for Joseph to respond, he repeated, "Very well, don't give in to despair. But for practical needs, Father, what's to be done about the back rent?"

"Didn't I hear," O'Bannon mused aloud, studying the broken pieces of clay pipe that Joseph had preserved on a shelf. "Didn't I hear of Colonel Mahon, scoundrel though he is, lustin' after Burke property to add to his own? Three or four years ago it was expressed to your uncle and rejected."

Joseph tumbled to the notion at once. "Sublease part of the property to Mahon and use the payment to make up the arrears? It might work at that. But Mahon is the worst of all landlords for squeezin' his tenants, Father. How can I do such a thing to them? Even if it only affects some?"

"We will pray that a better option presents itself," Father O'Bannon said. "But let us not neglect siftin' the ashes in search of the gold. Activity beats despair every time, even if the result is not what we expected."

15

Daniel O'Connell lifted his lionlike head to regard Osborne Davis and Beth Anne O'Toole. "This could not have come at a worse time," he said. "How can anyone raise the west when it is facin' a plague? Is there any word about how bad it is?"

Davis looked grim. "It is confirmed as smallpox, Daniel. There is no way to minimize what that means. The west is still so backward when it comes to medical care—one infirmary for almost four hundred thousand people, no vaccination." His words trailed off, but their significance hovered in the air like a thick layer of dark smoke. "They had no warnin', of course, and no time to get ready. We must be prepared for the worst."

"Which is?" O'Connell asked softly.

"A third of them will die . . . if Providence is gracious. More otherwise. But we are fortunate in two respects."

"Oh?" O'Connell said eagerly, grasping at even the slightest positive news.

"It is summer and relatively warm. That will help keep down the mortality from pneumonia. Also, the government clamped an immediate quarantine around the Burke townlands. No one gets in, no one gets out. If this truly is an isolated outbreak, the rest of Connaught may be spared its ravages."

O'Connell grunted at the irony. "A reason for us to be grateful for the efficiency of the British army. Can we send communication in to Joseph?"

"Yes." Beth Anne took over the answers. "Mail can be delivered, but none brought out."

"How long before we know the outcome?"

"With the absolute embargo, and no outbreak elsewhere, two weeks will show the depth of the disaster; a month will see them clear."

"We must let Joseph know that we hold him and his people up in prayer," O'Connell said. "Though we miss his efforts terribly, we must encourage him."

"That is exactly why I have sent Garrison O'Toole to Galway City, to our printin' office there," Davis remarked. "I wanted a reliable source of information closer to the scene and one to whom we can direct specific requests."

O'Connell scanned the shelves of the office on Baggott Street. They were laden with stacks of newspapers, broadsheets, and flyers that announced in excited terms the growth of the Repeal movement and the upcoming rallies taking place across the whole country east of the Shannon—two or three every week. Of special interest was the huge gathering planned for the hill of Tara in mid-August. The convocation slated for that thousand-year-old seat of the High Kings of All Ireland was expected to attract one million people or more. Excitement was reaching a fevered pitch. "Everywhere but in the west," he murmured.

Beth Anne offered, "My brother volunteered to go. He understands the importance of Connaught to the campaign and was most adamant that he be nearer, while I continue to operate the shop here."

O'Connell added his gratitude. "You are both doin' yeomanlike work," he observed. "Where would the movement be without you?"

Davis agreed. "It is so important to have reliable people around and through our organization. As close-knit as we are, there are still times when it appears that there are informers in our midst. The Castle seems to get word of our plans before we know them ourselves."

"Aye, and they fear us all the more now that they have seen for these months that the movement will not go away. An enemy who fears you is dangerous; we must be on our guards."

To this assertion Davis and Beth Anne both solemnly assented.

Martin was being sent home. "This is no place for you now, lad," Joseph said as he sealed the last envelope containing correspondence to the outside world.

"I'd rather stay," Martin protested. "What with Mary Elizabeth here and David Clooney bein' me dearest friend. No one can cheer them like myself. They'll need cheerin'. Can't you find things for me to do?"

"Your father sends word he needs your help." Joseph scooped up the pile of letters and placed them in the satchel. "There's nothin' you can do here to help your friend or Mary Elizabeth. You're secure from the pox. There are servants in this house, all of whom were inoculated when they were employed by the Marlowes. That's enough hands for the washin' and the cookin' and the cleanin' up. I'm sorry, Martin, but your da has only himself since Kate is here. As for Miss Susan, when the cowpox takes hold she'll be too sick to help him."

Martin hung his head. "Will David and Mary Elizabeth get well do you think, Joseph? And the others too?"

Joseph stood and clasped the boy's hand in his own. "I've never seen the course of the disease, but Dermott O'Neill says it will grow much worse as the days pass. Then, if they live for sixteen days they're out of danger. God knows such things. He asks only that we pray and do what we can."

"I could do more if . . ."

"Pray, Martin. Tend your father's herd. Do what's put in front of your face. That's what God wants of you."

Reluctantly Martin agreed. To go to Ballynockanor now when all the excitement was just beginning felt like a punishment. "I'll come visit them."

"We'll see." Joseph swung the leather case into Martin's arms. "Now then, one last errand. Take these letters to the barricade. Tell the sentries it's mail for the Galway coach." Joseph nudged him and smiled into his gloomy face. "Very important! Repeal business it is, at that. A letter for Daniel O'Connell and one each for all parish churches in the west. Don't dally now, boy. The coach arrives in an hour."

Martin crept into the sick ward to take his leave of David and Mary Elizabeth and the others. They did not look as ill as everyone said they were. David, however, said he felt as though he had been trampled by a herd of cattle. The rash by now had spread over every surface, but it was still only a rash, not much worse than something Martin had suffered when he fell into a patch of nettles.

"You'll be all right," Martin told Mary Elizabeth.

"My throat is sore," she replied softly.

"Sure, that'll pass. And you have all you wanted. To sleep and eat in one room full of children."

She remembered she had wished to be a permanent part of the Clooney tribe. "They can't be rid of me," she said. Then she frowned. "But I would love to see Little Tom. They say I can't see him since I'm sick."

Martin decided not to tell her that the baby had been taken to the Donovan dairy for the sake of safety. Instead, he made a cheerful farewell and carried the mail sack out to the main road, then along the quarter mile to where the soldiers blockaded the road.

Aware of their order to shoot to kill anyone who trespassed, Martin hailed them at a distance. "Ho! I've got a sack full of letters from Squire Joseph here! To be taken by the Galway mailcoach."

A tall, slim soldier who looked barely older than Martin raised his weapon in acknowledgment. The captain of the detail shouted to

Martin, "Bring it to the marker, lad! Come along! I'll tell you when to stop."

Martin knew they had been ordered to shoot anyone who came too close to them. This made Martin walk forward slowly, as if he were balancing on a log.

Impatiently the captain commanded, "Hurry along, then! Ten more paces! That's it! Drop it there by that stone. Now back with you, lad, and no dallying!"

Martin deposited the mail pouch, turned on his heel, and hurried back to the safety line. Loaded guns at his back made him sweat. He felt an unreasonable sense of relief to be back on the Castletown side of the boundary.

He did not slow down, but continued his odd, uneven jog halfway home to Ballynockanor.

Aidan Clooney, father of twelve children, master of the flute that had taught the feet of the poor of Ballynockanor to dance in spite of poverty, died first among the victims.

His sons and daughters, too sick to know their father was ill, were not told. His broad-hipped wife, two toddlers, and a baby, still miraculously well, were not allowed to attend the burial nor even to see his body one last time.

The trip through Castletown to Ballynockanor and the churchyard of St. John the Evangelist could not be risked. Before daybreak Joseph, the Tinker, and Father O'Bannon placed Clooney onto a blanket and carried him away from the house, away from the buildings, out to a field where a venerable solitary oak stood.

Dermott O'Neill dug the grave deep. Joseph expressed sorrow that Aidan Clooney could not lie in sanctified ground among his fathers.

Father O'Bannon answered that it was the Christian man himself who made the earth hallowed where he rested. And surely Christ would not leave him behind on resurrection day. Until then the music of Aidan Clooney would lie dormant for a while as what was mortal of the man melted into the hill and fed the tree. When that was accomplished his songs would rise again and sing of God's glory in the leaves. The branches of the oak would dance each day to his memory.

There was concern among the household staff that Molly would wander off to the barricades for a bit of a chat with the soldiers and get herself shot.

This fear was justified when Martin, delivering the milk and cheese to the manor house, found her at the perimeter shouting her usual greetings to the men of Queen Victoria's Irish outpost.

"Ye're all devils is what ye are!" She flung a handful of dust in the direction of the men. "Ye'd murder the children in their beds! Ye'd steal their Irish souls and sell 'em to yer master! Away with ye! In the name of Jesus! Be gone with ye!" Another handful of dust punctuated the last line.

Martin could see plainly that the sentries were hunched behind the barricade with their weapons unslung. What if the old woman attacked?

Martin pulled up the donkey and leaped from the cart. "Molly, darlin'," he called softly, "I've brought the butter and the milk and the cheese."

She turned at his voice. The former scowl melted into an expression of delight. "It's Martin, is it! Butter and cheese and milk is it? Sure, and I'll be takin' tea now."

"Come to the cart, Molly, or they'll shoot you." Martin took her arm.

"Shoot me, is it? Nay! I'm well armed against the fiery darts. The Lord favors little children and the feebleminded who cannot help themselves. My mind is feeble enough for ten. They'll not harm me. 'Tis the souls of the children they're after, Martin. Angels of light they claim to be, but I can plainly see the difference. They're in it for themselves. Father O'Bannon's prayers keep them at a distance. Aye! Speak the name of Jesus, and they turn ugly quick enough. I'll not be fooled. Lord have mercy!"

Through this babble Martin nodded agreeably and smiled. But sweat was pouring from his brow. He knew well that they would shoot her without reservation if she came too close. The muzzles of their guns were trained upon his back as he helped her toward the waiting cart.

"You mustn't go too close, Molly. They'll kill you, sure. They don't like you, that's plain enough, isn't it? Nor any of us."

"There are some who dwell within these walls that they like well enough. Men whose souls are bought and paid for who claim stolen tribute. The walls bear witness to their evil deeds. Sure, and the devils like those traitors well enough, for they keep company together. But it's hard to tell who is who in human kind. People are crafty. Speak the name of Jesus to an evil man and he can still say 'Aye,' smile, and hide the darkness. But a fallen angel, Martin . . ." She jerked her thumb over her shoulder. "Fear not! The barest mention of the name, and they run mad." At this she cackled. "I'm an old, old woman, and my mind is addled, but speak the name of Christ, and the rebels who are older than old and saw God at the beginnin' shriek and tear their hair." She wagged her head from side to side and sang loudly, "Let us proclaim the mystery of faith. Christ has died, Christ is risen, Christ will come again." More laughter. "Sure, and they're flyin' away in all directions now for certain."

"Aye, Molly." Martin shuddered. The madwoman made such mysterious sense. It made him look over his shoulder and squint into the air as though there really were something there. "Now come along home to tea."

"Tea. A grand idea." She counted on her fingers. "One. Two. Three. Which one is he, Martin? Sure, and he gives no sign. Seems a good fellow."

"What are you gabbin' about now?" He climbed into the milk cart beside her.

"Adam the first. Cain the second. Abel the third. So which is he?"

Martin slapped the reins down on the rump of the mule and guided him toward the lane that led to Burke manor. Someone would have to keep a sharp eye on Molly. These were dangerous times indeed for everyone, and she did not appear to fathom how near she had come to meeting her death.

It was late. The candle on the table of the sickroom was guttering when Joseph entered. The patients were mercifully asleep. He leaned against the doorframe and prayed for them. The disease had progressed to the point now that it was certain each face would bear the scars of this battle forever.

Joseph considered the information in Daly's letter for the hundredth time. Evil was loose within O'Connell's camp. Someone close to the cause of Repeal was in fact its enemy. The design to close off the west had succeeded, but at what awful cost! Never mind politics, Joseph thought. What was Repeal compared to the life of even one of these children?

Joseph knew that a soul controlled by greed and cruelty transformed the world around it into a mirror of itself. Here was an act so evil it made the loss of Eden look like an accident. This unknown man had willfully chosen to injure these innocent lives for the sake of something as eternally absurd as British political policy! It was, to Joseph, incomprehensible. As the first garden had fallen with the fall of man; so these sweet Irish blossoms now lay blasted by another's sin.

Joseph wondered if the man had imagined he acted for the sake of patriotism. Did he fool himself into believing that evil could be justified by an ultimate British triumph over the Repeal movement? For the first time Joseph felt rage and hatred not just toward the one who had done this, but toward England.

Joseph gazed over the little ones and prayed he would one day be able to avenge them with his own hand. Until he was free to leave the townlands, however, he would hope O'Connell could trace the villain. Perhaps O'Connell would catch Daly and discover who in the movement was responsible for this. If only Joseph's letter could arrive in time for Daniel to take action!

Caution would have to be observed, however. If news of this plot were made public there would be open Irish rebellion against the English Crown and its agents. How many Irish farmers armed with pitchforks and rakes would die in such an event?

Kate, who was sleeping beside Mary Elizabeth, sensed his presence and sat up. Quietly she lit a second candle and snuffed out the stub of the first. In the soft light, her eyes met Joseph's.

"I could use a cup of tea," she whispered.

He took her arm and led her to the hallway. "I'll send Fern down to keep watch with the children." He would not tell her what he knew about the origin of the contagion. Nor would he speak of it until the culprit was captured. Then the matter would be taken to the courts. Justice would have to be done—even in an English court.

"When's the last time you've eaten?"

Kate shook her head. "I . . . sometime . . . I can't recall."

"Myself as well. I was working on . . . a problem . . . and correspondence. Margaret scolds me about not eatin', so I won't be a hypocrite and scold you. She said she'd keep supper in the warmer for me. There's always enough vittles for three or four big men. It would please her if it were entirely gone when she got up tomorrow mornin'."

"We'll share, then," Kate said gratefully. "For Margaret's sake."

The two reached for the jug of milk at the same moment. Their fingers touched and entwined at the handle. Eyes, weary with the battle against sickness and affairs of a nation, locked and held steady in spite of the uncertainty of what tomorrow would bring to them.

The roasted chicken grew cold on their plates.

He spoke her name at last. "Kate."

She did not look away from his gaze for the first time in a year.

"I'm sorry," she said quietly.

He knew what she meant. Not that she was sorry things were going badly or sorry he was locked away here in the townlands like everyone else. Nor was she sorry for what had happened before with Brigit and with Kevin. But rather she was sorry for the times she had wasted hating him when the truth was, simply, she had always loved him.

He said to her, "This will pass."

She knew he was speaking of the hard times. In the passing of tragedy the river would run free again, and there would be birdsong above its waters. There would come a day when they could see and hear beauty again. The weight of trouble and grief would not make them deaf and blind. St. Brigit's cross would still stand and watch as the two of them climbed the hill together to share a loaf of bread upon the base. The memory of this horrible experience would grow into a song, and the song would become a legend to descend to generations of their children. The struggle of this one long night would become the victory ballad for the people of Ballynockanor.

It had always been so in Ireland. Pain born of the refining fire would ascend and dissipate like smoke. What remained behind in the ashes of remembrance would become forged steel, a plow to cultivate the fields with love or a blade with which to fight future battles.

"Whatever comes . . ." Kate touched his cheek.

"I can face everything with you at my side, Kate," he told her.

"Then I will walk beside you, Joseph."

16

Garrison O'Toole sat on the hearth rug in the upstairs office of the Galway City printshop. Though the day was balmy, a roaring fire was going in the cast-iron parlor stove. Spread out around him on the floor was a circle of letters in Joseph Burke's handwriting.

"To the bishop of Clonfert," O'Toole read, "encouragin' him to continue collectin' the Repeal rent and regrettin' the 'temporary setback,' as Burke calls it." O'Toole tossed the missive into the flames. "To the Repeal wardens of Kilrush, Knock, and Westport, the same." He also consigned these papers to the blaze. "To Archbishop MacHale, apologizin' for bein' unable to meet with him on the twentieth of July and askin' his prayers for God to spare the children." O'Toole chuckled. "'And a little child shall lead them,'" he quoted maliciously. "What did you say the boy's name was, Kenny?" he asked a thickset man missing his front teeth.

"Clooney, I think it was. That's it, ain't it, Ryan?"

Ryan, a slightlybuilt, nondescript character, concurred. "That's it exactly. Went off clutchin' the blanket like it was the treasure of the Indies."

"Life-changin' to be sure." O'Toole laughed. "Aha, here's a prize." He held aloft another letter. "To the Great Liberator himself."

Kenny and Ryan gathered around O'Toole to peer over his shoulder. "What's it say, then?" Kenny demanded.

"Give me a minute. Hum, hum, hum, 'so sorry, will try to make it up as soon as' . . . can he furnish details . . . Well!" O'Toole spun around on the floor with unusual energy. "Where did you say Schoolmaster Daly is lodged?"

"Down at the Albatross on Dock Road," Kenny responded. "He's usin' a false name, and he ain't goin' nowhere. We got a man watchin' day and night."

"And he does not know he is bein' watched?"

"Nah," Kenny responded after looking to Ryan for confirmation. "He's scared of his own shadow. He don't even go out for air."

"And his plans have not changed?"

Kenny shrugged. "Daly has likely chewed his nails up to the elbows, but no, he still has the same passage booked: The *Elizabeth and Sara*, bound for Boston, but hung up in port these days past, waitin' on a favorable wind so's she can make sail."

"Watchin' him is no longer enough," O'Toole instructed. "He must not be allowed to leave Galway City for anywhere."

"Why?" Kenny inquired. "What's happened?"

"Listen to Burke's question for O'Connell." O'Toole resumed quoting, "'Can you furnish details of who recommended Schoolmaster Daly to you for my employ?'"

"Ho, ho!" Kenny guffawed. "And that means you! Burke suspects somethin' was amiss with the teacher, and he can be traced to you!"

Garrison O'Toole did not look amused. "May I remind you that it is *you* who gave the Clooney boy the blanket? It is your neck in the noose even more than mine if Daly spills what he knows."

The grin on Kenny's face slipped, and his jaw tightened.

Ryan asked anxiously, "But if we fixes him here, there's liable to be a stink, ain't there? I mean, what harm can he do us in America?"

Kenny and O'Toole both grimaced. "They gets letters even 'cross the ocean, don't they?" Kenny challenged. "Better he don't have a chance to say nothin' again ever." The bulky man with the crooked nose gazed into the blaze as if finding inspiration there.

"Absolutely right," O'Toole concluded. "And another thing: consider this a practice. Clearly Joseph Burke, if he survives the pox, can never be allowed out where he might ask difficult questions, even if his source is . . . no longer available. See to the one tonight, and then we'll plan what comes next."

The little victories Kate had experienced on the farm became the strength she drew upon in the terrible battle against the disease that sought to take the Clooney children, Alan O'Rourke, and Mary Elizabeth.

When they would not swallow for the pain in their throats, Kate coaxed chicken broth into them with the same patience by which she had taught the orphaned calf to suck from a rubber nipple. Her only aim was to make them live long enough, like the calf, so they could eat on their own again.

Alan O'Rourke refused to eat, refused to keep breathing, though Kate commanded him to live. She demanded that he fight for the sake of his mother's heart, but Alan chose instead to rest beneath the oak in the far field.

Kate, remembering the calf, doubled and redoubled her efforts with the others. Alternately scolding, coaxing, and bullying, she ladled soup down raw throats. She slept among them and held to the manifesto ingrained in the heart of every good farmer: *when the calf sickens, do not let him slip away without a fight! While he lives there is hope that will not let you rest! If he dies, accept his relief and push on to save the others!*

Kate's fidelity to the creed reached through long nights. Every new dawn that her patients still survived was a triumph.

All the while she knew there was nothing more she could do. Oddly, there was comfort in that. The impossible was left in the hands of the Lord of Miracles. Night and day the prayers of Father O'Bannon were presented to God. Mad Molly said she heard the angels singing above the house and saw a glowing canopy of protection above the townlands of Ballynockanor.

Kate, who neither saw nor heard Molly's visions, nevertheless felt a presence and a strength much bigger than her own.

She often considered the pockmarks that would remain forever after the illness had vanished. Knowing what each survivor would feel when looking into a mirror made her love the little herd all the more. What would Da say when he saw Mary Elizabeth? Would he mourn for her lost perfection, or see it as a kind of living death? But Kate, who had been so long a prisoner of her own scars, knew life was more than beauty. Here she was, branded forever from another tragedy, and yet she was strong enough to fight for the ones who had no strength to fight for themselves.

The Tinker came into the sickroom and thrust a butter crock of dark, greasy ointment into her hands. His brooding eyes bored into her thoughts.

"You will not win life for all of them, Kate Donovan, but the Lord hears your prayers and sees your battle."

Before, she might have thought him presumptuous, but this enigmatic man knew things she only sensed.

"Aidan Clooney," she said. "Poor Missus Clooney. Her husband. And so many children on the brink."

"It isn't finished, so don't lose heart. There are some who must rest from this life and others who will go on."

The authority with which he spoke made her want to ask him if he knew how many more would die and who. But she did not.

"Quick thinkin' on your part, sir, to do what you did with the cowpox. Father O'Bannon says he believes it was done in time. No one else but these poor wee children has taken ill in the whole parish. A miracle, he says."

"That it is." O'Neill's thick finger tapped the ceramic container. "I've made enough of this to last, if you use it sparingly. A thin layer upon their faces night and mornin' will lessen the damage of the pox. There's not enough except for faces. There'll be no more after this. Their bodies will have to bear the wounds, and they will have to accept their imperfection as you have accepted your own."

She inhaled the aroma, catching the scent of mint and roses. The substance was dull sable in color, a reddish-black. "What is it?" she asked.

He smiled his reply, indicating that he would not say.

"Remember the salvation God sent to you upon the udders of your milk cow and don't ask me for the ingredients. If I told you, you would not believe it."

"And why can you not make more?"

Again the cryptic smile. "I've been called away."

"But we're none of us allowed to leave. The soldiers . . ."

"They'll not know I've gone."

"But . . . what . . . how will we manage without you, Mister O'Neill?"

"The struggle is on, make no mistake." He waved his hand around the room. "The barricade and the soldiers are nothin'. Have no fear of them. Politicians and queens are destined to be meals for worms, no better than beggars in the end. Know this: despair is your enemy, and it's despair you're fightin'. The weapons to join that battle are found only in the cross of Christ."

A hundred questions remained, but he cut her off. With a crook of his finger he commanded her to follow him. At the bedside of each child he knelt and, muttering the words, "In the name of Christ," he daubed on the mysterious ointment. The heavy, calloused hands of the Tinker coated forehead, cheeks, and chin of each sufferer, applying it thinly to cover the faces of the sick.

"Night and mornin'," he instructed Kate. "Exactly as I have done. On the sixteenth day any who will die will have died, and those who survive will be healed."

He did not wait for Kate to respond, but left the room without looking back.

And where had Dermott O'Neill got off to? the question was asked.

The Tinker was simply gone. His wagon vanished without a track or trace. Now the horses were restless, Old Flynn remarked. At night they whinnied and kicked and bumped against the walls of their stalls as though they sensed something evil. How had the Tinker sneaked past the British soldiers? Or was he a British agent allowed to leave in order to make his report? Speculation on the matter went wild. The talk of it was a pleasant diversion from the dismal reality of illness. There was something eerie about it, make no mistake.

On the heels of the Tinker's vanishing, Adam Kane arrived from Galway City on the English side of the line. It was hot beyond expectation. He was driving a huge wagon heaped with seed potatoes for planting. Warned by the redcoats that he could not leave again if he entered the poxy townlands, he shrugged and smiled.

Being an honest man who spoke his mind, he explained to the captain, "Sure, and I heard of the outbreak while I was at the port. I said to myself I could ship out to America, and who would miss me now? So I stayed a while in Galway City with that thought on my mind. Then I remembered the woman I've decided to wed. She'll be ready to leave here soon enough. I'm a bachelor these thirty-five years, and now I'll marry. Take down your wall and let me in, boys."

The soldiers wished him luck and waved him through.

Kate heard from Fern that Kane had arrived with the cargo of potatoes. Joseph had gone to meet him at the barn.

The thought of dealing with Adam Kane's attentions at such a time added heaviness to the twelve hours she had been attending the children. So much had happened since Adam left. How could she explain what she had rediscovered in her heart for Joseph? There had not been time enough for her to sort it out herself. No opportunity to take it apart and understand why loving Joseph was as much a part of her as breathing.

When Fern and Margaret arrived in the sickroom for their shift she retreated quickly up the stairs to her room and closed the door behind her.

The tin tub behind the screen was full of cool water. Shedding her clothes she immersed herself in the soothing liquid, leaning her head back to wash her hair.

"Better." She sighed. "Better."

No sooner had that one grateful word come out of her mouth than a slight rapping sounded at the door.

"Kate, darlin', it's Adam!"

"Welcome home, Adam. Now go away. I'm washin'!"

To her horror the latch of the door clicked, and the hinges moaned as he entered.

He neared the screen and said softly, "I know you're wantin' to see me as much as I want to see you!"

"Get out!" She groped for a towel to cover herself. "Come one step farther, and my da'll have you strung up for the arrogant lout you are! And Father O'Bannon will denounce you to the entire parish as a . . ."

"But, Kate," he said, sounding unconvinced, "I've come to tell you we're to be wed."

Furious, Kate tossed a bar of soap over the screen. "This may be the way courtin's done in Dublin, but not in Ballynockanor! And I have no intention of bein' married to the likes of yourself, ever!"

"Of course it's sudden, girl, but I've set my heart on you alone . . ."

"Then you might as well know straight out I'm in love with Joseph Connor Burke!"

"The squire himself, is it? Been cuttin' in on my dance, has he?"

"Get out, Adam Kane! Now! Get out!"

At that Joseph's voice demanded angrily from the doorway, "Aye! Get out indeed!"

There was the sound of boots on the floor. One loud smack followed another and another as the two men grappled and tumbled into the corridor.

Kane was perhaps the heavier of the two; Joseph had the longer reach. By the time Kate wrapped herself in a dressing gown and rushed to the hallway, the squire's ear was bleeding and the steward's right eye was swollen.

Kane used his bulk to force Joseph back against the wall, then pummeled his opponent's midsection with a pair of hammer blows.

Joseph, doubled up after his breath went out with a whoosh, flailed wildly. One of his overhand rights caught Kane on the bridge of the nose, knocking the steward away.

Kane shook his head to clear it, then bore in again. Two steps from Joseph he unleashed a sweeping punch, intending to step into the blow and take Joseph's head off with the impact.

Instead, Joseph dodged aside at the last second and Kane's fist slammed into an ancient shield that hung on the wall. The wood and metal oval bounced free and clattered across the hall, making Kate skip out of the way. "Stop it!" she shrieked. "Stop it, I say."

The combatants gave no sign of having heard. Kane flung himself on Joseph, receiving another blow on the point of his chin before his rush carried both men to the floor.

The two brawlers, fingers around each other's throats, rolled from side to side on the narrow landing. After bouncing against the wall on one hand, they tumbled over into the balustrade on the other. The oak spindles broke with a splintering crack, dropping five feet of railing down to the stone floor of the Great Hall. With Joseph on top, the coiled figures hung half over the edge of a twenty-foot drop.

Kate screamed and grabbed Joseph by the collar to pull him back from the brink.

Choking, he sputtered, "What are you about, then, woman?"

Kane took advantage of the distraction to club Joseph on the side of the head. Maddened to the point of blindness, the squire released his hold on Kane's throat and folded his hands together. Rearing upright, Joseph brought his clasped hands down with all his force on Kane's forehead.

The steward's head bounced once on the floor, popped up feebly, then his eyes rolled back in his head.

The normally cheerful demeanor of Adam Kane was subdued as he met with Joseph in the small study. Both eyes were blackened, and his lower lip was swollen. He tested his jaw.

"A stout right you have, Squire. And by right you've won her fair and square."

Joseph, who ached all over from the fight, observed, "Her heart was mine before the fight, Kane. It was your presumption that got you beaten, not Kate's affections."

"Sure, sure, sure." Adam Kane waved away the comment. "And here I am trapped like everyone else in the townlands. My feet are just itchin' to go to America. Maybe a year or so. In the meantime you need a good steward, and I need the work. So what do you say? Why should we let a woman disrupt the harmony? Let bygones be bygones, Squire?"

"You'll not trouble Kate with this again?"

"I'll tell you my mind on the matter. If the truth be known, I've had half-an-eye on Fern, in case Kate didn't fancy leavin' Ireland. Fern's younger and . . . not that there's anythin' wrong with Kate Donovan, Squire, but with your permission I'd like to try my luck with Fern."

And so the steward remained on. He tipped his hat to Kate like a perfect gentleman. He returned to his duties and turned his attentions full on Fern, the housemaid with the wee brain of a chicken.

The gloom of twilight was merciful for the sick children in the ward. The pustules had swelled and begun to rupture. Those with the most severe cases, like Mary Elizabeth and David Clooney, looked as though they had been beaten with clubs. Blood vessels beneath the surface of the skin erupted until there was not an inch of flesh unbruised. Mary Elizabeth, whose hair fell out in bloody clumps on the pillow, was unrecognizable. The value of the Tinker's concoction remained unproven.

The summer sun remained up late. Kate worried that Da would come visit Mary Elizabeth while it was still light enough for him to clearly see the extensive damage of the child's once-angelic visage.

Kate stationed herself beside the window and prayed that daylight would vanish or that Tom Donovan would be detained until the darkest hour of the night.

How proud Da had been of Mary Elizabeth's beauty. With Kate scarred, Martin's leg shrunken and crippled after the fire, Brigit dead, and Kevin banished, Mary Elizabeth had remained the one bright star in the old man's life. He had held her high on his shoulders as he marched across the hills and called her his beauty, his sapphire princess! What would he say when he saw her like this?

"Come, night!" Kate pleaded.

The sun dipped lower toward the ring of the mountains to the northwest. But details of the world and the room and the battered body of Mary Elizabeth remained too vivid.

Da had taken the pledge against the drink when Kevin had hovered so near to death last spring. The man had not broken his vow of abstinence to this very day. But Kate knew Tom Donovan had a history of drinking himself blind when what he saw was too much for him to bear. The suffering of Mary Elizabeth was nearly too much for Kate. What would Da do? She trembled for him.

Eight days he had stayed away at Father O'Bannon's insistence. But after Aidan Clooney's death, Da would be separated from his youngest child no longer. He sent the note to Kate with the good priest. "Tell Mary Elizabeth I will come to town after the milking and the churning are finished this evening."

Kate delivered the message, but Mary Elizabeth, clinging to life by a thread, had given no sign that she understood.

Father O'Bannon declared he had instructed Tom to prepare himself for what he would see. But even the stoutest warning could not ready a heart for this. When told he would not recognize her, Da declared she was his own wee babe and even the most dreadful curse could not keep him from her side tonight.

"Merciful Christ, hold Da back until the darkness," Kate prayed.

As though Joseph sensed her need of company, he joined her by the window.

"He's comin', is he? Your da?" Joseph asked.

"He won't be kept back any longer."

"Father O'Bannon did his best. But Aidan dyin' has made everyone in the townlands mad with worry. The Tinker says we'll know soon enough if the cowpox has prevented the spread."

Kate put a hand wearily to her forehead. "How can any survive?"

"The young ones have a better chance . . ."

"And then to live forever with the scars. Never to be loved by a man . . ."

He searched her face, somehow knowing she spoke of her own injuries. "Kate . . ." She knew there was much he wanted to say to her, but not in this place or at this time. "He needs to see her. If only to let her go."

"Another good-bye will kill him. Ah, Joseph, if only night would beat him here. Soften the blow of it. She's always been his favorite. Not only his, but mine." She glanced across the room at the scab-encrusted form of the child. Every breath was a struggle. Each breath caused a tremor of agony to pass through the fragile body. Kate looked quickly away.

"He needs to come," Joseph said again.

"I would have him remember her . . . laughing on his shoulders." Her spirit broke, and she bowed her head.

"He will wish her free from sufferin'. Safe in the arms of Jesus, playin' at the feet of Mary."

Kate was unable to speak. Closing her eyes, she pictured Mary Elizabeth lively, whole, and perfect again.

"Aye." Kate breathed at last. "But still . . . Joseph . . . I pray for night to come conceal her agony. His heart will be crushed and this time not be mended. I'm sure of it."

The light refused to yield to blessed darkness.

It was still light at half past nine in the evening when Tom Donovan, a bunch of wildflowers in his hand, came quietly to the sick ward.

He hovered outside the door like a timid schoolboy. Doffing his hat, he forced cheerfulness on his face and called Mary Elizabeth's name.

The child did not answer. Da did not enter, hanging back until Kate came out to him.

Her glance was one of pity. The flowers. Da's face. Hopeful, frightened eyes. And night had not come at her request.

She embraced her father.

"I brought her these." The old man extended the bunch of blooms for Kate's approval.

"She's sleepin', Da." Kate attempted to deflect his determination to see the child. "Can you not come again tomorrow?"

"I won't stay long, Kate. I just . . . Father O'Bannon says it's bad. I have to . . . you see. I won't wake her. Just to kiss her on the brow."

Kate did not tell him there was no clear inch where Mary Elizabeth could be kissed. "Are you sure then, Da? You know I'm here with her night and day. She'd want you to wait till she's better."

Tom wagged his head. "I want to see her, Daughter."

Kate tucked her chin in defeat and stepped aside. Tom hesitated, then stiffened his back and stepped forward into the ward.

The room was the monochrome blue of twilight. The patients, still laid out in neat rows on the floor, were of human shape, but flecked with dark crusts the color of the mahogany bookshelves. Eyes were swollen nearly shut, lips and noses lost in the swelling. Most were hairless by now, scalps raw and bloody. Ears were without detail. Except for some variation in size, the children looked the same.

Tom Donovan stumbled forward into the center of the carnage. Lowering the flowers he looked from left to right and managed to ask, "Where is she?"

Kate touched his elbow and inclined her head to the tiniest figure against the wall.

Da exhaled with a groan and took one step toward her. For an instant Kate thought he would fall, but he pulled himself straight and snapped the bouquet upright.

"Mary Elizabeth?" his voice quavered. "It's Da."

The puffed slits of the girl's eyes opened fractionally. And there was the bright sapphire blue. One gleam of familiar color and life.

Kate warned, "She can't speak, Da. It's in her mouth and throat, you see."

The old man nodded, extended his gift, and sank to his knees at the child's side. "I brought you flowers, see? On the hill above St. Brigit's cross they're growin'. Ye've got to get well. You'll miss the best part of summer."

A faint moan escaped her lips.

Da, trembling visibly, continued, "Lovely things, ain't they?" He placed the offering on her pillow, fanning out the blossoms so she could see the colors. "No, my sapphire princess. Ah, your pretty eyes are speakin' to ol' Da. Mustn't talk. Ye mustn't say a word." At this his throat constricted with emotion.

Kate heard him gasp for breath, struggle to control himself. He reached out to touch Mary Elizabeth, but there was no place that would not have caused her agony. Instead, his palms hovered over her as if in blessing.

"Talk to her, Da," Kate encouraged. "Tell her about Tomeen." At the mention of the baby Mary Elizabeth's eyes blinked. A certain request for information. "Aye, Da! Tell her about Little Tom! Mary Elizabeth! He's stayin' at the place with Miss Susan."

Da swallowed hard and took over. "That he is. He squalls like a norther when he's hungry. Bawls like that bull calf, he does. And sure I am that you'll be wantin' to get well and come home . . ." He faltered. "And . . . come home . . . and . . . be there with him. He misses his aunt Mary Elizabeth!"

Da pivoted to look at Kate with pleading eyes. The flowers were a grotesque contrast to the appearance of the girl. What was left to say? Good-bye?

Kate leaned forward slightly and in an artificially light tone said, "Da's got to be goin' home now."

Mary Elizabeth coughed a protest.

"But . . . I'll be back," Da promised. "That I will. You'll be good. Do as Kate says. When she tells me you're fit, I'll carry you home on me shoulders!" He stood shakily and turned away, lest Mary Elizabeth see his tears.

Kate grasped his forearm "Go on now, Da," she said gently. "You know I'll take good care of her."

The old man, devastated, nodded once and left the room.

Mary Elizabeth's bright blue eyes traced his going.

Kate knelt beside her sister and began to sing a ditty Mary Elizabeth so often sang to Da when he needed cheering up:

'Tis a look of his eye
And a way he can sigh,
Makes Paddy a darlin' wherever he goes;
With a sugary brogue
Ye'd hear the rogue
Cheat the girls before their nose. . . .

∾17∾

Galway City had declined in importance as a port from the days when the Spanish traders favored its quays in the exchange of wine and wool. Most folk of the west attributed the fall in Galway's fortunes to the resistance offered by it to the Puritan army of Oliver Cromwell. To spite the defeated inhabitants the tyrant stabled his cavalry horses in the Church of St. Nicholas and closed the port to international commerce.

Nevertheless, Galway's harbor still remained home to the coastal traders and fishermen in their black-hulled boats known as *hookers*. The anchorage also served as a foul-weather refuge for ships rounding the west of Ireland and as a last port of call for transatlantic sailors bound for the New World.

"Hear ye, hear ye!" a ship's crier announced to the darkened wharfside streets. "All 'e havin' passage booked aboard the bark *Elizabeth and Sara*, three hundred tons burthen, destination Boston, present yourselves at quayside no later than six of the clock for sailin' with the tide. Hear ye! Hear ye!"

The shouting of the news and the clanging of the crier's bell receded toward the Long Walk and the inns located there. "Whew!" Ryan observed to Kenny as the pair stood in the shadows across from the Albatross. "We didn't get here none too soon."

The Albatross on Dock Road dated from the late 1500s. Beneath its plastered exterior it was a half-timbered structure built in the style favored by the Tudors. Though its original thatched roof had been replaced with slate, inside it was still a maze of crooked hallways, low ceilings, and half-flights of steps. Only three stories high in appearance, it contained five different levels of tavern, gaming rooms, lodgings, and kitchen—six if the damp, smelly cellar was counted.

"How we gonna get him to come out?" Ryan worried. "What if he don't oblige?"

"Shut yer gob and let me do the thinkin'," Kenny ordered. "I got a plan, see? Now I been in the kitchen, and there's just the cook. She's fat, greasy, and has a better beard than you—just your type."

Kenny easily fended off a wild swing of the other man's arm. Spreading his palm across Ryan's face, Kenny pushed his partner back against the wall of the alley. "Her name's Matilda. Go in there and sweet-talk her, see? Tell her you want to buy her a drink. She'll be eatin' outta your hand. Take her into the snug and get her a pint."

"Then what?"

"Just leave the rest to me."

"How'm I gonna get shed of her?"

Kenny smirked, the light shining out from the tavern windows gleaming on the teeth on either side of the gaping hole in the center of his smile. It made him look hideous. "You'll know," he said. "Just when you hear me hollerin', come up the stairs double-quick."

Ryan grumbled and snorted but did as he was instructed. Within five minutes of entering the kitchen he had convinced Matilda that he could not live without her better acquaintance. The two were soon ensconced in the dim confines of the snug, deep in draughts of black beer. The kitchen was deserted.

Kenny entered through the rear doorway. The cook fire was banked, and there were still plenty of hot coals. Under his arm was a keg of whale oil. The wooden floor of the kitchen was soon awash in the highly flammable liquid, especially the piles of straw that Kenny distributed in every corner.

Retreating to the far end of the room and surveying his work, Kenny nodded with satisfaction and scraped a match on the wall. Very deliberately he bent over the nearest heap of hay and set it alight.

The blaze was soon roaring and licking the low ceiling, but Kenny waited until there was no possibility of extinguishing the flames before he gave the alarm. "Fire!" he bellowed. "Fire! Get out while you can!" He ran through the tavern shouting the same thing. The orange glare and volumes of black smoke that erupted from the kitchen rendered any other proof unnecessary.

The patrons of the pub scattered in confusion, some shouting for hoses and pumps, others screaming that their belongings were upstairs and had to be saved. The clamor suited Kenny perfectly. "Ryan!" he shouted. "Now's the time!"

The two cutthroats collided on the stairs, knocking a sailing-ship captain out of the way. Kenny threw a traveling linen merchant down the steps when he and his portmanteau blocked the flight.

"Where is his room?" Ryan said, puffing.

"Top floor," Kenny grunted in return. "Lively now. We're almost there."

Both men were still crying, "Fire!" as loudly as they could when they reached the landing at the top of the stairs. Daly's room was the only one opening onto the confined space.

"Could he have got past us already?" Ryan wondered. "Or out the window?"

"Neither," Kenny growled. "This is the only way down and the window's too small. I checked."

"Then where is he?"

At that moment the door of the schoolteacher's room opened, and he emerged in his nightshirt. Spotting the two thugs, he spun around and darted back inside, clicking the bolt behind him.

"Won't do," Kenny announced. "Can't take a chance on him gettin' down to some other window after we've gone. Stand aside." With one blow of his boot, Kenny shattered the door, the bolt, and the frame.

There was a brief struggle and much yelling for help, but the air around the Albatross was full of frenzied appeals. The schoolmaster was no match for the grip of Kenny's clenched right fist on his throat, let alone the table leg with which Ryan struck him from behind.

Kenny dusted off his hands, coughed at the fumes with which the room was already filling, and said, "Horrible accident, this. Time to go."

The Albatross burned completely to the ground. It was far from being the first cheap inn at the Galway City dockside to suffer a conflagration, so its destruction caused little comment. Fires were commonplace in the older buildings, and besides, only one life was lost, and that an unknown.

Tom Donovan did not return home that night. The next afternoon Martin found his da in Joe Watty's tavern. A half-empty bottle of whiskey was on the bar in front of him. He had been drinking alone since the tavern opened and was as drunk as he had ever been.

Martin cast an accusing look at Joe Watty who was drying pint glasses. Watty knew Tom Donovan had taken the pledge. Why then did he sell him the bottle?

"Sure, and he'll not be denied." The barkeeper shrugged, turning away.

Martin put a hand on Da's arm. "Come home, will you, Da?"

Tom considered his son through blurred vision. "She's dead then?"

The question was like a slap to Martin's face. It explained everything. Da had gone to see Mary Elizabeth and had ended the visit here. "She is not."

The man wagged his head as if he did not believe it. "Aye. She's dead. I laid her in the cold grave meself. Brigit, me own dear daughter."

Joe Watty gave Martin a look that said Da had been going on like this for some time.

"It's the drink, Da. You know you can't think clearly when you've been drinkin'."

Da downed another shot. His words ran together. "And why should a man wish to think clearly when the world is so confused?"

Martin pleaded gently, "Come home. It'll make sense if you sleep it off. The baby is home, Da. Sweet Tomeen. He's lookin' for his Grand, sure. I need your help with the milkin'. Miss Susan's finally come down with the cowpox and is unwell . . ."

Da's eyes widened with some terrible vision. He poured more of the drink and put the rim of the glass to his lips as though it were medicine, and he would die without it.

"Smallpox . . . Susan?"

"No, Da. The vaccination has taken hold, you see. She's sick, aye, but it's the lesser illness."

"Not what Mary Elizabeth has. For who could live with that? Aidan Clooney never more will play the flute."

"No, Da. Everyone in the townlands is feelin' poorly. But they're ill from the cure. It's the tenth day, and they've come ill from Daisy's cowpox, praise be to Christ. But they'll be safe from the plague, the Tinker says."

"The Tinker . . . Ah, I was too easy on Mary Elizabeth, you see. If I'd made her go to milk the cows she would have long ago been safe from this . . . this angel of death. But I didn't. I'm to blame. Killed her with kindness, I have. She was so young, and I never made her turn a hand to workin' like the rest of us."

"Kate's with her, Da. Now, please. Give up the bottle and come home."

"Did you see her, boy? There's no bit of her left but the blue of her eyes. Death has destroyed my little Mary Elizabeth while she lives. The sufferin'! Christ on the cross it is, Martin! Innocence crucified! What home have I to go to with my children gone . . ."

"Not all, Da. I'm still . . ."

"Gone or crippled," Tom finished, his words cutting deep into Martin.

At that comment Joe Watty turned and sternly remarked, "He won't listen to reason, Martin. He broke into the tavern last night. He was here and drunk when I came in this mornin'. The man is out of his mind with grief. They say your wee sister is dyin' for certain, if she's not flown away already."

"Dyin'." Martin said the word flatly and exhaled. "Mary Elizabeth? What should I do, Mister Watty?"

"Go fetch Father O'Bannon. He'll no doubt be at the manor house. Fetch him back here, lad, for your da is in a bad way. Father O'Bannon will talk some sense into him."

Martin nodded solemnly. "That I will, Mister Watty." Then to Da he added, "Do you hear me, Da? I'm goin' for His Honor, Father O'Bannon. He'll know what to do with you. You've broke your pledge, and I'm bringin' Father O'Bannon here to deal with you."

The sun outside the pub was too bright. Martin's head throbbed as he limped the mile toward the turning in the lane to Burke Hall. The street was oddly deserted and still. Every living person in the townlands was too weak and ill from the cure or perhaps too afraid to venture out.

The eerie loneliness of it made him quicken his pace. Suppose it was not the cure that had sent everyone to his bed? Suppose they were in the early stages of the pestilence and doomed? Suppose Martin was the only one who would be left?

At the gate of the manor house he glanced toward the barricade a quarter mile farther on where the British sentries lounged on the stone wall and smoked as they waited for the Irish within the boundary to die. Perhaps they were hoping someone would be foolish enough to challenge the barricade. Did they long for the opportunity to shoot and prove their worth as guards? Martin stopped in the road and glared at them. Unreasonably perhaps, he was furious at these languid jailors. He blamed them for what had come upon his people and his village.

"But we won't all die," Martin said aloud. "There'll always be some of us left for you to bully."

Returning to his purpose he ran toward the house. Calling for Father O'Bannon, he rounded the corner of the west wing and smacked into Margaret who was leading Mad Molly away. Both women were weeping.

"What is it?" Martin demanded.

"Why does it go on and on?" Margaret asked wearily. "Be done with it, I say!"

"Is it Mary Elizabeth?"

Mad Molly raised her hands to heaven. "My wee girl. My darlin' girl!"

Martin begged, "She's dead then?"

Margaret sobbed and put her apron to her cheek. "The poor thing. And what more will Missus Clooney have to endure?"

"Who is it has died then?" Martin asked anxiously. "Say it plainly!"

Margaret sniffed. "David Clooney himself. Poor boy. He's followed his father's soul not but an hour ago."

Martin rocked back on his heels. How could he be grateful when his best friend had just died? "And my sister?" he queried as fear drained the color from his cheeks.

Molly replied, remarkably lucid, "She is holdin' on, Martin. A fighter, she is."

"Where's Father O'Bannon?"

Margaret inclined her head up the slope toward the far field and the solitary oak tree. "They're buryin' that poor boy. The two of 'em are up there. Joseph and Father O'Bannon. And by the time this is finished we'll be buildin' a chapel beside the old oak to say prayers for the dead. If any are left to pray."

"I need his honor to help me talk sense to my da. Da's at the pub, you see. The drink has him . . ."

"There's more important things at hand," Margaret chided. "Did you hear what I said? David Clooney has died. Now get home with you, Martin. Tend your dairy. This is no place for a lively young boy."

Defeated, Martin hung his head in despair. The two women left him at the side of the house. Leaning heavily against the rough stone wall, he allowed himself to raise his eyes to where the grave was being dug. Earth splashed up beside the blanket-wrapped mound that had been David Clooney. David was dead, yet Martin felt nothing but relief. Mary Elizabeth was alive and fighting! Martin would take that news back to Da. He would lead his father home with hope.

Turning away from the scene Martin walked slowly back toward the gate and the main highway. He had covered no more than fifty paces of the road toward town when a disturbance behind him made the boy turn around.

The British soldiers were no longer slouching about in postures of bored indifference. They were up and posed, their muskets unslung. Several of them were shouting.

"Clear off, you daft bugger," one cried. "Get away with you."

The cause of the uproar was not easily seen. From the stances adopted by the sentries, whoever they were speaking to was hidden in the shadows of a bank of willows. A slurred voice from the cover of the willow branches challenged, "Clear off, yourselves, y'great herd of redcoated sheep. I'm goin' to see my daughter, and there's an end. So give me the road, or you'll suffer for it."

It was Da. He stepped from the shade into the light and shook his fist at the sentinels.

Somehow he had followed Martin from the pub and out the highway to the manor, but had lost the turning and was at dagger-points with the guards.

"No, Da," Martin shouted, starting to run. "Come back, it's this way."

It was not so serious, Martin told himself. The soldiers could hear that Da was drunk. Some of them were even laughing.

That was before Tom Donovan scooped up a handful of rocks and began pitching them at the guards. "Chase you off like a pack of dogs," he bellowed, shying a stone that made the English captain duck as it glanced off his bonnet.

Martin ran harder, stumbling on his bad leg. "I warn you," he heard the officer say, "come no closer. We have orders to shoot."

"Give it up," Da roared. "Whose orders? Queen's orders, that's what. Well, take this back to Queen Vic!" He slung the handful of stones at the British. The rocks missed, clattering against the stone fence, but Da was himself lumbering forward like the chained form of an elderly dancing bear.

"Sergeant," Martin heard the captain order, "I'll have one round over his head!"

"No!" Martin exclaimed again. "It's my da! He's drunk, y'see. I've come to fetch him home."

Martin's struggle to stop the soldiers, to warn his da, to reach his father and drag him back possessed the quality of nightmares. Martin's words seemed to fly no farther than his breath; no one heard him. He was running through molasses; no matter how hard he tried he was not closing the gap fast enough.

A musket roared, the crack reverberating past Martin to echo off a hillside and return again. A single cloud of blue haze drifted up between Da and the soldiers, like a spectral form rising into the heavens.

Still Da would not stop his advance. "My daughter," he announced again loudly. "Goin' to see my daughter." He was only a score of feet from the guards, rising up in wrath to throw another handful of stones.

There were only yards left for Martin to cover. He would grab his father from behind, turn him around, force him to retreat. He would knock him down if need be. He would . . .

"On my command," the captain barked. "Ready! Aim! Fire!"

Kate heard the rattle of gunfire and looked out the window to see who was hunting. Molly Fahey's cries drifted up. *She's weeping for David Clooney*, Kate thought.

Mary Elizabeth opened her eyes and spoke clearly for the first time in days. "Da was just here."

Kate went to her side. "Aye. You remember then? He came to visit last night."

"No," Mary Elizabeth insisted. "Just now, sister. Did you not see him?"

"Last night. Sure, and he was here, at twilight," Kate explained, pleased Mary Elizabeth was enough better to argue.

"No. Just now. He said the water of the river is beautiful gold and wide. He said I shouldn't cross over yet, but he'll go ahead and wait for me with Mother."

Kate's smile faded and foreboding filled her. "Only a dream."

"Not a dream! Da kissed me good-bye. Didn't you see him? Sixteen days, he told me, it will be spent. But I mustn't cross the river for a very long time. What did he mean?"

Outside in the yard the commotion grew louder, then retreated toward the main road. Kate resisted the urge to go to the window. "You were dreamin', darlin'," Kate replied.

Alice Clooney, who had hovered two days on the verge of death, said softly, "Your da was just here, Mary Elizabeth."

Mary Elizabeth replied, "I know." Then to Kate, "You see?"

Across the room Michael Clooney spoke clearly, "Tom Donovan said I should be a good lad and not break Mother's heart."

Alice Clooney added, "He says he's goin' to see my da, and I mustn't give up."

Kate rose from her knees, and as each child repeated some word spoken by Tom Donovan, she went to the window, knowing.

Moments passed before she saw the crowd bearing the body of her father toward the house on a wooden plank. She could not make out the features, but she had no doubt about the identity. Martin, limping at the side of the procession, clutched Da's hand. The boy was crying for help as Molly wrung her hands and fell to her knees. Joseph, Fern, and Old Flynn bounded out of the house and sprinted up the lane.

With the certainty that her father was dead, Kate felt oddly at peace. The scene of panic on the lane had a dreamlike quality, as though she were watching the world from the high vantage point beside St. Brigit's cross.

"Did he say anything else, Mary Elizabeth?" Kate asked.

"Aye. He says it's lovely, and I should never be afraid."

"I'm certain he's right," Kate replied in a whisper.

Morning came. Mad Molly, a streak of soot on her chin and tears on her cheeks, stoked the fire in the kitchen and put the kettle on to boil.

Tom Donovan was laid out in the parlor of the manor house, his coffin supported by two chairs and surrounded by candles. Kate and Martin sat the vigil at the head and the foot.

"There'll not be a proper wake," Molly said to no one as she set the teacup on the empty table. "Annie Rose can't come to keen. Nay! She's off singin' in the choir at Mullins Path with Emily, Edward, Peter, Sean, and the other Martin. Ah, well. God bless the queen. But they'll never let us out of Ireland alive after this. They shot Tom, didn't they? Tom was a good man when he was sober, make no mistake."

The old woman tapped her foot impatiently. The water was too slow to boil. Lifting the kettle she peered in at the liquid, then, with a sigh, replaced it on the crane.

"What's your hurry, Molly?" she asked herself. "None a'tall. It's comin'. It's comin'. What's hidden shall be known, and every eye shall see it by and by."

Peering up into the rafters she spied a cobweb and remarked, "Purified by fire . . . Aye. This house could use a good cleanin'. In the cupboards and in the walls. Betrayal and greed. Merrow Marlowe poisoned the father of wee Joseph Connor Burke for it. A long time ago it was. Too much grief and murder . . ."

She spied her reflection in a polished serving tray. "And just when Joseph was makin' it a happy home again! Well, Molly, it'll never be a joyous place after this. Now there's smallpox in the library and poor Tom lyin' stiff as a board and riddled with English lead in the parlor . . . Would he like a cuppa tay? Nay, Molly! Nay, ye old fool! It'll just run out the holes! Like melted lead it'll run out. There's a riddle for the riddled man."

She pondered her words and swept the floor. "When I think of the things I say, sometimes I envy the dumb!"

The water boiled. Molly fixed her tea and gingerly sipped the steaming brew. "That'll teach Tom Donovan to drink. Sure, and he's sober as a Puritan now."

PART III

Oh! the Erne shall run red
With redundance of blood,
The earth shall rock beneath our tread,
And flames wrap hill and wood,
And gun-peal and slogan cry
Wake many a glen serene,
Ere you shall fade, ere you shall die,
My own Rosaleen!
The Judgement Hour must first be nigh
Ere you can fade, ere you can die,
My dark Rosaleen.

—James Clarence Mangan
Translated from the Gaelic

❧18❧

It was raining. Martin raised his face to the clouds and let the plump drops conceal his tears. There were only four besides Martin at Da's graveside: Father O'Bannon, Kate, Joseph, Little Tom.

Martin considered how many of the family had been lost in the span of a year. If Mary Elizabeth flew away as well, would she be buried next to Da or beneath the oak tree beside the Clooneys?

All that could be said about Tom Donovan had been said. Father O'Bannon had carefully stepped around the fact that this final act in the tragedy need not have taken place.

Da had died because he was drunk and a fool, Martin thought. He was angry at his father for adding yet another layer of grief to already aching hearts.

Father O'Bannon put a hand on Martin's shoulder in a final charge to the living. "You are head of the Ballynockanor Donovans now. Live well in the sight of God and man, Martin. Live by the great virtues of wisdom. Aye. Remember livin' well is nothin' other than to love God with all your heart, all your soul, and all your efforts. Keep your love whole and uncorrupted; this is temperance. Let no misfortune disturb you; this is fortitude. Obey only Christ in word and deed; this is justice. Be careful in discernin' things, and don't be surprised by deceit or trickery; this is prudence."

Martin gazed down at the rain drumming hollowly on the top of the pine coffin. It came to him that if he was the head of the Donovan clan of Ballynockanor things were in a desperate state indeed. He wanted to say he would do a better job of it than Da had done. Instead he simply said, "I'll try."

So it was over with. There were cows to milk, butter to churn, and cheese to be made.

Joseph took Martin's hand. "I'll send Adam Kane out to help with the dairy for a while till Mary Elizabeth is well and she and Kate can come home again."

Martin could not bring himself to look Joseph in the eye. He did not believe Mary Elizabeth would ever come home. He and Kate would manage the dairy fine when Kate returned. It had always been the two of them doing most of the work anyway. "I thank you for it."

Kate, holding the baby, retreated to the carriage as Joseph and Martin walked slowly beneath the shelter of the dripping eves of St. John's church.

Joseph said, "This is not the time, I know. When things settle a bit I'll be wantin' a word with you as head of the Donovan house. It's about askin' permission formally to court your sister."

Martin stopped in his tracks. "You can't mean Kate?"

"That I do."

"Does she know about it?"

"That she does."

"And what does she say on the matter?"

"She's for it. That is, if the head of the house gives his assent."

St. Patrick's Cathedral, on Patrick Street just south of the center of Dublin, was first consecrated in the year 1192. Despite its early Catholic origins, and its location across the Irish Sea, the hallowed place was not safe when King Henry the Eighth decided to make himself head of the English church. His decree applied everywhere English writ ran, which included Ireland. Heedless of its dedication to the Irish patron saint, after the sixteenth century St. Patrick's belonged to the Protestant Church of Ireland.

So it was not a cause for comment that Burtenshaw Suggins walked into the cathedral late on a sunny summer afternoon. The roses were blooming on the grounds, and many officials of the British government were taking their ease there. Suggins pretended to be absorbed in the exterior stonework before wandering inside.

Jonathan Swift, dean of St Patrick's during the early 1700s and author of *Gulliver's Travels,* was buried inside the church. Suggins looked around the almost-deserted interior before strolling over to read Swift's epitaph. Swift, an unusual and outspoken satirical critic of British treatment of the Irish, had penned his own commemoration:

> *He is laid where bitter indignation can no longer lacerate his heart. Go, traveler, imitate if you can one who was, to the best of his powers, a defender of liberty.*

On this occasion, Suggins paid no attention to the inscription, if indeed he ever had before. The official was merely waiting for an elderly verger to disappear behind a column so that Suggins's next movement would be unobserved.

Halfway down a darkened aisle was a medieval chapel. A stone grating separated it from the body of the cathedral proper and there was a door, but Suggins did not enter the enclosure. Instead he leaned nearer to the grating and whispered, "Are you there?"

"Indeed, my lord," returned Garrison O'Toole. "The key you supplied fit the outside door."

"We have heard of the situation in the Burke townlands," Suggins said in a hoarse, breathy whisper. "Your scheme succeeded perfectly. Not only has it confined the Burke and his zealots, but the effect elsewhere has been superb. The west country is afraid of the mass meetings and suspicious of strangers who pass through. You have cleverly squelched the rebellion west of the Shannon."

"Thank you," O'Toole responded. "There is one lamentable fact, however."

"What?" wheezed Suggins.

"It appears that Joseph Burke himself did not fall to the disease. Also, we suspect that our agent in Burke's home may have hinted about what he knew or suspected."

"What?" demanded Suggins again, his apprehension increasing the volume of his whisper to a strangled shout. The footsteps of the verger were heard echoing toward the source of the disturbance. "Quickly, man," Suggins inquired, "what's to be done?"

"Remain calm, my lord," O'Toole said. "The traitorous agent has been dealt with. It has not been possible for the Burke to communicate with anyone outside the barrier these past weeks. We are continuin' to intercept the mail. As soon as the quarantine comes down, I have reliable men who will see to the Burke. And we have another agent on the scene."

"But what about O'Connell himself?" Suggins said.

A shaft of bright sunlight stabbed the gloomy interior as O'Toole slipped outside once more. To the ears of Suggins came the final reply, "All in good time, my lord. You may rely on me."

And so the period of dreadful suffering came to an end. From the hour of Tom Donovan's violent death and his appearance to the children in the sickroom, the recovery of the afflicted was rapid and astounding. No further cases of the illness occurred.

It was considered a miracle that only three had died of the pestilence. These dead, Aidan Clooney, his boy David, as well as young Alan O'Rourke, were properly waked in the gardens of the manor house and within view of the oak where they rested. Joseph provided the vittles and refreshments.

These deaths were considered tragic but a matter of the natural order of life. The loss was accepted by friends and family with a sorrow untainted by bitterness. Those who had died had only passed from this life to another, and there was unwavering assurance of that fact among the mourners.

Squire Joseph rallied the men and provided the materials to build a new house for Mrs. Clooney. The widow, with so many practical matters to consider, bore her tragedy with dignity. With eleven youngsters remaining, half of whom were old enough to manage the farm, she expressed her gratitude that the Clooney name would not die out. Squire Joseph promised they would not be left destitute and mentioned, Had not Aidan left his mark on the world? If children were a sign of treasure, then Aidan Clooney left behind an enormous legacy.

On Sunday at St. John's the whole parish gathered as Father O'Bannon declared a special mass of thanksgiving for the reprieve God had granted to the citizens of Ballynockanor. On behalf of the three smallpox victims he gave a gentle homily from the book of Wisdom, chapter three.

"We offer tribute to our fallen . . . ," he began.

Mad Molly's head bobbed eagerly. "Tribute! Aye! The very thing!"

The priest, looking slightly worried that Molly's commentary should begin so early in the proceedings, continued, "But the souls of the just are in the hand of God, and no torment shall touch them. They seemed to be dead, and their passin' away was thought an affliction and their goin' away from us, utter destruction. But they are at peace. Chastised a little, they shall be greatly blessed, because God has tried them and found them worthy of Himself. As gold in the furnace He proved them . . ."

At these words Molly stood in the congregation and shouted, "Glory be! Gold in the furnace! That they are! Ye'll see! That ye will!"

Molly's daughter clamped a hand over the old woman's mouth and forced her to sit.

Father O'Bannon cleared his throat loudly. ". . . As sacrificial offerin's He took them to Himself. In the time of visitation they shall shine, and shall dart about as sparks. . . ."

There was no holding Molly. At this she shrugged off the firm grip of her daughter, stood, and cried, "Aye, Your Honor! Pay attention! That's just as it shall be! Little sparks and offerin's!"

Father O'Bannon looked up from the book with a sigh. "Molly darlin', if you don't mind. You're cheerin' the readin' of God's Word like it's a horse race from Westport to Castletown."

"And so it is, Your Honor! In the shadow of the devil's mother! Ride hard! Westport to Castletown! Sure, and he'll have to ride fast as Brian Boru! Where's the Tinker? Where's Dermott O'Neill?"

"Hush now, or I'll have you taken out."

"And that's what they want! Take Joseph out feetfirst like poor Tom Donovan! It's a tribute they're wantin' for themselves! But there's a million on the road to Tara!"

Father O'Bannon put a hand on his hip and scowled at Molly's daughter as an unspoken command that the woman was to be removed out to have a bit of a chat with the headstones.

Molly knew the look. Chastised, she hung her head like a petulant child, fell silent, and went out quietly.

Acceptance of a death caused by illness was one thing. The shooting of Tom Donovan at the barricade was something else again.

"Murder, it was," said Joe Watty to Old Flynn and a group of a dozen men at Tom's wake. "Pure and simple. The murderin' English could see plainly he'd had a wee drop. And they shot him dead just the same!"

Old Flynn snatched off his hat and held it to his breast. "A fine way to die, it was. Tom Donovan would be a proud man if he were alive to see how he died."

"Sure," said O'Flaherty. "Like the men of '98 it was."

Flynn protested, "Like '98 is it? They didn't dip him in tar or chop off his head. I saw the body plainly, and he was shot full of holes, but he looked quite happy for a dead man."

The wake was held at the Donovan cottage a full twenty-eight days after the first outbreak of the plague. Tom had been buried long before, of course, but his send-off had to be put aside until the people of the townlands were no longer afraid to gather together. In two days the quarantine would be lifted. It was then that Tom's friends would dare the British soldiers to ride through Ballynockanor and face the villagers who gathered tonight.

"And I'll have a little somethin' for the assassins if they come by here!" O'Brien held up his fist. Never mind that O'Brien was blind. He would be relying on Watty to direct him to the fray.

O'Flaherty, owner of the pub in Ballynockanor, hooked an arm around Martin's shoulder as the boy passed. His breath thick with whiskey and tobacco, O'Flaherty said, "Along with a bit of treason against England which your da would have approved, we're plottin' the downfall of them as murdered himself."

Watty sighed. "Ah, that Tom could have been here to plot with us the revenge against his murderers."

Martin had said little since the day his father died. Tonight friends and neighbors crowded the cottage to honor his da. And here was the truth of it: Martin resented the manly backslapping and good-manning of those who sought to draw him in and pull details from him.

"Here's to brave Tom Donovan!" cried O'Brien. "As brave as one of the men of '98! A true man of Erin! Courageous in the face of the enemy!"

"Death to the English!" Martin said sullenly.

This sentiment from the son brought a loud cheer.

And Martin meant it too. The English had sent away Kevin, dishonored Brigit, and broken her heart. And now Da. Martin thought each night that if he were grown he'd join the Ribbonmen, and there would not be a Crown agent or soldier of the queen left standing in the west.

But what was the truth? Martin had confessed to Father O'Bannon that he feared Da may have intentionally charged the soldiers at the barricade. Not an act of bravery as those in this crowded room now claimed, but the act of a man weary of living.

This fear shadowed Martin. It was a burden equally as heavy as grief. The boy did not want to talk about it. Nor did he want to think about what might happen if Da's well-meaning friends took it upon themselves to avenge Da's death.

"Did you hear, boy?" asked Watty, slurring his words. "An eye for an eye."

O'Rourke added, "A tooth for a tooth."

Martin heard Father O'Bannon's voice behind him. "Here's a point to remember. Sure, and the English can put out more Irish eyes and pull more Irish teeth than we ever can of their's. They'd have the Irish blind and toothless, one and all, if we're not careful. Remember their motto: Ireland without the Irish."

This sentiment sobered the celebratory atmosphere that infused the men of Ballynockanor when they spoke of killing English soldiers. "Sure, Your Honor, can't you let a man dream a bit of blood and glory?" asked Watty. "Their blood. Our glory."

"Tint your dreams with common horse sense," cautioned the priest. "The devils who shot down Martin's da would like nothin' better than to have each of us upon a gallows. They're out there now at their barricades. You can see their weapons by the light of the campfires. Hold your tongues and forsake the drink. 'Twas that which killed Tom as surely as a British bullet. I've done enough buryin' in this parish for one month. Now! The meetin' at Tara's comin'. On the same hill where our ancient Irish kings were crowned, Squire Joseph says a million men will march with O'Connell for Repeal. A million Irishmen, Catholic and Protestant, united and peacefully gathered in one place? That'll kill the English with fright."

Watty raised his glass. "Then here's to killin' rats." He drank deeply, and the others followed. "And here's to our own Irish kings upon the Hill of Tara!"

The last of the quarantined children had been released. Miss Susan and Tomeen were back at the manor house, while Kate had gathered Martin and Mary Elizabeth and returned home.

Joseph sat in the small study. His head was cradled in his hands, and he stared out the window at the waving green boughs of high summer without seeing it at all.

Two days before the partition had been lifted, Joseph received a peremptory letter from the trustees of the National School, informing him that in as much as he had not appeared before the hearing, the fine was now due and payable. He was also forbidden to reopen the school.

The communication, which would have roused Joseph's angry indignation before the pox, now provoked only a shrug. It did not matter; particularly, not next to the back rent demand.

There was a tap at his door, and Father O'Bannon appeared. "Yes, Father?" Joseph said, shaking off the brown mood into which he had fallen and rising from his chair. "Was there something you wanted?"

"Now, that was *my* intended question," the priest said. "Dermott O'Neill informed me you wanted to see me."

Joseph shook his head. "My wits are tangled about many things," he said, "but I believe no one has seen the Tinker these many days past. What did he say I wanted?"

"Ah, there's the nub," the priest said, sitting down in an oak armchair. "As I recollect his exact words, he said you 'needed' to see me."

"I gave no such order," Joseph replied, his eye falling on the letter from the rent collectors. "Perhaps he knows my mind better than I do myself," he admitted. "I must go see that blackhearted Colonel Mahon about takin' over part of the Burke lands. That thought alone troubles me enough."

"We'll pray that another solution presents itself, then," offered Father O'Bannon in a matter-of-fact tone. "Now about the Repeal business."

Joseph was shocked. After the plague and the deaths and the back taxes, how could the priest even think for one instant that Joseph would still be involved in something not close to home? "I imagine you're wantin' my suggestion for another lieutenant to raise the west, since I have failed," he ventured.

"And why would I want that?" O'Bannon retorted. "Are you not the man chosen by Daniel O'Connell himself for the work?"

"Daniel," Joseph repeated slowly. "He has not pressured me, but I know I have disappointed him. He'll be better off without me."

"Very likely, from the way you sound," said Father O'Bannon sternly. "But would you? Oh, Joseph, what did I warn you of? Trials and temptations and at the last, despair. Will you let the Evil One have the victory because you say, 'Poor me. All my work is worthless'? I tell you, now more than ever is the time to get fire in your belly and steel in your backbone!"

Joseph was surprised at the priest's vehemence. "And go on as before?" he inquired.

"No! You must go forward with twice as much energy, twice as much determination. The sickness, the back taxes, even the school closure, are part of a wicked plan. If you give in to despair, you are agreein' to a lie: that He that is in you is not greater than he who is in the world."

Joseph crushed the back tax letter in his fist and thought of Tom Donovan's children, whose father was stolen from them. He thought of lives cut short. He felt his indignation rising.

"And another thing," O'Bannon continued. "The more intensity you devote to justice for Ireland, the more mercy you will see here at home. Doin' what is right, even when it costs you dearly in the small coin of your life, is always repaid in golden blessin's."

A shock of wild hair popped around the corner of the doorway. "Golden *tribute*, Father," Molly Fahey corrected. "The Burke always takes the lead here in the west." She patted the paneling of the study and nodded vigorously. "Even the walls bear tribute to the Burke of Connaught." Then recollecting why she had climbed the stairs to the study in the first place, she inquired, "Cook wants to know if His Honor will be wantin' milk with his tay?"

It was the same table at the Green Bough Coaching Inn in Castletown and the same cast of players as had assembled back in the spring. But instead of a scowl, Colonel Mahon wore a satisfied smirk. Squireen O'Shea looked as nervous and skittish as ever.

"Well, Burke" Mahon chuckled as Joseph arrived. "Seen the light at last, have you? Looking for a better class of friends than bog-trotters and rabble-rousers? I said to O'Shea here, 'He'll come around to our way of thinking.' Then I heard you wanted to see me and knew I was right."

Pulling up a chair for himself, Joseph sat down across from the other landlords. "You would lose that bet, Colonel," he said. "What I have for you is a business proposition."

"And what could the leader of Galway's rebels have that I might be interested in?"

Joseph shrugged. "Perhaps I was wrong then." Moving his chair so that his back was to Mahon, Joseph addressed O'Shea. "O'Shea," he said, "I am minded to sublet some of my property. Now I wonder . . ."

"Whoa!" Mahon demanded, scooting his chair in turn so that he crowded in on O'Shea. "What's this? I was the first to make an offer on some Burke lands. You should be speaking to me."

"I thought you weren't interested."

"I never said that. What do you have in mind?"

Briefly Joseph outlined the fair and reasonable terms of the agreement, then said, "It will apply to all property adjoinin' yours lyin' east of the Allintober road."

"No, that's no good. I will have Ballynockanor or none. There's good grazing in that valley for my cattle."

Without spelling out the crux of the problem, this was exactly what Joseph feared. If Mahon got hold of Ballynockanor, he both could and would turn out the crofters, and make the farms into pasture. It was a complete dilemma: to save some of the Burke inheritance, Joseph must give up some. But to save it at such a cost—the tossing and eviction of his friends and neighbors, including the Donovans—made such a victory hollow at best.

"Mister O'Shea," Joseph implored, "what about you?"

"I might be able . . . ," the squireen began. A fierce glare from Mahon stopped him. "That is, no, I . . . perhaps some piece, after Colonel Mahon, of course."

Mahon was smirking again. The colonel sensed that Joseph was without options, and he was gloating. More than anything else Joseph wanted to take the satchel full of lease papers and stuff them down Mahon's throat. He checked himself. "Mahon," he said, "I have lost my father-in-law and other friends, good people all. If there was another course you would see no more of me than the back of me goin' out of your sight. But I know this about you: the one thing darker in your soul than your arrogance is your greed. As it is I have until October to satisfy the arrears so I reserve the right to cancel the deal until then. Fair?"

Mahon waved his hand airily. "Never know who your real friends are till you get in trouble. Seems unmannerly to spurn them, then beg their help, eh, O'Shea?"

Joseph stood, knocking over his chair in fierceness. "Colonel, I don't have to like you to deal with you, and if there is any other way I won't deal with you. Despite how you and others of your kind feel about it," he said, stretching upward till he towered over both seated men, "despite what you have done to stop it, Repeal is goin' forward. The back rents are not due until October. October is the climax of the Repeal campaign. It may well be that after October I won't need either of you or your money. In that case, the bargain is off."

Joseph gave instructions for the signing of the documents and their delivery to his solicitor's office. O'Shea's fingers were twitching nervously, as they always did when he contemplated money. Mahon was more stoic, but nevertheless, Joseph noted that the colonel fully understood the advantages he would gain.

"There is one more thing," Joseph added after one step toward the door. "Neither of you has any time to be muckin' about in politics. You tell your master, whoever he is, that he has gone too far. You will not allow your neck to be substituted for his in a noose."

It was a shot in the dark, but from Mahon's reddening glare and O'Shea's fearful gulps, Joseph knew it had struck home, at least to a degree. It was the only comfort in a bitter draught.

Father O'Bannon was in the Church of St. John the Evangelist. The good priest was kneeling before a row of lighted candles at the feet of Jesus, lost in his devotions. Joseph likewise knelt and prayed so as not to interrupt.

"And have you been dancin' with the devil?" the priest said, approaching Joseph and sitting next to him on the rude bench. "Meanin' Colonel Mahon, of course."

"That I have, Father," Joseph acknowledged. "It is well that we had our discussion first. If it is a mark of respect from the enemy to be dosed with things to bring on despair, I swear I have swallowed a bucketful this day." Joseph explained the difficulty, beginning with Mahon's insistence that the sublease agreement include Ballynockanor.

"And he'll turn the people out, sure," the priest admitted.

"It is such a snarl," Joseph said. "All I can think to do is pray that another option presents itself before October."

O'Bannon said gently, "We think of prayer as a last resort, rather than comin' to it in the first place. But then, our lovin' Father knows that weakness about us, just as He understands the rest."

"I have thought of one more possibility," Joseph confessed. "I can sell the manor house. If Mahon ends up with Ballynockanor, I can raise enough money to at least resettle the people on other property."

Looking Joseph up and down, O'Bannon said approvingly, "You are every inch your father's son, Joseph Connor Burke. He is prayin' for you this day, but smilin' on you as well." The priest brushed imaginary dust off his hands. "Now," he concluded, "you have spoken a large truth to Mahon and the English overlords. If Repeal becomes fact, there will be enormous changes in the way the law runs hereabouts, and you will have no need of Mahon or of sellin' your fine house. Therefore, you must go out and redouble your efforts to see that Repeal happens."

"Indeed," Joseph concurred. "My thought exactly."

Kate and Joseph walked beside the Cornamona. The village of Ballynockanor lay behind them. Above them was St. Brigit's cross. The heat of high summer shimmered in the air. Joseph said little, and there was a sadness about him that told Kate something was wrong.

"Why are you sorrowing, Joseph?"

"The passin' of time. I'd stay with you here, today, forever if I could."

"A grand plan." There was a poem in such a thought.

"But I can't stay, Kate," he finished, and the poetry evaporated. She would miss him, and the thought of missing him made her lonely even though he was with her.

They continued along the path, with the rush of water to their left and the hush of the winds above them.

"You're leavin', are you?"

"That I am. I must."

"For O'Connell?"

"That, first of anything."

She did not reply or ask what the second reason was that called him away.

He slipped his fingers into her palm and glanced up toward the ancient cross. "You love it here. Ballynockanor, I mean. You'd hate leavin' the place. And why wouldn't you?"

"Leave? Sure, and it's all I've ever known, Joseph. My family. The dust of this valley is made from the bones of everyone I loved who has gone on. A thousand years of Donovans are here at least. I want to stand beside them when Christ comes." *Leave Ballynockanor*, she thought. *It would be easier to cut off an arm.*

Her reply, though honest, creased his brow and troubled his blue eyes. "The Burkes have held this valley since the time of King Brian."

"I know how you love the land."

"You know I love you, Kate," he said after a time.

"I don't doubt it."

"And what if there were no more Ballynockanor?"

"The days of Landlord Marlowe are over."

"Kate . . ." He pressed his lips together in consternation. "The legacy of Marlowe lives still. He left me with five thousand pounds in back rent due to the Crown. You know what that can mean?"

The information struck her like a blow. She stopped in her tracks and searched his face for some solution. There was no reassurance in his expression.

"The agents of the Crown'll sell the lease out from under you and all of us then?"

"That they will. Unless . . ." He told her of Colonel Mahon's offer to take the lease on the townlands that encompassed Ballynockanor. He explained that the village could be settled elsewhere on the Burke estate, new houses built, the church reestablished. He finished sadly, "But the dust cannot be moved and sure, my heart is breakin', for I have no other answer for it. If Repeal fails, then Ballynockanor must be sold to save at least a part of the Burke lands."

The scene around her became sharper. Blades of grass on the slope. Boulders in the river. White foam of the water as it flowed. The songs of perching birds were distinct voices, all familiar, each calling Kate's name.

"This isn't your doing."

"No. But it's my problem."

"And ours as well." She looked up at the cross. The boundary of the village, St. Brigit's cross, would belong to someone else. "There isn't so much money in Galway."

"If it's up to Mahon it's certain Ballynockanor will be tossed, there is no doubt. I offered him another section of land, but he wants this valley and no wonder."

"Then it's settled."

"No. I have until October to pay my uncle's debt. Or until Repeal passes." He hesitated. "I have one more thought on the matter. Another buyer who might want the eastern section."

"And who is that?"

"Lady Fiona Shaw." He swallowed hard. "I intend to pay a call at her estate in Limerick. Make the offer. She lusted after the Burke highlands."

"She lusted after you."

"There are no tenants, and the tract would be fine for grazin'."

Kate touched his arm reassuringly. "Do what you can, Joseph, but don't let the woman talk you into a marriage of convenience. My heart may be here in Ballynockanor, but it will die without your love to nourish it. Do what you must for O'Connell and Repeal. Speak to that woman for the sake of Ballynockanor. Only come home to me, and I will be truly home, wherever you take me."

The worry on his face softened as he pulled her to him. His lips moved against the nape of her neck. "Ah, Kate." He sighed. "My Kate." He kissed her gently again and again until the rushing of the Cornamona blended with the drumming of her heart.

Lady Fiona Shaw welcomed Joseph as though they had not parted company under less than ideal circumstances. Extending her hand to him, she swept down the staircase of her manor house.

"Joseph!" She rolled the name on her tongue with pleasure. "My almost-priest. Come to hear the confessions of a lonely woman, have you?"

"I've had some business nearby."

She took his arm and led him toward the drawing room. "For your cause, is it?"

He smiled and did not reply. Her eager welcome caught him off guard. He had expected a decided coolness.

She tried again. "I heard you had a bit of a scare. Smallpox, was it?" There was a genuine concern in her voice. Her eyes reflected a knowledge and dread of the disease.

"We lost three to it."

"Only three? But how?" They sat on the apricot-colored settee. Joseph noted how the colors of the household decoration—yellow, pale blue, and apricot—complemented Fiona's hair and eyes. He wondered if she had arranged it.

"There was a man on hand, by the grace of God, who knew about vaccination. A miracle really."

"Indeed, Joseph? I'll have him treat my tenants as well if you'll send him to me. I'll pay for it."

"He's gone."

"Gone where?" She leaned close to him to pull the bellrope to call a servant.

"There's no way to know." Joseph frowned as the fact of the Tinker's disappearance troubled his thoughts again.

"A pity. If death came to Galway and was repulsed, he'll certainly show up on the doorstep of Limerick."

"I pray not," Joseph offered soberly.

"If your mystical man shows up again, remember your dear friend in Limerick, will you?" She flashed a dazzling smile.

The maid entered, curtsied, and asked what was required. Fiona spoke to her in a familiar, friendly tone, and requested tea to be brought. Joseph noted how relaxed and unpretentious Fiona seemed since he had seen her last.

"Life is good to you here?" he asked.

"I love the country. But I could use a bit more in the way of handsome visitors." She grasped his hand. "I'm afraid I acted a bit spoiled when I was at Burke Hall. And such a beautiful home. It makes my place look like a cottage. I should have written to apologize."

This unexpected contrition embarrassed him. The truth was, he had hated every minute of her visit. She was another person altogether when she was on her home ground and without the guidance of Suggins and Lucas.

"You liked Burke Hall."

"I envied you. Coveted that baby boy of yours. And how is he?"

"Untouched by the illness." He searched his mind for a way to approach her with the true purpose of his call.

She brought it up herself. "Sure, and you did not come to Limerick on a social visit. Have you come to try me again for Repeal? Enlist the Lady Shaw for O'Connell's cause? It's not that I haven't admired it, mind you, but I'll not be losin' everything I married for, to gain a political independence I'm not certain is a good idea."

"The very subject."

"O'Connell? I'll not march with your millions at Tara."

"No, Fiona. The subject I meant was . . . losin' everythin' for the cause."

Her mouth twitched. "So they've turned the heat up? I knew they would."

"It's the estate."

"Burke lands?"

"My uncle, Marlowe, left owin' nearly five thousand in back rents to the Crown. I'll have to sell off a part of my lease to pay."

"Or?"

"Or I'll lose everythin'."

She looked away and raised her eyebrows slightly as she considered the predicament and his offer. "This has the smell of Suggins on it."

"That may be. But the question of who has forced it can't matter to me now. I've got a thousand open acres."

"Beggin' your pardon, Joseph, but a thousand acres in Galway isn't worth five thousand pounds."

"But with the house and parklands . . ."

This information stopped her. "A lovely place. Your uncle must've put the unpaid rents into fixin' it up."

Joseph shrugged.

"I'll want to see it again before I commit. And I'll not be needin' your housekeeper. Molly, is it?"

"Aye. Molly Fahey. I'll take her with me." Fiona's answer lifted an enormous weight off his shoulders. "If Repeal passes perhaps there'll be no need for any of this."

She closed one eye and considered him as though he were not entirely in his right mind. "I wouldn't count on that."

"But I do."

"Then you're mad as a hatter. But a handsome madman at that." She paused as the tea was delivered on a silver tray. The servant left again, closing the doors at some imperceptible command of Fiona's. "Where was I? Handsome and mad. A true son of Ireland."

"At your service."

She considered him over the rim of her teacup for a long moment. "An interestin' thought."

It took him a second to tumble to her meaning. "No. Not a'tall. I mean . . . Fiona . . . I'm in love."

"Why didn't you say so?"

"With a truly grand woman from Ballynockanor," he blurted.

She relished in his discomfort. "Does she get along well with your housekeeper?"

They laughed, and Joseph relaxed again.

Fiona, who was proving to be a decent person, poured them each more tea and in a serious tone noted, "I have it you're a marked man."

"By whom?"

"Them. Who do you think?"

"It would be better if you'd put a name to them."

"Agents of the Crown. Men in high places and low. Aye. And they've got a mark on O'Connell too."

"How do you know such a thing?"

"Rumor mostly. But there's truth to be found in it, or your name would not be so strongly connected to what is bein' called *The Rebellion* in London." She tapped the china cup pensively, then continued, "They say Burke is becomin' another name for *fool* in England. You get your inheritance back and then proceed to find ways to make people want to take it away. Is it worth it?"

"It is."

"No, Joseph. I like you well enough. You're a man of conviction, even if I can't go along with it. What I mean is this. Is it worth it if you lose? If O'Connell fails and takes you down with him? You'll lose everything."

Joseph considered the question. It deserved an honest answer, but he was not certain he had one to give. "If I pray and weep for freedom from the tyranny of kings, how can I accept the yoke of bein' owned by things? That is another tyranny, sure, but slavery of my soul, just the same. Do I belong to my possessions? I ask myself sometimes. If I can't give them up for freedom's sake, then I am not a free man."

19

The road back from Westport, County Mayo, was long and tire-some, running as it did between the Partry Mountains and the Sheffrey Hills in the valley of the river Eriff. Joseph had already been away from home for a week, and it felt to him like a month at that.

Ever since the raising of the quarantine around the Burke town lands, Joseph tried to regain lost time and momentum by pushing himself to the limit for the cause of Repeal. Instead of visiting one village a day, he took in two or sometimes three. To speed his travel he even denied himself the relative comfort of a carriage and the companionship of a driver and rode the black hunter instead.

The main road continued westward as far as the long finger of Killary Harbour, but Joseph intended to save a half-day's travel by means of a shortcut.

Just below a peak named the Devil's Mother, there was a trail of sorts that took off due south, climbing the heights and eventually skirting Ben Beg. It would bring Joseph back to Ballynockanor and home without him being carried so far out of his way and having to backtrack.

At the waterfall where the Eriff tumbled into Killary, Joseph nudged the hunter aside from the post road and set him to climbing. The horse leaned into the grade but did not fight it, leaving Joseph relatively free to think over the experiences of the past days.

Mayo was even more on fire for Repeal than Galway, Joseph found. The Repeal wardens there had been zealous in collecting the pennies of Repeal rent, and they were eager to pass it along. Daniel's last letter on the subject had mentioned that more than two thousand pounds a week were coming in across the country, and the offering was still climbing week by week. Joseph patted the leather satchel strapped behind the saddle. The next report would reflect an even higher total; Joseph was transporting in silver coin fully one hundred pounds and from the poorest county of them all.

His destination with the collection was Archbishop MacHale in Tuam, but it would only take an additional day of riding for Joseph to sleep at home one night out of ten. The thought was very pleasant.

So was the recollection the he would see Little Tom again this night. In a smaller leather pouch tied opposite to the Repeal rent was a silver baby rattle, a bell made in the shape of a shepherd's crook. Joseph smiled when he imagined Tomeen reaching out to grasp the toy.

Other thoughts were less enjoyable. Something that recurred over and over again to Joseph was the question he needed to pose to Daniel O'Connell: Who had recommended Mister Daly as an instructor?

Joseph was convinced that behind Daly was a lurking, plotting murderer and that O'Connell's memory held the key to the mystery. Through the enforced isolation of the epidemic, he had never received a reply to his letter to Daniel.

In the aftermath of the plague, with its deaths and all that had to be seen to, the matter had slipped to the back of Joseph's mind. He had not had even the opportunity to post a letter on this whirlwind tour of Mayo, but it was at the top of his list of things to do as soon as he again sat at his own desk.

The trail Joseph was following was almost extinct by the time he neared the top of the two-thousand-foot-high peak. Local lore called it haunted for its conical shape and the thin mist in which its summit was perpetually wreathed. Then, too, there were the ravens that appeared in great numbers above the heights of the Devil's Mother. Clearly, the old ones said, the presence of such ill-favored birds was proof of the evil nature of the summit.

Joseph was still lost in his thoughts of another kind of evil when the black hunter snorted. Joseph rose in his stirrups and scanned both behind and before; there were no other travelers to be seen. The afternoon, while not brightly cheerful, was not far advanced, and the haze atop the peak did not extend down to where Joseph rode.

There was a rumbling sound from the pinnacle. What caused the noise? The clouds were not heavy enough for it to be thunder, and yet the booming and crashing noise grew in volume and intensity.

Staring at the top of the slope provided the terrifying answer: it was a rockslide. A hundred feet higher in elevation and only two hundred yards away, an army of black boulders was cascading downward, directly toward him.

Ducking his head, Joseph jabbed home the spurs, though the already nervous mount needed no urging. The black shot forward as at the noise of a starting gun, leaping over low places and charging headlong around the curve of the hillside.

Outrunning the slide was the only hope. The incline was too steep, the downhill slope too precipitous to risk descending. A hurried glance upward showed the avalanche spread from horizon to horizon. It was as if the entire top of the mountain were falling. Colliding rocks bounded into the air like startled goats. Already the stones on the leading edge of the rockfall were bouncing across Joseph's path.

A cabbage-sized boulder drove straight toward horse and rider. Before Joseph could even react, the black horse instinctively turned uphill, letting the rock plunge past only five feet ahead.

Then the mass of the slide was around them. Boulders the size of Joseph's desk thundered by. "Go!" Joseph urged. "Go! Go!"

A pair of stones as big as bathtubs converged only a dozen feet above the path. Their collision made the air hum and spattered Joseph and the horse with sharp fragments, but the impact flung the boulders apart, leaving the path clear.

There was a bulge in the slope up ahead. If man and beast could reach that bend upward, there was the faintest possibility they could shelter below it as the rest of the slide divided to pass around it.

The black leaped over a pair of cannonball-shaped stones, then reared, bucking, as a slab with the contour of a dining table slid by. A rain of fist-sized stones showered down. It was nearly the last of the avalanche; the deluge of rocks was slowing, and the size of the chunks diminished again.

Joseph felt the satchel of money slipping and made a futile attempt to grab it with his free hand. A fragment of granite no bigger than a doorknob hit him in the back of the head. He was thrown from the horse to land just below the lip of the trail and right on the edge of the precipice. The black neighed and galloped away, dashing off around the incline.

A sprinkle of rocks and pebbles and gravel and grit continued to drizzle across Joseph, but the projecting edge of the path protected him from all but the most minor impacts. Of this he knew nothing; he was unconscious.

Joseph struggled back toward the air from what felt like the bottom of a mud-choked pool. Every movement was torturously slow, every breath painful, every thought laborious.

Nearing the surface at last, he heard voices. As a child he had fallen from a shaggy brown pony and struck his head on a tree stump. On that occasion his father had been the first to rush to him, to lift him up. Maybe the words echoing so hollowly belonged to his father, coming to lift him from where he had fallen.

But no, that was wrong. Joseph was a man grown, his father dead. He had been doing something, going somewhere, though those details now seemed unimportant.

Someone was speaking again, but the words in the piping treble made little sense.

"A good job, ridin' to the top like we done. Two more minutes and he would have been clean away."

"An' it looks like an accident," a gruff voice agreed. "That's a right stroke."

Joseph's mind protested this nonsense. He'd really had an accident. Why did the voice insist it only looked like one?

"Kenny, when you pushed over them rocks, like you done, I thought the whole mountain was gonna fall on 'im. I said to meself, that's torn it, I said, the whole sack of boodle is buried forever. But look where it lies, perty as a picture."

A swirl of cool air played with Joseph's hair and on the cheek that was upward as he lay on his side. He wanted to open his eyes, but he had forgotten the method. The orange of the sun shining against his eyelids dimmed to gray.

"Say, Kenny," the higher-pitched voice inquired, "this ain't like robbin' God or nothin' is it? I mean, he picked up the swag at a church."

"Give me that!" the one named Kenny demanded. "You'll do murder, but you won't rob no church? Give it up, Ryan, you're balmy."

"I just don't like this place," Ryan complained. "When we first got here it was clear. Where'd all this mist come from anyways? I can't no more'n see my hand in front of my face."

"Fine by me," Kenny grunted, rolling Joseph over onto his back and riffling his pockets. "Then I don't gotta see your ugly mug neither."

Through the barest slit of one eyelid, Joseph saw Kenny's ugly mug: gap-toothed and broken-nosed.

There came a new faint sound in the eddying mists: a chiming like a church bell heard from a distant mountainside.

"What's that?" Ryan hissed. "There's someone comin'."

"You're daft," Kenny returned, removing the money from Joseph's waistcoat and a pair of letters from his jacket. "There ain't . . . hist!" he said urgently. "You hear that?"

Joseph wanted to say he heard the noise, that it was a tinkling sound like rain on a pond, but he could not speak.

"Let's get out of here," Kenny said. "We've got what we come for. Let's go."

"What about him?" Ryan wheezed. "What if he ain't dead?"

"He will be after I toss him off this cliff, see? Sad accident still."

The jangling sound crept closer.

"Move!" Kenny urged.

Joseph tried to oblige. He wrinkled his forehead, and his chin came up a bare half inch from the gravel that was cutting a diamond pattern into his flesh. Then he was being lifted, his body floating free of the weights tying him down. He was flying, cool mist whistling in his ears.

The landing was mercifully quick. His right arm, extended before him, absorbed most of the shock, then his shoulder and back. Joseph never knew he bounced three times before coming to rest on a granite slab, never knew his assailants had fled the scene even before his battered body stopped tumbling down the slope.

The black hunter ambled slowly up the trail, returning to the place where he and his master had parted company. A silver baby rattle jingled on the saddle.

When Joseph awoke, it was pitch black, although whether this was due to nightfall or some defect of his eyes, he could not judge. He drew in one breath, tried to raise himself on his right arm, shrieked as a jagged spear of agony pierced him, and passed out again.

When next he came to his senses, he lay still, trying to force the pain into a manageable corner long enough to reason. He could not immediately remember where he was and only knew that he was lying on a rocky hillside. He was unable to recall how he had come to be there, but guessed he had been thrown from a horse. This time he knew it was truly night, for a range of stars twinkled overhead.

Also, his right arm was broken, perhaps shattered. The slightest twitch of that limb was enough to send his senses reeling, to push him near the brink of a yawning pit.

Lying perfectly motionless, he tested every part of his frame. His head ached abominably, feeling swollen to thrice normal size. The vision in his right eye was blurry. The left was bruised and swollen nearly shut.

He had at least one broken rib, he judged. Shallow breaths were no problem, but inhaling deeply caused a stab of pain that was echoed by the outraged nerves in his arm.

His internal parts seemed uninjured, at least not so violently that their protests outweighed the others. The same verdict applied to his legs.

It was enough. Exhausted, but in some obscure way satisfied with his investigation, Joseph prayed briefly, thankfully, for his life, asked for daylight to come soon, then allowed himself to slide gently backward into darkness.

Sometime during the long night, he dreamed. Joseph saw a man with missing front teeth grimacing down at him, saying something about money.

Had he been robbed, or was it a dream?

In another vision, someone asked his identity, but he could not provide it. The Christian name *Joseph* came quickly enough to mind, but he was not convinced that it was really his. This lapse did not trouble his sleep, however.

What did nag him was an unresolved inquiry, made more disturbing because he did not know what the issue had been. Over and over again, he told himself that he was seeking something important, that he must find a solution, to which another part of his tormented mind responded, *Willingly, if you will just remind me of the question.*

B right sunshine warmed Joseph's ear. He roused with a clearer head and a diminished sense of outraged body parts, except in his right arm. It not only refused to respond to any commands he sent, it spitefully retorted by making him violently ill whenever he tried to move it.

After he finished retching, Joseph again studied his situation. It was nearing noonday, and no one had found him. How long had he been blacked out? Was it only one night or several?

By degrees Joseph hoisted himself into a sitting position. He used the right coat sleeve to pull his injured arm across his chest and hold it there as he scooted toward vertical. Joseph cringed at what the fingers of his left hand discovered under the fabric: his right arm possessed a new joint, a sharp bend midway between wrist and elbow.

"I'm thirsty," he said aloud. There had been a water-filled gourd in his satchel. But where was that item? Inching gingerly around in a circle, Joseph scanned the slope above him. A slightly flattened rim marked where the trail must be, but it looked impossibly far away. Even if he had been thrown from a horse, how had he come to land so far down the hillside? The incline was covered with basalt and granite boulders. By Providence alone, Joseph had fallen between two of them, landing in a crevasse partially filled with moss and gorse. The shrubbery had broken part of his tumble. More than that, lodging in the cleft kept him from being tossed over another sheer drop of fifty feet or more.

It was well he had not been able to get up in the darkness; it would have cost him his neck.

The important business at hand was to get back up on the track. Either someone would come along or Joseph would follow the trail and find help. The question was, How to get there?

The rubble-strewn grade presented no clear route to the top. Every direction offered only boulders that would have to be surmounted by crawling. The thought made Joseph shudder.

His first attempt involved a thrust of his legs and a lunge to propel himself as far across a granite slab as possible. This worked adequately until it came time for him to claw the rest of the way across the rock. In order to stretch out his left arm he had to drop the right. At the first contact between the broken bone and the solid stone, Joseph gasped and spiraled away from his wits once more.

By the time the warm day was succeeded by a chilly, fog-swirled evening, Joseph had advanced no more than half the distance to the path. He had crawled, lost consciousness from the pain, reawakened and forced himself onward more times than he could count, and he was still well below the rim of the path.

Using his jacket, he had contrived a sling to keep his injured limb bound against his body and that had helped. He struggled over three basalt lumps in fairly quick succession, then almost gave up in despair. In his frenzy to regain the road, Joseph had hurtled over obstacles without adequate planning. After the third lunge he found himself at the base of an insurmountable granite monolith, pillared on either side by unclimbable rubble. What had appeared to be a slanting course toward his goal turned out to be a trap.

It took him three hours of agony to backtrack down the slope, then regain as much along another course.

Joseph pressed his mouth against a slick rockface, sucking the condensing moisture from the stone. It helped his thirst, but the brisk air of twilight was making him shiver and sapping his strength. He used a break in the cloud to get some bearings for the coming struggle.

Huddling below the stone, cradling his arm, Joseph allowed himself the time it took for the last rays of the setting sun to sink below Ben Gorm before making himself try once more.

He was still troubled by something, nagged by a puzzle he knew to be important. But the more he struggled with his memory, the farther from his grasp it slipped. He tested every single part of his life to see if one of those memories would jog something else. He considered Little Tom, Kate, Daniel O'Connell, Mary Elizabeth, and others, but nothing resonated. The only conclusion he recognized was that out there alone on the mountain, the only things of importance were people he loved; nothing else mattered.

Joseph had traveled as far as he could, and it still was not enough. How much time had passed, Joseph did not know. He was a mere twenty-five feet from the trail, but he could not cross what remained. The slope was at its steepest and the rubble-strewn surface its most jagged.

Days without either water or food and nights without warmth had sapped Joseph's strength. Twice he had heard, or thought he heard, the voices of passersby. He might have been hallucinating, but it made no difference anyway; his voice was a feeble groan incapable of being heard more than a few feet away.

Worse still was the fact that he had crawled to where he could not be spotted from the roadway, being below the angular outlines of several boulders. Even if some chance traveler should look over the rim, they would not spot him.

Joseph resolved that he was going to die. He was not panicked by the thought, though he regretted many things left undone. He was sorry he would not be around to watch Little Tom grow up. He lamented that he would never have one last chance to speak to Kate of his love for her, that they would have no more chances for a future together. He bemoaned the fact he would leave Tomeen and the Burke estate so unguarded in what was sure to be a period of enormous turmoil coming upon the land.

These things he committed to the Lord as he prepared to leave his body behind. It must be almost the moment, he thought. He could hear someone calling his name, but far away and dreamlike.

"Joseph," the voice whispered. "Joseph, get up once more."

"I can't," he protested. "There is no strength left in me."

"Joseph . . . Joseph . . . Joseph Burke," called the voice again, repeating his name with concern and urgency. "Joseph Burke, where are you?"

Joseph's swollen eyes opened, and he drew a shuddering breath. From the depths of his soul he shouted, "Here! Here I am!" Even in his own ears it sounded feeble, useless, and impotent.

Yet scarcely three minutes later Dermott O'Neill picked his way down over the boulders. He splashed water across Joseph's face, then aided the squire to drink from a leather flask. "How did you find me?" Joseph asked when he had swallowed half the water and could speak again. "How?"

"The black came home without you," the Tinker said. "I got him to show me the way back here."

"And then you heard me call out to you?"

The Tinker looked puzzled. "No," he replied, "I heard nothing but the wind. But I turned aside when I found this beside the track." O'Neill opened his mammoth palm to display a silver baby rattle.

The big man cradled Joseph against the expanse of his broad chest as tenderly as if he were ministering to the needs of a newborn foal. His hands, though huge, were gentle and sure. The Tinker apologized over and over for causing the squire pain when all Joseph could say was, "Thank you for saving my life."

The blade of a bone-handled knife flashed in the sun next to Joseph's injured right arm. The edge hissed through the fabric of Joseph's coat and shirt, and the cloth fell away. The Tinker whistled softly at what he found there.

"You know, Squire," he said, "the arm is broken, and one of the bones is poked through the skin. I'll have t'straighten out the damage before I bind it up."

Joseph knew what an open fracture meant. Besides the excruciating suffering, there was the real possibility the wound would be so infected as to threaten life itself unless an amputation was performed. The longer resetting the bone was delayed, the slimmer the chance of keeping the limb.

"I am sorry for the pain," the Tinker repeated, "but we'd best get it done."

"Go ahead, then," Joseph said, already gritting his teeth against what he knew was coming.

O'Neill pressed the silver child's toy into Joseph's left hand and closed the fingers around it. "Sure, and He has kept you alive for a reason," he said. "He'll not be failin' you now."

The Tinker bathed the wound in water, washing it carefully before holding the limb across his lap and gripping wrist and elbow in his two great fists. Delicately he rotated the arm, seeking the perfect alignment. Choosing the moment when Joseph was as relaxed as he was likely to be, the Tinker pulled sharply in opposite directions.

Joseph gasped and would have jolted off the rockface but for the weight of the Tinker pressing him down. Then he blacked out.

When he came to, his right arm was bandaged, splinted between the stiff leather soles of Joseph's boots torn off for that purpose and tied again in place. "I'm sorry about your boots," the Tinker said. "In this place I could find nothin' else for braces." Then he added in a brighter manner, "But I did find moss growin' about. I have made a poultice and pressed it over the wound. It will serve to draw out the poisons."

The Tinker hoisted Joseph upon his shoulder as if the squire were no more bother than a collop of thatch. He picked his way with surefooted steps up the rockface, and the two men were soon back on the road.

The black hunter stood watching over the brim with pricked ears and interested eyes. Beside him was a bay draft horse, more suited to the Tinker's bulk. "Your pardon, Squire," said O'Neill, "but I think you are in no fit condition to ride. You sit in the saddle in front of me, and I'll keep you from fallin' off."

It was like being a child again, but Joseph did not object. His head was constantly near a swoon, and the very thought of falling again and landing on the splinted arm made him sweat. "Just get me home," he said. Then, as a thought struck him, "No, wait. I remember a satchel. Was it on the black?"

"No," O'Neill replied. "Perhaps you were robbed and left for dead."

"I don't know," Joseph said honestly. "And there is some other mystery that has been troublin' me, but I can't work it out."

"Well, don't fret yourself," the Tinker advised. "It'll come to you in God's own time."

❧ 20 ❧

Joseph lay on Kate's bed opposite Mary Elizabeth. The child wanted the company, and her presence consoled Joseph.

It was a fiercesome break. Kate winced on his behalf as she changed the bandage and applied a fresh moss poultice as the Tinker had instructed. Joseph turned ashen.

Mary Elizabeth, propped on her elbow to watch the process, commented, "You blend right into the wall, Joseph. I never saw anyone alive as white as you."

He could only nod once and grit his teeth.

When it was finished he inhaled deeply, looked at Mary Elizabeth and remarked hoarsely, "You're as pale as I, girl. And not one scar on your pretty face."

This was not the case with her arms and trunk, but the skin of her face was luminous. Kate credited the healing of the children's skin to the ointment the Tinker had provided. It was because of that and other proofs of his ability to heal that Kate followed every instruction he had given in regard to Joseph's arm.

"Will I ever have rosy cheeks again, Kate?" Mary Elizabeth asked.

Kate replied, "By Christmas, Dermott O'Neill says. You'll be strong and fit as ever by Advent."

"What was in the ointment he made you put on me?"

"I asked him yesterday." Kate wore an amused expression. "He told me it was faith."

"I wish he had put faith on my hair." Most of her black curls were gone. The rest was clipped very close to her scalp. She wore a bright red scarf that she adjusted as she swung out of bed and announced she was going to see Queen Maeve.

Her course past Kate and then outside to the privy was slow and unsteady. But she was stronger every day.

"I'm glad to have a minute with you," Joseph said.

She touched his head and said in a quiet voice, "As for my faith in you, sir. Will you promise to be well soon?"

"Much sooner. We'll climb the Hill of Tara together, you, me, and Mary Elizabeth. And I'll be a married man before Christmas. Molly promised she'd dance with me on my weddin' day. I'll need strength for that." He smiled up into the warmth of Kate's brown eyes. "But I could stay here forever if I had you to look at."

She knelt beside him. "Stay here forever? Anywhere with you, Joseph. I thought I'd go mad when you didn't come back. When I thought I'd lost you."

"I don't remember any of it. Days are all a tangle in my brain. I was ready to die. I regretted losin' only my future with you and Little Tom. As for the manor, it's a tiny price to pay. We'll live here."

"You saw her then. Lady Shaw?"

"She'll come inspect the house after the Tara meetin'. She's a better solution than Colonel Mahon. Not a bad sort. You'd like her, I think."

"The blow to your head knocked the sense right out of you then."

"Ah, well. Fiona Shaw in the Burke manor. I'm more home in a cottage than in that empty barn of a house."

Brushing back wisps of his blond hair she kissed his forehead. "If we lost everything it wouldn't matter. Kevin's happy enough in America. If you said come to America with me, what would I have to hold me here?"

"A thousand years of Donovans?"

"All I care about is today and tomorrow with you. I know that now." She kissed his ears and his nose and his chin as though he were a child.

"I'll rise up sooner if you'll kiss me the way you did the day I left you." He smiled and pulled her close to kiss her mouth with surprising strength. Breathlessly he whispered, "Sure, and I'll be strong long before Advent. The first day of Advent is a fine day to marry. What do you say, Kate?"

"I will."

Martin Donovan rode on the driver's box of the Burke coach. It was a huge source of pride for him to be atop the shiny black conveyance as it surged along the rutted roads. Nor was the boost to his self-esteem in any way diminished by being seated on the exterior. Handling the ribbons of the matched team of bays was Dermott O'Neill. The Tinker's immense size and brushy black beard conveyed an additional sense of awe to any onlookers, an intimidating reverence in which Martin was glad to share.

Given the glories of the August weather, the only drawback to Martin's position was being placed next to the final occupant of the driver's box: Mad Molly Fahey. In between muttering and crooning, Molly had an unfortunate habit of patting Martin on the head or pinching his cheek. After a few miles of this treatment, the Tinker spoke to her in an unknown tongue, and at least the patting and pinching ceased.

There was an altruistic glow for Martin as well: the interior of the rig was so packed with folks that forcing them to ride in the enclosed coach with Mad Molly would have been very severe indeed. Squire Joseph, his arm freshly poulticed with clean moss and suspended across his chest by a silk scarf, rode inside. So did the other Donovans:

Kate and Mary Elizabeth. The nurse, Miss Susan, and Baby Tomeen were aboard as well.

What occasioned this togetherness was the Repeal monster meeting at the Hill of Tara. Across the breadth of Ireland they were going, to County Meath in the Province of Leinster, farther away from home than Martin had ever been or ever dreamed of going.

Joseph Burke had invited them because, as he said, this was a chance to be a part of history. To join forces with a million of their countrymen, uniting in one place and one time and for one purpose was something not to be missed. It was said that one out of every eight Irishmen would be present at Tara. More than that: there was another monster meeting taking place a hundred miles to the south, and it was expected to draw another quarter of a million souls.

As Mad Molly said, "There'll be lots of company for dinner."

At which observation Squire Joseph laughed and noted that Daniel O'Connell was certain the British would feel the same.

Given Martin's sense of adventure, it made him no less excited about going to overhear Joseph explain a slightly different motive for the summons. "I could leave them at home with you to watch after them, Dermott," Joseph had said to the Tinker in the stable. "But I feel better havin' those I care about under my eye as well."

So, leaving the Burke estate in the care of Steward Adam Kane, they were three days on the journey. After spending the first night in Roscommon and the second at a coaching inn in Trim, today they swirled ahead of a plume of dust toward the fabled Hill of Tara.

Or rather, they had swirled along for the first mile or so in the early light of dawn. Then as Molly jabbered and pointed, Martin stared at rolling hills that looked to be thickly planted with swaying rows of tall, dark grain.

Coming from a village that never had more than a hundred people abroad at any one time, even having been to the Mallow rally did not prepare Martin for this: as far as the eye could see, every hill, every valley, every pasture, and every trail was covered with people converging on Tara. It made Martin shiver to hear Mad Molly describe it as being as if the graves were opened and the dead coming forth at once.

The carriage slowed to a walk. The hordes of pilgrims were more than willing to make way for the Burke of Connaught and the family of Brigit Donovan, but even if they moved aside, what then? Stretching off toward the knob on the distant horizon that marked the seat of the High Kings was an unbroken line of sojourners. The mass of bodies filled the road fifteen across.

Still, by creeping progress, the coach made its way toward the Golden Hill of Tara. There was no immense city of fierce knights and elegant ladies. There was no feasting amid the splendor of the court that exercised exalted judgement over clan disputes. There was no longer a Great Assembly Hall as there had been in the days of King Cormac, but never mind; the green mounds that were the remaining legacy of the High Kings of All Ireland were this day witnessing the greatest assembly in the history of the Celtic peoples.

Martin found himself looking from face to face for some telltale sign. What if Mad Molly was correct and among the stalwart, committed features seen on every hand were some that belonged to chieftains newly returned to the fight for freedom after a thousand years in the grave?

As if reading the boy's thoughts, the Tinker said, "She's almost right, you know. The blood of Cormac MacArt and of the bold warriors of the Fianna is still in the veins of those you see around you . . . and in your own."

Martin, who had believed himself already bursting with pride, felt his height expand six more inches at that comment.

Though standing on the platform as a celebrity, Martin was still lost in a throng: the dais was constructed to hold six hundred dignitaries and was actually occupied by close to a thousand. It was already impossible for any more people to crowd around the knoll on which the stage was constructed. For more than a mile in every direction the grass was packed solid with onlookers, the count passing one million before nine in the morning. At six altars around the perimeter of the scaffold, continuous prayers were offered for justice, for freedom, and for peace.

The platform was surrounded by banners that would not have been out of place in Cormac MacArt's palace. Green and fluttering, bearing images of harps and wolfhounds, of stone crosses and rampant horses, of sailing ships and shamrocks, hundreds of flags proudly announced the origins of those who had walked for days to join the rally. Kells and Kildare, Cork and Killarney, Ardee and Altboy, Dublin and Dundalk, all were represented, and a thousand more towns and villages besides.

Troops of mounted men, twenty-five in each company, four hundred companies in all . . . ten thousand members of the newly formed Repeal cavalry, wearing hats that sported green cockades on one side and Repeal Association membership cards on the other, formed a column that stretched from Tara halfway back to Dublin. They had ridden out to meet Daniel O'Connell as he came from his Merrion Square home. It took the cavalry almost two hours to escort Daniel through the press of the last mile of the journey.

Bounding upon the stage in a display of endless energy and enthusiasm the sixty-eight-year-old Liberator wasted no time in preliminaries. "We are here at Tara of the Kings," he boomed to boisterous and surging cheers, "the place from which emanated the rights to dominion over the farthest reaches of the land."

There was the briefest of pauses as the implications sank in. Tara, the hub from which the authority of the High Kings flowed out across Ireland, was the emotional center of the Irish nation. To Martin it was like the gathering of the children of Israel below Mount Sinai. *We are Ireland*, he thought. *How can anyone rule Ireland without the approval of those gathered here?*

It was apparent that the entire multitude felt the same. In the next instant the response was massive and beyond deafening, beyond overwhelming. The shouting of approval was a physical presence; Martin could feel it pushing him, kneading him like human hands. He saw Tomeen crying in terror in Miss Susan's arms but could not hear one of the infant's wails, even though the child was less than one foot away.

Daniel O'Connell gave words to the vibrant emotions, acknowledging the power gathered there: "The strength of the national movement was never exhibited so imposingly as at this great meeting. Such an army . . . for you have the steadiness of trained men . . . no free state would willingly see in its bosom, if it were not composed of its choicest citizens."

The gauntlet was plainly thrown down at last. *Resist the vigor of Repeal if you dare*, O'Connell suggested to the British government. *This mighty force is controlled and law-abiding, but those qualities do not reduce the fact that it is the mightiest force ever assembled.* "Greater than the armies that fought at Waterloo," he bellowed.

O'Connell then launched into his nine-point plan for restoring an Irish parliament, but Martin ceased to listen. He was still musing on the assembled power. Not just bigger than the army of Napoleon or the British force that defeated him, this gathering was larger than both armies put together—six times larger.

In the faces of the crowd Martin saw the city dwellers from Dublin and poor country farmers like himself from the hills of Wicklow. Fisherfolk from the port of Drogheda stood shoulder-to-shoulder with tanners and weavers and carpenters and quarrymen. Between Catholic and Protestant there was no way to distinguish, nor did any in the gathering make the attempt. They were Irish men and Irish women, one million and a half strong, bred of the blood of the ancient kings and born to rule their own destinies. That was the sum of their identity at the Hill of Tara.

A renewed clamor from the throng brought Martin's attention back to O'Connell.

"I say it to you again," the Emancipator cried, "step-by-step we are approachin' the goal itself, but with the strides of a giant!"

The cheering that followed these words lasted for over an hour. Martin could see O'Connell was pleased and in no way flustered. He spent the hour circulating around the stage, shaking hands, speaking mouth-to-ear with the special guests, including Martin.

"Young Donovan," he shouted into Martin's hearing. "You see what a movement you are part of? Not intimidation nor even smallpox nor murderous attacks, nor murder itself . . . and your father was a good man; none better in the land . . . nothing can stop us now, eh?"

Martin felt his face flush as the closest ten thousand in the audience studied the features of the youngster whom the Liberator had singled out for a private word.

Returning to the lectern at last, O'Connell asked, "And where do we go from here? Well, throughout the land, to be sure. But soon we shall be there." He stretched out his arm, hand rigidly extended like a signpost, toward Dublin. "At Clontarf, where Brian Boru, Brian of the Tribute, defeated the army of the Danes. At Clontarf, within hearing of Dublin Castle itself. That is where we shall be, in a gatherin' to make today's assembly look like a caucus in . . ." O'Connell looked around the stage and smiled at Martin. "In Ballynockanor. And then don't you think the British government will give us what we want?"

As far as Martin could tell, though it was twenty miles to Dublin from Tara, the shouts of "Yes! Yes! Yes!" from fifteen hundred thousand throats undoubtedly reverberated in the ears of the Lord Lieutenant and his henchmen right then.

It was supposed to be a private celebration after the immense success of the rally at Tara. Midway between the Hill of the Kings and Dublin's fair city, in the upper room of a crossroads inn named for King Brian Boru, Daniel O'Connell held court with a few of his closest friends. Joseph was asked to attend. The rest of the Ballynockanor entourage waited downstairs. Outside, in the summer air that smelled of freshly mown hay, was a gathering on a different scale altogether. An immense part of the day's crowd gathered brush and built campfires, sleeping on the stony ground and toasting dry bread for their suppers. These hundred thousand were ready, willing, and only awaiting the word from the Liberator to loose them to storm Dublin Castle and toss the British out on their ears. In the meantime they did not want to go home. By hundreds they gathered to sing "The Men of Ninety-Eight," and "Rory O'Moore":

Oh lives there a traitor who'd shrink from the strife
Who, to add to the length of his forfeited life
His country, his kindred, his faith would abjure
No! We'll strike for our God and for Rory O'Moore!

Far from being fatigued, O'Connell was more buoyant than ever. He stood at the window, gazing out over a sea of fires. "Biblical proportions," he exclaimed jubilantly. "Must not the government be quakin' in their boots this night? Surely they must now see what a force of sentiment is here gathered. How can they resist our demands any longer?"

In the wake of having close to 20 percent of the populace stand up for freedom on the same day, it was difficult to dispute Daniel's optimism.

Osborne Davis, for one, was not about to ignore the positive signs. "Now we rally the whole country," he explained. "Between now and the Clontarf meetin', the air will be electric as those present today go home and spread the word. *The Nation* will fan the flames until we might have three million Repealers there."

"To commemorate the destruction of the Danes by Brian Boru," Garrison O'Toole chimed in. "And to prophesy the same for the British."

There was loud approval in the room for these sentiments, but now O'Connell sought to voice a word of caution. "We must be more canny than ever," he said. "Electrify, yes, but in guarded language. More than before, we must not give Dublin Castle any excuse to charge us with treason or revolution."

"Like today when you accused Queen Victoria of ignorin' the will of the people?" Davis commented dryly.

O'Connell waved away the rebuke. "Nothin' but politics in that remark," he said. "If you think it necessary, I'll even apologize to Her Majesty in tomorrow's paper. But enough of tomorrow. For now, let's just savor today."

Gingerly draping his arm across Joseph's shoulders, O'Connell took a moment to thank the young man for extraordinary effort. "You see, Osborne," he said, "Burke's arm is still in a sling from where he was set upon by hoodlums in the employ of the government."

"We don't know that for certain," Joseph cautioned. "They may have been common thieves, for aught I know. I still can't recall anything about the attackers."

O'Connell shook his head sympathetically, his broad features etched with concern. "Nearly killed him. Broke his arm. Bashed his head till he's lost part of his memory, and still he comes clear across the country to support Repeal. What do you think of that, Davis?"

"Heroic," the newspaper editor agreed.

"And one day soon his addled wits will recover, and then those hooligans had better watch out, eh, O'Toole?"

"They will rue the day," the printer concurred. "Shall we sit? I see that the places are set and the wine poured."

O'Connell rubbed his hands together with gusto. "I'm famished," he said.

In the jostling while the group was being seated, Joseph, who was placed next to Osborne Davis at the head table, knocked over the editor's glass of wine.

"Here, take mine," Joseph apologized, passing over his goblet of dark red fluid.

"Let me get you another," Davis offered.

Joseph declined. "My head has never completely stopped achin' since the mountainside beatin'," he said. "It's better if I don't tax it with the drink anyway."

"A toast!" O'Connell announced, raising his glass. "To the spirit of Tara . . . on to Clontarf!" The Emancipator continued poised, his glass held aloft till all should drink and then he, with a finely tuned sense of the dramatic, would drain his at the last.

"On to Clontarf," the room echoed, everyone except Joseph tipping their glasses.

A bewildered look crossed Davis's face, and he grabbed Joseph's injured arm with a grip of iron. "My throat," he said, coughing, his eyes bulging. "I can't breathe." The newspaperman gasped for air, levered upright, staggered, and toppled over.

"The wine!" Joseph shouted, leaning across Davis to dash the container from O'Connell's lips. No more than a single drop had reached the Liberator's mouth.

The room erupted in screams and pandemonium. At the other end of the head table, Garrison O'Toole likewise cried out. "The wine! I've been poisoned." He also started from his chair, flecks of foam around his mouth, then fell heavily to the floor.

Shouldering through the milling crowd that shouted, "Murder" and "Assassination," Joseph hurried downstairs to find Dermott O'Neill.

"What's happened?" the Tinker said, meeting Joseph at the bottom of the steps. "The commotion is even louder than the singin' outside."

"Poison," Joseph said tersely. "Can you come?"

"Aye," the Tinker said. "I've got to get a bag from the carriage first."

Vouched for by Joseph, O'Neill was allowed to dose both stricken men with a thick syrup from a tear-shaped vial. Immediately both were retching so as to turn their insides out. O'Toole, who had swallowed only a tiny sip of the toast, was soon sitting upright, though extremely pale and drawn.

Osborne Davis remained in a twilight state, between awake and asleep.

"Now we'll need to watch him close," the Tinker pronounced. "But I believe they have been relieved in time before any permanent harm was done."

"But why these two?" O'Connell mused aloud. "Why attack two newspapermen?"

"Perhaps the poison was meant for you," suggested Mr. Daunt, O'Connell's secretary, "but the assassin could only guess which seat was yours, so he placed two or three tainted glasses near the center of the table."

This was conceded to be a likely explanation, especially after Joseph explained that Davis's glass had originally been his. What he did not mention was that his seat was farther from the center than that occupied by Davis.

"A cowardly assassin that," O'Connell cried, recovering his fire.

"If he wishes to take me on, I'll stand and let him shoot for a shillin' a ball. To be given to the Repeal rent, of course."

The meeting in the private function room at the Stag's Head Tavern was supposed to be clandestine and furtive, but from the beginning the outraged voice of Burtenshaw Suggins rattled the windows. Despite efforts by Secretary Lucas to make him lower his tone, Suggins could not help bellowing at Garrison O'Toole.

"Who gave you permission to try such a thing? What a dunderheaded stunt! The whole country is exploding with the news that someone tried to . . ."

It was only by vaulting over an ottoman, his hand raised as if he would clamp it over Suggins's mouth, that Lucas managed to prevent the word *poison* from echoing down Dame Lane all the way to Trinity College. Suggins's shock that someone of lower rank was about to touch him alarmed him sufficiently to make him stifle the word.

Garrison O'Toole, his back to the wall and the expression on his face as hunted as was ever worn by the mounted stag's head over the mantel, could not bring himself to speak. Anticipating this reception had motivated him to bring his sister to this meeting, and he let her do the talking.

Coolly, she said, "Who gave permission? You did, my lord."

His face swelling and purpling visibly, Suggins was nearly apoplectic with rage. "Not within the sight of a million potential rioters!"

Hastening to avoid another injudicious outburst, Lucas offered, "If you will allow me to do the questioning, sir?"

Suggins stuffed a lace handkerchief in front of his mouth as though preparing to gag himself, then nodded for Lucas to proceed.

"Why, on the very day when O'Connell had whipped a million people to a frenzy, did you decide to attempt murder . . . and fail besides?"

"It is simple," Beth Anne O'Toole explained. "We had no idea that Joseph Burke survived the attack on the mountain until yesterday.

He says he has no recollection of the events there, but who knows if that is the truth? Or who knows when he might soon recall enough to backtrack to Garrison? And if that happens, gentlemen, the Repealers will find . . . you."

"Great thunder!" Suggins rumbled around his fat, cloth-filled fist. "He must be taken care of at once!"

"Precisely," Beth Anne acknowledged. "And except for an unfortunate mischance, he would have been."

"Were you trying to poison O'Connell as well?" Lucas asked.

Recovering a fraction of his spine, Garrison O'Toole replied, "No, that was not the intent. And I did manage to divert suspicion by feignin' to be poisoned myself."

Having recovered from plum to merely ruby in complexion, Suggins admitted, "That was well done, that. But what's to be done now? Yesterday's demonstration proved what the government has feared all along: O'Connell's force is powerful, hugely powerful. One word from him, and we are plunged into civil war."

"Which is precisely the same tightrope O'Connell is walkin'," Beth Anne pointed out. "We understand your concerns. These monster meetin's must cease. In particular, the one at Clontarf must not be allowed to happen. If we can do that while discreditin' O'Connell at the same time, then we have won."

"How can that be accomplished?" Lucas asked.

Garrison and Beth Anne exchanged a look of consultation, then the sister allowed the brother to proceed. "Though the poisonin' of Osborne Davis was accidental, we can turn it to our advantage. He will recover, but will be unable to see to his editorial duties for some time. That leaves me . . . us," he corrected, with a nod at Beth Anne, "in charge. In a short time we can give you adequate reasons to arrest O'Connell for rebellion and prohibit the gatherin'."

It was the turn of Lucas and Suggins to exchange glances. "Very well," Lucas agreed. "Is there anything else you need?"

"Only the freedom to deal with Burke," Beth Anne announced fiercely. "He could destroy us."

∽21∽

It was Mad Molly who first brought the broadsheets announcing the Clontarf Repeal Rally to Joseph's attention. She came into the kitchen clutching a bright yellow flyer in each hand and muttering to herself, "Clontarf . . . Brian Boru, may he rest in peace. And the Sassenach will never get the treasure. Never, never, never. Where's the squire?"

This last query was addressed with vehemence to Fern, who jumped and squeaked much the same as she did in the presence of a mouse. "Was you speakin' to me?" she inquired.

"You see what it says here?" Molly demanded, thrusting the document under the maid's nose. "It says here 'Clontarf.' It's for the master."

Margaret intervened. "It's just another bit of a paper about another monster meetin'," she said, sniffing. "Nothin' to be botherin' the master with, and him so thick with O'Connell already. Doubtless he's already seen it."

274 BODIE & BROCK THOENE

"Clontaaaaarf!" Molly squealed, in appearance and intensity much like a thin, grizzled hog stuck under a gate. "Clontaaaaarf!"

Whether Joseph should be disturbed about the flyer or not was soon moot since he came at a dead run downstairs from his office to see what the racket was about.

Molly shoved the paper under his nose. "See," she ordered, "Clontarf. Brian Boru. Cast out the Danes, he did, but the other Sassenachs came, didn't they? Where is Brian of the Tribute now?"

"Calm down," Joseph urged. "It's just a broadsheet, Molly. And Clontarf is just where the rally's to be held."

It seemed the only word Molly actually recognized on the paper was the name of the gathering place. The rest was spinning out of her own fertile wits. "But it's all right, Molly," Joseph said kindly. "Here, I'll read it to you."

Beneath the date and the words *Monster Rally for Repeal,* in letters three inches tall the broadsheet carried the word *CLONTARF.* And then it said:

Join the Repeal Cavalry!
Four thousand mounted men wanted!
Hundreds of Thousands more to arm themselves and
MARCH!

Joseph was thunderstruck. This was exactly the dangerously militant language against which O'Connell and Davis had been on guard. It mattered little that the fine print continued:

Arm yourselves with Repeal membership cards

Because the next lines announced in giant block print,

NOW IS THE TIME!
STRIKE A BLOW FOR LIBERTY!
THE SHOT FIRED AT CLONTARF
WILL BE HEARD IN LONDON!

O'CONNELL AND THE SPIRIT OF BRIAN BORU! DRIVE THE INVADER FROM OUR SHORES FOREVER!

"Molly," Joseph said, taking the woman's gnarled hands in his and looking into her eyes, "I apologize. This is of the utmost impor tance. I must go see Daniel right away. Tomorrow, in fact."

At nine o'clock in the evening in a darkened corner of the Surinam Coffee House and Restaurant, just off Merchants Quay beside the river Liffy, Beth Anne O'Toole patted a lump of frowsy blond curls back into place behind her right ear. It gave her head a lopsided appearance, exaggerated by the fact that she leaned her left cheek on her palm in what she thought was a winsome pose.

"And so, your lordships," her brother continued to Burtenshaw Suggins and Edward Lucas. "You can see we have completely fulfilled our allotted tasks. The newspapers, flyers, and broadsheets practically call for armed insurrection at Clontarf. They have gone out over the entire countryside, and it is now far too late for O'Connell to call them back."

"You have done well," Lucas applauded. "Even if the Great Liberator chooses to distance himself from them now, we can still justify his arrest on a charge of fomenting rebellion."

From the depths of the high-backed, barrel-shaped leather chair in which he was almost hidden, Suggins rumbled, "And if O'Connell decides to play out the hand we have dealt him . . . really call for revolt, I mean . . . we are ready for that eventuality. Two extra battalions of troops and two warships . . ."

Lucas cleared his throat violently and Suggins subsided. "And the other matter?" Lucas asked, smoothly transitioning away from Suggins's indiscretion. "Joseph Burke. What of him?"

O'Toole and his sister exchanged their first uneasy glance. "We are still workin' on that score," O'Toole admitted.

"What my brother means is that we are usin' the utmost caution,"

Beth Anne explained. "Lord Burke suspects he is a target. Our agents report that he is always in the company of a large, black-bearded man. It may be his bodyguard. We will, of course, succeed in the end."

"Of course," Lucas agreed in a friendly tone, forestalling a grumpy question that arose from the barrel-backed chair. "In regard to your latest payment . . . ," he added.

"Yes?" both O'Tooles responded eagerly.

"Would midnight tonight on Ha'Penny Bridge be acceptable?"

"Certainly, my lords. Always glad to be of service." The O'Toole brother and sister bowed and simpered their way out of the room in the coffeehouse.

"It appears to me that our instruments have outlasted their usefulness," Lucas observed.

Suggins contradicted the secretary. "It appears to me they are a positive liability. Can it be resolved soon?"

"Would midnight on Ha'Penny Bridge be soon enough?"

"Excellent," Suggins approved. "Now let's sample the bill of fare at this establishment. I hear their steak-and-kidney pie is excellent."

Joseph's dreams were troubled again. For several nights in a row he had experienced the same nightmare. Every time he turned over in his sleep, the action set off the vision of an avalanche. Tons of rocks crashed down toward him. He could not move fast enough to escape the torrent of boulders, and they piled up around him, hemming him in like a stone-sided coffin.

An ugly, gap-toothed face peered down at him, but when Joseph appealed for help, the figure disappeared, leaving Joseph trapped.

When this vision had happened three times on the same night, Joseph woke covered in sweat and trembling, almost afraid to go back to sleep. His arm, though healing properly thanks to the Tinker and to Kate, throbbed as if newly broken.

Joseph forced himself to think through what was troubling him. The image had become a daily occurrence. It must mean something.

There was something important he was still trying to recall, some elusive question that needed to be satisfied, but he could not recapture it. He needed a tool to dig out what his mind was trying to suggest.

He wrestled with the problem until he heard a clock chime three, then fell back to sleep. Almost at once the vision appeared again. This time, though, the Joseph of the avalanche was carrying a turf spade and a hammer as the rocks began to roll. He did not cry out for help, but set to work using the tools to free himself. *Even if it happens daily,* he thought, *I can free myself. Even if it happens daily.*

Mad Molly appeared in the vision for the first time. "Oh, tool of the devil," she chattered. "Even one you see daily may be a tool of the devil."

Joseph bolted upright in the bed, his mind racing. Schoolmaster Daly! That had been the question for Daniel O'Connell. Who had recommended Daly for the post? What traitor in O'Connell's camp supplied the spy in Joseph's household?

Even as his subconscious finally supplied the troubling inquiry, Joseph was certain he had received the correct solution. He must still confirm it with O'Connell, but Joseph was already convinced he would find that Instructor Daly had been endorsed by none other than Garrison O'Toole.

The black expanse of the river Liffy flowed underneath Ha'Penny Bridge in silent rebuke to the puny efforts of mankind around its banks. The Vikings who had vexed the freedom of Ireland eight hundred years earlier had vanished together with their whole civilization. Where are they now, the water murmured, where are they now?

Garrison O'Toole, deaf to the censure presented by the river, played with the silver coins in his pocket and looked at his watch with impatience.

"It's five minutes past the hour," he complained to his sister.

"They're late. That constable made his rounds ten minutes ago already and may be back this way soon. I'd not like to have to explain what we're doin', loiterin' here at this time of night."

"Calm down," Beth Anne instructed. "We have been well taken care of up to now. Why not this time?"

As if in agreement with her assertion, a match flared at the north end of the bridge, illuminating the face of a short man lighting a clay pipe. Behind them, at the opposite extremity, a much larger figure did likewise, and then the two smokers converged on the center.

A spiral of the river breeze made one of the pipes flare up, revealing the features of the man known as Kenny.

"What are you doin' in Dublin?" Garrison O'Toole demanded angrily. "You are supposed to be watchin' Burke Hall."

"Well, now," Kenny drawled, moving closer to the O'Toole siblings. "As to that, you see, Master Lucas bid us come to town."

"That's right," commented Ryan's voice from the other direction. "We thought you'd be pleased, seein' as we brought your payment."

"You did?" Beth Anne prompted. "Let us have it."

"Oh, it's right enough all here," Kenny responded, lowering an obviously weighty sack that had taken both hands to carry. "Take a look."

As Ryan struck another match and held it above the drawstring, Kenny parted the top of the pouch. Garrison reached hastily toward the glimmer of coins, but Beth Anne's fingers got there first. "Lovely," she whispered.

Not to be outdone, Garrison nudged her aside and dug deeper into the bag. He appeared not to care for what he discovered. "What's this?" he asked, pulling out an oblong object and holding it near the flame. "Lead bars? Do they think they can cheat us?"

"Not just cheat," Kenny said, slipping a coil of rope from around his waist and tossing the loop over the necks of both O'Tooles and yanking it taut. On the other end of the cable was a steel hook that Kenny quickly thrust through an eyelet in the pouch.

"What?" came in a choked cry from Garrison's mouth, but nothing more as Kenny counted out loud.

"One, two, three, heave!"

O'Tooles and weighted bag made an impressive splash in the river Liffy. "Let's be off then," Kenny suggested to Ryan.

"Aye, and only one more job to do and then it's America for the likes of us," the slighter man said. "A sea voyage for our health."

When the constable whose beat included Ha'Penny Bridge strolled by moments later, there was nothing unusual to remark except a thin stream of bubbles, which soon after ceased.

It was two nights before what Daniel O'Connell promised would be the climactic Repeal rally, the biggest monster meeting of the campaign. Three million souls were on the roads, the tracks, and the lanes leading toward the ancient site of Irish pride: Clontarf.

Every byway was jammed with people speaking in glowing terms of King Brian Boru, Brian of the Tribute, of blessed memory. He who rid the country of the Sassenachs just after the turn of the first millennium had dropped his mantle from heaven, and it had alighted on the Great Liberator.

For seventy miles outside Dublin Joseph heard cheering and singing like that on the day of the Tara gathering, but this jubilation was happening days beforehand. The entire nation was on the move, eager to see the finish of British rule and home-rule for Ireland begun.

There were even Irishmen who had chartered ships to bring them to the rally from their jobs across the Irish Sea: stevedores from the docks at Liverpool and day laborers from Clydeside. Some had spent their last shillings to go home, if only for one day, but what a day it would be! A new day dawning for Ireland, a day of freedom and justice at last.

Joseph and the Tinker thundered down the highway, past the Clontarf gathering place north of the city. Their pace was slowed in the last stretch by the crowded conditions, but these travelers were not pilgrims; they were soldiers. And they were not headed into the capital, but rather toward the countryside.

"Faster," Joseph urged his black-bearded coachman. "Something is amiss, and we can't get to Daniel too soon!"

Dermott O'Neill did not need to use the buggy whip. He clucked his tongue softly and said something to the team who pricked their ears to listen and agreed to greater speed.

There was something terribly wrong. The double file of soldiers who parted in the middle to let the coach proceed were not constables, not militia, but British redcoats in battle array. Joseph recognized the insignias of the Sixtieth Rifles and the Twelfth Dragoons; both groups looking serious and businesslike with rifles on shoulders and cartridge pouches bulging with ammunition.

The two arrivals from Connaught drew up in front of 58 Merrion Square just as dawn was breaking. The windows in O'Connell's home were ablaze with light, showing the Liberator was already alert.

Leaving the Tinker to care for the coach and horses, Joseph entered the drawing room, which he had not seen since Brigit's death and Tomeen's birth ten months before. The room was full of Repeal leaders: Archbishop MacHale, Secretary Daunt, Gavan Duffy, John Blake Dillon and, looking pale and wan and wrapped in a comforter in the chair nearest the fireplace, Osborne Davis.

"Joseph," Davis croaked hoarsely, still not recovered fully from his bout with the poison, "so you've heard, then?"

"Heard what?" Joseph demanded. "I must see Daniel at once. Is he here?"

The door to the adjoining study opened, but the man who entered looked more like an O'Connell grandsire than the Emancipator himself. Daniel's shoulders slumped, his head was bowed toward his chest, and his complexion had the gray of the terminally ill. He stared with unseeing eyes through Joseph, not recognizing his friend at all.

From the room behind him stalked a British officer in the dress uniform of the Sixtieth Rifles. His tall black boots bore a high gloss, and his sandy mustache was neatly clipped, as were his words. "I take it, then, you understand me fully and will comply?" he said to O'Connell.

His hand barely rising above his waist, as if the effort were too much to lift it farther, Daniel O'Connell gestured his agreement, but did not speak. The officer saluted and marched out of the room.

Aided to a chair, it was some time before O'Connell explained the purpose of the soldier's visit. "Captain Drummond has brought a message from the Lord Lieutenant, Earl de Gray," he said, then more bitterly, "an order, rather. The meetin' is prohibited."

There was dead silence in the room.

O'Connell, peevish-sounding at what he took to be a lack of understanding, repeated himself. "Do you not understand what I'm sayin'? The Clontarf meetin' is proscribed, forbidden. There will be soldiers on the field, and there are warships in the bay within cannon range of Clontarf. To go forward would mean civil war."

"Then let it come!" Gavan Duffy announced. "We're ready! The people are ready! Give the word, Daniel, and we will strike a blow for liberty!"

"No," O'Connell said firmly, echoed by Archbishop MacHale and others. "No. I have said no single drop of Irish blood is worth Repeal. I will not soak this country in blood now. We must turn them back." The last phrase was spoken so softly that Secretary Daunt had to ask O'Connell to restate it. "The millions on the road. We must send our own people out on every highway to turn them around. If they meet up with the redcoats and are ordered to turn back, then the thing we are tryin' to prevent may happen in spite of us."

The frozen tableau broke up into a swirling hive of activity. Assignments were given, messages sent, riders dispatched, all for a purpose that was distasteful to every man in the room, and yet one they knew to be essential.

When the space had cleared, Joseph sat down between the weary O'Connell and the invalid Davis. "Daniel," Joseph said, "I know it matters little at a time like this, but I believe I have discovered a spy in your ranks. It is Garrison O'Toole!"

"Ha!" Davis laughed bitterly. "An excellent conclusion, but too late, friend Burke. O'Toole and his sister have hung the charge of treason around our necks, and we can only pray we do not hang from it."

"The broadsheets," Joseph commented needlessly.

"The same, and now that the O'Tooles have betrayed us before Clontarf, doubtless they have escaped to enjoy their thirty pieces of silver."

"Joseph," O'Connell said, lifting his head slowly as though an immense weight hung there, "I need to compose a message; a communiqué to the Irish people. I must tell them to obey the Repeal wardens without question. If we are to rally to lift the banner of Repeal another day, it must be so. Will you carry it to Daunt for printing and see to its publication throughout the streets?"

"Of course, Daniel," Joseph consented. "Anything else I can do?"

"You have your Tinker friend with you? Good . . . please send him to Clontarf. I'll write a note to the workmen there to begin dismantling the platform. We must accede willingly to what the Castle demands, or they will still say we are rebels."

Joseph had never seen O'Connell so beaten down.

Adam Kane galloped onto the Burke property at a pace that announced he was bearing news.

Martin, who was helping Old Flynn groom the carriage horses, dropped the brush and sprinted for the stable door at the shouting.

"Clontarf!" rose the alarm. "They've thrown us back at Clontarf!" Adam leaped from the back of his still-moving mount. The mare charged past Martin into the barn. Old Flynn stumbled hastily out of the way, snagging the agitated animal by the reins. Then when Adam Kane's message penetrated his brain, Flynn's eyes widened, and he hurried out into the yard to stand beside Martin.

Kate, clutching Little Tom, ran from the house with Mary Elizabeth, Molly, Miss Susan, and Fern behind her. Questions erupted from every mouth.

"What do ye hear?"

"What about Clontarf?"

"Are there many dead?"

"What of Joseph and O'Connell?"

Adam, out of breath and visibly shaken, bent down and grasped his knees. "Sweet Jesus." He shook his head and stood erect to face the horrified crowd around him.

Wiping sweat from his brow, he told what he had heard from the driver of the Galway mailcoach.

"There were the flyers . . . the ones you brought, Molly."

"Aye," said the old woman. "A call to arms."

Adam exhaled loudly. "So said the English. And they landed shiploads of troops at Dublin to face off our people. There are warships still in the harbor, cannons pointed toward the hills. It's a failure. Turned back some three million who came. Three million, I say! Turned back by the English because O'Connell would not have even one drop of Irish blood shed." Adam raised his eyes skyward. Tears brimmed and spilled down his cheeks.

At the sight of his weeping, Fern gave a cry and rushed to put her arms around him. She began to cry as well. "Ah, me darlin', Adam! What's it for? What's it for?"

Mad Molly dropped to her knees and started to keen as though ten thousand had died. Though no Irish blood had been shed, Martin knew that the defeat at Clontarf meant the death of a dream in every Irish heart. Repeal of the Union with England, the hope of freedom, was finished. Even Mary Elizabeth was struck by the tragedy of it. She clung to Kate's waist and sobbed.

Martin held back his emotions with difficulty.

Darby, who had been polishing the silver, wandered out late to the news. "What's this, then? Who's died?"

"Ireland," Kate remarked hollowly as she cradled Little Tom. "Our future here."

Adam Kane embraced Fern, sighed, and covered his eyes with the back of his hand. "And here's the worst of it. The Liberator is to be charged, it is said, with treason. Punishable by hangin'." He directed his gaze at Kate. "Aye. And himself, your own betrothed, Squire Joseph . . . may be taken up as well."

22

Joseph spent three days running errands for Daniel O'Connell. The time was occupied in posting Daniel's proclamation of non-resistance, or as he put it, "biding our time." There was much grumbling at this position, and Dublin remained a powder keg for forty-eight hours. The compliance in which not a single violent act took place spoke well of the immense regard in which O'Connell was held and of the incredible discipline of the Repealers.

After the mass of pilgrims had departed, the situation was mostly defused. That was when the British government struck. Four days after the Clontarf meeting was prohibited, the authorities in Dublin Castle arrested O'Connell and all the executive committee of the Repeal movement on whom they could lay their hands, including Joseph. The charge was "conspiring to unlawful and seditious opposition to the government."

A day later Joseph was released, there being not enough evidence to connect him with a conspiracy and his name, happily, not being found on the list of the Repeal leaders. He needed no urging, but being met by Dermott O'Neill, left immediately for home.

It was night when the coach passed through Castletown. Joseph, weary in body and sick at heart because he saw the failure of Repeal as the end of the Burke inheritance, was brooding in silence.

He made no response when the Tinker observed, "There's a great light up ahead." It could have been the sun rising in the west for all Joseph cared. He was mentally reordering his life, parting with Burke Hall, and becoming a farmer husband to Kate when Dermott clucked to the team and said with quiet urgency, "It's a fire."

From the small mound over which the highway ran Joseph could see an orange glow swelling into the sky over toward the manor house. By the time they reached the turn onto the gravel drive the coach was flying, skidding around the curve. Flames were visible in the downstairs windows.

Kate was sleeping in an upper-floor bedroom with Mary Elizabeth. Miss Susan and Tomeen were in the nursery, and Martin had a bed on a sofa in the small study.

The Donovans had moved into the manor house so as to be present when Joseph returned from Clontarf.

Though she slept in a high-ceilinged room on a four-poster bed, Kate was not dreaming of grand style or of being Lady Burke. Rather her thoughts were filled with sweet, commonplace things: keeping a tiny cottage neat as a pin, being surrounded by a flock of little ones who tugged at her skirts and called her *Mama*. And of cooking supper for Joseph—the way he looked into her eyes and the way she gazed back with equal fervor. A draft in the chimney tossed a handful of smoke back into the room. Kate frowned in her sleep. Perhaps the stack wanted cleaning, or perhaps it was not quite tall enough to prevent that sort of draft.

The odor of smoke grew stronger, hotter, and more present. Kate's eyes snapped open. The smoke in the air was real; the manor house was on fire.

"Mary Elizabeth!" she ordered sharply. "Wake up! There's a fire!"

The girl, who Kate often noted could sleep through an earthquake, was no different this time. "What?" she said sleepily. "Tend the fire yourself, sister. It's not time to get up."

Gathering the dozing child up in her arms, Kate hurried along the corridor, shouting for Martin and Miss Susan. The knot of frightened people moved down the corridor toward the staircase, found it ablaze, scurried back toward the servants' stairs, and found the dark passage full of choking black smoke.

"I'll go," Martin volunteered. "I can shinny down and bring help." Before Kate could say either yes or no, the boy clambered over the railing and descended the trellis to the ground.

The Tinker jerked the team to an abrupt halt in front of the main entry. Tongues of flame were jutting out of the French doors and the windows all along the front, licking the stonework and devouring curtains and trim.

Joseph saw Martin climbing down and ran toward him, but the Tinker got there first and lifted the boy down the last six feet. "Help them," Martin panted. "Kate and them are trapped upstairs."

Lunging toward the doorway, Joseph found that Dermott O'Neill was grasping him by the left shoulder. The Tinker pointed at Joseph's bandaged arm. "I'll go," he said. "You and Martin see what you can do about the fire."

The Tinker kicked open the door, ducked as a blast of heat roared as out of a furnace, then, ducking low, sprinted into the Great Hall. "Run to the servants' wing," Joseph instructed Martin. "Rouse Old Flynn and Mister Kane."

There was no need. Before Martin had gone six paces Adam Kane and Old Flynn rounded the corner of the house, followed by Margaret, Darby, Fern, and Mad Molly. The two men were dragging the tarp-shrouded cart of the hand-operated water pump and the hose reel. "Where's the baby?" Kane shouted at Joseph over the crackling roar of the blaze.

"The Tinker's gone in to get them," was the reply. "Throw a hose into the fountain, and let's see what we can save!"

With one line coming from the pond in the center of the circular drive and Darby and Kane sawing the pump handles, Joseph, clamping the hose under his left armpit, directed a stream of water into the broken-out windows. The women gathered a heap of pails and formed their own bucket line, working at the side of the Great Hall where the fire was not so well established. The combination of the home's stout masonry and the jet of water checked the conflagration.

"Hey, below!" boomed a voice from the balcony. It was the Tinker. He was rapidly knotting together a series of bedsheets into a makeshift rope. "Someone hold it steady for the women to climb down!"

There was a thundering of hooves on the roadway. Neighbors coming to help fight the fire, Joseph thought.

A trio of men, one masked, one with a corkscrew nose, and a slightlybuilt third, galloped straight toward the pump. The ugly one yanked Darby away from the pump. "Let it burn!" he commanded. Then to his accomplice he shouted, "Ryan, take care of the squire!"

"Right-o, Kenny," Ryan agreed.

"It wasn't supposed to be like this!" Darby protested. "Nobody said nothin' about burnin' us out!" The valet ran from the pump and into the night.

The stream of water died, and the flames burst out with renewed intensity.

Three combats took place on the driveway: Adam Kane leaped on the crooked-nosed man and bore him to the ground. Old Flynn tackled the masked man, assisted by Martin, who swung a bucket at the disguised figure's head.

The smaller attacker made straight for Joseph, grinning at the prospect of an easy victory over a one-armed opponent. Letting the villain come to close quarters before reacting, Joseph snatched up a length of fire hose and spun it like a whip. He cracked Ryan across the teeth with the heavy brass nozzle, knocking the man back.

Kate bustled from window to window, staring down at the chaos in the yard and urging the Tinker to "Hurry, hurry!" It was her worst nightmare revisited: a holocaust had destroyed her family and nearly her life six years earlier. Now another conflagration was threatening to complete the doom of the Donovans.

"Help me, here," the Tinker directed. "Tie a loop under Miss Susan's arms. I'll lower her and the baby first, but you'll have to aid me."

It tore at Kate's heart to set Mary Elizabeth down, but she did so and rigged the hoop as requested.

"Are you afraid?" Dermott asked Miss Susan.

With chin held high, the nurse responded in an unquavering voice, "You think I'm gonna let any evil take another chile from my arms? Fear don't signify; only savin' this baby counts!"

Together, O'Neill and Kate assisted Miss Susan, with a squalling Tomeen wrapped tightly across her chest inside a shawl, as she climbed over the balcony and hung, suspended, in midair. "We'll need to lower you fast as to get you past the flames," the Tinker said.

"Lower away!" Miss Susan directed. "Don't worry 'bout me none."

Mad Molly stood aloof from the confusion and commotion around her. As if her routinely jangled mind drew on some hidden reserve of calm, Molly was not frantic nor did she act upset. "Purified by fire," she crooned.

The hooded man, in his fine boots and with a build that looked much like Colonel Mahon's, punched Old Flynn in the wind, then was himself battered over the head with another swing of Martin's bucket. The man backhanded the boy, sending Martin stumbling away, when another pail, wielded by Margaret, crashed into his chin.

Adam Kane and Kenny slugged it out, toe-to-toe. "You murderin' swine!" Kane said, breathing noisily through his bloody, battered nose. "You'll hang for this."

Kenny laughed and swore coarsely, but the threat must have been overheard by the masked attacker. Pummeled from three sides by Old Flynn, Martin, and Margaret, the slender figure broke free and ran for his sleek horse.

"You blasted coward, M . . . ," Kenny shouted, nearly saying the name of the deserter before a solid right hand from Kane splintered what was left of Kenny's mouth. "You'll be sorry you did that," Kenny snarled, whipping a knife from his belt. "Orders was just to burn the place, but now you're goin' with it!"

Joseph was keeping Ryan at bay with sweeping blows of the fire hose, but behind him the heat from the blaze was growing intense. If the clash did not end soon, there would be no saving the house anyway. As Ryan circled warily, looking for an opening, Joseph abruptly threw aside the hose and charged. Putting his left shoulder into Ryan's midsection, both men crashed to the ground, Ryan aiming deliberate strikes at Joseph's injured arm. Enraged with the pain, Joseph brought the top of his head down sharply across Ryan's nose. The impact resulted in a crunch and a spray of blood.

Miss Susan and Tomeen reached the ground in safety, and the impromptu harness was hauled back up. "You're next, Mary Elizabeth." Kate coughed as she spoke, expressing more composure than she felt. "Mary Elizabeth?" In the deepening clutches of the smoke, the little girl had disappeared. Composure abandoned at once, Kate darted toward the door to search for her sister.

The Tinker caught her. "I'll get the child," he said. "Hurry now, and I'll send her right after."

Amazing herself, Kate agreed, strangely accepting of the Tinker's confidence. She allowed herself to be looped into the sheets and swung out over the rail.

Adam Kane watched closely and jumped back as Kenny slashed with his knife. "Cut you and cook you!" the murderer threatened, the blade making a savage arc through the air.

"Here," Flynn shouted. "This'll even things up."

The stablemaster slid a wooden-tined pitchfork across the ground toward Kane, but as the steward stretched for it, Kenny sliced downward again. The blow ripped through Kane's shirtsleeve and scored his bicep.

Ryan pounded his fists on Joseph's broken arm, making the squire cry out with pain and release his hold. Jumping up, Ryan also drew a knife and menaced Joseph with it. "Keep back," he hissed. "Kenny! Kenny! It's blazin' now. Let's go, mate!" The smaller man ran to Kenny's side. The distraction allowed Kane to shoot forward and grab the pitchfork.

The flames from the French doors shot thirty feet into the air. The fire was eating its way through the floor above. Beams cracked with pistol shots as the weight on them exceeded what the weakened spans could bear.

Halfway down to the ground, Kate slipped in the loop. Having not enough strength in her good arm, she screamed as she slid downward. The Tinker paid out the rope faster, hoping to set her down before she fell, but the speeded-up descent and Kate's struggles made the escape line swing toward the blazing windows.

Joseph, hearing her shout, ran toward her and with his sound limb caught her legs and dragged her backward from the flames, just as her body fell free of the coil.

"Let us pass," Kenny growled with menace. "Let us pass, and no one needs to die."

Kane shook his head, though all he had with which to fend off the knives was the wooden pitchfork. "Not a chance," he said. Flynn with a turf spade and Martin with his bucket flanked the steward.

"I warned you," Kenny said with a shrug.

Overhead, as Kenny and Ryan stood with their backs to the manor house there came a rending crash. The fabric of the building itself was tearing apart and the stone facade above the terrace, no longer bound to the whole, tumbled outward.

Ryan heard the splintering noise and turned. Kenny craned his head back and looked up.

"Get back!" shouted Adam Kane as a half ton of rock and mortar crumbled and toppled.

Kenny and Ryan were not able to leap clear in time. They were buried under an avalanche of stonework.

After rescuing Kate, Joseph released the knotted sheets to send them back to the Tinker. But in the brush with the window, the fabric ignited and the cord burned in two. The remaining piece was far too short to reach the ground.

The Tinker appeared at the window with Mary Elizabeth in his arms.

"Dermott!" Joseph called. "Get back. Go another way."

"No time," the Tinker shouted. "It's all ablaze. Get something to catch the girl."

Joseph jumped for the canvas in which the water pump had been covered. In a moment it was stretched between Kane, Old Flynn, Margaret, Martin, and Fern. Mad Molly took a corner. Joseph and Kate, with one good hand each, together grasped the remaining space and pulled the tarp taut. Maneuvering under the window Joseph yelled, "Now, Dermott. Let her go!"

As Mary Elizabeth plummeted earthward, a shaft of flame shot out a crack in the wall, trying to impale the girl with a blazing fork. Miraculously, the fire parted as she dropped, and she landed safely in the center of the canvas.

But the jet of heat that hurtled out of the dying manor house curled upward like an explosion. The entire front of the building was engulfed in flames.

Though they called and called, Dermott O'Neill never reappeared at the window. In less than three minutes, those gathered in the yard had to back away as the house disintegrated, slumping its floors into a single, massive inferno.

The charred ruins of the ancestral manor of the Burke of Connaught still smoldered into the next afternoon. The foundation stones of the centuries-old castle lay scorched and exposed in the destruction. Tenant farmers brought their families to witness the end of a long Galway history. A lot of ancient dreams were dying, it seemed. The attempt to duplicate the heroic actions of Brian Boru at Clontarf now was ending with Ireland's greatest defeat.

"Sure, and Daniel O'Connell's shown himself a coward," said Joe Watty. "Not a shot fired by a few English soldiers, but three million men strong of Ireland are commanded to cut and run. Our fathers are spinnin' in their graves. Spinnin'!"

"'T'weren't only English hirelin's done this burnin'. Brought on by the ghost of the Old Burke. He's set the torch to this place in shame," agreed Widow Clooney. "And now the Tinker's dead. A fine-lookin' man he was for a Tinker."

Those of the household staff were smudged with soot and without so much as a clean shirt to wear. Every person's effects were in ashes. Fern, Adam, Flynn, and Margaret huddled in a tight group beside the stables and talked about the vile informer, Darby.

"A true Judas that one," said Margaret, scowling. "And to think I thought well of him. Welcomed him into my kitchen anytime for a cuppa. Never made him ask for a bit of this or that."

"Aye," squeaked Fern. "Betrayed the squire and the rest of us as well. They've burned the house, and now where'll Darby go?"

"They'll have some lackey post for him in Dublin Castle no doubt. Lickin' the boots of the English lords," Adam sneered.

"If ever he lives so long," Flynn snarled. "Traitorous vermin. Sure there's a code for dealin' with scum like him. It's his fault that my dear friend Dermott O'Neill died in the fire. A good man, the Tinker, and now he's gone forever. Aye, he's gone. We'll find the stump of his knife in the wreckage. Thirty years I knew Darby and never trusted him a day of it. What can you say about a man who spends his life polishin' silver? But the minute I laid eyes on the Tinker I said he was a good man. Sure, he was a man who knew a fine horse. How will I manage without him?"

Across the lawn was a jumble of those few belongings that Adam had managed to rescue from the inferno. There was the portrait of Joseph's mother and another of his father. A high-backed, red leather wing chair had somehow survived after being thrown from a window. Mad Molly sat in it, more haggard than usual, silent as stone. She had been staring at the rubble since morning.

Father O'Bannon, Joseph, Kate, Miss Susan, and Little Tom shared a patch of lawn beside her. Mary Elizabeth and Martin wandered off to examine the reeking pile of rocks and blackened timbers.

"Lady Shaw'll not be wantin' the house, I suppose," Joseph said.

Kate studied him for a moment. "God be praised for small blessin's. I can't say I'm sorry she'll be stayin' in Limerick."

Father O'Bannon caught the drift of Joseph's meaning. "Repeal dead. The manor house gone. What you're sayin', Joseph, is that you'll have to sell the Ballynockanor lease to Colonel Mahon."

Silence among the group. Little Tom smiled up at Kate and then turned his face to her breast. Kate kissed the baby sadly and passed him to Miss Susan for his meal.

Joseph inhaled and bit his lip. "Sure, Father, and that's what it means. It'll have to go to Mahon now."

"Well, then." The priest gazed steadily at a tumbled chimney. "If that's the way it must be, that's the way, and we'll live with it. Twenty farms. A hundred people. St. John the Evangelist."

"We'll survey my tract to the east. Every man'll have more than he has now."

Kate took Joseph's hand in hers as she spotted Colonel Mahon striding through the crowd of spectators. "Speak of himself, the devil. Comin' to gloat, no doubt."

She was not far wrong. Slapping his thigh with a riding crop Colonel Mahon was the only smiling face in the assembly. Joseph stood to meet him.

"Ah, Squire Burke. I saw your bonfire from miles away last night. Lovely glow in the sky." He scratched his cheek thoughtfully. "You won't miss the place, I assume, since you intended to sell it to Lady Shaw." With a snap of his fingers he emphasized his sarcasm. "Well, well. I suppose she won't be wanting it now."

"No." Joseph reddened at the calloused attitude of the man who was prepared to toss twenty families off his land.

"And Clontarf did not go well, I hear. Glad to see you're temporarily out of prison." He cleared his throat and tipped his hat to Kate.

"The situation leaves only yourself as buyer." Joseph spoke with tense control.

"Sorry to disappoint you. But why should I buy the lease on measly Ballynockanor when I will have it all for the same money?"

"What are you sayin'?"

"You should've taken my first offer. Business is business. Talk from the higher authorities is that Joseph Burke will not remain free for long. Additionally, all your property is to be confiscated directly and sold for the Crown rent due." He bowed to Kate, who glared at him. "A pity about the house," he said to Joseph. "Your uncle Marlowe tore it apart and put it back together."

Molly shouted, "Aye! That he did! But he never found it!"

Taken aback by the outburst, Mahon continued, "I should have liked to have it. But then it had to go, didn't it? What with Lady Fiona also wanting it. As for the rest of your tenants, sir, best tell them they have two weeks before Colonel Mahon buys this little coop. Two weeks and they'd better have another roost. I want my lands perfectly untenanted."

There was nothing more to say. With a happy wink at Miss Susan, Mahon turned on his heel and strode back to where a child held his horse. Moments later he cantered lazily across the lawns toward the gate. No doubt he was calculating the size of what would soon be his parkland.

"Then we're finished." Joseph sank back to the ground. "I don't mind so much for myself. But everyone here will be given notice."

"America is the place." Kate tried to be brave, but the certainty of eviction, of everyone on the road, shook her.

Miss Susan frowned at Mahon's back. "What did that devil mean this house had to go?"

At this Mad Molly sat up. "Mahon, is it? Devil indeed! It's right the place burned down, a wicked old pile of stone it was too. Blood, blood, everywhere. See it ooze! Out of the chinks like melted lead. A good cleanin', that's what this house needed. Purified like gold in the fire. But I'm not fond of him who burned it."

Father O'Bannon interrupted. "I wouldn't put it past Mahon to have some part in this. He's full of brass, that one."

Kate was on her feet. "America, I say. Father O'Bannon, we'll rebuild St. John's in America. We'll leave soon, Joseph. They'll not take you away to prison."

Father O'Bannon did not acknowledge her attempt at hopefulness. "And the first Burke, Miles de Burgo, is spinnin' in his grave to see it come to this. Fought with Brian Boru he did. Laid those foundation stones. A thousand years of history gone up in smoke. And an Englishman in control of the Burke lands. I had hoped to be buried by me chapel. Sing in the choir of the churchyard with me old friends one day."

Molly Fahey persisted in a lively banter. "Uncle Marlowe killed your father for it. Remember, Joseph? But he never found it. I knew, but I never told him. He would've burned it down. It's there! It's there! Sure, and I've been watchin' for it all day." She capered and danced as if hearing the strains of fiddle and pipes.

Father O'Bannon clasped Molly's arm in a viselike grip in an attempt to lead her away. "Come along then."

"Where?"

"Just away."

"Nay! Look! There's Martin and Mary Elizabeth! To the kitchen for a cuppa tay!" The children were poking with a stick at a fallen beam lying where the kitchen used to be.

"The kitchen's burned down entire."

"Aye! Blood and murder. Purified by fire it is! Oozing from the chinks in the original castle walls! Marlowe'll never get wee Connor's treasure. I promised the Burke upon his deathbed. Keep it safe in the pantry with the porridge and potatoes. Do you not remember?"

She broke away and began to run toward the ruins where the kitchen used to be.

Departing men and women stepped aside. Poor old thing. The fire had been too much for her. And what would become of Mad Molly if the whole village were tossed?

Joseph stood beside Kate and watched Molly run with her arms waving in the air as though she were trying to fly off the lawn like a bird. Finally she hopped three times on the flagstone path and began to laugh as she neared the broken portal of the kitchen entry.

Molly stretched out her hand as if to pull a nonexistent latch. In pantomime she opened the door and stepped across the threshold to where a heap of rubble lay. She could go no farther.

Putting her hands to her cheeks in dismay she left two black prints on her face. "Oh, little Connor!" she cried. "Come help Molly! King Brian gave it to him. It's here in the kitchen, I'm certain of it!"

Joseph exchanged a glance with Father O'Bannon. What was she talking about?

The stump of the kitchen chimney poked sadly out of a heap of rubble and tumbled, scorched beams. A pair of blackened timbers were crossed before the remains of the hearth like the coat of arms of a chimney sweep.

"By fire!" Molly said, pointing at the chimney. "Brian of the Tribute said save it for Ireland's need. Look!"

The old woman pointed an imperious finger at the devastation.

"Come now, Molly," Joseph said. "There's no reason to . . ."

A glimmer of something shining in the sun caught Joseph's eye. He stepped across a mound of stones, around a heap of charcoal that had been a ceiling. Then he yanked at a beam blocking the fireplace and . . . gold!

Melted gold, liquefied by the intense heat inside some ancient hiding place, had oozed and dripped out of the cracks in the rocks. Puddles of gold resolidified on the hearth. A shallow basin of stone layered over with gold gleamed like a ceremonial temple basin, a vessel fit for a king.

"Neither crown nor collar," Molly sang triumphantly. "And they never found the tribute . . . till now."

About the Authors

With twenty-four novels to their credit, over six million books in print and seven ECPA gold Medallion awards, Bodie and Brock Thoene have taken their works of historical fiction to the top of the best-seller charts and to the hearts of their readers.

Bodie is the storyteller, weaving plotlines and characters into stunning re-creations of bygone eras.

Brock provides the foundation for Bodie's tales. His meticulous research and attention to historical detail ensure that the books are both informative and entertaining.

The Thoenes' collaboration receives critical acclaim as well as high praise from their appreciative audience.

Thanks for taking the time to look further into book two of The Galway Chronicles, *Of Men and of Angels*. We hope that you take pleasure in following the lives of Kate, Joseph, Martin, and Mary Elizabeth. (And Mad Molly too, of course!) As we spend years researching and months writing, the characters become like close family and very dear friends, even though the real people on whom they are based walked the Irish countryside one hundred and fifty years ago!

A frequent comment expressed in our mail is that the reader found himself or herself praying for the characters. We consider this to be one of the highest compliments possible. Our suggestion if you feel that degree of involvement is to direct your prayers toward the success of the fragile peace accord recently enacted in Ireland.

After having read *Of Men and of Angels* you certainly grasp how dear is Irish liberty and how difficult to achieve What a struggle it has been through the ages for peace, freedom, and tolerance to exist side-by-side on the Emerald Isle!

Now, it seems, the great majority of those in both the Republic and in the British province of Northern Ireland have spoken in a remarkably united way: we want Irish voices having the greatest say in Irish affairs; we will no longer accept terrorism in the name of Christ.

May God bless them and you!
Bodie and Brock Thoene

Now that you have completed *Of Men and of Angels*, you may want to ponder the following:

- Father O'Bannon remarks, "When God has shown you the way out of one wilderness you thank Him, and then when you come to the next bit of dark forest you say, 'Where is He? He has abandoned me.'" What does he mean? What examples from your own life can you think of? When facing trials what should be our response?

- What do you think of the Tinker? Did he immediately seem good or were you suspicious? When were you certain that he was a benevolent character? Since we used the Tinker in several literary levels do you think of him as more realistic, more allegorical, or more spiritual?

- Why does Kate think she will never be able to love Joseph? What does she say to support this conclusion? Is she speaking her true mind or giving herself rationalizations? When and why does her attitude change?

- To what does the title refer? Are both men and angels represented in this book? Does anyone speak like "sounding brass or tinkling cymbal?" What does scripture indicate is the single most important component in our dealings with others?

- From British officials Sudgen and Lucas to traitors Garrison and Beth Anne O'Toole and on to thugs like Kenny and Ryan, several different levels of villainy are represented. Is one group more evil than another? What examples of different strata of wickedness have you experienced in your own lifetime?

- After his appearance as a supporting character in *Only the River Runs Free*, Daniel O'Connell returns in *Of Men and of Angels*, as a much more important historical figure. Does this treatment-make you want to reread the "Daniel" passages in book one? In what ways is O'Connell the same character as presented in book one? In what ways is he bigger?

- As this millennium draws to a close, we tend to think of "mass meetings" as a distinctly Twentieth Century phenomenon. Yet it is obvious the Irish Repeal gatherings that numbered over half a million out of an eight million population were hugely significant. Why did the repeal cause fail? Was O'Conell right to insist on non-violence? If O'Connell had released the forces of Irish nationalism, what might the outcome have been?

- When Joseph faces both the back rent demands and the charges for operating an illegal school he falls into despair. Father O'Bannon advises, " circumstances are never as damagin' to us as how we take on about them." What does he mean? Is he right? What is the proper response?

- One of our goals in painting accurate history in *Of Men and of Angels* is to emphasize that the support for Repeal came from both Irish Protestants and Irish Catholics. How did the British Government undermine this alliance? On a purely spiritual level, are there as many doctrinal differences between Catholic Christians and Protestant Christians as you once thought?

- The Tinker says "Those who look for wisdom find it in everything livin'. . . . Every plant and tree and creature contains some heavenly antidote against evil." Do you believe this is correct? Do you think the Tinker means for it to always be taken as literally true? How do the words of Proverbs (and other passages of Scripture) suggest similar themes?

You may reach the authors by sending correspondence to:
P.O. Box 542
Glenbrook, NV 89413